SHATTERED JEWEL

KETLEY ALLISON

CIMMERIAN COURT PLAYLIST

Dolls - Bella Poarch

Crazy - Natalie Jane

Don't Blame Me - Taylor Swift

I'm Her - Natalie Jane

Not to be Dramatic - Zoe Clark

The Things I Do For Love - bludnymph

Beggin' - Chris Lake, Alan

Blood//Water - King Kavalier Remix - grandson, King Kavalier

Dirty Thoughts - Chloe Adams

BOYTOY - Halle Abadi

Listen to the rest of the playlist on Spotify:

CHAPTER 1
ELARA

My legs tremble as I sink to the floor. The plush carpet scrapes my knees. Kaspian reaches for his belt, the metallic clink punctuating my surrender.

I keep my eyes downcast as he frees his cock, already hard and leaking at the tip. He fists a hand in my hair, yanking my head back.

"Open."

I relax my jaw and he thrusts forward, filling my mouth. I gag as he hits the back of my throat but he doesn't relent, fucking my face with ruthless strokes.

Tears leak from the corners of my eyes. Drool drips down my chin. Kaspian grunts, his grip tightening painfully.

Through the haze of tears, I notice movement. Axe and Wilder have inched closer, pure lust darkening their features as they palm their erections through their pants.

Only Cav hangs back, watching the scene with hooded eyes.

Kaspian pulses on my tongue, his thrusts growing erratic. With a guttural groan, he spills down my throat, forcing me to swallow every bittersweet drop.

He releases me and I slump forward, coughing and gasping for air. But there's no respite.

Axe is there, fisting his cock, the thick length jutting obscenely from his open fly. He hauls me up, bending me over the edge of the bed.

The cool silk duvet presses against my heated skin as he notches his cock at my entrance. With one brutal thrust, he hilts himself inside me.

I cry out, my pussy clenching around the sudden intrusion. Axe sets a punishing pace, pounding into me from behind while his fingers dig into my hips hard enough to bruise.

Wilder appears in my line of sight, his eyes dark with lust. He grips himself, guiding the swollen head of his cock to my parted lips.

"Suck," he commands.

I open for him and he slides into the wet silk of my mouth. I hollow my cheeks, working him with lips and tongue while Axe rails me from behind.

Their dual assault overwhelms me until I'm mindless with it, reduced to nothing but a receptacle for their greed.

But am I? My nipples beg to be pinched and sucked on, my clit demanding more than one man to please her, my mouth happy to welcome every one of them. My moans are muffled, but they're present. My pussy is slick with both cum and need.

And then the orgasm builds, the last piece of evidence falling into place. It crashes over me as Axe finds his release, spilling hot and deep. Wilder follows seconds after, his seed flooding my mouth.

They withdraw and I collapse onto the bed, my limbs shaking, my breath coming in ragged pants.

I swallow the rest of Wilder's cum and wipe the droplets from my chin. My pussy throbs with a strange ache, satisfied but wanting more, dripping with Axe's cum. I reach down and bring it to my lips so I can taste it, too, slightly sweeter than Wilder's and Kaspian's.

I peer through my lashes while I lick my fingers, finding Cav as he stalks closer and runs his large hands over my body like he has the right to touch me however he wants.

His fingers dip into my pussy lips, collecting some of Axe's cum and bringing it to his nose for a deep inhale. "You smell so good when you're covered in us."

Cav shoves me onto all fours on the bed and spreads my cheeks, exposing the most vulnerable parts of myself to him. "I want to taste you."

And then he's there, tongue circling my tight entrance, making me moan despite the previous orgasm still echoing through my body. It feels so different from when Axe was inside me—slower but equally as intense. He tests the walls of my pussy with each lick until he finds just the right spot that has me writhing on his face.

He teases with his tongue while he inserts his middle finger, searching for hidden spots of pleasure. Axe climbs onto the bed behind me, holding my hips to keep me still—or from suffocating Cav from how hard I'm grinding on his face.

Wilder leans in, watching our session at a better vantage point, and Kaspian moves to Cav's bar, sipping on a glass of scotch while he spectates.

My breath comes in shallow gasps. I try to stay collected and sexy while panting and staring at Kaspian, transfixed by the power in his repose, my lips still tingling from his rough thrusts.

My mouth stays wet and desperate, saliva mixing with their cum, their taste lingering like forbidden fruit.

I'm forced to look away from Kaspian first when my eyes roll back as Cav's finger finds a spot inside me, sending waves of radiance over my vision. I cry out, moaning incoherently as Cav laps up what remains of me, the world blurring under the weight of their demands, losing myself completely to the sensations they so expertly elicit.

I don't try to resist anymore. I want them all. But there's a lingering unease.

How can I be so aroused and still want to run away, to escape these men who've taken my body and mind hostage?

Another orgasm comes, ripping the worry away and following the path Cav maps out with his mouth and fingers.

It's a struggle to draw in breath when Cav finally stops. He helps me flip onto my back, still trembling with the orgasm. I reach up to touch him, traces of me glistening on his lips, but he grabs my wrist, his fingers digging in painfully.

Wilder elbows in, taking Cav's place between my legs and running a single finger along the slick folds of my entrance. His touch is too hard—like he's staking his claim.

I squirm away, gasping when he slaps my thigh.

The sharp sting jolts me out of the haze of ecstasy. I wrench out of Cav's hold and scramble off the bed, grabbing the blanket on the floor and wrapping it around me.

Kaspian takes another slow sip of his scotch, still watching from the bar. His eyes are bored, but his grin is diabolical as he finally speaks up.

"Do you think we're little boy virgins in cloaks, chanting with our candles and *Ouija* boards in our mothers' basements and singing devil's hymns?" Kaspian asks with faint traces of amusement on his lips. "No, beastie. We are from the under-world, honed to inflict pain, trained to torment anyone deemed an enemy by the Sovereigns. And for our failures, we suffer punishments equal to our transgressions, which we've now passed on to you."

In a simple blink, these men can turn into executioners, uncaring of whose head is on their block.

Even if it's mine.

"You've never truly seen us at work," Cav adds, his mouth and chin sheening with my arousal. He hasn't bothered to wipe it away. "All you know is our talents in pleasure. We possess pain in equal measure, and you've been deliberately separated from it. Don't make us further prove this to you."

Stupid, stupid girl. How could you think they'd be anything more?

I flinch away from the cruel internal voice.

The sound of the initiates below, lost in their partying vices, streams into Cav's lavish bedroom, filling the air with moans, laughter, and clinking liquor bottles.

But all I can focus on is the erratic pounding of my heart.

Axe moves to shut out the cold wind from the balcony with a flick of his wrist against the open French doors. Wilder helps to resettle the blanket around my body, bringing with it a warmth I can no longer feel.

It's uncharacteristically gentlemanly of Wilder to maintain my modesty, and he proves that when he unleashes his half-cocked smirk and slides his palms down my arms as he smooths the cashmere. His touch, once familiar and pleasurable, sends a shudder through me that I struggle to suppress, blinking back tears.

Clutching the blanket tightly around my shoulders, I face Kaspian squarely, searching his face for the answers I deserve.

I get nothing in return.

It's with a mixture of indignation and disbelief that I whisper, "I did what you wanted. Now you owe me. How do you know Maverick broke the ruby in half? And why would you *ever* believe he was killed for it?"

Kaspian doesn't react. His gimlet eyes hold mine as he responds over the rim of his drink, "I have my ways. But trust me when I say that the Sovereigns will stop at nothing to find where he hid the other half."

Frustration bubbles up like acid, searing any remnants of desire until it's nothing but ribbons of smoke. This isn't a joke, even though it's clearly amusing to them.

"Maverick was my brother," I manage to say, my tears blurring the four men surrounding me. "He was only 21 when he died. Younger than any of you here. He had less than a year at TFU before his murder. I—"

I cut myself off with a gulp. This year, I'll be older than him. The realization nearly undoes me.

Kaspian studies me for a moment. Is he feeding off my pain or empathizing with my grief? His granite expression refuses to hint at either.

Finally, he sighs. "I suppose I do owe you a reward for doing what you were told and being our dirty, obedient darling. There's more to the Heart than meets the eye. It holds power, ancient and deep-rooted."

Oh, that is *it*.

I snarl, "*Fuck* you. If you start spewing magic at me right now, that my brother was killed because some maniacs think this is a *fucking* school for wizards and spells—"

"Not magic," Kaspian calmly interjects. Though Cav's expression shutters like he doesn't entirely agree. "It's a symbol. Status, history, evidence of atrocious deeds. The Sovereigns want the Heart to maintain their iron grip over the Court and every high ranking individual they can blackmail and control. They've used it against our fathers, and they'll use it on us. In any way they can."

"But why involve Maverick?" I press. "He had nothing to do with the Cimmerian Court. He liked video games and books and related more to online friends than real-life ones. What did he have to do with any of this?"

Cav speaks next, allowing my "reward" of information to continue.

A bitter thought surfaces. *Well, at least they're true to their word.*

He says, "Your brother had Anderton blood in him, same as you. Not only that, he uncovered something he shouldn't have. Combine those two things, and you will get some very vengeful Sovereigns. Something made him break that ruby and prevent the Court from possessing its full value or even their ability to prove it's the lost Heart. That tells me your big brother discovered something about the Court's past that might just be more valuable than the ruby itself."

I struggle to process his meaning. "What are you saying? This is a gemstone. A piece of jewelry. It's not like it could sit down and tell Maverick its history. And he'd have to be interested to study Sarah Anderton, which is just not like him. He wasn't passionate about the history of Titan Falls. We had enough going on at home."

I avert my eyes after the confession, heat moving from my neck to my cheeks. I've never admitted the state of my home life to anyone except Sasha.

But even without looking at them, I'm incredibly aware of their unblinking study.

I fight off the urge to argue against their callous answers—that I've stared at this necklace with the jagged ruby and gnarled metal finishes for so long, my eyes crossed. It gave me no answers as to why so many are hungry for it. It didn't do anything but bring me in front of these men, made me vulnerable enough to care for each irredeemable quality they possess, and ripped my brother away.

If Maverick was involved with the Court, with these corrupted men and a poisoned secret society operating around campus and spreading their erosion across the globe...

No. Not him. *Not my sweet, quiet older brother.*

"The Heart isn't just some sparkly rock," Cav continues over my internal agony. "It carries its weight in blood. If Maverick was after it and broke it, then there's something either he or the Court is desperate to keep hidden."

My mind starts to form a complete picture. One I really don't like. "Why would the Court kill my brother before getting an answer on where he put the other half? And if they knew my family had it, why all the smoke and mirrors with the four of you? Why not just kill me—"

"Don't say it," Axe growls.

I jolt, so intensely focused on the two men giving me

answers that I failed to remember the predator at my back, silently observing until he prowls to the forefront. And Wilder, his arms crossed as his hunter's eyes assess Cav's and Kaspian's responses.

"Don't finish that sentence," Axe adds, half his profile bathed in columns of moonlight streaming through the panels of the balcony doors. "The Court isn't going to kill you, too. Or get anywhere near you."

Cav nods, ceding Axe's point. His stare scrapes over me with invisible claws. Moments ago, our real nails were doing just that, memorizing skin, gouging our claim into one another.

Yet so much has changed in such a small amount of time, minutes separating our pleasure far from my grief.

I blink out of it.

Out of falling for *them*.

Wilder's opinion rumbles to life. "We may never know why Maverick died when he did, because that's how our Sovereigns operate. Riddles, shadiness, lies, manipulations."

"I refuse to let that be the answer," I say. "We find it. We find the other half of the Heart and expose the Sovereigns for who they truly are."

Even though I *still* have no idea how a ruby will do that.

The continued chill in the room despite being cut off from the rest of the cavernous manor seeps into my bones, goose bumps rising on my exposed skin. The blanket around my shoulders does little to shield me from the drop in temperature … or these men.

But I forge on, because the only softness in this room is the cashmere. "Wilder, you lost someone too. How would you feel if this were you? Being told Maverick was killed because of mind games, but never getting to the bottom of it? Never getting your *revenge*?"

"Careful, sweetwitch. Your mouth is way too innocent for that word," Wilder murmurs. "And you don't want to know the kind of revenge I seek."

His words are firm, but his eyes betray all the past horrors he's endured. Clinging ghosts I'm starting to recognize all too well.

I imagine what he must've endured that night, the mania and anguish that would have coursed through him when his friend Teagan was shot and killed. He tried so desperately to save her, but sometimes even the most tenacious efforts fall short.

But even as I sympathize with Wilder's loss, my anger at his inaction surpasses it.

"How long will you bide your time?" I ask him then, motioning to include the other three. "How long will all of you keep enduring their punishments and their orders and their torture?"

I hone in on Axe, the one who carries the most physical evidence of the Sovereigns' wrath. His unreadable gray eyes carefully hold mine, sensing my hyperawareness of every brutal slash made on his skin. I have the feeling that out of the four, I could get through to him first.

Stepping toward him, I ask, "How many more scars will you carry until it's too much?"

The room, deliberately quiet before, falls into deathly silence.

Axe flinches under my scrutiny, his throat bobbing as he struggles to find the right words.

"Finding the ruby... it's our only chance to gain the Sovereigns' favor," he says hesitantly, avoiding my question.

"Enough with the vague answers," I press. "What are you afraid of if we fail?"

A long pause fills the air before Axe continues, his tone gravelly and barely audible. "I'm torn between my loyalty to the Court and my growing distrust of the Sovereigns. I always will be."

I stare at him, trying to comprehend. The man who had saved my life in the forest, who had touched me with a tenderness men like him shouldn't possess, would still serve the very organization responsible for my brother's death?

"How can you say that?" I demand, my voice rising with each word. "After everything they've done, after what they did to Maverick, to *you*, how can you even consider remaining loyal to them?"

Axe's jaw works, his expression hardening. "It's not that simple. The Court, the Sovereigns, they brought me out of hell."

And dropped you into another one, I silently retort, but wisely keep my mouth shut. Even when Axe infuriates me, I don't want to hurt him. I don't know if I ever could.

"Turning my back on them," he continues, "is not something I can do lightly."

I shake my head in disbelief. "But they're murderers, Axe."

"We all are."

I pivot, confronted by Kaspian's unsettling smile after that confession.

"So that's it then?" I ask with a tremble. "You'll just keep following their orders, no matter how many people get hurt? No matter how many lives are destroyed?"

With deliberate slowness, Axe advances, his hand outstretched. "Elara, it's not that simple—"

I recoil from his touch. "Don't. Don't try to justify this. There's no excuse for what you're choosing, for what the Sovereigns have done."

Wilder sighs, running a hand through his thick chestnut hair. "We're not asking you for forgiveness, sweetwitch."

Their indifference carves a hollow space beneath my ribs, eating away at my hope that I meant something to them. "You thought revealing Maverick's fate would break me. You're wrong, all of you. Instead, you've armed me with a fury that'll turn your world to dust."

I look at each of them in turn, my heart breaking with the realization of just how deep the Sovereigns' corruption runs. These men, once proud and strong boys, reduced to mere puppets, dancing on the strings of their masters.

"I can't do this," I whisper, backing away toward the door. "I won't be here anymore."

Kaspian intercepts me, his eyelids fluttering once, twice, like chameleon sensing the need to reveal his true self. "You can't go rogue on us, beastie. You'll fail."

I glare at him, my hands clenching into fists and tangling with the blanket. "Watch me."

I shove past him, ignoring the pitying looks on the others' faces as I storm toward the door. I wrench it open, the sounds of the debauchery below flooding the room.

"I'll find out the truth about Maverick's death, with or without your help. And when I do, the Sovereigns will pay for what they've done. To him, to all of you."

The door slams behind me, the sound fading as fast as it came.

I've just lit the fuse. But as I stride away, I wonder:

How long before they light theirs?

CHAPTER 2
ELARA

The coldness of the hallway creeps under my blanket as I round the corner and bring myself further away from Cav's room and the men reclining within it.

I'm vulnerable, exposed, my chest gaping with a fresh wound —betrayal. It's with that sick, unyielding ache that I push forward, refusing to linger in this house of nightmares.

My feet barely touch the cold marble tiles when Axe throws open Cav's door and catches up to me, his ash-blond hair like a muted halo in the soft light of the sconces along the scarlet walls.

He doesn't say anything or apologize for so lithely cutting into my path and blocking my escape.

Axe stands motionless as I take him in. His features are a study in paradoxes—beauty hewn from cruelty, softness ruined by misery. My attention lowers, catching on the patchwork of scars peeking from his sweater's neckline. His arms extend, offering clothes and a cloak. When our eyes finally collide, Axe probes for a reaction, but he'll only find the impenetrable wall they put there.

"You need to cover up," he murmurs. "Before you leave our wing. Cameras are everywhere."

"Oh, so your lords have decided I can leave? How benevolent of them."

Axe's carefully sculpted expression doesn't crack.

His concern comes off as an obligation, not care. I want to scream, to unleash the cyclone inside me. Here is a man who knows my brother's blood was spilled by those he serves, yet remains tethered to them like a phantom refusing to stop haunting this mansion.

"A car will be at the front," he adds.

"Thank you *so much* for your thoughtfulness," I spit back, the words tasting like acid on my tongue.

I hate that I'm beholden to them to get out of here. As soon as I stormed out of Cav's room, I realized my mistake. I could've at least sworn to go against them *after* I'd put clothes on and arrived home. There's also the issue of finding Sasha in this gigantic manor, and once I do, there's no way we can make that same trek through the forest Axe led me through.

Also, I have no clothes.

Even if I'd had the sense to grab my dress off Cav's floor, it's in shreds.

From Cav's fury. His need. His total, utter dominance and my submission to anything he wanted to do to my body.

Only my breathing fills the space in the quiet corridor, and my fingers loosen their grip on the blanket. It slips, cascading to the floor with a whisper, leaving me bare before Axe.

Axe, the statue, the pillar of self-control, falters. His eyes widen a fraction—an imperceptible flinch, but it's all I need.

"What's the matter? You've seen it all before," I say, the challenge clear.

Break, damn you, I want to add. *Just show me something. Some form of remorse, of shock ... of regret.*

Advancing toward him, each step measured, I close the gap that separates victim from traitor. He doesn't move, doesn't breathe, as I pluck the shirt and cloak from his rigid hands.

Fabric whispers against skin as I dress in sweatpants and a plain white T-shirt under his gaze, never breaking eye contact.

There's power in this silence, in this defiance.

"Elara—" His low rumble is almost a plea, but I've no patience for it.

Axe isn't about to apologize or win me over. No, he wants to explain his loyalty to the Court. My brother's *murderers*.

"Save it." I interrupt. My tone is ice, my posture regal despite the disaster that churns within.

The cloak settles around my shoulders, a black velvet shield against the scrutiny of Sovereign gods and men alike.

Without another word, I pull the hood over my head.

For one painful second, Axe looks like he might say something, but his mouth tightens and he turns away from me instead.

I do the same, the cloak billowing behind me like dark wings.

The grand staircase unfurls before me as I move downward, my focus split between stealth and tracking the never-ending initiate party moving from room to room in between selecting blind-folded girls to play with. The cloak's fabric brushes over me like a protective shroud, but it does little to stifle the heat of anger coursing through my veins.

When I spot Sasha standing at the base of the staircase, relief surges, quick and sweet. She's safe, her warm brown eyes meeting mine with an expression that mirrors my own.

"El," she says with a big smile, and there's a universe in that single word. Her familiar features are balm to the raw edges of my soul.

"Thank god you're okay," I say, rushing down the rest of the stairs.

She's wearing the same type of cloak I am, the hood drawn

back, her flowing black hair seeming to become part of the fabric.

We don't waste time catching each other up with what happened once we were separated. Sasha falls into step beside me as we navigate the maze of hallways leading to the main entrance.

It won't hit me until later, but it eventually will—the ease with which Sasha turns through each hallway, her chin up and her attention directly ahead … like she knows exactly where she's going because she's done it plenty of times before.

As promised, a black car idles on the circular driveway outside, its sleek form barely visible through the stained glass of the manor's doors. We slip into the back seat, the heavy door closing with a definitive thud that seems to seal my exit from this world.

Their world.

"Hey," Sasha begins, her voice soft and tentative so the driver doesn't overhear. "What happened in there?"

I glance at her, registering her earnestness. Sasha's been here before. She's comfortable in this world of sexual decadence. Yet I'm reeling from the fact that she's known about these secret gatherings and tasted their forbidden fruit without ever whispering a word to me.

"I…"

How do I even begin to unravel the night's events? The touch of Cav, Kaspian's goading, Axe's corrupted loyalty, Wilder's deliberate ignorance, my brother's murder. I bear scars that mar more than just flesh—they etch deep into the fabric of my being.

It's not just about the ruby Heart anymore; it's about revenge and justice for Maverick.

"Elara," she presses gently, her hand finding mine in the darkened space between us.

I should feel repulsed, disgusted perhaps, at the thought of Sasha reveling in such anonymous, high-risk escapades. But the emotion doesn't come, smothered by the weight of horror I bear, by the black tar that clings to my heart.

So I squeeze her hand, seeking solace in the familiarity of her touch.

"Let's just go home," I say, my voice barely above a whisper.

"Home," Sasha echoes, her smile a tiny flicker of what it usually is.

The car's engine purrs, a soothing undertone to the chaos spinning in my head. Outside, the estate fades into a blur of stone and wrought iron as we drive far away.

"Hey," Sasha teases, nudging my arm. "You're getting that face again where you look like you're plotting world domination."

A laugh escapes me, bitter and short. "Feels more like the world is dominating me right now."

Sasha leans closer, her brown eyes glowing bronze under the passing streetlights. "Want to talk about it?"

I turn my gaze out the window, watching the stars flicker in a black sky. How do I voice the tangle of hurt and anger, the sting of betrayal that lingers like Maverick's ghost on my skin?

"It's all just ... a lot," I admit.

Sasha releases a sob. The driver glances in the rearview, then dutifully away when Sasha buries her face in her hands and sobs again. "I'm sorry."

"Sasha?" I lean forward, clasping her forearms. "Sash, talk to me."

"It's because of me," she says, her voice escaping through the gaps between her fingers. "I shouldn't have just thrown you in there like that. But I've been so lonely—it's like this giant secret I've kept, going to their parties, participating in anonymous hookups. With your history with Kaspian or maybe Axe, I thought you'd be open to coming along and seeing what it's like, but then I couldn't find you. God, what was I thinking by bringing you? You must hate me now."

I absorb Sasha's confession, the weight of her loneliness and desperation settling like a stone in my chest. The car hums, engine vibrations thrumming through the seats as he takes the narrow, winding roads back to campus.

Sasha's face remains buried, her shoulders shaking.

I grip her forearms tighter. "Sasha, look at me."

She raises her head, tears streaking her cheeks, eyes glistening in the passing white glow of the moon.

My gaze doesn't waver as she searches my face.

"I could never hate you. You're my best friend."

Sasha's bottom lip trembles. "But I put you in danger. I was selfish, wanting to share that world with you without considering the consequences."

I shake my head, a small, wry smile tugging at my lips. "Danger seems to find me regardless. It's not your fault, Sash. None of it is."

She releases a shuddering breath, leaning into my side.

The car swerves, tires screeching against the asphalt. We lurch sideways, Sasha's shoulder slamming into mine. The driver curses, maintaining a white-knuckle grip on the wheel as he rights our course.

"What the hell was that?" I ask, heart pounding against my ribs.

The driver meets my eyes in the rearview, his expression grim. "Something in the road. An animal, I think."

Unease coils in my gut, a serpentine whisper of intuition. I twist in my seat, peering out the back window. The road stretches behind us, a ribbon of black fragmented by the red glow of our taillights.

And there, just at the edge of the illumination, a figure stands motionless.

Watching.

Waiting.

Recognition slams into me, stealing the air from my lungs. The figure's stance, the breadth of his shoulders, the tilt of his head—it's Kaspian.

But it can't be. We left him at the manor. He's bound to the Court, his loyalty unbreakable.

He's a proud killer.

"El?"

Sasha's voice cuts through my thoughts, her hand gripping mine. "What is it? What do you see?"

I blink, and the figure is gone, swallowed by the night.

A trick of the light, a manifestation of my frayed nerves. It has to be.

"Nothing," I say, tearing my gaze away from the window. "Just nocturnal animals, like the driver said."

Sasha's brow furrows, but she doesn't argue. We settle back into our seats, our mutual silence broken only by the engine's hum and the rush of tires on the pavement.

But as the car speeds onward, carrying us closer to the illusion of safety, I can't shake the feeling that the shadows are watching.

Waiting.

Biding their time until they can drag me back into their depths.

The key clicks in the lock, and Sasha swings our dorm room door open with a familiar creak. The smell of our mixing perfumes is so comforting, I nearly collapse with gratitude as we step inside our messy, mostly pink room—the exact opposite of the Court's Gothic grandeur.

I kick off my shoes near the foot of my twin bed.

"El," Sasha says, her voice quiet. "You're shaking."

I look down. My hands are indeed trembling.

Sasha's eyes—those warm coffee pools—reflect an array of emotions: concern, affection, but also ... anticipation? An odd sense of distrust ripples through me. How much can I trust her now that I know she's been sneaking off to a place where I am

100 percent certain there are stone tables, iron chains, and electric clamps in their basement? How much can *I* trust myself after willingly enduring it?

Or rather, how much can *she* trust herself before she ends up down there, too? It wouldn't be Axe, Wilder, Cav, or Kaspian tying her down, men who put my pleasure above theirs. It would be the initiates, the ones with no limits on what they can get away with when they lock the door behind them.

My voice barely rises above a murmur as I tackle the topic we've been tiptoeing around.

"This mansion you're going to for the anonymous sex…"

Sasha doesn't flinch at my open reference to her secret indulgence. Instead, her chin juts out slightly—a stance that bespeaks pride rather than shame. The hint of a smile tugs at my lips in silent respect.

I'm not about to shame her. It's not for me to judge what avenues she chooses to explore in her pursuit of pleasure.

All I want is for her—*us*—to stay safe during our uncommon pursuits.

"Thornhaven Manor isn't filled with rich playboys looking for a bit of fun, Sasha."

My confession comes as a faint whisper; low enough not to shatter our cocoon of faux normalcy within these four walls. "There's something far more evil about them. It's not just hedonism but something … perverse. You've realized that, right?"

Sasha's gaze lingers on mine, her expression unreadable. One I've never seen before on her open, cheerful face always behind a strumming guitar, or crunching on cheese puffs after a particularly bad day, or offering a pep talk when I tell her about hellish exams.

Do I know this person? Does she know me?

"I know something about them is off," she eventually admits. "But that's part of the allure, isn't it? The risk, the forbidden thrill of it all."

I search her face, trying to understand the emotions swirling beneath the surface. There's a hunger in her eyes, a longing for something more than the mundane existence of college life. But there's also a flicker of dread, a recognition of the chances she's taking.

"Sasha, you can't keep going back there. You don't know what they're capable of, what they might do to you."

She shakes her head, a rueful smile playing at the corners of her lips. "I can take care of myself, El. I've been doing this for a while now."

I want to argue, to make her see the folly of her actions, but the words die on my tongue. Who am I to judge her choices when I've been drawn into the same web?

The truth is, I'm just as lost as she is, just as trapped by their allure.

Sasha crosses her arms, her gaze dropping to the floor as she starts to turn away.

Before I can second-guess myself, I blurt, "Maverick was involved with them apparently. And his murder—it might be connected to that house. Or some of the people in it."

That gets her attention. "I knew there was more to them than just wealth and good looks. I've seen glimpses of it in the way they move, the way they speak." Sasha's throat bobs. "But I never imagined ... murder."

And there she is. My friend, who I feel like I've known forever and believes me without a second thought.

My shoulders relax at the recognition, though my answering nod is stiff. "They killed him. Kaspian, Cav, Wilder, Axe— they're sure of it."

Sasha's expression softens, and she reaches out, taking my hand. Her touch is grounding.

"Who are *they*? Tell me everything," she urges, guiding me to sit on my bed.

We sink into my familiar comforter, the scent of my laundry detergent adding to the calm, centering me.

Breathing out, I start from the beginning. The moment in

class when I became the center of the Court's attention. Cav Nightshade with his cruel smirk, Kaspian Valenti with his green eyes full of cruelty and arrogance, Axe Devereaux with his silent intensity and insatiable need, and Wilder with his possessive, rough touch.

Once I start, the truth is a spool of thread unwinding from my lips.

Their ruthless quest for the ruby Heart. The Cimmerian Court Secret Society and the three Sovereigns…

Sasha listens carefully, her eyes growing wide at times, slanting at others.

The old-fashioned cat clock on our wall ticks by unnoticed as I tell her about Maverick's alleged involvement with the Court and how this ruby necklace seems to connect all the dots. How he found the ruby Heart and split it in half. How one piece ended up in a necklace and was put in my hands by Gram on the day of his funeral.

And how I suspect the other half is still out there somewhere —possibly even within my reach.

As well as the Court's.

By the end of it, I'm curled up at the head of my bed, knees drawn to my chest, as Sasha paces the room.

The glow of our desk lamps throws her shadow against the walls, elongated and fluttering.

"So you're saying…" Sasha knits her brows together. "These men—Cav, Kaspian, Axe and Wilder—are after the ruby Heart? That they want to find the other half? And if they don't … they're toast?"

Nodding, I watch as she stares off into space.

She looks back at me suddenly, her face ashen. "What are you going to do?"

"I don't know," I admit. My voice is hoarse from all the talking and the growing trepidation. "But I can't just stand by and do nothing."

Sasha studies me for a long moment, her gaze probing. Then she nods. "We'll figure this out. We've faced worse before."

I chuckle softly at that, the sound devoid of true mirth. "Have we? Have we really?"

She gives me a pointed look. "Your goldfish died during our freshman year. That was pretty tragic."

Despite myself, a real laugh bubbles out of me, genuine and cathartic in its release.

Sasha climbs onto my bed, curling around me protectively. Her warmth is the softest blanket, and despite the chilling topic of conversation, I feel safer.

"Above anything else," she says into my hair as her fingers trace soothing patterns on my arm. "You're not alone in this. I may not be able to stand up to those brutes physically, but there are other ways."

Her voice lowers ominously on the last sentence.

"I have to find the other half of the ruby Heart before they do," I say.

Sasha pauses, shifting to look at me with newfound concern etched deep in her face. "I was thinking we call the cops on them. Schedule a raid. Or forge a letter from one of them to the Dean admitting to inappropriate relations with a professor."

"That's not enough," I counter softly. "Maverick made this my fight when he unknowingly brought disaster upon himself. I became the necklace's custodian when he died, so everything is intertwined. And if I don't step up now, the Court will, and they'll keep covering their asses. Maverick's killers will never be found."

"And the guys? Do you care what happens to them?"

I sigh, avoiding the question and rubbing my temples. I'm so tired, but sleep is a luxury I can't afford right now.

"I just ... I need to find the other half of the ruby Heart and end all of this before it gets any worse," I murmur, gazing blankly at the worn carpet between our beds.

Sasha's arms tighten around me as if she's trying to lend me her strength through that simple gesture. "They might care for you too, in their own twisted way."

Her words hit home. As much as there is a bitter rivalry and reckless manipulation between us, there's also an undeniable connection—an addicting brew of attraction and my unrelenting wish to save them before this gets worse.

I stiffen in Sasha's hold.

Save them. Like I have any idea what I'm saving them from. They said they were killers, but their hands do nothing but elicit ecstasy from me. They claim to be the Sovereigns' slaves, but the savage glint to their eyes tells me they enjoy viciousness over escape.

"I don't trust them," I say to Sasha. "Not completely."

"But...?" Sasha prompts, her eyes reading the hesitation in mine.

"But, I feel there's more to them than what they present to the world." My gaze falls onto my hands. "Maybe they're not entirely to blame for the actions they've been forced to take."

It's a thought that grew stronger the more I broke the story down for Sasha.

Sasha cocks her head to the side.

"So you think they're victims too?" she asks skeptically.

"In their own way," I admit. "Does it excuse what they've done? No. They still have the necklace they manipulated me into giving away. They still answer to the Sovereigns."

"Elara," Sasha begins, her tone cautious. "These men are in deep with this Court thing. If you decide to go after the ruby Heart..."

"They might be killed if they don't succeed first," I state grimly. "They said as much."

Her grip on me tightens, and she swallows audibly.

"I think I know where to start looking," I whisper shakily into the quiet room.

Sasha raises an eyebrow, curiosity spiking. "Oh?"

"Maverick's old room. My mom keeps it like a shrine. If he found the ruby and split it in two, there might be clues there."

Sasha nods. "It's worth a shot. And it sounds like the only lead we have right now."

The hidden study I found at Gram's place shifts into focus in my mind's eye, but I blink it aside for now. There's no evidence Maverick knew about William Jonquil's 19th-century office constructed behind an old grandfather clock at Wraithwood Estate. And I've already confessed enough to Sasha without making her head explode. I'll look through that study after I've sifted through everything Maverick left behind.

Sasha abruptly stands, jolting me on the mattress. She strides to the closet, yanking out a backpack and tossing it onto her bed.

"What are we waiting for? Let's go."

I blink, surprise momentarily overriding the fear coiled in my gut. "Now? It's the middle of the night, Sash."

She shrugs, already stuffing clothes and supplies—for her, that means snacks, a charger, and a can of Coke—into the backpack.

"Are you sleepy? Because I'm sure as fuck not. No time like the present. Besides, the cover of darkness might work in our favor."

"I hate to break this to you, but we're not professional burglars. I can just unlock the front door."

Sasha snorts. "Way to shatter my dreams, El. Here I was, fantasizing about scaling walls and crawling through air vents."

She throws the backpack over her shoulder and gestures toward the door. "After you, Agent Wraithwood."

I muffle a laugh and push off the bed. Despite it all, Sasha can still make me smile.

She's right, though. A certain thrill to this makes my pulse quicken. A high risk but necessary adventure.

But as I rise to my feet, my laughter dies down, replaced by terror. Reluctance. Panic.

Everything I thought I knew is being turned upside down, just like the men who've invaded my life and my heart. And Maverick, my treasured memories of him corrupted. How could he be involved in this?

What if I don't like what I find?

"Hey." Sasha elbows me, redirecting my attention.

As if sensing my indecision, she tosses me a small pocketknife from her desk drawer.

"For protection," she explains, her jovial tone fading into seriousness just for a beat before her lips pull into a fierce grin. "Let's go kick some secret society ass."

CHAPTER 3
CAV
THE PUPPETEER

The summons is expected.

A heavy *thud-thud-thud* against my door has all our heads turning.

We know that knock.

Dawn slides through the cracks in my blackout curtains like a goddess's fingers determined to illuminate her enemy's crypt.

The succinct snap when I draw the curtains shut snuffs out her progress.

"The Selection must be over," Axe says from his favored spot against the far wall.

Kaspian frowns at the small licks of fire struggling for survival in the hearth. "You'd think the Sovereigns would've stretched out their time with their own Selections."

"Those fuckers are so ancient, they fart bone dust," Wilder bites out, capping the crystal stopper of my scotch decanter with a sharp *clink*. "No way could they get through one thrust in sweet, young pussy before drowning the poor girl in a cloud of spores."

"Now, there's a vision I didn't need behind my eyes." Kaspian lowers his head and pinches the bridge of his nose.

Three knocks come again, the space between them shorter.

"Messenger boy grows impatient," Wilder croons, swirling the ice in his third—maybe fifth—drink.

We're all coping in our usual ways after Elara's illustrious exit a few hours ago. The fact that we're even coping is a huge red flag in itself. Accusing us of cold-blooded murder and subterfuge is a compliment. We didn't join the Court for anything less. But to be accused of it when we *didn't* do it ... that's what bothers us.

It's an insult.

Neither of us participated in Maverick's death or knew of it. That was confirmed the second after Elara slammed my door.

I went for their throats—Kaspian first.

He kept his smooth grin the entire time I hooked his neck, but I believed him when he said he had no fucking clue until he discovered the evidence yesterday.

Wilder dodged my physical restraint, choosing to run for my bed and jump on it like a goddamned toddler, daring me to catch him. In the pauses between my snarls, he denied any knowledge.

Axe preempted my interrogation by sneaking up behind me while I was distracted by the jumping idiot and coiled his arm around my neck, murmuring into my ear that if I thought he'd hurt Elara that way, I'd be dead before realizing I was incorrect.

These are my brothers. Not by blood, but *soul* brothers.

If they say they don't have any further information about Maverick Wraithwood, I believe them.

At the time of Maverick's death, we were seventeen and about to graduate from our various high schools. We would've just received the coveted invitation to officially join the Court as their members by enrolling at TFU.

The Court has global scouts who troll schools, clubs, and streets for the talents required to join their ranks. When looking for gifted criminals, they deliberately avoid juvenile detention centers or other justice systems since they have no interest in those who've been caught.

It makes me wonder how they scouted Maverick, the all-around golden boy and doting big brother. We didn't let Elara know he was an initiate. With the way she reacted to his involvement with the Heart, damning him further would've been too much for her.

Despite what it looks like, we *do* care about mental health.

Sometimes.

It's another question mark to add to my lengthy mental list regarding Elara Wraithwood.

With a long sigh, I stride across the bedroom, passing Wilder and Kaspian, neither of whom made a move to answer the knock.

I open the door to find a hulking initiate adorned in a black velvet cloak and the upper half of his face obscured by an ivory mask.

His chapped lips part to reveal his chipped front teeth.

"The Sovereigns request your presence immediately," he intones.

"Just me? I'm flattered."

The initiate isn't amused. Clearly, he didn't partake in the Selection, or if he did, he was one of the … colder ones.

He sneers, "All of you."

"Understood," I reply, my voice dripping with the usual frigid calm.

Snapping the door shut, I glance back at Wilder and Kaspian, whose expressions have all but morphed into masks of indifference.

But they're like me, and my blood boils underneath.

Closing my eyes as I take one last swig of my drink, an image of Elara pressed between me and the wall flashes across my mind; her body writhing under my touch, her sweet lips parting in gasps as I explored every inch of her. The thought sends a jolt into my cock.

Elara may be furious at me right now, but I'd love to fuck her while she's angry.

She'd be ferocious, clawing at my skin, biting, kicking, then tilting her head back and screaming in pleasure as I gave it all back to her tenfold.

I am abruptly brought back by Wilder's voice.

"What's the plan, Cav?" he asks with an intrigued smirk, clearly reading the lust-filled thoughts crossing over my features.

I send him a look that sends initiates screaming in the other direction. He merely cocks a brow.

"We tell them nothing," I answer.

Axe doesn't give any indication whether he agrees or disagrees with my decision. Wilder shrugs, and Kaspian frowns.

The floorboards creak under my weight as I head back to where Wilder and Kaspian are lounging and carelessly toss the crystal decanter in Kaspian's direction.

He catches it in midair without glancing toward me, or it.

Instead of telling them to take one last swig before we leave like I was going to, I begrudgingly ask, "What's on your mind, Kasp?"

He doesn't hesitate. "We can use this as leverage."

I frown at him, aware that Wilder's attention perks up at the scent of a good deal. "Leverage?"

Kaspian's eyes glint, as if he's already several steps ahead of us all.

"We use Maverick's involvement with the Heart as a bargaining chip," he explains. "We tell the Sovereigns we know more than they do, but we want something in return."

Axe scoffs in his corner, but doesn't deny that Kaspian has a point.

"Then we might as well tell them that Heart is broken. We can give them Elara's necklace, our one piece of leverage, so they can promptly kill us for destroying their sacred artifact," I counter.

Kaspian smirks and pours himself another drink into his empty glass on the side table. He'd never sully himself by drinking directly out of the decanter.

"They need us," he says matter-of-factly.

"They need us until they don't," I say as Wilder plucks the decanter from him and tips it to his mouth. "They seek every opportunity to punish us."

"We've gotten further into the hunt for the Heart than any other members. Ever," Kaspian adds.

Reluctantly, I motion for him to continue. I'm conscious of the Sovereigns waiting for us.

"We've outsmarted even the Vultures," Kaspian says. "We have a piece of the Heart. If the Sovereigns kill us, we can go no further, and that wouldn't bring them any closer to this ruby, now would it? Telling them about Maverick and the Heart, since clearly they weren't aware of his possession when they had him killed—as well as some of what I've found, perhaps the encrypted files in Maverick's flash drive that the Sovereigns can't access immediately, could buy us more time to present the Heart to them once it's whole."

"They could still torture it out of us."

Axe's voice, lower than hell itself, draws all of our attention.

And our answering silence backs up his point.

"It's nothing we haven't endured before," Kaspian says while swirling his drink.

He's right, damn him. We've all been on the receiving end of the Sovereigns' brand of "motivation"—it's how we all ended up here in the first place.

I'm saved by agreeing with Kaspian, maybe even changing my plans, when Wilder throws back his head and laughs, coarse and hard.

He says breathlessly between laughs, "You've got to be fucking kidding me! You want to blackmail them?"

Kaspian sets down his glass and rises, straightening the lapels of his blazer. "Do you have a better idea?"

"No, no, go ahead, use that as your bargaining chip. They own everything we have and everyone we've ever known. But sure, give the Court the one thing we've kept for ourselves.

Make sure to spread our legs for them, too, so they can fuck us fully."

"Wilder," I start to say, but his laughter cuts off and he looks directly at me, his gaze fierce.

But the flint in his eyes is fueled by something else entirely. Elara's introduction into our lives has brought his loss of Teagan back to the forefront, the two women becoming the same person: one he can't save.

It's consuming him from the inside out.

Giving the Sovereigns Elara's necklace, or exposing Maverick's brief possession of the whole Heart, means leaving Elara vulnerable, ensuring the Sovereigns' continued interest in her, perhaps bringing her to their chambers and doing god knows what until they discover what she knows. Even then, they might keep her out of pure, vindictive enjoyment, exactly like we do.

Save for our willingness to keep her whole.

My lips stiffen. Twist. Turn bloodless and feral.

Wilder has a true and striking point.

They can't have her.

"We hold on to all of our information for now," I say with surprising calm against the spreading wildfire in my head. "Including the necklace. Until we're certain it won't backfire on us."

Kaspian doesn't look happy about it, but he nods, understanding the hierarchy and that I'm in charge, which is also shocking. I have to believe he's come to the same conclusion—presenting Maverick on a silver platter means that Elara will be the Sovereigns' dessert.

"I can access Maverick's encrypted files, given some time," Kaspian says. "The bastard was good at tech, I'll give him that. Or he knew someone, but I guarantee you they won't be as good as me."

I say to Kaspian, "Find more about what Maverick knew, take us to where you discovered this flash drive, and we'll go from there."

"What are we supposed to do about the summons?"

At last, Axe creeps from the shadows after asking the question, his face pale and angular from the play of dark and light against his features.

I set my jaw. "Leave the Sovereigns to me."

Exhaustion gnaws at my brain as I lurch down the underground tunnel leading to our ritual chambers. I need to rest, but the thought of Elara fuels the thrashing tension within me. My body rebels against the distance from her, every muscle straining in her direction.

But in order to return to her, the Sovereigns have to be satisfied in some way tonight.

My gaze slants to Axe, his hulking frame mere inches from my right shoulder, a sentinel poised to intercept any threat. Wilder prowls to my left. His movements are fluid and predatory, a jungle cat stalking its prey. Kaspian guards our rear, his keen eyes scanning for any anomaly.

Our fighting circle was trained in us at a young age. Indeed, it was ingrained in us the instant we were torn from our beds after the Court's invitation, which conveniently did not list a date or time to arrive.

How old were we when we had to audition to become initiates? Thirteen?

It's a branding iron that has left an indelible mark on my psyche. Torn from our privileged homes, thrust into a world of violence and brutality, molded into the weapons the Court desired. The training, the torture, the endless trials designed to break us, to reshape us into their twisted image.

As legacies, our parents expected the abduction, but didn't warn us. They didn't get a heads-up, so why should their offspring?

We should be thankful we were legacies, which meant our

invitations were inherited but not our membership. Those scouted and chosen, the random selections around the globe, were taken with a lot less grandeur and much brutality.

Those initiated with us died, ran, or were cut down by their own family for their cowardice.

All for the promise of power. Control. Heedless and hedonistic for the rest of our lives.

Yet we endure. We survive. *We thrive.*

I will not falter. I cannot. Not when Elara's fate is woven with mine.

The thought of her, ignorant and vulnerable because of her brother's deadly mistakes, causes my hands to clench into fists, the knuckles cracking like gunshots in the quiet underground of the tunnel. I will not let them have her. I will not let them break her as they broke us.

The stone corridor winds directly under campus grounds, passing below the dorms, scholarly buildings, and recreation centers, with direct access points all if we choose to sneak in and alter papers, fuck co-eds, seduce professors … anything, really.

We reach the end of the tunnel, the massive iron doors looming before us like the gates of hell itself. I square my shoulders, drawing in a deep breath that fills my lungs with the stale, musty air. With a nod to my brothers, I step forward, my hand reaching for the handle.

The door swings open with a groan of protest, revealing the cavernous circular chamber beyond. The Sovereigns sit upon their stone thrones, their faces obscured by the emotionless masks clinging to their faces. The air is thick with the stench of decay, the coppery tang of blood, and the incense meant to diffuse the stench, a miasma that burns the back of my throat with each inhalation.

Black-robed figures ring the periphery, still as statues. In the center, atop a dais of obsidian, the three Sovereigns await.

I stride forward, my gaze unwavering as I move in front of the Sovereigns. I've never seen their true features or called them anything but the three Sovereigns, but I've always imagined them behind their disguises and how they likely regard me with a mixture of contempt and amusement, their lips curling into cruel smiles that promise only pain and suffering.

I mount the steps, spine straight, shoulders back. Kaspian, Axe, and Wilder flank me in a united front.

And we kneel.

The middle Sovereign fixes his bottomless gaze upon me. Firelight dances across the porcelain mask. "You took your time in answering our summons."

I incline my head, finding the Sovereign's stare through the eyeholes of his mask. "We came as soon as we received your summons, my lord."

The Sovereign leans forward, his robes rustling. "Yet you tarried. What pressing matters could possibly take precedence over our command?"

The undercurrent to his words runs deep. *Someone will be punished for your tardiness.*

I fight not to look at Axe.

And I refuse to tell them the information Kaspian uncovered. About Maverick. The files. This supposed hidden library underneath Thornhaven.

Do the Sovereigns know about this forgotten room?

The question gives me pause.

Everything I say must remain one step ahead. Half-truths. White lies. But never, *ever,* complete deception.

My attention flicks to the silent Sovereign, motionless, yet I can feel his study like spiders crawling under my shirt. To invoke his wrath—

We've never done it. For good reason.

The silent one hasn't moved, his gaze cold and dispassionate like the mask that conceals his face. A chilling reminder that he always watches. Always waits.

And I wonder how long it will be before my turn comes to kneel before him.

I choose my next words with care. "We were discussing the Heart, my lords. Strategizing on how best to retrieve it for the Court."

The center Sovereign leans back, his fingers steepling. "Is that so? And what, pray tell, have you discovered?"

I hesitate, weighing my options. To reveal what we know about Maverick risks exposing Elara to their machinations. But to lie outright invites the creativity of the silent Sovereign.

"We believe we have a new lead, my lord. One that may prove fruitful. But we need more time to pursue it."

The Sovereign's mask betrays nothing, but I sense his displeasure. "More time? You have already had ample opportunity to retrieve the Heart. Yet it remains lost."

I lower my chin, acknowledging the rebuke. "You are correct, my lord. But this lead is... delicate. Rushing in blindly could jeopardize everything."

The Sovereign's fingers drum against the armrest of his throne, a staccato beat that grinds against my ears. "And what assurances can you offer that this lead will bear fruit?"

I meet his gaze squarely. "None, my lord. Only my word that we will not rest until the Heart is in your hands."

A long, tense moment stretches out, the Sovereign's scrutiny boring into me like a physical weight. Then, abruptly, he nods. "Very well. You have one week. One week to bring me the Heart. Fail, and the consequences will be severe."

I bow my head, relief and alarm clashing. "Thank you. We will not fail you."

The Sovereign's masked gaze shifts to Kaspian, Axe, and Wilder. "And what say you three? Are you as confident as your leader?"

They bow their heads in unison.

Kaspian murmurs, "We will not let you down, my lords."

"See that you don't," the Sovereign growls before motioning with a bone-white hand. "Rise."

A weight lifts off my shoulders as I rise, my brothers along with me.

And that is my mistake.

The righthand Sovereign croons from his stone perch, "Kaspian."

Kaspian stiffens yet says with unaffected calm, "Yes, my lord?"

"You show much faith in Cavenaugh's leadership. Dare I say as much, if not more, than your faith in us, if you're willing to follow in his steps and allow this delay."

Sensing the direction of the conversation, Axe steps forward, bracing his posture for the worst. I shoot him the most murderous look in my arsenal, freezing him in place.

Leave the Sovereigns to me.

That is what I promised them.

Closing my eyes, I take a deep breath, thinking of the last person to touch me. The woman whom I settled between with such utter perfection, I no longer want anyone else. The way her lips split for me, her mouth, her pussy, her moans and whimpers as I soaked in her heat and felt oblivion for the first time.

I open my eyes.

And say, "As their leader, punish me for forcing them to heed my delay."

The chamber erupts in a frenzy of whispers and speculation. The black-robed initiates in their half masks shift and murmur like a swarm of agitated insects. The middle Sovereign raises a hand, silencing them.

My heart thunders in my chest, but I keep my expression impassive. "Let my punishment serve as a reminder to all. The Court's will is absolute."

After a beat of silence, the middle Sovereign nods. "Very well."

He motions to the black-robed initiates, who surge forward like a tide of shadows. Rough hands seize me, dragging me toward the center of the chamber. I don't resist, even as Axe lets out a low growl and Wilder's muscles bunch under his skin, ready to spring. Kaspian's lips pull back like he wants to confess, the finishing stroke to all of us.

My mouth wrenches into a snarl when I catch his eye. *Don't.*

Each of them obeys, though I can see the fury in their eyes, the helpless rage at watching me suffer for their sake.

I don't resist as I'm dragged toward the circular floor, its surface stained with the blood of countless punishments. They force me down, the cold stone biting into my back through my shirt.

Rough rope binds my wrists and ankles, then are tied to four wooden pegs one initiate has happily shoved into designated holes, stretching me out like a sacrifice upon an altar. I stare up at the vaulted ceiling, picturing Elara in this position. Envisioning nothing but her pleasure with my pain.

The second Sovereign—not the silent one, thank fuck—looms over me, his mask a death's head in the flickering torchlight. "You will learn obedience, Cavenaugh. One way or another."

He raises his hand, a glint of metal catching the light. A blade, its edge honed to razor sharpness. My teeth clench, a fortress holding back a flood of sound, bracing for the burn of fresh cuts.

The knife descends, slicing through my black shirt, parting fabric and flesh with equal ease. Blood wells, a crimson tide spilling across my skin. I bite back a scream, my body fighting the restraints.

Each cut is a masterpiece of agony. He peels back skin, exposing muscle and sinew. I writhe, swallowing my howls until I'm suffocating and unhinging my jaw to the point of dislocation.

My world narrows to white-hot fire.

Time loses meaning, reduced to an endless cycle of torment. The Sovereign's blade dances, leaving ruin in its wake. My blood paints the ground, rivulets filling the symbols carved into the stone underneath me.

Through the haze of pain, I cling to one thought, one image. *Elara.*

I will endure. For her. For the chance to hold her again, to lose myself in her warmth.

She hates me, but her body is made for me.

As I might be made for her.

An eternity passes before the Sovereign retreats, admiring his handiwork. The lead Sovereign begins chanting in a language I don't understand, part Latin, part guttural horror.

The curse. He's reinforcing it onto my flesh. I'm doomed. My life is forfeit…

I lie shattered, my chest a ruin of flayed flesh. Each breath is agony, my lungs straining against the ravaged cage of my ribs.

"Cross us again, and this suffering will seem a mercy."

My depraved surgeon turns, his crimson robes swirling, and strides from the chamber. The lead Sovereign finishes his chant. The initiates release my bonds, their hands slick with my blood.

I struggle to rise. Every movement is a new discovery of pain. Kaspian and Wilder are there, lifting me and supporting my weight. Wilder looks like he wants to throw up at the sight of my chest. Kaspian deliberately keeps his attention on me from the neck up. I'm too exhausted and dizzy from blood loss to see what, exactly, they've done to me.

Axe stands guard against the overexcited initiates, his face pensive.

We stumble from the chamber, leaving a trail of ruby droplets in our wake. The tunnel stretches endlessly before us.

I'm not going to make it. *Am* I ever going to make it?

I lean on my brothers, drawing strength from their presence.

The iron doors slam shut behind us with a final, punctuated clang.

We pass under the girls' dorms, where Elara is likely sleeping, completely unaware of the eternal cruelty occurring beneath her feet, leaving nothing but blood beneath her dreams.

CHAPTER 4
ELARA

The moon is a thin crescent, barely casting a glow on Farrow Estate as Sasha and I make our way through the small garden path on the west side. Farrow Manor, my mother's sanctuary and prison, looms like a sleeping dragon, its silhouette an ominous cut against the starless night sky. Sasha and I slip through the wrought-iron gates, our presence nothing more than whispers, fully committed to sneaking in.

I unlock the towering oak door, then inch it open. My racing mind juggles apprehension and courage while I scan the unlit corners for any sign of my mother's notorious traps.

"Remember that time your mom set up fishing line at ankle level?" Sasha whispers behind me as we creep in. "I'm pretty sure I still have a scar from tripping into her 'intruder alert' system."

I warn, my own voice barely above a breath, "She's gotten more creative since then."

"Booby traps by Elara's Mom: because who needs home security systems when you've got yarn and bells?" Sasha replies with a grin that I can feel rather than see.

I stifle the need to admonish Sasha for talking about my mother that way. "She doesn't trust any security installations or the people who install it."

Sasha has always had this knack for slicing through tension with her humor, even in the most harrowing situations, and I know she's doing it to help, not to insult. It's absurd, the lengths my mother will go to protect herself. Paranoia paints her world in bright colors of danger—every shadow a potential threat, every silence a harbinger of death—but I will always want to defend her, even as she peels off a bit of my soul every day she doesn't get better.

"Seriously, though," Sasha adds, her voice dropping an octave. "Yell out if you spot anything that looks like it came out of a spy movie."

"Will do." I keep my focus sharp, aware that one wrong step could send a homemade noisemaker blaring throughout the house. We navigate the hallway, a maze designed by a mind that sees enemies in every corner. It's a strange duality, living with someone who crafts fortresses out of fear, yet here we are, tiptoeing through the latest iteration of her makeshift security.

"Elara," Sasha says, her hand gripping my arm. "Stop."

I freeze. "What? What is it?"

"Look." She points at the floor where a nearly invisible thread stretches across our path, glinting faintly in the scarce moonlight filtering through a distant window.

"So she's kept the fishing line after all," I breathe out, stepping carefully over the tripwire. We continue on, hyperaware that one misstep could mean disaster—or, at the very least, waking the banshee that is my mother by springing her traps.

Sasha's presence is a constant comfort, even as adrenaline gets me up the stairs, through the winding hallway, and in front of Maverick's door.

I take the time to use my phone and illuminate the door-frame, well aware that out of all the rooms in the manor, my mother's and Maverick's are her top priority to protect. Finding nothing *yet*, I inspect the door's handle.

"There," I whisper. "You see it?"

Sasha peers over my shoulder, adding her phone's light to mine. "Nope."

"A piece of her hair." I motion to the subtle shine of a hair strand, wavy and long, laid over the lever. "We have to make sure we put it back when we leave."

Sasha nods. "Got it."

After carefully laying the strand of hair on the neck of the handle where we won't disturb it, I push the door open.

We slip inside, the moonlight casting a ghostly glow across a life cut tragically short. I can almost hear Maverick's laughter, a lost sound from a happier time that now feels like a distant dream.

Sasha lets out a low whistle, her gaze sweeping over the motley collection of posters and gamer trophies. "Do we have to worry about any traps in here?"

"No. Mom wouldn't disturb Maverick's stuff. This is like a shrine to her now. We have to return anything we touch or move exactly as it was."

A pang of sadness clogs my throat at seeing my brother's world exactly as he left it the day he died. It's as if he could walk through the door at any moment, flashing that quiet smile before burying his head in his computer or comics.

"Hey, check this out," Sasha says.

She's holding up a CD stacked with others on his desk, the cover emblazoned with the bright, grinning faces of a once-famous boy band. "Maverick had a thing for these guys?"

"Shut up," I retort half-heartedly, the corner of my mouth twitching upward despite myself. "They were popular back then, even to him."

"Sure, sure." Sasha laughs under her breath, carefully placing the CD back onto the shelf.

My fingers glide over the spines of books, tracing the faded titles and worn edges of his fantasy series collection that line his shelves. Holding them creates a physical connection to him.

Mavvy was always such a book nerd, reading on his beach chair during our rare family vacations while I splashed him from the pool, begging him to join me.

Sasha picks through his desk drawers, her forehead wrinkled in concentration as she hunts. The reverent hush of the room is broken only by the soft shuffling of papers and the occasional creak of the floorboards beneath our feet.

I slowly straighten the sheets of Maverick's mattress after checking under it, ensuring they're as crease-free as they were before.

Glancing at his closed laptop, I remember Maverick's obsession with *Warcraft* and his deep involvement with the online gaming community. Maverick was smart, levelheaded, and popular. He avoided trouble, yet attracted the most popular kids in school, who'd invite him to underage parties and offer him drugs, sex, and trips on their private jets. My middle school friends told me that Maverick's hotness overrode any geek in him, including his love for elves, castles, and dragons. Girls found it adorable.

Sasha and I search the room meticulously. Our hands glide over the surfaces of Maverick's belongings, and our eyes scan for any clue that might lead us to the answers we seek, my heart twisting as our disturbance causes the last remnants of his cologne to waft into the air. I resist the urge to bring one of his shirts to my face and inhale deeply because of the risk that I'll break down.

I was never allowed in Maverick's room after he died. The one time I tried, Mom collapsed at the threshold and wailed so terribly, I didn't do it again.

A loud creak from the hallway snaps my head toward the door. Sasha and I freeze, ears cocked.

Silence.

Sasha mouths, *What was that?*

I shake my head, straining to detect any sound. When I hear none, I gesture for her to keep looking.

It's when I turn back to Maverick's bed, one side shoved up against the wall, that I see…

There—almost hidden in the everyday—is something odd. A pattern on the wallpaper that doesn't quite belong.

Farrow Manor came to my mother in its original state when she inherited it from her parents, including the ancient, yellowed wallpaper in almost all the rooms. Renovation was prohibited in both the wills and testaments of my ancestors and historical home laws unless necessary. Mavvy and I tried to get around living like 15th-century children by asking for modern items, but the clashing of state-of-the-art furniture against the traditional furnishings upset my mother so much that we took down our posters, matched our sheets to the wallpaper, and chose wooden bed sets.

Maverick's room has arabesque wallpaper, and I only know that because it creeped me out so much, I had to reverse-image search it on the internet. It's a mixture of flowers, foliage, fruit, and animals, coming together in intricate lines, almost appearing like lace from far away. The complicated pattern causes the eye to skim over small details until I catch the pen marks.

"Look at this," I murmur to Sasha as I crawl on to the bed, my fingertips brushing over my brother's … drawings?

A series of dots and dashes, so small you'd miss them unless you knew where to look.

"Whoa." Sasha leans in beside me, squinting at the deliberate marks. "Was Maverick known to doodle on his wallpaper before drifting off to sleep?"

"Definitely not." I angle my phone to illuminate it better. "Do you think he's trying to tell me something? Maverick knew how much I hated this wallpaper, which meant I had to learn everything about it to make sure it wasn't haunted. He laughed at me while I did it, but … maybe he figured I'd notice the difference one day if something happened to him."

Because the Maverick of my memories is no longer the brother I thought he was. Maverick got himself involved in something evil, a situation requiring coded messages and secret enclaves and death.

I swallow.

"Do you think we can look it up?" I ask Sasha, leaning away to give her space.

Sasha whips out her phone, the screen flooding the dim room with bluish light. She snaps a picture, taps furiously, and waits. Whatever app she chose churns, grinding through possibilities until—

"Got something," Sasha exclaims. She holds the phone out to me, and I lean in to see the screen. "It's Morse code."

Sasha's app translated the code and spat out numbers and degrees.

"Coordinates," I murmur. "Latitude and longitude."

"Yep." Sasha bites her lip as her thumbs fly across her screen. "Whoa. Look where it leads."

I read the screen when she flips it my way. My chin jerks back in surprise. "Gram's house?"

A headache blooms, my brain cramping with the possibilities. We played at Wraithwood Manor all the time, hide-and-seek being one of my favorites. And Maverick held parties to impress girls there whenever he could get away with it. We were both incredibly familiar with the layout, the best rooms to hide in, the places that—

"Oh shit," I whisper.

"What?"

"I found a hidden room a few weeks ago. An old office. Like *old* old. From the 1700s. I figured I was the first person to find it in decades, hundreds of years even, but maybe Maverick found it first." My heart speeds up. "That would be the *perfect* place to hide important, evil things."

Sasha slowly lowers her phone to her lap. "You Wraithwoods are a weird-ass family, you know that? Lovable but ... weird."

"Tell me about it."

"So I take it we're breaking in there next?"

I nod. "I won't be able to sleep until we do."

Sasha slips off Maverick's bed. "Onward, Agent."

We perfect Maverick's room, ensuring nothing is out of place or will disturb my mother when she visits next, until I open Maverick's door, the coordinates burning a hole in my head.

"Ready?" Sasha says.

I nod, tucking my phone into my back pocket. But before we can move, a creak echoes down the hallway like a warning shot. Instinctively, we stiffen, our eyes locking.

Another step makes the wooden floorboards groan, closer, louder.

"Hide!" Sasha hisses, and we shut Maverick's door and scramble for his closet, throwing ourselves inside just as the bedroom's door handle turns with an ominous click. The closet is cramped, the musky scent of leather and moth-bitten clothing wrapping around us.

Sasha's hand finds mine in the dark, squeezing tight. "It's just your mom, I'm sure. We have nothing to worry about."

Through the narrow slits of the closet's panels, a black-clad figure, disguised from head-to-toe, tears through Maverick's things without any regard or respect.

No.

I don't realize I've stepped forward until Sasha jerks me back.

His silhouette is jittery, movements erratic, like a marionette being yanked by unseen strings. I can tell it's a man from the broad set of shoulders, the tapered waist and thick thighs. He wears gloves and a ski mask, the eyeholes flashing the whites of his eyes as he turns and walks through the slit of moonlight through the window.

I don't recognize him.

"Come on, come on," he mutters to himself, fingers combing through Maverick's desk drawers with frantic urgency. Papers rustle, and objects clatter.

He's searching for something—desperate, obsessed.

"Elara…" Sasha breathes, so quiet it's almost part of the stuffy closet.

"Shh." I press my finger to my lips even though I know Sasha can't see it. My heart thuds against my ribs, so loud I'm sure it's threatening to give us away.

The man upends a vintage wooden box Maverick stuffed his knickknacks in, its contents spilling across the floor—a cascade of memories, trinkets, and pictures frozen in time. He moves to Maverick's bookshelf next, pulling out his beloved books one by one, flipping through pages, then tossing them aside without care.

The sight snares my breath and tears at my heart; these are sacred leftovers of my brother's life, treated as nothing more than obstacles in a frenzied quest.

"Please," he whispers to no one, or perhaps to Maverick himself. "Where is it?"

His voice is too low. I can't link it to anyone I know.

The air in the closet is getting thicker, heavier. I dare not blink, dare not breathe too loud. Beside me, Sasha's grip is a lifeline.

The man pauses, his head cocked, listening for something we can't hear. For a moment, I think he's sensed us. It's only a matter of time before he decides to search the closet. I wish I'd picked up a weapon on my sprint here. Even Maverick's NYC snow globe from 2004 currently rolling across the floor would do.

My pulse hammers in my ears, but he resumes his search, tearing through Maverick's belongings with renewed fervor.

What is he looking for? Will he notice the wallpaper, the message hidden in plain sight?

"Elara," Sasha whispers again, a question laced in her tone. *What the fuck do we do?*

Keep still, I mouth soundlessly, my gaze never leaving the sliver of space that allows me to witness this man's unraveling.

Eventually, the frenzy subsides, his shoulders slump, and he stands at the center of the mess he's created. A low, pained sigh escapes him, and I feel it—a sharp twist in my chest.

This is pain, raw and unfiltered.

He turns slowly to the closet.

"*Elara...*" Sasha says once more, her voice a stretched thread close to snapping.

The truth is, other than scream and scratch our way through him once we're revealed, I don't know what we can do. I clench my phone in my hand, ready to use it as a mallet against his head.

A distant thump, like something heavy hitting the floor, sounds out in the hallway. We share a concerned glance at the same time the man whips his head toward Maverick's door, his leatherclad hands fisting.

Moving with silent precision, the man slinks out of the room, quietly shutting the door behind him.

Sasha jerks forward, but I stop her by clamping my hand around her arm.

I mime, *Wait.*

After five minutes of hearing nothing out of the ordinary, I inch the closet door open, wincing at every unwilling sound we make.

But my mother is alone in this house. Her fears are realized by a man rifling through our things. If she stumbles upon him, or worse, if he seeks her out...

"God, El," Sasha exhales as we step out of the closet and into the aftermath.

I can't think of cleaning up right now. We have to get to my mother.

"Did you see his face?" I ask as I creep toward the bedroom door, lending half an eye and all my fear to the hallway beyond.

Sasha shakes her head, her eyes clouded with concern.

"Do you think he's complicit, or a victim in all this?"

Sasha's question makes my shoulders tense.

"Both? Neither?" I answer while battling a sobering thought.

The intruder could be like us—pawns thrown to the mercy of a merciless Court, scrambling for answers in desperate places.

Those answers still elude me, but one truth stands out—that man is not welcome in our home.

The hallway stretches dark and still. I motion for Sasha to follow as I slip out, eyes roving for any tripwires, other traps, or more men in black ready to jump us.

At the end of the hall, a door hangs open a crack.

My mother's room. She always shuts and locks her door.

I dart forward, the dread of something happening to her thick in my mind.

Sasha's hand finds my arm, pulling me back. She shakes her head minutely, mouthing, *We need to call the police.*

I shake my head in return. The police, with their blinding lights and chaotic storm of authority, would only push my mother further into her madness. The man wasn't after her; he was looking for something.

Sasha hisses a warning breath as I near Mom's door, where a faint rustling becomes audible. I grip the door handle, heart thundering in my ears. With a deep inhalation to steady myself, I push it all the way open.

My mother cowers in a corner. She's tangled in bedsheets she tore off her bed and muttering unintelligibly. Bottles of medication and supplies litter the floor around her. She doesn't seem to register our presence.

I carefully enter the room, sidestepping the debris. "Mom? It's just me, Elara. We need to get you to safety."

Mom's eyes, lost and feverish, clash against mine.

"*Stay back!*" she shrieks. "*You're not real! You're not my daughter!*"

Sasha moves to my side, hands raised in a calming gesture. "Hi, Mrs. Wraithwood, remember me? I'm Sasha, Elara's roommate. We're not going to hurt you."

"Lies! *Liar!* You're shapeshifters, you can't fool me!"

The accusation flies from her lips with venomous certainty.

Mom grabs blindly at the clutter around her, seizing an antiquated revolver.

"Fuck, fuck, *fuck*."

Sasha's panicked whisper hisses through her clenched teeth.

Mom levels it at us with trembling hands and a deranged look in her eyes.

CHAPTER 5
ELARA

"Is that thing loaded?" Sasha asks in a wet whisper.

The truth is, I have no idea. My mother is paranoid enough to ensure the gun's chamber is filled with bullets, but she's also scared enough to leave it empty in case it's ever used against her.

Mom stares at me, into me, with wild, untamed hatred, her eyes shining with furious tears over the barrel of the gun.

"Fifty-fifty," I say to Sasha, who deserves nothing but honesty.

"*Fuck*." Sasha inches back a step, her hands raised. "How good is her aim?"

I'm too focused on my mother to answer. Her finger tenses on the trigger, knuckles blanching white.

"I know who you are," she snarls. "And you're not my daughter. You're not going to do to her what you did to my son. I'll make sure of it."

Sasha trembles, a choked sob escaping her throat. "Please, don't, Mrs. Wraithwood."

I raise my hands slowly, palms out. "Mom, listen to me. You don't want to do this."

"*I am not your mother!*"

"You are." The sob finally comes, swelling in my throat before releasing with a painful keen. "You're Caroline Wraithwood, your son was Maverick, and I'm your daughter, Elara."

Her eyes, manic and darting, turn dull and lifeless with a single blink. "My son is gone."

I nod despite Sasha frantically warning, "Don't say anything to upset her!"

"But I'm still here. I'm alive, with you," I plead, my hands raised, fingers shaking. "Maverick's with Dad now, and you and I have each other. You'll always have me, Mom."

With a single jerk of her chin, her paranoia returns. "*You're not her*! You were in here, in black, and now you've shapeshifted because I saw you trying to hide. I *saw* you despite your attempts to deceive me, you fucking devil. And now you beg me? Make me think you're Elara? Liar. Liar, *liar*, LIAR!"

"Change tactics," Sasha pleads to me. "Change them real quick, El."

But I'm at a loss for words as my mother raises the gun higher, its barrel aligned with my chest.

"Mom," I sputter out, desperate and yanking at any memory I can to prove to her I'm real, "I heard you. I heard what you said to me when you thought I was asleep, when you snuck into my room when I was eight, remember?"

She pauses, her roaming stare locking onto mine.

Drawing on the memory, I say, "You'd just come home from your first gala since Dad died. It was so hard for you, you said, so impossible to do without him even though eight years had passed and you should be better by now. But then you ..." I swallow against the swelling in my throat. "You said how you remembered who was waiting for you at home. Your reason for surviving, for enduring for as long as you have. Me. I was your last piece of Darian Wraithwood, and I was so small, your baby, his baby, and I needed you. You couldn't leave me, and I helped you keep going. Do you remember that? How could I know that if I wasn't truly Elara?"

Mom's grip loosens on the trigger. "Elara?" she whispers.

"Yes, Mom." I nod, tears streaming down my face while I keep my hands up. "It's me. I'm here."

Her gaze darts to Sasha, then back to me. "You're... you're not one of them? You're not here to take me? Not like your father?"

The mention of my father in her harrowing question sends a jolt through me. "What do you mean like Dad?"

Mom's eyes fill with an eerie, distant look. "He was born into it, groomed for it."

Sasha and I exchange shocked expressions. Her arms must ache as much as mine, the way we're holding them aloft, not daring to lower them.

"Dad was part of the Cimmerian Court?" My question comes out in a hushed murmur.

"Mavvy." Mom's hoarse voice is barely audible, yet it commands my full attention. "He knew... knew too much. Tried to shield us all."

My heart clenches at my mother's words, the weight of Maverick's actions suddenly pressing down upon me. What did he uncover, and why had he felt compelled to protect us at such a cost?

"Hidden truths," Caroline continues, her gaze piercing through the haze of her delusions. "In the walls, beneath the floors, in the heart of our houses."

I exchange another look with Sasha, seeing my own confusion reflecting back. The Cimmerian Court, my father, my brother, the ruby Heart...

Mom mutters under her breath, lowering the gun slightly as she retreats into her head.

I hesitate, desperate to ask her more, to understand the giant skeleton my family has kept hidden. But more questions will only agitate her fragile mind.

Sasha touches my arm, nodding toward the door. "We need to get her help. You can't do this by yourself anymore, El."

"But I…" I wrench my stare from Sasha back to my mother, who no longer responds to us, lost again in her cursed world.

She was forced into this breakdown, I want to argue. *Someone was actually here, going through our things, scaring the shit out of my mother, breaking her where she was already fractured…*

The argument turns to ash in my throat.

Tears slip down my mother's cheeks as she stares at spirits I can't see, the gun dangling in her hands. It doesn't matter who incited her tonight. Sasha could've been hurt. Killed. Mom could've killed me, too, and she'd never recover from that.

"I love you, Mom," I whisper.

She doesn't respond.

Sasha tugs at my arm, a pained grimace on her face. "How do we—I mean, can we leave her here with the gun while we call the EMTs? Or do we … take it?"

I gently pull out of Sasha's grip, taking another step, then another, until I'm close enough to reach out and touch Mom.

"Give me the gun, Mom," I say softly, holding out my hand. "You don't need it anymore."

She lifts her gaze, and for a moment, I see a flicker of the woman she used to be—strong, loving, fierce in her devotion. Then her eyes cloud again, and she shakes her head.

"No, no, I have to protect you. From them. From the Court. They'll come for you like they came for your brother, your father…"

Fighting to keep my composure, I push away the burning questions threatening to consume me. I have to focus on the present, on getting the weapon out of her hands.

"I know, Mom. And you have protected me all these years. But now it's my turn to protect you." I take a deep breath, steeling myself. "Give me the gun, and let me take care of you."

A heartbeat passes, then two. Mom's eyes search my face, as if looking for a sign, a reason to trust. I let her study me, pouring all my love, all my desperation, into my returning stare.

The door creaks behind me, and I stiffen as someone else's footsteps calmly wander in.

No. Not when I was getting through to her.

I risk turning, meeting the eyes of the person ruining everything—

—is it him? Is it the burglar dressed in black?—

And see Kaspian dressed in his impeccable suit, holding a polished handgun and directing it at my mother. "Kaspian? What the—Get out! Stop pointing that at my Mom!"

His flat, snake-colored stare regards my mother. "Put down the gun, Caroline."

Mom screams, spittle flying onto the barrel of the gun as her grip tightens and shakes madly.

"You're one of them!" she shrieks. "Here to take me, to silence me like you did Darian and Maverick!"

Then I do something stupid. Mind-numbingly dumb. But I can't stand by and watch Kaspian, who shouldn't be here, doesn't *belong* here, threaten my mother.

I position myself between them, Kaspian's gun at my chest, my mother's at my back.

"Oh, Jesus fuck," Sasha cries out.

The skin around Kaspian's eyes reacts with a minuscule flinch at my boldness, that I'm now staring down the barrel of his gun, but his aim doesn't waver.

Kaspian's finger curls around the trigger. "Last chance, Caroline. Drop your weapon."

"Kaspian, don't," I gasp out. "She didn't mean to. She's not in her right mind."

"Oh, I think I've grasped that part of the situation."

"I'd calmed her down!" I shout. "She wasn't going to hurt us."

Kaspian acts like he doesn't hear me. "Put down the gun, Caroline, or I shoot your daughter."

My stomach turns to ice, though I hold his stare, ensuring

the silent accusation in mine speaks louder than words ever could. "You wouldn't."

The Kaspian who stands in front of me is a stranger. This isn't the man who promised to break me so he could put me back together with feverish, orgasmic care. His face doesn't burn with that brutal oath, nor does his cold, calculated expression crack the way it did when he pushed into me the first time.

No, I'm looking at the face of a killer. A trained, brutalized assassin who follows orders, not pleas.

"I'm not here to debate, beastie. Your mother is unstable and a threat."

Mom's shrill voice pierces the air behind me. "You won't take my daughter! I won't let you!"

I raise my hands, palms out, my heart thundering. "Please, both of you, just stop! Kaspian—leave. Why did you even come?"

His heartless expression doesn't shift. "There was a situation with Cav that led me to believe something might happen to you, too. I tracked you here."

I bare my teeth once he voices those words. "You were the one who broke in? Who tore through Maverick's room and put my mother in this state?"

He blinks, his hardened exterior pulling before snapping back. "Wasn't me." His finger tightens on the trigger as he looks over my shoulder, and I stiffen. "Last warning, Caroline."

He's not going to shoot me. I know this in a place deeper than bone or marrow, surer than a heartbeat.

Sasha inches closer, her hands still raised. "Kaspian, please. She's not well. We need to get her help, not threaten her."

At that moment, time slows.

I read the certainty in Kaspian's eyes that he *will* shoot Mom and can sense the madness in my mother's at my back. I feel the weight of the burdens they both carry, the cursed legacies that have driven us to this point.

And I make a choice.

I lunge forward, reaching for Kaspian's gun. He reacts instantly, twisting away, but my fingers brush the barrel, throwing off his aim. The shot rings out, deafening in the confined space, and I hear Sasha scream.

I whirl around, terrified of what I'll see. But my mother is unharmed, standing now as she points her gun at Kaspian.

"You missed," she hisses. "But I won't."

"Mom, no!"

Too late.

CHAPTER 6
ELARA

Tempest Callahan and Miguel Rossi stride through the front door of Farrow Estate like they own the place, leather and scruff highlighting their preference for darkness. The Vultures' presence makes the hairs on the back of my neck stand on end even though I'm the one who looked up Tempest's number in the online campus directory and blubbered out my need for incognito medical help.

Kaspian was shot, my mom did it, and I'm desperate not to call the police.

Both men are incredibly handsome, but my attention lands on Rossi and doesn't move for a good few seconds. Maybe because I'd already dissected Tempest's good looks when he cornered me in front of an abandoned mine a few weeks ago, and Rossi, former Professor at TFU, is now a whispered myth around campus.

His dark chocolate hair flows back from a sharp, jaded face. The golden undertones in his skin and subtle streaks of white in his hair aren't enough for the angel to win over the devil. He's tall, huge, and, according to Tempest, a former surgeon.

My eyes drop to Rossi's hands. Ones that when spread, could cover my entire face with ease.

I meet them at the base of the staircase, my arms tight at my sides.

Sasha's still shouting in the background as Kaspian tries to fight her off and staunch his own wound, and my mother's monotone voice is the percussion as she discusses the situation while shut in her bedroom with my invisible, dead father.

"Thank you for coming. He's in here," I say to them once Rossi's bottomless, black stare meets mine. Tempest merely arches an ebony brow over wintergreen eyes.

I lead them into the dilapidated sitting room, where Kaspian slouches forward on a tattered sofa chair, pale and sweating, but stubborn as an ass. Sasha huffs behind him, glaring at the back of his head. Kaspian's eyes narrow at the sight of Tempest, who lets out a low whistle upon noticing him. "Well now, this is turning out to be an interesting evening."

"Shut up," Kaspian snarls.

"Make me." Tempest smirks. "Unless you want to finish what your girlfriend's mommy started?"

Kaspian's lip curls into a sneer, rage simmering beneath the surface. "I wouldn't come to you buzzards for help if my head was on a block."

"Enough," I snap, even as my stomach flips at the fact Kaspian didn't deny the *girlfriend* part of Tempest's sentence.

Yes, I am either so in shock or so unhinged that I'm actually delighted at this moment.

"I asked them here. I had no choice," I say when Kaspian unhinges his jaw, likely to say something heinous. "No one else picked up their phone, including Cav."

They turn to look at me, Kaspian's anger fading into surprise.

Kaspian's lashes flicker, temporarily shading the toxic green of his eyes before he schools his expression. I resist the urge to question him on what awful news would keep the guys from answering my calls, choosing to focus on the present.

Rossi lowers his brows, snuffing out any shred of light from his eyes. "Believe me, Mr. Valenti, I'd much rather return to my manor where I was rather enjoying my weekend away from the city with a beautiful woman. You've interrupted. So rather than bleed out on Elara's chair, let's make this quick for all of us."

Kaspian grits his teeth as Rossi approaches with his medical bag, the former surgeon's movements precise and efficient.

I didn't notice that Sasha had sidled up to my side until she squeezes my arm. She says so only I can hear, "I heard Rossi's in the mafia now. There's a mafia don in your fucking. House."

I nod, like this is normal.

Rossi kneels beside the sofa chair, setting down a black leather medical bag and unzipping it to reveal an array of surgical instruments. Kaspian eyes the scalpels and forceps with suspicion, his muscles tensing beneath his blood-soaked white shirt.

I raise my brows at Sasha, impressed she got the blazer off him.

"He told me he'd turn the blazer into a noose around my neck if I so much as touched him," she mutters to me. "God forbid I try to use Armani as a tourniquet."

"I don't need your help," Kaspian growls at Rossi, even as his face drains of color.

Rossi ignores him, donning black latex gloves with a snap.

"Hold him down," he instructs Tempest, who stands behind Kaspian, gripping his shoulders.

"Is he going to be okay?" I ask.

The way Kaspian's body torqued backward after the bullet hit him, the surprise on his face, the idea of him *dying* at my feet...

I suppress an agonized moan at the thought.

"He'll live," Tempest says, his tone bored. "Rossi's patched up worse."

I hover nearby, my throat aching as I watch Rossi cut away the fabric around Kaspian's shoulder. Blood wells up from the bullet hole, dark and viscous. Rossi swabs it away dispassionately.

"The bullet's still in there," he announces after a moment's probing. "I'll need to extract it before I can close the wound."

Kaspian blanches but remains silent, his jaw clenched so tightly I fear his teeth might shatter. Sasha whimpers, releasing me hand to cover her mouth.

"If anyone feels the urge to vomit, I suggest you leave."

Rossi selects a long pair of forceps from his bag.

"This will hurt," he warns Kaspian, almost as an afterthought before he inserts the instrument into the gory hole in Kaspian's flesh.

"I'm going to go sit with your mom," Sasha says, almost sprinting for the door.

Kaspian lifts his head and finds me, the green depths glazed with pain. I step closer, my hand finding his. I keep the shock from my face when his fingers tighten around mine, his grip crushing.

Tempest tightens his hold on Kaspian, biceps flexing as he pins Kaspian against the seatback. I look away, bile rising in my throat, but I can't block out the wet squelch of metal in meat or Kaspian's agonized groans.

Rossi makes quick work of the rest, irrigating the wound and stitching it closed with brutal efficiency. Kaspian has gone limp, his head lolling, unconscious from the pain and blood loss.

Maybe the one, the only time, I'll see him weak.

"He'll need some recovery time," Rossi says, stripping off his gloves. He packs up his supplies and rises to his feet. "Keep the wound clean and dry. Change the dressings daily."

I nod mutely, not trusting myself to speak. Tempest releases his hold on Kaspian and steps back, cracking his neck.

"Kaspian will be out for a while," Tempest says. "Don't move him until he wakes."

"Thank you for your assistance." The words feel wooden on my tongue. I owe the Vultures a debt for saving Kaspian's life, but that doesn't mean I have to like them. I called Tempest because I had no other option, but his reasons for accepting remain a mystery.

Why *did* they help me?

Rossi gives me a once-over, as if sensing the direction of my thoughts. "He'll be all right, Elara."

His quiet assurance makes me want to sob with relief, but I hold myself steady.

"Care to explain what occurred here?" he asks.

"My mother, she's not well," I say hoarsely, still clinging to Kaspian's limp hand. "If you don't mind, could you take a look at her next?"

Rossi doesn't move. I grimace, preparing for the word *please*, until he says, "We know all about your mother's illness. After a few phone calls, there's a vacancy for her at the a private psychiatric facility in the city. With your permission, she can be settled there by morning."

My eyes grow hot, and it hurts to raise them, to meet his black, tarred gaze—

Until I'm absorbed by the warmth in them. The care.

Is this what the girl he's with sees? The water under the ice, the promise of life once he thaws?

I manage to respond, "I appreciate your help, truly. But I need some kind of assurance that my mother will be safe and cared for."

"You have my word," Rossi says. "That alone is enough."

The rigid conviction in his tone almost makes me fall to my knees and assure *him* that I believe him so he doesn't kill me.

I nod, my throat constricting. Entrusting my mother's well-being to the Vultures feels like a deal with the devil, but what choice do I have? Involving the police would bring more scandal, more questions, implicating Kaspian and the Court. Involving the Sovereigns.

I crush Kaspian's hand in my grip. *I can't let that happen.*

"We won't tell anyone about tonight," Tempest adds a bit reluctantly.

"Why would you help me?"

I shouldn't ask it, what with looking a gift horse in the mouth, but I can't confidently let them leave until I hear some sort of reason as to why the Vultures would help a member of the Court. Help *me*.

Rossi inclines his head. "You're involved with the Cimmerian Court. I have a particular weakness for women who aren't afraid of dangerous men and have acquired an insatiable need to protect those who deserve it." He glances down at my white-knuckled hand on Kaspian's. "You strike me as one of them."

"I don't know how I fell in with them," I find myself saying, "But as much as I've tried, I don't want to leave them."

Rossi's lips curve in the barest hint of a smile.

"Are you still after the ruby Heart, Elara?" Tempest asks.

Any softness is ripped from Rossi's face as he whirls on Tempest. "What did you just say?"

Silence descends, broken only by Kaspian's labored breathing.

I shuffle back, my gaze darting between Tempest and Rossi. The latter's face hardens, his eyes narrowing to obsidian slits, and I get the feeling Tempest's question was made with deliberate timing to alert his leader that I've bitten off more than I can chew.

"The Heart is a dangerous artifact," Rossi tells me, his voice low and warning. "It's not something to be trifled with."

"Oh, so you believe it exists, now?" I swallow after blurting the question, my mouth suddenly dry.

Thankfully, Rossi ignores my sarcasm, his attention fixed on Tempest.

"What are you implying?" His voice is hard as metal, each word sharp as his scalpel.

Tempest holds his ground. "Sarah Anderton's legendary ruby Heart. Elara's been asking around about it."

"And you didn't think to mention this sooner?" Rossi advances on Tempest, his movements volcanic.

I find my voice, though it wobbles. These are *scary* men. "What do you know about the Heart?"

They both turn to me, Rossi's gaze sharpening, Tempest's lips curving. "Enough to know my warning to you still stands."

Rossi silences him with a look before recentering on me. "A lot of people who've searched for the ruby Heart and its fortune have died, Elara. Whatever Cavanaugh Nightshade has told you, what you think you know, whatever you're planning, stop. Now."

"I can't." I force my chin up for what I'm about to say next. "I'm not one of you. Or part of the Court. But I'm someone with a vested interest in that ruby."

I leave out the bombshell that I'm Sarah Anderton's descendant. If Tempest and Rossi are holding back information, then so will I.

I straighten my spine. "I need it."

"For what?" Rossi's voice is low, a mere purr in his chest.

I hesitate, glancing down at Kaspian's pallid face, his blood staining my fingers. Just last night, I was determined to go against them and find my own answers about the Heart and why it was so important that Maverick had to die for it. Then my mother held a gun, pointed it at Kaspian—

And I realized I don't want to be their enemy. I can't be on the other side of that gun, pulling the trigger against them.

I've lost Maverick. I can't lose…

"To save them," I whisper.

Tempest barks out a sound close to a laugh, but not quite. He scrubs a tired hand down his face. "Great. Haven't heard that one before."

I include both Tempest and Rossi when I say, "The Court is more than just a group of violent men. They're important to me, however fucked up that might seem to you."

"Oh, believe me. It makes sense," Tempest replies dryly. "I have a sister just like you."

Then Tempest shrugs. "But in defending them, you side with the Court. Kaspian and his brothers are slaves, exactly the way we were, and they do their Court's bidding."

At Rossi's sharp look, Tempest doesn't explain further, but works his jaw as if he doesn't enjoy being silenced.

I don't know what to say to that, so I just nod, my attention drifting back to Kaspian's unconscious form. His chest rises and falls with steady breaths, but his face is still pale, his features drawn.

"Are you sure you know what you're doing?" Tempest asks at his lowest decibel. "That's a dangerous fucker who would sooner bite your hand off than cling to it for help."

"You don't know what Kaspian's been through," I retort, but my voice cracks, desperation leaking through. "Or what *I've* been through. This jewel killed my brother. I have to know why."

Rossi closes in. I fight the urge to back away and put distance between us. "Your brother is dead, Elara. If it is indeed real, the Heart can't change that."

"Yes, but it can give me answers. For so long—too long—I accepted his death as cruel and terrible bad luck. I was willing to live with that open wound and just cover it with a bandage. But now? When the answers are so close, and four incredibly skilled men want to find the Heart as much as I do, how can I say no? Why would I ever stop? You don't know what finding the Heart could do—"

"I know enough." A muscle knots in Rossi's cheek. "I know the price of involving yourself in Sarah Anderton's lost treasure. I know the destruction the search for it leaves in its wake. And I know that no one, not even you, should unearth what she was willing to die for to keep hidden. What her daughter was willing to die for."

Tears burn my eyes, blurring my vision. I blink them away,

refusing to let them fall. "I have to try. I can't just let his death go."

For a brief instant, the hard lines of Rossi's face relax. "I understand your grief. But this isn't the way. Searching for the Heart will only bring you more pain, more loss. Let the treasure stay buried. Let your brother rest."

A sob catches in my throat, my chest aching with the weight of it. I want to scream, to rage against the unfairness of it all, but I push it down, Kaspian's hand my anchor.

"I can't," I whisper. "I'm sorry."

Rossi sighs, rubbing a hand against the stubble on his jaw.

"Then I'm sorry, too." He looks at Tempest, and a silent communication passes between them. "We can't let you do this, Elara. Sarah's treasure is too dangerous in anyone's hands. Our job is to keep it from ever coming to light."

Fear prickles my skin. "What is that supposed to mean?"

Tempest draws closer, reaching into his jacket. If I knew him better, maybe I'd believe the line between his brows means he feels somewhat regretful when he says, "What we have to, so we can keep *our* loved ones safe."

I stumble against the sofa chair, Kaspian's dead weight nearly toppling us both over. "No, wait—"

Tempest draws a gun from his coat, its muzzle gleaming in the dim light.

Rossi moves to block the door, his broad shoulders filling the frame.

CHAPTER 7
KASPIAN
THE BOGEYMAN

Through a wasteland of black and white noise and nothingness all at once, the voice I would never choose to hear first says, "Don't make this harder than it needs to be, Miss Wraithwood."

Rossi.

Fucking Miguel Rossi.

I haven't heard from that old man since he left campus last year, with Cav smirking at Rossi's back as the former professor walked away from his assassin's life and carved a name for himself through the city in his enemies' blood.

I open my mouth to welcome him back to my turf and then promptly stab him, consequences be damned, until two things hit me at once.

One, my tongue is too big for my mouth, and it's sticking to the roof, brushing along my gums like a dehydrated, mewling street cat. And my throat pulses with swelling irritation. Like I've been screaming.

And two, Rossi said her name.

Elara.

My eyelids swing open.

Rossi's form snaps into focus first, his large, oversized body taking over the doorway—the one exit out of this sitting room.

At Farrow Estate. Elara's mother's house, where I'd headed to after being forced to endure Cav's mutilation and wondering who would be next, who else will fall victim to our failure to secure the whole Heart…

And Cav had looked at me, his face speckled and painted with his own blood. Looked at me in a way that his thoughts lined up with mine. *Find her.*

Yes, it's all coming back to me now. Rossi had worked on me, using his expertise and sadism to make sure my shoulder was stitched up nicely. And the reason he was here was because Elara called Tempest… because her mother had a gun … yep, and fucking shot me.

Rossi says to Elara, who's gripping my hand like I imagine a python strangles an alligator, his voice almost gentle, "We're not going to hurt you. We just need you to come with us, and it's clear you won't follow willingly."

"Like hell I'm going unwillingly, too," she spits, and my initial confusion morphs into fury.

Tempest—*Tempest*, that motherfucker—cocks a gun at Elara, the click echoing in the sudden silence. "Don't be stupid, Elara. You're outnumbered and outgunned."

I hear the hurt seeping into Elara's words when she responds, "I called you for help. I thought you were helping me. Why would you do this when none of it has to do with you? Other than tonight, I haven't asked you for anything. And I'm not leaving him." She tightens her grip so my knuckles almost crack. "I'm not leaving my mother. I'm not leaving my *home*."

"We only want to keep you safe." Tempest risks darting his attention to me. I catch his intention in time to shut my eyes, pretending drugged stupor while I coil.

"We're taking you away from the Court," Tempest says to Elara. "They will kill you if you stay. Kaspian and his brothers will be at the front of the line—"

"Say that again."

Tempest cuts himself off at the sound of my haggard voice. His attention lowers to me again, but this time stays there.

Well, at the gun I'm holding, pulled from my ankle holster, though it hurt like a motherfucker to swiftly grab it before Tempest caught on.

Caroline Wraithwood, sweet, half-starved, aimless widow that she is, got me in my good arm.

"You're not taking her anywhere," I growl, having to scrape my vocal cords together to do so. "Elara stays with me."

Tempest's gaze hardens, his grip tightening on his own weapon.

Elara's nails dig into my skin. "I don't think adding another gun to the mix will help."

Rossi intercedes, his hands raised in a placating gesture. "Let's all just calm down. There's no need for violence. We only want what's best for Elara."

"Fuck you," I spit, my gun never wavering from Tempest's face. "You have no idea what's best for her. None of you do."

"You included," Tempest retorts. "To involve her in this, to drag an innocent girl into this vile, corrupt world where nothing but bodies pile up on our shoulders … Be ashamed, Kaspian, not proud, that you've fucked her life over so badly."

I respond with an answering, jackel's smile, though lopsided and weakened behind the barrel of my gun. "It's not my fault you can't separate your own shitty situation from mine. Elara is not your little sister, and I'm fairly certain she can speak for herself and make her own decisions."

Tempest's lips curve in a vicious sneer. "Big words for a guy who can barely hold up his gun long enough to aim it."

"You're right, I can't," I say before my focus swings behind Rossi's shoulder. "But he can."

Tempest spins in time to see Axe with an arm around Rossi's neck and a knife to his cock.

"Rossi probably needs his big swinging dick to keep, you

know, being a big swinging dick," I say idly to Tempest, though my vision grows spotty.

I refuse to pass out, though, and leave Elara to these overprotective carrion eaters.

A low, dangerous laugh escapes from Axe, but it sounds too far away, like I'm sinking in deep water. I blink twice, trying to clear the stars dancing in my vision.

"Axe…" Elara's tight whisper resonates throughout the silenced room.

Her tone communicates what I'm thinking, which is abject relief at my silent, lethal comrade who knew enough to follow me through the woods and get to Elara, too. A man who answers to the same beautiful, chilling call of this woman.

My relief is short-lived. Fresh blood seeps through my shirt, staining it a dark red.

"Fuck," I curse under my breath. My grip on the gun wavers as a wave of dizziness hits me. I manage to keep my aim steady and hold on to consciousness by sheer stubbornness alone.

"No one has to get hurt," Tempest says, his tone surprisingly calm, given the circumstances.

But his words trigger something inside me. A savage rage that's been simmering beneath the surface for far too long.

"No one has to get hurt?" I repeat, my voice laced with pure venom. "That's rich, coming from you."

I can feel Elara's hand trembling in mine, her fear tangible. It fuels my anger and ignites it into a raging inferno.

Elara's under my protection because she deserves more than this shit show. And besides that … there are things about her that draw me closer. Things I'm still trying to define.

Gathering every ounce of strength left in me, I push myself off the chair and stagger forward.

"Stay away from what's mine," I declare. "And if you or any of your buddies try, I'll kill every last one of you. And don't doubt me. I've done it before and will do it again."

Tempest's finger twitches on the trigger, and I brace myself to fire a shot before he does. But before he can pull it, a deafening boom shakes the room.

Shielding Elara with my arm, I pivot sharply and discover Caroline Wraithwood standing in the doorway, a shotgun clutched in her bony hands. Smoke curls from the barrel, and a gaping hole mars the doorframe beside Rossi's head.

"I'm not asking," she states, her eyes wild and feverish.

"Mom!" Elara screams.

"Christ," I grit out. "Where does she keep getting this shit?"

Sasha sprints up behind her, Axe and Rossi shifting slightly to face the two new wild-eyed women in this fight.

"I tried to stop her, El!" Sasha rasps, out of breath as she puts her hands to her knees and drinks in oxygen. "But she tricked me by asking me to go into her closet and get her favorite—"

"Not important," I snap as Elara wriggles from my shield and runs for her mother. I don't have enough strength to hold on to her, aim at Tempest, and communicate via our coded hand signals to Axe. So I go with reason. "Listen to the woman of the house, gents, and get the fuck out."

Elara darts between Tempest, Rossi, and Axe, none of whom attempts to detain her. That would've been the perfect moment to grab Elara, or strip Caroline of her shotgun, or twist out of Axe's delicate hold on Rossi's balls...

I glance at Caroline, who remains in the doorway, though the shotgun now hangs limply at her side.

She senses my study, turning to me, her eyes hollow. "She's all I have left. I won't lose her too."

Rossi is the first to respond. "Look, this is not what we wanted when we came here. Last year, we were part of a search for Sarah Anderton's treasure, and we found it. The Heart wasn't there. It doesn't exist, and you are putting this girl through hell for no reason. All we want is to remove her from the curse of your secret society and give her a decent life."

I guffaw, half leaning sideways as my adrenaline loses steam. "Because you're so wholesome?"

"Listen to me, boy," Rossi snarls. My brows jump at his tone. "The Heart *does not exist*. Communicate that to your superiors, deal with the fallout, and leave Sarah Anderton's legacy alone."

"But it does exist," Elara pipes up.

Axe growls it before I can. "Elara, *no*."

"Enough of this alpha male bullshit," she snaps at both me and Axe. At the entire room, really. "Everyone put down your guns—you, too, Mom, give it to Sasha, please—"

Sasha looks sick at the idea of handling a gun, but she does what Elara requests and holds the shotgun practically with two fingers.

"The Heart exists," Elara states, "Because we found half of it. Half of the largest ruby in the world. My brother broke it so it could never get in the Sovereigns' hands, the leaders of the Cimmerian Court."

Tempest's and Rossi's faces are so immobile that they must be caught off guard. Caroline moans, rocking back and forth on the balls of her feet.

I groan, slumping into the chair and ideally giving in to sweet unconsciousness. Cav is going to blow *a gasket*—until I remember what state he's in, too.

"Is that what you needed to know?" she dares Rossi and Tempest.

There's fear in Elara, but also something else that makes my pulse quicken and my palms itch with the need to bring her back to me. I relish in the delicious anticipation and stifle a laugh at the absurdity of the situation—how this delicate creature could be holding two deadly former assassins rapt, as well as her two trained killers of a different sort.

Tempest turns my way. "She's serious?"

A dramatic sigh escapes me. If the plot twists of tonight have taught me anything, it's that me, my boys, and Elara are currently fucked. The Vultures, in all their feather puffing, might have some use.

In for a penny, in for another mic drop... "You're looking at Sarah Anderton's descendant, so yes, she speaks the truth."

Tempest sputters, "I'm sorry, what the fuck?"

Rossi remains ominously still.

Axe shifts, knife still poised at Rossi's groin. "Time for you to fly away home, birdies."

Rossi extricates himself from Axe's grip with exaggerated care, hands raised but expression menacing. "This changes things."

"You think?" Sasha shrieks, still holding the shotgun like it'll randomly shoot her.

"You have your answer," I say on an exhale, my voice strained but steady. "Now leave."

Tempest hesitates, his finger still poised on the trigger. For a tense heartbeat, no one moves. Then slowly, deliberately, he lowers the gun.

"This isn't over," he says.

I bare my teeth in a lopsided, feral grin. "For you, it is."

"We'll schedule another time to ... discuss this," Rossi adds. "You may not see it this way, but we're trying to help."

"For patching up my shoulder and getting Elara's mom the help she needs, I'll let you live. If last year taught me anything when you worked with Cav, you guys aren't complete assholes," I grind out. "But don't ever try shit like taking my girl while I'm weak again. Because I will always, *always*, find the strength to end you."

"Elara—" Tempest says, but Elara cuts him off with a sharp shake of her head.

"Go." The single word cracks like a whip. "Violence may be second nature to all of you, but it's not always the answer. You could've just talked to me."

They retreat, footsteps heavy on the hardwood. The door slams behind them with a resounding finality.

In the sudden stillness, I sag further into the chair, the gun clattering to the floor. Black spots dance across my vision as the adrenaline drains away, leaving only wretchedness and exhaustion in its wake.

Elara rushes to my side, a shuddering breath escaping her.

I inhale her scent, letting it … even though I shouldn't … letting it ground me.

Cool air hits my face as she retreats, possibly fighting the same emotions I am and not letting them win.

Around us, the others mobilize. Axe secures the perimeter. Sasha sets down the shotgun and moves to comfort a weeping Caroline while they wait for a private ambulance to escort her to a secure facility.

But at this moment, in this single suspended heartbeat, there is only Elara and the promise I made her.

The promise I will keep, even if it kills me.

I will scorch this earth before I let anyone take her from me.

CHAPTER 8
CAV
THE PUPPETEER

Blood. So much blood.

It coats my skin, the sheets, the air—a metallic perfume I can't escape.

I suck in oxygen, pain ripping through my body with each choked breath.

What happened to me?

Who did this?

I blink, struggling to focus.

Three shadowy figures hover nearby, their hushed voices urgent. My brothers. They did their best to patch me up, but this is beyond them.

We're in danger. All of us.

I have to remember what happened.

Who attacked me.

Why.

The room spins slightly as I try to piece together the fractured memories of what brought me here.

Sovereigns.

The knife plunges into my flesh, carving agonizing sigils of worship meant for the Sovereigns, not me.

Do the Sovereigns' talons now have a permanent grip on my soul?

I trace the fresh cuts, hot and swollen under the bandages, the ridges forming a map of ancient insignia across my chest that seem to dance and shift under my touch.

I've been here before, trapped in this cycle of torment. How much more can I endure before their perverse faith consumes me completely?

The Sovereigns' monotonous chant during our constant rituals creeps into my thoughts—rhymes uttered by candlelight, marks that bind, and curses that follow bloodlines.

My eyes sting with a mercurial rage I can't quell. "What have they done to me?"

My voice sounds foreign, clogged with the dust of defeat.

But the pain is almost welcome in its intensity. It's a reminder that I'm still here, still fighting, even when my soul screams for surrender.

The boys may not believe in the dark magic the Sovereigns like to tease or the ravenous beings the Sovereigns are beginning to serve and covet, but I do. They've *made* me believe in dark things, writhing things, terrible creatures that will hunt and hunt and send you to madness if you don't fulfill their orders.

I groan, wincing as my fervor tightens my body, tensing the sliced muscles and prodding me to beg for mercy.

How does one fight an enemy that brands your flesh and leaves you destroyed in the darkness of your room? How do you combat a curse that has torn through generations, leaving nothing but ruin in its wake?

The symbols on my chest throb in response, sinister heartbeats mimicking my own.

The moment dawn peeks through the gap in my curtains, I push myself up, ignoring the protest of my battered body.

The ruby Heart—this is the key. It has to be.

Sarah Anderton's legacy, this curse, has clung to the Nightshades through centuries. But now, with each throb of the symbols etched into my flesh, I feel it—an urgency that borders on madness.

To find the Heart is to break these chains.

The door swings open, followed by several pairs of skilled, stealthy footsteps, as well as a singular, lighter pair, darting in the lead.

Elara's hooded face appears in my vision, her amber in her eyes piercing through the gloom coating her face. She pushes back the hood of the cloak and presses a hand to my forehead. "How long has he been like this? He's feverish."

She doesn't falter at the sight of me, half naked and wounded. Her attention rakes over my bandaged chest, blood leaking through where the marks cut the deepest, the Sovereigns' symbols seeming to glow beneath her gaze.

They want to hurt her. The Sovereigns want her.

"Damn, Cav, you look like hell," Kaspian quips as he slinks to the foot of the bed, clutching his left shoulder tenderly while his left arm is in a sling, his posture stooped.

"No worse than you," I slur, pushing to rest higher against the pillows, but my eyes are on *her*, capturing every detail. The way her chest rises with each breath, the honeyed fire in her gaze that burns brighter than any ire within me.

"Sit down, you stubborn ass," Wilder chides Kaspian as he wanders in last, pointing at an armchair near the fireplace, but still where I can see them.

"Elara," I murmur. "Come here."

She huffs like she's reached her limit on taking orders tonight but obediently perches on the edge of the bed, close enough for me to feel the warmth radiating off her. My eyes roam over her appreciatively before returning to hers.

A villainous grin tugs at my lips.

She slants her eyes at my study. "What?"

"I want you."

The words slip out effortlessly, and a startled silence blankets the room.

Her eyes widen slightly, then quickly harden again. Elara's lips part to say something—

But I beat her to it.

"I mean it. I want to fuck you, right here, right now."

My hand shoots out to grip her wrist, my fingers curling around the fragile bones there.

She makes an annoyed sound in her throat but doesn't yank herself free from my grasp. Instead, she asks the room, "When was the last time he's had his fever treated? Or drugs?"

"Mmm. Drugs and partying and fucking. That's what I like to hear," I purr back at her, staring deep into those fiery orbs as if they hold all answers to this fucked-up world. "That's what normal college assholes do. Let's do that instead of … instead of …"

The memory of what happened, what I endured, starts to leach into the edges of my vision.

"Axe," Wilder says sharply from across the room. "Grab some ice water in case we need to cool him down."

Axe's mouth tenses grimly, but he leaves the room without protest, leaving the four of us remaining in uneasy, I dare say *worried*, quiet.

Well, if I'm good at one thing, it's breaking the silence. I glance over at Elara again.

My smirk deepens. God, how I long to trace every inch of her skin with my fingertips.

"Now," I murmur, my thumb gently stroking her wrist, "let's deal with this fever the right way."

My attention shifts from her flushed face to my own aching body. The pain is a distant, dull throb as I guide her hand past my angry chest to the large tent of my cock beneath it.

Elara's gentle hand on mine pulls her wrist away, her fingers tracing lightly over the blood-soaked bandages. Her touch is careful, but it's enough to set my nerves on fire. I hiss through gritted teeth but make no move to recoil.

"Easy," she murmurs, her fingertips moving from the bandages to ghost over my skin, leaving trails of delicious tingles in their wake.

My vision tunnels with need as I watch her every movement. The way her lips part slightly as she concentrates on refreshing my bandages and treating my wounds under Wilder's guidance and how her strawberry lips purse with concentration. It's fucking thrilling.

Wilder clears his throat, shifting his attention from my cock to my face with a look that says he's seen far too much for one evening. Kaspian merely smirks from his spot by the fire, his eyes flicking between Elara and me with the kind of amusement that tells me he was recently in a similar situation with her.

Axe returns with a pitcher of water, refreshing the untouched, room-temperature one on my bedside table. He takes in the sexual tension in the room with suspicious eyes, keeping the pitcher aloft like he's willing to douse me in it should I get too out of control.

I beam at his discomfort before returning my attention to Elara.

"Did you miss me while I was cooped up in the basement?" I ask her, my voice dropping lower, something ominous lurking beneath my tone.

Elara rolls her eyes, but not fast enough. I catch the lash of pain my question causes her as she comes face-to-face with my mutilated chest before she retorts, "You wish."

Ignoring the twinge of my consciousness at the utterly destroyed look in her eye, I return my focus to Elara's touch as she applies the ointment to my wounds. Her hands are cold against the fevered skin of my chest, but they bring relief—a sweet torture I can't get enough of.

I lean in closer, ignoring the sharp stab of pain that shoots through my ribs from my wounds. "I want to make you blush so hard, your pussy turns a different color, too."

My voice is barely a vibration, but she hears me.

Her fingers hover for a moment over my body before her defiance comes back in full force. "You'd have to try harder than that, in the state you're in."

A challenge. Fuck, how I love a good challenge.

"I don't try," I point out, noting her shiver, "I conquer."

"All right, that's enough, big guy," Wilder says, approaching my other side. He holds up a bottle of pills and shakes it. "Time to go night-night."

I wince as Wilder shakes the pill bottle, the rattle piercing my skull. Elara resumes her ministrations, applying salve to my wounds with a gentleness I don't deserve. The sensation unravels throughout my body like satin ribbons, desire and pain intertwining until I can barely distinguish one from the other.

"Open up," Wilder commands, holding out two white pills. I glare at him, rebellion at the forefront, but Elara's touch on my jaw draws my attention back to her.

"Take them," she murmurs. "I'm worried about you. You need to heal."

I want to refuse, to pull her down onto the bed and lose myself in her, but the throbbing ache in my chest reminds me of my limits. I open my mouth but snarl until it's only Elara who can place the pills on my tongue. Axe hands her a glass of water, which she brings to my lips, and the cool liquid soothes my parched throat.

As the medication takes effect, my eyelids grow heavy, the room blurring at the edges. Elara's face swims in my vision, her features softening with concern. I fight the pull of unconsciousness. The meds aren't working yet, but my efforts to fuck her are certainly taking their toll.

I snake my arm around Elara's waist, pulling her flush against my bandaged chest. The movement sends a bolt of agony over the need, but I welcome it with the pleasure of having her at my mercy.

She gasps, hands splaying over the bloodstained fabric as if to prepare herself.

Wilder grimaces. "You're going to feel that tomorrow, brother."

I don't care.

My fingers dig into the supple flesh of her hip under her shirt, a promise and a claim. Elara's breath stalls, her pupils dilating with a heady mix of annoyance and arousal. "Cav, stop. You'll hurt yourself."

"Fuck my injury," I snarl, capturing her by tangling my fingers in her hair at the back of her head. "I want to feel something other than this goddamn curse."

Kaspian chuckles from his seat, the sound low and knowing. "Better give him what he wants, beastie. You know how obstinate he gets."

I grind my hips against hers, my hardness evident through the thin fabric of the sheets. Elara grits her teeth, her lower back arching, unconsciously seeking more contact.

Axe shifts to the side of the bed. The tension in the room changes, morphing into carnal hunger.

Elara's denial is on the tip of her tongue, but I silence her by yanking on her hair until we meet with a bruising kiss.

I pour every ounce of my frustration, my pain, my thirst into the clash of our mouths. Her resistance is fleeting. She melts against me, her fingers relaxing against my chest.

I break the kiss, panting, "I wasn't about to pass out until I showed you what you were missing by stomping off last night, butterfly."

I'm pretty sure the grin stays on my face as I lodge her against me and, at last, allow the nightmares to claim my mind.

Refusing to let her go.

CHAPTER 9

ELARA

I pace the hallway, boots thudding on the marble, my bones clanging with each step.

Cav's bedroom door creaks open, and Axe emerges, his storm-gray eyes finding mine, turbulent and clouded. Kaspian and Wilder trail him, faces grim, Kaspian wincing as he adjusts his injured shoulder.

It took mere minutes for Cav to surrender to the pain medication and fall asleep. I slipped out of his unconscious arm-lock with more flexibility than I thought I possessed, Wilder promising to explain everything after we made Cav comfortable.

I thought my mother shooting Kaspian was bad. Now, after tending to Cav and pulling away the thick bandages on his chest to reveal that … that *horror*…

I rush to them, questions spilling out. "Is he going to be all right? What did they *do* to him?"

Axe drapes a muscular arm across my shoulders, pulling me close while maneuvering me away from Cav's room, no doubt sensing my urge to lock Kaspian in there with Cav to keep both of them from further death-defying injuries. "He'll heal, Elara."

Axe's assurance rings hollow. I twist under his arm to stare at Cav's door, fighting the impulse to charge in and demand answers. The fever, hallucinations about a curse—Cav needs more than ointment and pills.

I glance at Kaspian, but his jaw only clenches, refusing to meet my stare.

"We need to get you both to a hospital," I insist, my voice rising with each word. "Whatever they did to Cav, it's beyond our ability to treat. And you, Kaspian—can we really trust how Rossi treated you after what happened?"

For that reason, Sasha stayed behind with Mom after we both verified with the EMTs of the private ambulance who they were associated with, confirmed where they were going, and forced them to link our phones so we could track their movements. Sasha climbed into the ambulance with my mother the minute Axe muttered into Kaspian's ear, and Kaspian—*Kaspian* —turned pale.

I'd spent enough time desperately trying to read my mother's lips while she silently chanted, worried that she might be planning to hurt herself, that I read Axe as saying, *Cav's getting worse.*

It didn't take me long to convince them to take me, considering both were reluctant to let me go after the Vultures recently tried to take me away.

Now, Axe tenses into living stone. Wilder vocalizes Axe's concern, asking Kaspian in a low, menacing undertone, "Explain what went on with you and Elara. I didn't press you in front of Cav and politely refrained from interrogating you the instant you smuggled Elara in, but Kasp, you vanished after the blood ritual."

Blood ritual? My mind instantly flashes back to the angry slashes across Cav's chest. Sigils carved into his flesh, carrying some terrible meaning.

Kaspian dismisses Wilder's questions with a weary shake of his head.

He says to me, eyes hooded and bleak, "Hospitals are too risky."

I start to argue, but Axe interrupts. "Trust us, Elara. We handle this regularly."

His arm constricts around me, meant to comfort but only stoking my frustration. I shrug him off and plant myself in their path, halting our progress.

"This isn't right. Look at what's being done to you. It's not worth it." I shake my head, thoughts churning and tears building. "Maverick's fate was undeserved, and Cav's is no better. Look what your leaders inflicted on him." I point behind them with a shaking, furious finger, indicating where we just came. "*Look!*"

Seconds tick by. They don't move.

Kaspian shifts his weight and flinches, the motion jarring his shoulder.

Axe's jaw flexes, a muscle jumping beneath his stubbled skin. He glances at the others, communicating in their private language.

That just enrages me further. "I am a part of this. My Anderton bloodline *gave* you a piece of the ruby, so don't you dare use your secret society eye language in front of me—"

Wilder steps closer, hands raised. "Elara, we can't risk—"

"I don't care about the risk!" The words rip from my throat, echoing in the vast hall. "Cav's hurt. Badly. And so are you, Kaspian, because of my mother." I bark out a heartbroken laugh. "My fragile, emotionally wounded mother *shot* you. This is what it's come to. No, it's all because of this fucking *jewel*. Because of the Sovereigns."

Kaspian sighs, raking a hand through his hair. "We don't have a choice. You may be an Anderton, but you don't have a clue about the Court."

"Then do me a favor and enlighten me," I snap.

Behind Cav's door, a crash sounds, followed by a strangled cry.

Surprise twists into concern when I recognize the voice as Cav's. I lunge into the space between Axe and Wilder to race back to the room, but Axe intercepts me, his large frame blocking the way.

"Let me through," I demand, straining against his hold. "You said he'd be knocked out. That Cav would rest."

It was the only way they could convince me to leave him.

Kaspian interjects, "You don't want to see him like this."

Another roar rips through the air, raw and agonized. It tears at my heart, my very soul. I thrash in Axe's grip, desperate to reach Cav and somehow ease his suffering.

Wilder shoulders past us and disappears into the room, the door slamming shut behind him. I sag against Axe, tears building as Cav's shouting grows more tormented, more inhuman, with each passing second.

"What have they done to him?" I ask brokenly.

Kaspian's gaze darkens, his hand tightening into a fist. He says in a tone edged with hunger, "If they've crushed him beyond repair, I'll tear them apart myself and happily suffer the consequences."

The violence frightens me, but I understand the sentiment. Ever since I've learned about the Sovereigns, I've entertained similar thoughts.

"Come on," Axe says, moving me along with little effort. "There's nothing more we can do here. We'll wait for Wilder in the kitchen."

I somehow let him guide me down the hallway as Cav's howls chase us. Each one pierces me, a blade twisting in my gut. But these guys have been with each other for years. Wilder would know what to do to calm him.

"I'm tainted! It's inside me now. The curse melts my bones, tars my blood. You can't stop it. YOU CAN'T STOP IT!"

Wilder's deep, soothing voice follows the screams.

The kitchen is as cold, sterile, and dim as last time, as if these boys can't stand the light. All stainless steel and marble, hard and imposing.

Axe deposits me in a chair at the island, then moves to the fridge.

He stands with his arm slung over the fridge door, blinking rapidly. He gives a rough jerk of his head with a furrowed brow, mumbling something close to, "I'm getting her food," before his confusion clears, and he glances over.

"You want anything?" he asks, his voice gruff.

I shake my head, not trusting myself to speak. My hands tremble where they rest on the cool countertop. Kaspian comes in and collapses onto a stool with a groan, his face ashen. He fumbles in his pocket and withdraws an orange pill bottle, shaking out two capsules. He tosses them back dry.

"What are those?" I ask.

"Antibiotics. Painkillers." He shrugs with his good shoulder. "Whatever Rossi gave me."

"And you trust them?" I ask again. "After what he tried to do?"

Kaspian levels me with a look. "No. But I don't have much choice, do I?"

Their private chef silently walks through the doors, setting down green tea, before he disappears from wherever he came from. I stare down at it, not seeing hot tea, but steaming guilt.

I forced Rossi on Kaspian, asked for the Vultures' help when I knew full well they're the enemy. And it's not just college fraternity level dislike. The animosity between these two groups runs deeper, closer to warring factions who deal in death than campus rivalries.

"I didn't have a choice," I say more to myself than to Kaspian. "It was either that or call the police and get my mother arrested, or do nothing and let you die."

Kaspian arches a brow in a way where he clearly expected me to choose the latter.

"Mom doesn't deserve to go to jail for protecting me from you, and I would never leave you to die," I clip out, then pick up the teacup. The porcelain is so delicate, with painted purple irises. So different from the brute force currently surrounding me.

Axe sets a glass of water in front of Kaspian, then leans against the counter, crossing his arms. "We need to talk about what happened with the Sovereigns. The blood ritual. And then we can go over what you did to cause Elara's mother to point a gun and actually shoot you."

Axe's tone indicates Kaspian is substantially better at avoiding targeted bullets than what he demonstrated today.

He's right. I focus on Kaspian with a little more concern. What made him so distracted that he couldn't use his expertise to disarm my mom in time?

Me?

Kaspian's nostrils flare. He glances at me, something indecipherable cracking through the winter in his eyes, before looking away. "Not now."

"Then when?" Axe pushes off the counter, muscles under his thin T-shirt clenching. "Cav is in there screaming his fucking lungs out, carved up like a Christmas ham. You've got a hole in your shoulder. And Elara's caught in the middle of all this shit."

I flinch at his rare, harsh words and their honesty.

Kaspian must notice, too, because he sighs, scrubbing a hand over his face. "Then you fucking explain it to her."

Kaspian drops his hand from his face and regards his brother-in-arms. At Axe's lowered brows, a deliberate shading of emotion.

Kaspian realizes it at the same time I do: Axe goes quiet because he can't recall everything.

"The ritual Cav went through was to bind us to the jewel," Kaspian says finally, his voice flat. "It's meant to make us into... controllable weapons for the Sovereigns to use, or that's what we've figured, ever since they started on Axe. They want something, or someone, to possess us."

Horror floods me. "I'm sorry, what?"

"You *saw* what they did to him!" Kaspian slams his fist on

the counter, making me jump. "It may sound ridiculous. It's fucking deluded. But the Sovereigns believe it. They believe this ruby has magical properties going all the way back to Sarah Anderton."

I take in a quivering breath. "Do you all really think we're searching for a supernatural ruby with powers?"

"Fuck, no. Axe, Wilder and I—we know there's no such thing." A muscle ticks in Kaspian's jaw. "But Cav..."

Axe lifts his chin, his features sharpening as he latches on to Kaspian's story and is able to continue it. "The Sovereigns believe that the Heart possesses dark properties that can grant them immense power and control over others. They intend to harness this supposed magic to strengthen their hold on the Cimmerian Court and extend their influence beyond our secret society."

I fold my hands over the sides of the teacup, seeking warmth. Needing it. "The blood ritual Cav went through, it's just the beginning, isn't it?"

Axe gives a solemn nod.

Kaspian adds, "It was punishment, too. Binding him to the Heart will make him find it faster. That's what the Sovereigns believe. And he endured it. Cav didn't say a word about the half you gave us. He kept it safe."

The tea I was about to swallow gets caught in my throat. "And Cav seriously believes the Sovereigns succeeded?"

"They took him young," Kaspian says in lieu of an answer. "The Nightshades have been part of the Court since its inception. Cav's father wanted him involved as soon as he knew he was having a boy. They took him and tore at him, piece by piece, until he was nothing more than a vessel. They forced him to endure trials that would break lesser men."

The small sips of tea I managed burn in my stomach, then reaches up as if to burn my heart, too. "How... how did he survive?"

Kaspian's smile returns, but this time, it's tinged with a fierce pride. It's a strange, foreign expression for a man who is proud of so little and only invokes duty. "Because he's a relentless fucker. Even now, he fights. His belief in the ruby's curse—your ancestor's curse—is a burden he may never fully escape, but one we'll help him bear."

I'd gotten it so wrong. Blaming them for Maverick's death, confronting them when they refused to help me and demanding they put Maverick first—put my *grief* first—when all the while, they are a group of men who shoulder the worst in humanity and want nothing more than to help each other.

They have no obligation to me. They never have. Yet...

Kaspian came to my aid at Farrow Manor tonight the second he understood why Cav endured the Sovereigns' punishment. They were to keep half the Heart, and *me*, safe.

The thought of having these men's loyalty, as brutal and vicious as they are, makes my belly flip in concerning ways.

I don't want to change them and turn them into moral men. I want these caged animals to fight by my side, fangs and scars and all.

Axe speaks, drawing me out of my stark revelation, "The Sovereigns plan to use the ruby in a final ritual that they believe will give them abilities. Their ultimate goal is to create a legion of unwavering followers who will blindly obey their commands. This current batch of initiates is just the start. They're undergoing trials, tasks, and skill training that are vastly different from how we were brought up the ranks."

As Axe trails off with tight brows, Kaspian continues without missing a beat, "They're willing to go to any lengths to acquire the ruby. Tonight was just a flex."

"This is insane," I whisper. "This is the real world, not a supernatural *realm* where witches and curses exist."

I gesture around dramatically as if to prove the non-existence of magic through the air alone.

Neither of them need to argue. Cav's unhinged screams filtering down the hall say it all.

Whether or not it's real doesn't matter.

I squeeze my eyes shut as fresh tears threaten. He sounds just like my mother when she's at her worst. *This can't be happening.*

The kitchen door bangs open and Wilder strides in. Sweat dots his brow and blood stains his hands. My stomach heaves at the sight.

"How is he?" Axe asks.

"Let's just say the sleeping pills didn't take."

He goes to the sink and starts scrubbing his hands, the water running pink.

Then Cav screams again, an inhuman roar that sends ice down my spine. *"Carve out the poisoned flesh, seal the curse! The Sovereigns are in my head! Kill me, let me die before they—"*

I'm out of my seat before I realize it, teacup tipping over and splashing across the counter, porcelain shattering. I run for the door.

Kaspian lunges to block me, but I dodge him in his less-than-invincible state. I race down the hall, my heart a wild drum in my chest, and wrench open Cav's door, stumble to a stop, then freeze.

Cav writhes on the bed, his body arching grotesquely as he roars, clawing at his chest. The bandages are soaked through, more red than white, his skin stretched taut over straining bulges of muscle. His eyes roll wildly, unseeing. Lost in a purgatory I've only just begun to imagine.

"Oh god, Cav," I choke out.

I start forward, reaching for him, desperate to soothe, to help, to do something. But then his head snaps toward me, and he snarls, baring bloodstained teeth. I recoil with a scream caught in my throat.

"You think you can save me? You have no idea what I've done or what I'm capable of. The curse won't let me go, and it's hungry. For you. For your Anderton blood." His mouth splits into a twisted mockery of a smile. *"Can I tear off your wings, little butterfly?"*

That's not Cav. It can't be. Whatever the Sovereigns did to his mind ... it's not my Cav in that bed anymore.

It's a demon wearing his skin.

The instinct to give in and run, flee from this nightmarish scene, is all too real, but my feet remain rooted to the spot. Behind me, I hear the thundering footsteps of Axe, Wilder, and Kaspian.

Cav arches off the bed with a howl, blood spraying from his lips. His nails gouge into his chest, tearing at the bandages, ripping into his own flesh. "*Carve it out!*"

Wilder swears and dives forward, grabbing Cav's wrists and pinning them to the mattress. Kaspian takes the other side of the bed until they're both focusing restraining him. Cav bucks and contorts beneath them, inhuman strength fueled by madness.

"Help us hold him!" Wilder shouts at Axe over his shoulder.

Axe surges forward, taking Cav's flailing legs. They wrestle Cav down, sweat pouring down their faces as they strain against his manic thrashing.

"Cav!" Kaspian snarls, pulling out of his sling and using both arms to hold down one of Cav's, heedless of any pain it might cause his shoulder, the stitches it will tear. "Remember what we've said. What we say to each other when it gets too much. *The Court isn't our destiny.* It is *not* our death. There is no curse. You're hurt, the Sovereigns fucked you up, but you are fine. There is no dark magic. Nothing holding your mind. Just us. Your brothers, and Elara."

I hover, hands pressed to my mouth, tears streaming down my cheeks.

Cav's face whips toward me, his eyes seeking mine. For a moment, just a split second, I swear I see a flicker of recognition. A glimmer of the man who so furiously claimed me in this very room, succumbing to that rare emotion of his, the one that binds, the one that parts the black clouds of his life and finds the sky.

And I know what to do.

With trembling fingers, I untie my cloak. The boys are too occupied restraining Cav to notice me undressing behind them.

I unbutton my pants and peel off my shirt, my bra and underwear with a light *whoosh* of sound.

Wilder glances up sharply as if scenting my nakedness. His pupils dilate at the sight of me, with my hair flowing past my shoulders and curling under my breasts.

I start forward. He doesn't stop me.

Movement in his periphery draws Axe's attention, too. He looks at me with a mixture of awe and protectiveness, his arms bunching with corded muscle as he grips Cav's thrashing legs. Yet he only watches me as I move toward them.

Kaspian's focus is on Cav, trying to get him to calm down. But it's like as soon as I get too close, his head snaps up, and his snake-green eyes center on me.

There's no hesitation in my step at their targeted, heated attention, and I crawl onto the bed next to Cav, feeling the cold, sweat, and blood-soaked sheets against my bare knees, and then slide on top of Cav to straddle him.

"Careful, beastie," Kaspian warns.

I run my shaking fingers over Cav's bloody cheekbones. He's now watching me carefully, his teeth poised to snap. Leashing my own terror, I try to reclaim his attention.

Slowly, so slowly, I lean down and press my lips to his bloodstained mouth, tasting the saltiness of his sweat and the metallic tang of his ichor. Cav stiffens, and then something shifts ... his arms relax against Wilder and Kaspian just a fraction. His body goes slack for one sweet moment before he bucks again, but there's less violence in it this time. Less anger.

And it's mainly in his hips, directly below my parted folds.

Kaspian meets my gaze over Cav's twitching form and nods once—sharp enough that I understand that he's curious enough to allow me to tread carefully. I reach down and grasp Cav's hand in mine while Wilder holds his wrist, pressing our palms together. My heart hammers out a rhythm only heard by him now.

"Breathe with me," I say against his ear as I match his shallow breaths with mine.

Cav's hips arch again, his cock twitching under me. Only a single sheet separates us from each other.

Kaspian moves to capture his arm again, but I stop him with a hooded look before turning my focus back on Cav.

"Look at me," I murmur to Cav, my chest rising and falling with his.

Cav struggles for a moment before his gaze clashes with mine, a battle of wills. His hand flexes under my palm in a desperate plea, breaking my heart and turning me on all at once.

Wilder rumbles low in his throat, his gaze rapacious as he takes in the scene.

"Fuck," he mutters under his breath. "I want her, too."

"Get in line," Kaspian murmurs, his eyes as vulturine as Wilder's.

A rush of warmth drenches my pussy at the sight of the three of them staring at me like I'm better than dinner. Like I'm the whole damned five-course meal.

I can't see Axe, but I sense his utter stillness behind me, and have no doubt where his attention lingers while he gets a perfect view of my backside.

Boldly, I reach down and stroke along the length of Cav's cock, another form of soothing, of complete and utter distraction from agony.

"Feel me," I breathe.

Cav's bloodied, chapped lips part, his mouth finally relaxing.

Wilder grabs my hair roughly and yanks my head back, forcing our eyes to meet. His grip on my hair is painful, but it only adds to the growing ache between my legs.

"Fuck her, Cav," he says through clenched teeth without taking his eyes off me. "Fuck her until you come back to us."

Cav doesn't need further instruction. He thrusts into me slowly, letting his hips choose the rhythm as he moves in and out.

The feel of him filling me up makes me moan softly.

"Yes," I whisper, arching my back slightly to take all of him.

Axe's hands press against my ass cheeks as he watches Cav fuck me from behind. I can feel the heat emanating from him, making my pussy clench around Cav's cock even tighter.

In response, Cav picks up the pace, slamming into me harder and deeper with each thrust.

"She's so tight," Cav groans between breaths, his hips moving steadily as he takes control of our connection.

"That's the first logical thing you've said all night," Kaspian says, his tone wicked with sexual approval.

Kaspian's mere voice, velvet and grit and arrogance, soaks my pussy further.

Wilder keeps his grip on the back of my head, holding my gaze captive as Cav's movements grow furious.

Suddenly, Axe grabs both my hips and pushes down roughly, forcing Cav deeper.

Kaspian watches us intently from the other side of the bed, his eyes shrouded with lust as he runs a hand through his usually well-groomed hair.

"She's ours, Cav," Kaspian says. My pussy clenches around Cav's cock in response. "Your only curse is that you have to share her with us, because I'm not fucking letting you have her all to yourself."

With Axe now in control of my hips and Cav's arms free, Cav threads his fingers around the back of my neck, pulling on it gently as he drives himself deeper. His rhythm matches Axe's guidance, making every stroke feel like an electrical current coursing through the three of us.

Kaspian leans closer, his presence adding another level of excitement to the mix. He runs a finger lightly down my cheek before capturing my lower lip under his thumb. It's enough to send sparks flying through every nerve ending in my body.

"You like that?" he asks.

I nod as much as Wilder's hold on my scalp allows, unable to find the words to express how completely overwhelmed I am by these four men.

Even now, they take care of me.

Wilder's grip on my hair tightens as he angles my head back, exposing the column of my throat, the motion dragging Kaspian's thumb until my lip pops free from it. Wilder's teeth graze my pulse point, sending shivers cascading under my skin.

"You're doing so good, sweetwitch," he growls. "Taking Cav's cock to save him."

The slap of skin against skin echoes obscenely in the room, mingling with Cav's and my pants and moans.

Cav's gorgeous blue eyes, once wild and unfocused, now bore into my bouncing breasts with a searing intensity. The madness recedes, replaced by a primal hunger that has my pussy fluttering.

He rasps, his voice hoarse and strained, "I ... I need..."

"I know," I say on a current of breath.

Wilder releases his hold on me, and I lean down to capture Cav's lips in a blood-soaked kiss. I pour everything into it—my worry, my desperation, my stubbornness to convince him that we make the only magic in this world.

As if spurred on by my nips and sucks, Cav's hips snap up with renewed vigor. He fucks into me with abandon, chasing his release.

"Come for me, Cav," I plead against his mouth. "Come back to me."

With a guttural roar, Cav slams into me one final time. His cock pulses as he spills himself deep inside me.

I cry out as my own orgasm crashes through, my walls spasming around Cav's twitching length. Spots dance across my vision.

As the last of the tremors subside, I want to collapse onto Cav's chest but know I can't. I sag sideways, caught by Wilder and settled against his hard chest.

Cav follows my movement, clear-eyed but weary. "Hello, butterfly."

Tears prick at my eyes as relief floods through me. I glance up at Kaspian, Wilder, and Axe, noting the same sentiment reflected in their expressions.

Wilder says above my head with an amused tone, "I don't know whether to call you sweetwitch or curse-breaker, now."

I did it. I brought Cav out of his madness, an ability I thought I didn't possess. A sob of relief escapes me.

I'm not a failure. I can still save someone.

Wilder tightens our hug. Kaspian's cool, weighted study shifts away from me as if he's actually offering a sliver of decency while I collect myself, and Axe stands stoic, a thousand buried thoughts behind his gaze.

The fugue of an orgasm ends too quickly.

With Cav's fresh torture and the Heart split, if tonight proves anything, it's that we'll have to fight like hell to keep our half of it.

But for now, at this moment, I let myself bask in this small victory over the Sovereigns.

They'll soon learn that you don't come between a girl and her men.

CHAPTER 10
AXE
THE PHANTOM

After what Elara did with Cav, for Cav, in front of all of us, Wilder immediately invited her into his bed to stay the night. I kept silent, my dick straining, as I waited for her choice. I'm not like Wilder. I don't baldly assume a passionate fuck even though I expect it.

At Wilder's invitation, Kaspian sneaked away, likely falling back on his injured shoulder as an excuse not to take Elara to his room even though I know the truth. He pretends Elara doesn't affect him like she does the rest of us, like she's one of his many collector's items over the years who he fucks with, then discards as soon as he's stunningly bored with them.

But she's not like the rest, and he knows it.

Hence his quick exit after watching her ride Cav, the little sounds she made, the sweat shining on her perfect body, her hair begging for our fingers, her ass ready to be spread for all of us…

Unfortunately for all of us, Elara instead chose the couch in our private common room, closest to Cav's door, and she spent most of the night on her phone talking to her friend and sorting out her mother.

I clear my throat, shifting position on the armchair opposite Kaspian to better accommodate my stiff cock. Now, the morning sun filters through stained glass windows as we gather in the common room.

Kaspian slouches in an armchair, nursing his wounded shoulder. Wilder splays on the couch, flipping through streaming services on the flat-screen TV above our fireplace.

And Elara's curled up on the other side of the wide couch, the blankets she used overnight bunched around her legs. Her long hair is mussed from sleep but cascades down her shoulders, and her eyes—those damn eyes—seem to reflect the rainbow of light coming from the stained glass.

I itch to feel the softness of her skin the way Cav did, to trace the curves currently hidden by her leggings and an over-sized sweatshirt.

Elara's gaze lingers on the empty space between her and Wilder, a spot she seems to be wishing Cav were using, before she turns her rainbow eyes on me. "Did you sleep at all last night?"

The question jars me. I expected her to ask how Cav was doing or what the next steps were in finding the other half of the Heart, or updates on her brother's killers.

So many subjects to cover, yet she chooses … me?

I shrug in answer. Memories of violent homes and punishing schools haunt my restless mind. It's as if all those memories that elude me while awake manage to find me in terrifying detail through my dreams. Sleep is a luxury.

Kaspian straightens, grimacing. He grunts as he stands, his left arm reluctantly back in a sling.

I'm surprised he put it back on. Is it for Elara's sake that he's pretending to be a good boy, or is he using it as a distraction while he compiles all kinds of horrendous shit in his head to use against the Sovereigns?

My vote's on the latter.

Kaspian pushes to his feet, stalking over to the bar and pouring himself a drink. The amber liquid sloshes against the sides of the glass as he knocks it back in one gulp.

Elara's brows knit together, her lips parting as if to caution him against drinking first thing in the morning, but he prevents it by saying, "I'm off the pain pills. It makes me too vulnerable. So a shot of bourbon it is."

I lean forward, resting my elbows on my knees, asking her, "How did *you* sleep?"

Elara wraps her arms around her shins, curling her legs in close. "Okay."

She didn't choose Wilder. Or me. Nor did she sleep beside Cav or dare to knock on Kaspian's door. She wanted to sleep out here, in our common room, perhaps embarrassed at how she revealed herself to us last night—or struggling with the implications of it.

If she thought we wanted her before...

Therefore, Wilder and I slept in here, too, both taking armchairs and watching Elara more than we chased sleep.

Elara shifts, the blankets falling away as she plants her feet on the floor. "I want to help with whatever you guys are doing today. Tell me what I need to do."

My gaze rakes over her, from the wild tumble of her hair to the hard set of her jaw.

Even now, with everything at stake, I can't ignore the obsession that churns in my gut at the sight of her.

Kaspian slams his glass down on the bar, the sound ricocheting through the room like the very gunshot that ravaged his shoulder. Elara jumps, likely remembering the same thing.

"You've done enough already," Kaspian snarls with his back to us. "We don't need your help."

Yep, Kaspian is exceptionally unhappy about his current state.

Elara flinches as if he'd struck her, hurt flickering across her face before she smooths it away. She stands, squaring her shoulders as she faces him. "I'm not going anywhere. Didn't last night show you anything? You need me. You wouldn't have half the

Heart if not for me. I'm a part of this now, whether you like it or not."

Wilder whistles low under his breath, his gaze darting between them. I watch the scene unfold, tension crackling in the atmosphere, lightning readying to strike.

Kaspian's hand flexes at his side, his fingers curling into a fist. For a moment, I think he might lash out, his anger is so palpable.

I rise from my armchair, my erection straining against my jeans. I cross the room in a few strides and take the bottle from Kaspian's hand and pour him two more fingers. "You're cranky. Drink."

"I don't need a fucking nursemaid—"

I shove the drink into his hand. "You are a genius and we wouldn't be where we are without you, but when you're wounded, you're fucking intolerable, so drink."

Kaspian grunts, but tosses the liquor back, swallowing in one gulp.

Elara stands by, her cautious attention switching between Kaspian and me. And, appearing to have discovered our weakness, she stretches her arms high above her head as she gives herself a full-body stretch.

Her sweatshirt rides up, revealing a strip of smooth skin above the waistband of her leggings.

My cock throbs at the sight. I want to cross the room, yank those leggings down her legs, and bury my face in her. I want to feel her clench around my tongue, hear her moan my name when I make her cum.

But I don't move. I can't. It wouldn't be right, not after what I've been forced to do. To her, to my brothers…

If she knew, Elara's sweet expression would turn to hate. I never want her to look at me that way. It'd be the one time I'm thankful for my memory lapses.

Wilder sits up on the couch, tossing the remote onto the

coffee table and saying out of the side of his mouth, "Shit, Elara's as ruthless as you, Kasp."

His focus doesn't stray from Elara's belly button. "Where's that bourbon? I suddenly want to do body shots this morning."

Elara drops her arms to her sides and pads across the room, her bare feet silent on the hardwood.

She stops in front of Kaspian and reaches up to brush a strand of hair from his forehead, revealing those disturbing eyes of his at their full charge. "How's the shoulder?"

I struggle not to gape, though she's essentially just booped a shark on the nose and called it cute.

Kaspian answers through a barely controlled voice, "It's fine."

"Liar." Elara's voice is soft, almost tender. She traces her fingertips along his jaw and down his neck before retreating. "I'm sorry my mom did this to you."

"I don't need any apologies."

There's the snarl.

"True, but you do need an extra set of hands." Elara shrugs. With both shoulders.

Kaspian glares at her.

I step between them, placing a hand on Kaspian's chest and reminding him, "We're down a man. We can't lose you, too."

Kaspian's nostrils flare. For a moment, I think he might punch me, and I prepare for a fight. But then he barks out a laugh, the sound harsh and bitter. "Fine. But she stays out of my way."

Elara's eyes grow small with indignation, her lips pressing into a thin line. But she doesn't argue.

Wilder pushes himself off the couch, stretching his arms above his head and ensuring Elara gets her karma by showing a slice of toned abs. "I'll start digging through the initiates' archives downstairs, see if there's any mention of Maverick."

Kaspian smirks at Elara, fully aware that she can't go with Wilder and reveal herself to the rest of the Court. Not without raising questions and snagging the Sovereigns' attention.

I turn to Kaspian. "Elara can help you on the tech side. You're not leaving our wing and you can't properly type with your arm in a sling."

Kaspian looks like he wants to eat me whole. "Dictation, asshole. It's a thing."

I counter in a low voice, "Then why don't you tell her about the hidden library in the manor that hasn't been seen for hundreds of years—until it was discovered by Maverick and he hid his flash-drive confessing to breaking the Heart there?"

Wilder pauses with his coffee mug halfway to his lips.

Elara's jaw falls to the floor. "*What?*"

Kaspian now wants to turn me into a slow-cooked meal. "That was not your find to reveal."

"Clearly," I say with an innocent expression.

Kaspian informed me of his discovery shortly before we all met up in Cav's room while the Selection continued downstairs. With the Sovereigns at our heels and the danger posed to Elara, he hadn't yet revealed it to anyone else, and I was beginning to wonder when he would. Thankfully, I'd typed his words into my reminder app as soon as I got the chance, and had a lot of time to read last night.

Elara moves nearer, her eyes wide with a mix of shock, hurt at being left out, and excitement. "A hidden library? Containing evidence of what my brother did? Take me. Take me there right now."

Wilder sets his mug down with a thud, coffee sloshing over the rim and ready to move onward. He wipes his mouth with the back of his hand. "Lead the way, brother."

Kaspian pushes off the bar. He presses close to me until we're nearly nose-to-nose. "After this, we're going to have a long talk about when, and *who*, to reveal crucial intel to."

I don't flinch, holding his gaze steady.

Kaspian's eyes shrink to slits before he spins on his heel and strides out of the room, his shoes thudding heavily against the floorboards.

Expecting us to follow.

Elara hurries after him, her bare feet slapping against the wood. She throws a glance over her shoulder at me, offering a small smile of gratitude. I smile back, a flicker of … life … igniting in my chest, before she disappears into the hallway.

Wilder charges after Kaspian and Elara, but I hang back a moment, surveying our common room, the discarded blankets on the couch, the half-empty bottle of bourbon on the bar. Evidence of the unrest that's entered our lives.

I stride into the hallway. Ahead, Kaspian leads the way, his injured arm tucked close to his body. Elara keeps pace beside him, her hair remaining a wild tumble down her back. Wilder brings up the rear.

What does Wilder see when he looks at Kaspian and Elara together? Is he envisioning Teagan and himself, the girl who died on his watch?

I pull out my phone, typing this down as a question to ponder later.

We wind through the manor, taking turns and climbing staircases I've never explored until we're in the attic. The air grows musty, thick with the scent of leather, tobacco, old books, and dust. So much fucking dust.

Finally, Kaspian stops in the middle of a cobwebbed corridor in front of a large painting. He flicks on the flashlight of his phone, spotlighting the painting in full detail.

"It's Thornhaven Manor," Elara says.

"And the gold star goes to Miss Wraithwood," Kaspian drawls.

Elara appears ready to dig her finger into the bullet hole on his shoulder.

I incline my head, drawing closer to the painting and studying the manor as it would have been in the late 1600s. The gardens surrounding the gray stone, the pristine turrets and spires, the widow's walk, the unmarred west wing.

I glance between the silhouette in the garden, painted in

shadow despite the sun shining down on him, and the west wing that no longer exists—

Kaspian's hand darts in front of my vision, preventing what I'm certain I was about figure out, his index finger locating two pressure points in the painting. The figure and where the garden meets the west wing.

The wall behind us groans before a panel slides open.

Elara turns at the sound. Well, we all do, but she's who I'm most interested in watching, because her expression doesn't change, even though a secret wall in an ancient manor just opened up before her because Kaspian touched a painting.

She notices Kaspian's inscrutable study before she does mine.

"What?" she says to him sweetly. "Do you think you're the only person who's discovered a centuries-old room in an old mansion?" Elara peers over her shoulder at the painting with an unimpressed arched brow. "Mine involved a grandfather clock."

Her statement stops me short. While Kaspian and Wilder respond to her with reluctant questions and intrigue, respectively, I can't find any words. My voice has sunk too low into my gut, churning in acid along with my conscience.

How many of us are keeping our own secrets? For a brotherhood, a team, we're fractured where it matters most: trust. If we want to beat the Sovereigns, we have to work together, yet none of us do.

For the first time, I'm prevented from voicing my thoughts not by my bruised brain, but because I can't, out of sheer hypocrisy.

I carry my own betrayals, nestled in the cavity where a heart should be.

With lowered shoulders, I stare into the yawning darkness revealed by the wall panel with a pained sigh.

But write it down anyway.

Then hit send.

CHAPTER 11
WILDER
THE HELLHOUND

I release a low whistle, craning my neck to see down the endless spiraling staircase hidden behind the wall.

Which opened because of a painting. Jesus, these colonial fuckers were creative.

"Maverick found this place, too?" I ask.

"Apparently." Kaspian parts our rapt cluster and starts his way down, no hesitation.

I step aside, inviting Elara to go next, ignoring the thrum in my blood to go first. Even though I want to see it all first.

Kaspian may be in an epic bitchy mood, but his instincts are never dulled by emotion or injury. With him at the front and me protecting Elara's back, whatever else is in this hidey-hole won't have a chance to come at her.

I glance at Axe over my shoulder before entering behind Elara. He's focused on his phone, brows knitted and mouth tight.

"You okay?" I ask. "Who are you talking to?"

I'd caught a glimpse of a message screen before he subtly angled away.

"Cav." Axe shoves the phone into his back pocket. "He asked to be kept updated on everything we do today."

I nod. "Good call."

Axe gives me a half smile, his eyes darting away from mine and toward where Elara just faded to black. "After you."

I study him for a beat more, caught by the strange loop in my mind that keeps playing when Axe put his phone away and met my gaze.

Shrugging the strange feeling off, I step into the stairwell, my boots thudding on the worn stone treads as I descend. The air grows colder with each step, a damp chill that seeps through my jacket and raises the hair on my body. Elara's silhouette is just visible ahead, her slender form swallowed by the darkness. Her breathing echoes off the narrow walls, and I strain my ears for any sound that might signal an incoming threat. Kaspian has vanished, but I can hear his casual gait.

The four of us reach the bottom of the spiral staircase, emerging into a cavernous chamber that I cannot believe has been buried underground this whole time. Row upon row of bookshelves line up like neglected soldiers in front of me, their tops almost reaching the domed ceiling above, both blurred by black and dust.

Four blue-white spotlights arc over the shelving and forgotten debris strewn around the windowless stone cavern. Our phones' lights reveal the extent of the library's decay— tattered books lying scattered across the stone ground, their pages yellowed and brittle with age. Chunks of stone have fallen from the walls, cracking the cold gray floors.

Everywhere I look, I see the remnants of a once-grand collection. Broken sculptures, their features worn smooth by time; elegant furniture, now little more than kindling, haphazardly strewn about; and ornate globes on tarnished gold stands, their continents obscured by a century's worth of grime.

The intrusive thought wins.

I spin the closest globe, causing such a screech of unused mechanisms that even Kaspian's shoulders go tight.

Screws loosen, the globe wobbles and then falls off its stand and onto the floor with a crash that makes Elara wince.

"Wilder," Kaspian admonishes.

I slowly step away, hands up, and I don't hide my amusement when Elara gives me an embarrassed glance before heading to the row Kaspian walked into.

Fuck, she's cute when she's flustered.

Despite the icy chill wrapping around us, my blood heats at the sight of her. Her cheeks are flushed, her lips parted slightly. It's a sight that has me picturing her beneath me, pink for entirely different reasons.

Holding back a groan, I shake away those thoughts. Now is not the time.

Plunging my hands into my pockets, I saunter over to Elara. "Stay close."

I catch her by the arm to steer her into my side and away from any more potential mishaps, now that I'm being a good boy.

It's just my excuse to touch her, really. The feel of her skin against mine sparks my nerves in such a pleasant way. I haven't felt a *zing* like this since Tea—

No. Nope. Not going there.

I press closer to Elara, my arm snaking around her waist. Her warmth seeps through my motorcycle jacket, chasing away the subterranean chill. I don't question the ease in which she leans into me, too. Last night was surprising, eye-opening, and one I will never forget as long as I breathe.

The shape of her body on Cav, the way she slid onto his dick and fucked him back to sanity—by god, I can't wait to go insane.

But even without fucking her, I *felt* Elara, like she was a part of us now, giving herself fully not only to Cav but to us. I was the one who stared into her eyes while she shattered. I'm the one who got to scrape his teeth across her pulse when she screamed.

She gave herself to me as much as she did Cav. And for that, she's not his. She's *ours.*

The thought triggers an alpha need. I want to claim her right here, scattering dust and bringing this grand library into the now, reminding it that it exists through Elara's cries. I'll mark every inch of her skin, starting with that full lower lip of hers, and make her beg and crawl for my cock.

Fuck, that image alone rouses an urgent hunger.

I clear my throat, fingers spasming before I force my grip to loosen on her waist.

Kaspian's footsteps echo off the towering shelves as he weaves between them, scanning the spines with a critical eye.

Axe hangs behind, his gaze still fixed on his phone. His thumb taps the screen, checking for a signal.

"Anything interesting?" I call out to Kaspian, my voice reverberating in the cavernous space.

We reach the center of the room, where a massive oak table dominates. Its surface is strewn with yellowed maps and crumbling scrolls. I lean in to examine one of them.

"This is about where I found Maverick's flash drive," Kaspian says, pointing at a piece of yellowed parchment. "First, I found his name on that list right there. Past initiates dating back to the Cimmerian Court's founding."

I whistle and tuck my hands back in my pockets. "Not so forgotten, then."

Kaspian makes a low noise of agreement. "Someone is using this room. Whether it's for good or evil is up to us to decide. I haven't had a chance to return since first discovering the place, so now's as good a time as any to search for anything pointing at who that someone is, or hell, even finding the other half of the Heart. Maverick could've stashed it here, too."

Elara's jaw tightens at the mention of her brother's name. Not that it was said, but the way in which Kaspian voiced it.

Emotionless. Cold. Almost bone-chillingly bored.

I catch her eye and give her a sympathetic wince. *Welcome to the club. Kaspian would treat a fluffy kitten the same way.*

I turn back to Kaspian. "You said someone."

Kasp arches a brow at me. "And?"

"Why not someone*s*? How are you so certain it's only one person?"

It's for an eighth of a second, but a muscle in Kaspian's jaw pops out at the question. Then his face smooths, and he quickly answers, "You're right. It could be multiple people."

"Like the three Sovereigns?" Elara asks, oblivious to Kaspian's almost imperceptible tells.

Kaspian indicates that it's possible by waving a hand. Elara launches into further questions, focusing on where Kaspian found the flash drive (under a hideous golden raven statue) and what it contained.

While Kaspian deigns to answer, I scrutinize him closer.

That's two brothers now who I think are holding something back. Because I can bet you that Axe is up to something, and also wager that for whatever reason, Kaspian is keeping his certainty that only one person has breached this room close to his chest.

I can't remember the last time I was suspicious of one of my brothers. We've gone through hell together—through fires so hot that our souls were forged into molten metal. And we didn't emerge until every last one of us was out.

I search Kaspian's gaze for any hint of deception, but he remains impassive, a mask of cool indifference.

Elara purses her lips at Kaspian's non-answers to her questions. I can't blame her. We're three predators in one room, and she's the delicate deer caught in between.

She asks, "Could it be the same person who killed my brother?"

I catch her chin gently between my fingers. She looks up at me with those fearfully innocent eyes; so poignant and irresistible. I also see the hope burning there.

It's then I know I'll rip this library to shreds if it means finding her brother's killer for her.

I have to rein in the surprising emotion by blinking it back. There's no room for softness in this body.

Squeezing her jaw tighter, I grin. "Only one way to find out."

Elara sucks in a breath when I release her as fast as I caught her, snatching up a large square of yellowed parchment from the table and filled with symbols and diagrams, ignoring Kaspian's hiss of protest. Dust billows as I shake it out, ancient grit raining down.

I pull it closer, scrutinizing the faded lines. Something clicks in my mind. "That's the original sigil of the Cimmerian Court."

Elara, recovering faster than I gave her credit for, peers around my arm. "A flower?"

"A nightshade, specifically."

Elara's brows come together at the same time Axe pockets his phone, joining us at the table. He says, "Cav's family helped start this society. It was small then, limited to four original families of Titan Falls. When it grew, gaining power, influence, and reach outside this town, the founding families lost their iron grip on the Court and its rules. The sigil was changed to what it is now —the profile of a skull facing left with a celestial crown formed by two crescent moons—in the 1950s."

"To Nightshade's credit, they held on to it like a lady clutching her pearls for a good hundred years," I add.

Elara thinks this over, her nose scrunching and bringing her freckles closer together as she thinks. "Are you saying the Cimmerian Court started out … nice?"

Kaspian barks out a laugh, jarring in such a stifled room, but no less disturbing. "No. We were always ruthless and chose violence over friendly negotiation. It just became more brutal."

"That's what happens when you breed your own manner of beasts," Axe murmurs.

We fall into contemplative silence.

I flatten the map on the table, redirecting everyone's attention to our very pressing issue in the present, not the past. "Look at these markings. I think this is the layout of the library itself."

Kaspian is the first to snap to attention. He races a fingertip over a series of interconnected circles. "Then this must represent hidden chambers. Rooms we haven't found yet. Interesting, considering the last person rifling through these maps was Maverick, and he left this on top."

Excitement sizzles through my veins, hot and electric. The promise of more answers to uncover, of lost knowledge waiting to be rediscovered. My fingers twitch with the urge to pick this place apart stone by stone.

Axe shakes his head. "Either Maverick or whoever else uses this place. Kaspian is right. We can't assume we're the only ones who have access."

Elara glances up at me, her eyes almost golden in the gloom. "Then we have to find the other half of the Heart first. Maverick could've put it in one of these rooms and left this as a clue."

"Or a trap," Kaspian points out.

I shrug. "Does it matter? We're trampling through, anyway." Jerking my chin at a towering bookcase along the far wall, I add, "According to this map, one entrance is behind that bookshelf. Help me move it."

Axe and I throw our weight against the shelf, muscles straining as we inch it aside. Stone grinds against stone, a teeth-rattling screech that pierces through my skin and ricochets off my bones.

As the bookcase scrapes out of the way, stale air gusts out of a person-sized hole in the wall, reeking of mold and decay.

Kaspian produces a flashlight and aims it into the opening. The beam illuminates a narrow passageway, the walls glistening with moisture and crawling with pale roots.

I shoot Elara a shameless grin over my shoulder. "Ladies first."

She pulls her lips in, gnawing on them before she squeezes

past me, her hips grazing mine in a way that sends fire licking at my dick. I bite back a groan at the same time Axe sends me a damning look.

Fuck.

I was too distracted by her ass to realize—

"I didn't expect her to actually go first," I say to Axe's receding back as he shoots forward to catch up to her.

Only to catch a line of fire come back my way.

CHAPTER 12
ELARA

When the line of fire reaches Kaspian and Wilder, I swear I notice a smirk at one corner of Axe's mouth when he hears shouts coming from the entrance to the corridor.

I'm noticing he enjoys surprising people in the worst of ways.

Axe nearly sent me out of my skin when he gripped my shoulder to pull me to a stop in the pitch black passageway. Not that I complained, since I responded to Wilder's dare to enter first like a stubborn idiot. Something in me never wants Wilder to win at his dares, thus I traipsed into the unknown despite my current history of traps and gunshots with faux bravado.

So when Axe cautioned me to stay close while he flipped open a lighter from his pocket and held it to the wall, I did. His tiny flame illuminated a carved horizontal line spanning the corridor and I observed with interest as a combustible powder reacted to his flame and sent an impressive *whoosh* of fire lighting our way down.

And back.

I don't realize I'm grinning, too, until it falls from my face the minute I behold Kaspian's unbound fury, stoked by the orange line of fire along the wall. And Wilder positioned behind him, gun in one hand and knife in the other.

Kaspian's rage ignites the shadows clinging to the corridor. A vein throbs at his temple. He stalks forward, fist balled at his side.

I backpedal, hands raised in supplication. "Kaspian, we didn't mean to scare you—"

Kaspian pounces, seizing Axe by his shirt's collar and slamming him against the opposite wall. Pebbles rain on us at the impact. I look at the ceiling with worry. "Kaspian, stop."

"You think this is *fun*?" Kaspian seethes, face inches from Axe's inscrutable one. "Sneaking around in the dark, springing traps on each other?"

I have one foot forward, ready to intervene, but Wilder's hand at my elbow stops my approach. He's pocketed those weapons I never even knew he had and shakes his head slightly, watching the scene unfold while saying to me out the side of his mouth, "Let him get it out. Axe wants him to. He can handle it."

Kaspian's lip curls. He shoves Axe harder against the wall, then releases him with a disgusted headshake. Though his throat has become bright red with Kaspian's chokehold, Axe stands strong, arms at his sides.

Kaspian rounds on me, jabbing a finger in my direction. "And you. Waltzing in first like a fool. Letting Wilder goad you into being an idiot."

I lift my chin, meeting his glare. "I don't let anyone goad me into anything. I make my own choices."

Kaspian snorts. "Clearly."

He spins on his heel and stalks down the corridor, the firelight casting his elongated shadow against the walls, storming behind him like his pet poltergeist.

Axe pushes away from the wall, hands balled at his sides. He still won't massage the mark on his neck or even acknowledge it's there.

"Guess Kaspian wants to be the leader," Wilder says at my side.

I don't respond. I'm watching Axe, trying to read his expression in the flickering light. His face is a veneer, but there's a glint in his eye that I can't place. Amusement? Anticipation?

He meets my gaze, and his mouth quirks, just for a moment. Then he turns and follows Kaspian into the depths of the corridor, leaving Wilder and me alone in the wavering firelight.

He regards me with a look that is part appraisal, part amusement, his lips curving into a faint, knowing smile that suggests he likes what he sees.

As he walks by, something about him feels different. Stronger, perhaps more focused and way less playful now that the threat of danger commanded his attention. His prowl is fluid and undeterred by the weapons I'm now aware he holds against his body.

"You okay?" he asks without looking back.

I scan our rocky surroundings while I resume walking. "Let's just get this search over with."

While continuing down the passageway, my feet scrapes against the uneven stone. I really should've worn shoes.

Ahead, Kaspian marches onward, his broad shoulders rigid with anger.

We round a corner, and the path opens into a cavernous chamber. Stalactites drip from the ceiling like jagged teeth, and the air is thick with the stench of damp earth and something else, something rotten.

Kaspian stops abruptly, his hand shooting out to halt our progress. I peer around his sheer size, and my breath catches in my throat.

A stone altar lies in the center of the chamber, illuminated by a shaft of sickly green light. Its surface is stained with dark rust-colored patches and symbols are carved into the sides, tangled and coiling like serpents.

Axe is the first to move closer, his face blanched of color, and circles the altar slowly, running his fingers over the symbols at the top.

The slab is just the right length to splay out a human. My eye is drawn not just to the carvings, but the finger-sized gouges along the rough edges.

"What is it?" My voice sounds too loud in the oppressive quiet.

Kaspian slowly shakes his head. "Nothing good."

Wilder moves to the far side of the chamber, scanning the walls and running his hands along thin, vertical marks. He asks in a voice matching the gravel around him, "Do you recognize the symbols, Axe?"

Axe nods.

Then peels off his shirt.

"Oh my god," I say. No, I don't *say* anything. I moan it through my fingers as they cover my mouth.

Many of the same markings on the altar are ones that the Sovereigns have carved into his back.

His muscular form flexes and strains with each movement, the raw, tortured maleness of him seeming to make the symbols on his back come alive in the eerie green light.

Axe looks at me over his shoulder, his eyes dark pools that the light can't reach. The resigned look on his face twists something in my chest, and I reach for him—

"Do you like what you see? What Axe has become?" Kaspian asks, a crooked smile accompanying his snide remark.

I recoil, my cheeks burning at the same time I hiss, "I'm not going to apologize for having a heart. Not even to men who clearly have no idea what it's like to feel one beating in their chest."

Kaspian returns his attention to the altar in clear dismissal. I wonder what I did to make him despise me so much. Opening myself up to Cav while they watched, at the time seemed ... right. Beautiful, even. But Kaspian, with his unhurried disdain and reluctance to have me at his side now, makes me think I did something shameful.

And I hate him for it.

I am not ashamed.

Axe's guttered eyes meet mine for another fleeting instant before he turns away, pulling his shirt on.

Wilder draws closer to Axe, his attention flicking between Axe and the altar. "You know what this means, don't you?"

I edge closer, morbid curiosity overriding the hurt Kaspian brought forth.

Axe traces a finger over one particularly intricate carving.

"It's some kind of ritual," he mutters. "Blood magic, maybe. Something dark and ancient."

Wilder shifts uneasily, his hand drifting toward the gun at his hip.

I dare to venture, "I thought your current Sovereigns were the only ones to bring dark magic into your rituals."

"Yeah, that's what we thought, too," Wilder says, his eyes not leaving the stone altar.

I turn to Axe, my voice soft but firm. "Do you have any idea what these symbols might mean? Anything at all?"

He shakes his head, his expression unreadable.

"Leaving the question," Kaspian says as he comes up behind me, "why does Axe have carvings on his back that are the same as ones found in an untouched chamber hundreds of years old?"

"Not untouched," I breathe out when something catches my eye—a glint of metal at the altar's base.

I crouch down. There, nestled in a crevice, is a small silver flash drive.

"Guys," I say, my voice cracking as I push to my feet.

I hold up the flash drive. Kaspian snatches it from my hand, examining it closely. "Your brother sure does love his scavenger hunts."

"He was trying to be safe," I reason. "Would you rather he leave everything in one place for the Sovereigns to find?"

Kaspian's eyes flare at my tone, but I refuse to be cut down by him again. Not when, for the first time in years, I feel closer to my dead brother just by finding another clue he left behind.

Kaspian's grip tightens around the flash drive, the whites of his knuckles bursting through.

"Your brother's games are going to get *my* brothers killed." His voice is a low snarl. "You realize that, don't you?"

I match his glare. "Maverick knew what he was doing. He wouldn't have hidden evidence here if he didn't think it was important."

Kaspian's attention lowers to my lips, his expression stirring with a mixture of lust and fury. The oxygen seems to evaporate from my throat, leaving me light-headed and struggling for air. Under his unrepentant study, the frustration between us undeniable.

It comes with so much heat, my core is melting with it.

For a long moment, Kaspian says nothing, just stares at me with those toxic, burning eyes.

Until Axe comes between us, dampening our fervid scrutiny of each other.

Kaspian straightens, his expression smoothing and his stare becoming bland and bored, like I never interested him in the first place.

I hold back the insult on my tongue by clenching my molars together and listening to Axe.

"We need to find out what's on that drive," he says.

Wilder produces a small tablet from his pack, holding it out to Kaspian. "No time like the present."

I hesitate in agreeing, my focus returning to the altar. The stains seem to shine in the sickly light, and a wave of nausea rolls through me. Yet I don't tell them to stop.

Answers about my brother overrides literally anything else.

Kaspian inserts the drive into the tablet's port. The screen flickers to life, lines of code scrolling across the display. He leans in, his brow furrowing as he deciphers the encrypted message.

"It's coordinates," he says after a moment. "And a warning."

Axe inclines his head, his attention locked on the tablet's screen. Wilder leans closer, a pensive frown on his face. After a few taps, his expression almost serene, Kaspian opens up a video.

The sound that comes out of me isn't human. It's an inhale of pain so ancient, every being on earth has felt it.

Grief.

Kaspian's hand clenches around the tablet at the sound, the veins in his forearm pushing against his skin. Axe closes his eyes like he feels my pain.

"You don't have to watch, sweetwitch."

Wilder's sudden proximity is a live grenade, his voice the pin that, once pulled, sets off a chain reaction of explosive sensations that tear through me.

I never saw him move, never felt the breeze of him closing in.

But I can't take my eyes off the close-up of Maverick's face, his face thinner, almost gaunt, as his amber eyes blaze. His hair, a twin to mine, is tousled and matted with sweat, like he's been clutching the sides of his head and pacing, a habit he had when he was stressed out and needed a moment to think.

"Play it," I say in a voice I don't recognize.

"You sure?"

I stare at Kaspian, surprised he even cares. "Yes."

Wilder settles an arm over my shoulders and pulls me close. At least if I explode, he'll cover me to lessen the impact.

Kaspian taps the screen, and Maverick comes to life.

"Sis, Ellie, I'm-I'm so damn sorry if you're seeing this. No, not if. When. When you find this." Maverick pauses, squeezing his eyes shut. The camera tilts as his hold on his phone loosens while he records. But with a shaky sigh, he centers the camera on his face again and continues. "I'm holding on to the hope that you'll find everything I've hidden while also praying that you won't need to. This isn't what I ever wanted for you, but ... but if …" His words catch as if something inside his body strangles his voice.

He visibly pushes past the lump in his throat, forcing the words out with a doggedness that belies the tremor in his voice. "If you're watching this video, it means I'm dead, and it wasn't accidental or from natural causes. Playing this video means I was murdered, and you're stopping at nothing to find my killer."

A tremor runs through me, a brief but undeniable quivering that I can't quite suppress at those damning words. They're true. His death has been a fact for six years, but *god*, it still hurts.

"You're sixteen, just a kid, but I see it in you. There's a force brewing in your soul, one that I doubt was extinguished after I died," he says, a hint of pride seeping through the despair in his voice.

A tear escapes, tracing a warm path down my cheek before falling to the filthy ground.

"I can't protect you anymore," he admits, another painful truth laid bare. "But I trust you can find your way out of this, because I've done everything I can to help you bring the Sovereigns down."

Wilder's arm turns to iron around my shoulders. Kaspian, who hasn't blinked since Maverick started talking, gives a single eye twitch of acknowledgment to Maverick's confession that he was trying to do exactly what we are. Axe lifts his chin, his attention tunneling into the screen.

"What I'm about to tell you goes against everything you think you know about Titan Falls, about its so-called elite Sovereigns who rule every aspect of this town and the powerful people outside of it." Maverick pauses, lost in thought.

He leans in closer to the camera. "I found something, Ellie. Proof of a secret that could bring their whole empire crumbling down. That's why they want me dead." His voice drops to an urgent whisper. "There's something called the ruby Heart. If you've gotten this far, I hope you know about it."

I nod, though there's no way he can see me.

"I found it. There are so many people looking for it, bad men, bloodthirsty ones, killers. But I found it before them, and I broke it. The other half, the one that will help you reveal everything, I've hidden it where they'll never find it. It's the only leverage I have over them."

Maverick glances over his shoulder, his jaw working nervously before he turns back to the camera. "Inside this drive are documents—photos—of what Sarah Anderton compiled centuries ago. Records, transactions, communications. I took photos of everything I discovered in the Grand Library underneath Thornhaven Estate. Hard evidence of the Sovereigns' true origins and the means by which they seized control."

Kaspian's stare lasers into the tablet's screen as if the threat of his eyes alone could force Maverick's ghost to provide more details.

As if predicting such intimidation, Maverick continues, "I won't risk going into detail in this video in case it falls into the wrong hands, but I will tell you one thing. The place where you found this drive is where Sarah Anderton was imprisoned, tortured, and killed."

I suck in a breath. My stare immediately locks on to the gouges in the slab, the vertical marks Wilder noticed.

Nails. Desperate, clawing fingers belonging to a woman.

"Sarah's death wasn't through official or lawful means," Maverick says, redirecting my grief. "Not after her trial. The Sovereigns kidnapped her and held her here for weeks—"

A crash sounds behind him. Maverick's head twists toward the noise, then swings back into focus, and he's talking faster and with more panic.

"Someone's coming. Find the second half, unlock the Heart, and expose their lies. Change *history*, Ellie. You have what it takes. You're the only one I trust to finish what I started … and please, *please*—"

Another sound clangs, then a shout. "Mavvy-boy, you in here?"

"—don't trust anyone other than family, Ellie," Maverick says in a rush, the camera shaking now. "You hear me? *Family* only. No matter how many years separate them from you. Members of the Cimmerian Court will try to manipulate you and sway you to their side, but these are not good people. Everyone's a liar. We're bred to kill, to work for the Sovereigns, and destroy anyone in their way—"

"Mavs! Where you at?" a disembodied voice yells somewhere behind him.

"I love you," Maverick chokes out. "I love you so much, Ellie. And I hate that you'll never see me again. There are no more USB drives. Just the three. Be safe. If there's a way to still be here after death, I will do everything that I can to stay with you."

The screen goes black as Maverick cuts the video.

I close my eyes against the anguish of his confirmation. The deep cut of his vow. Maverick was part of a brutal secret society and never breathed a word of it.

My shoulders slump as the final image of Maverick's drained face is seared into my mind.

The second I saw him on the screen, alive and talking, I had hoped for answers, maybe even a, *"If I'm dead, it means [insert name here] killed me."*

But it was a false hope. I should know that this world, these people, don't deal with their problems upfront. No, they stalk, and circle, and study, until their prey is at their weakest. Maverick, good man that he was, would've been trained in the same way.

My god. *Trained.*

For how long? How long did the Sovereigns have him for?

More questions, more worries, swirl inside my head.

What is the full extent of the Cimmerian Court's influence in Titan Falls—and beyond? How far back does their power truly reach? And most importantly—where the hell has Maverick hidden the other half of the ruby Heart?

I can't shake the cold, phantom fingers brushing along my shoulders, chilling my skin and raising the hairs on the back of my neck.

Don't trust anyone.

I slowly become aware of the others in the altar room. Wilder's arm still wrapped tightly around me, more possessive than comforting. Like he's saying through his strength, *You're not going anywhere, no matter what your brother just said.*

Kaspian watches me for any reaction, a python waiting for its dinner. And Axe's calm presence unsettles rather than soothes me.

I'm alone in here. Utterly alone among these evasive and dangerous men who likely know far more about my brother than I ever did.

Everyone's a liar.

CHAPTER 13
ELARA

*R*un, my instincts tell me., Maverick's spirit whispers to me. *Run, and don't look back at them while you do.*

Kaspian breaks the stillness. His tone is a low, feral thing, more animal than human, a snarl lurking just beneath the surface. "Now, where would your brother hide a piece of a multi-million dollar ruby?"

"I'm not letting you take over or order me around like I'm one of your initiates," I say. "Maverick entrusted this to me."

Wilder's fingers flex on my shoulders, a subtle warning. "We heard him, too, sweetwitch, but there's a lot your brother couldn't have predicted. You can't do this alone. You need us."

His tone carries an edge of menace, masculine expectation, beneath the concern.

I shrug out of his hold.

"I don't *need* anyone." The words taste wrong on my tongue, but I force them out. "Especially not those my brother warned me against."

Axe drifts closer. "Maverick was one of us, Elara. He knew the Cimmerian Court inside and out. If he left clues, we have the best chance of deciphering them."

I snort, a harsh sound in the oppressive stillness of this

ancient, *awful* room. "Right. Because you've been so forth-coming with information up until now." Sarcasm drips from my words, sharp and biting. "Where's my necklace, by the way? Do you want to tell me where you've stored it?"

Kaspian's eyes become guarded slits, a wall slamming down behind them. "Watch your tone, beastie. Don't make the mistake of making us your enemies. Again."

I notch my chin. "Does that mean you're still greedy for me, Kaspian? Because it doesn't seem like it, and I certainly don't need your threats."

Of its own will, my hand snatches the dagger at Wilder's hip, the blade rasping as it clears the sheath. I clench the hilt, the weapon an unfamiliar weight in my grip.

Wilder follows my movement, a humorless smile twisting his lips while his arms stay relaxed at his sides. "You really think you can take us on? You're in over your head. Maverick's video has you panicking."

I thrust the dagger forward, the point wavering inches from Wilder's throat because he didn't back away. His honed instincts would've seen me coming before I rose to the balls of my feet.

Wilder stares at me over the shine of steel, his eyes flashing with a dare.

He moves forward enough that the knife's tip dents the skin above his Adam's apple.

"There was someone else at my house yesterday," I say. "An intruder dressed in black. Searching for something, and he wasn't invited. Sasha and I were forced to hide from him. Was it one of you?"

Kaspian answers with a low, "If it were one of us, we wouldn't have been caught, least of all by you."

Wilder cocks a brow, heedless of the deadly tip at his throat. "Do you really believe we'd hide our faces from you at this point? It wasn't us. All that proves is there's someone else just as interested in your family history as we are."

He adds with a mocking tone, "Can you think of any group who would want to stop us, sweetwitch?"

"It wasn't the Vultures," I insist through the sinking stone in my stomach. "They came after and must've spooked the intruder. Kaspian can attest to that."

"I'm not agreeing to anything," Kaspian says mildly. "There are five active Vultures that we know of, and we only saw two."

"They're not interested in finding the Heart," I reason as best I can while holding a weapon to Wilder's throat. "They don't believe it's real. So why would they break into my house to search for it? Just—back off. All of you."

Kaspian scoffs, a harsh bark. "Or what?"

Axe shifts his stance, subtly angling himself to leap between me and Wilder if he has to.

"I'll be the judge of that," I retort, glaring at Kaspian. "And you can wipe that smug look off your face. I may not have grown up in this deranged multiverse of yours, but I'm a quick study."

Kaspian's beryl green irises flicker with something akin to tolerance and … is that amusement? "Oh, beastie, no one ever accused you of being slow-witted."

"No, just naive."

Cav's voice sounds out behind me, and I whirl toward it, knife first.

He strides out of the corridor's black hole and into the altar room, his blue eyes shimmering turquoise in the eerie light.

"Stupidly brave, maybe," he continues, his attention on me.

Despite Maverick's warnings ringing in my head, I scan Cav head-to-toe, searching for any spots of blood leaking through his white shirt, any indication of a wince on his face.

Only an arrogant swagger and a cocky smirk on his pale face answer my silent worry.

"I may have been sliced into, but I recover just fine, butterfly," Cav says. Then he adds in a low voice, "Thanks to you."

Relief threatens to take hold of my muscles and soften them

in his presence. To wrap my arms around his neck and whisper gratitude into the air that he is okay, despite the scar that will linger, the ghastly combination of circles and triangles and dark, hellish worship imbued in the scalpel that harmed him.

My knuckles blanch around the knife's hilt. The blade wavers, catching the pockets of light leaking into the room.

Kaspian's lip curls, his expression showing no surprise at Cav's unexpected appearance. "Put the knife down, Elara. We both know you won't use it."

I don't lower it. It's the only thing I have standing between me and them, a temporary blockade while I collect my thoughts and pick through Maverick's last words. These four men weren't at Titan Falls when Maverick was here. My brother died six years ago, and the current Court has walked through—and under—campus for four years. Yet there are over twenty initiates currently angling for these men's spots.

It occurs to me to ask, "How many initiates were with you before you became members?"

I don't ask it to anyone in particular.

Axe answers, "Around twenty. Why?"

"Would that have been the same for Maverick? He was with nineteen others?"

Kaspian gives a slow nod, his eyes growing small as he assesses me.

"And what happens to the rest of them?" I keep my knife between us. "The ones who don't make it."

Cav considers this. At last, I get my proof that he's not superhuman when he crosses his arms, then grimaces at the contact to his chest. He lowers them carefully. "They're disposed of accordingly."

"What's that supposed to mean?" I ask.

Cav advances, and I scurry back.

He continues, undeterred, "You asked us not to lie to you anymore, and I will keep that promise. You also have to understand that we are monsters of a different make. Highly intelligent, with honed bodies and killer instincts. Even when chosen as children by the Sovereigns, we displayed those talents." He dips his chin until I have no choice but to focus on the preternatural brightness of his eyes. "Do you understand what I'm saying, butterfly?"

I give a small nod, my throat aching with unspent emotion. "Maverick has—had—the same traits."

"Yes."

"So … do you kill each other off? Is that what goes on in your underground *Hunger Games*?"

Kaspian releases an amused chuckle. "No. Though some do die. Others are paid handsomely to keep their lips sealed about our existence, and if they ever loosen their lips, they meet unfortunate, tragic accidents. Some of our first tasks are to do just that and orchestrate untimely—"

"Don't finish that sentence," I demand hoarsely. I stare at him out of the corner of my eye, the buttery softness of his tone crawling through my ear like a centipede.

"Ah." Wilder folds his arms across his expansive chest. "She's getting it, boys. It's finally sinking in that we actively murder."

I say through my increasing rapid breaths, my chest rising and falling, "Maverick."

"He did the same despicable things, beastie," Kaspian answers, frowning with false concern. "You might as well be pointing that knife at your own family."

I shake my head. The soles of my feet scrape across the floor as I instinctively retreat.

"Your brother said to only trust him," Axe says, his face covered in more shadows than light. But his is the only voice I can sense honest concern in. "But he was one of us. So can you really?"

Axe moves in. I whip the blade in his direction, but he continues, heedless. "There is no good side versus bad. There is just us and our need to control our own futures again. Maverick wanted the same. We all have similar goals, and we need to work together to win. I believe Maverick would want that."

A jaded laugh escapes my lips. "You expect me to—"

Wilder's hand darts out, seizing my wrist in an iron grip. He twists, the dagger clattering to the stone floor. "Hate to break it to you, but you're not up for a solo mission if you can't keep hold of your only weapon."

I wrench my arm free, stumbling back, my gaze darting among the four men. They idly watch me, their relaxed stances hiding the bunching of their muscles and their ability to strike.

I know I can't outrun them, can't outfight them. My problem is, I don't know what to *do*.

The weight of Maverick's warnings press down on me, suffocating in their urgency. Yet the revelation of his own involvement in the Cimmerian Court's vile deeds sows doubt in my mind.

Kaspian's grin is a crown, a regal emblem of his unassailable belief in his own abilities, perched atop the throne of his vindictive confidence.

Wilder's grip on my wrist lingers, a reminder of his strength and the futility of my resistance. Axe's calm demeanor belies the tension crackling beneath the surface, and his words, while kind, are a calculated attempt to sway me. Cav's presence looms, alert and assessing despite the wounds marring his chest.

My throat constricts as I grapple with the impossible choice: To trust in Maverick's final plea and run, leaving behind the only connection to my brother and the truth he fought to uncover. Or to stay, to navigate the violent terrors of the Court and unravel the secrets they guard so fiercely.

In the end, it's the legacy of Anderton blood that settles around my bones. I meet the men's gazes, one by one.

"Maverick may have been one of you, but he was also my brother. Fiercely protective, loyal, and smart. Too smart to have joined your ranks blindly. And I can't rest until I find out what happened to him and why he left me that message. I'll keep working with you for now but on my terms. I'm not an initiate for you to order around."

Kaspian's lips pull in a humorless smile. "You'll learn, in this world, there are no rules."

"Then I'll make my own."

I stand there, surrounded by the type of monsters Maverick once called brothers, and I'm fully aware that my path ahead will be full of temptation and deception.

Because as much as I try to fight it, these monsters are my lovers.

Cav reaches out, his fingers ghosting along my jaw. "We'll see how long that bravado lasts, butterfly. When the darkness comes, we'll be the ones keeping you safe while you're hiding under the covers."

I jerk away from his touch, my skin tingling from the contact. "I don't need your protection. I need answers."

Axe clears his throat, drawing our attention. "Then let's start searching. Maverick was here. Meaning, we must've missed something in the Grand Library."

I nod, thankful for an excuse to move. "Lead the way."

As we retrace our steps through the corridor and into the neglected library, I feel the weight of their presence around me.

Predators, each one of them, their power caressing me like a living thing.

But I am not prey. I am descended from Sarah Anderton and forged in the same fire as Maverick. I make my own rules.

Trust no one. Find the Heart. Expose the truth.

Don't fall in love.

CHAPTER 14

KASPIAN

THE BOGEYMAN

"Axe, did you take notes on Maverick's video?"

I turn from a pile of dust-crusted books where I'm balancing my laptop and toward Elara's voice. Frowning, I watch Axe hand over his phone so she can go over his notes on the video we all were forced to endure.

It's amazing how Elara's gone from knife-wielding fury to phone-borrowing damsel.

Though I can't blame the girl for being a little shell-shocked and emotionally confused. First, we sexually manipulate her into giving up her family heirloom, then she's informed her brother was an initiate of our noxious, gruesome Court, then I'm shot by her mother, and finally, today, Elara watches another cryptic message from her dead brother confirming that he has indeed broken a jewel that our Sovereigns will commit unspeakable horrors to obtain if she doesn't do something about it first.

Sure, dead brother, beg your blissfully ignorant little sister to solve a homicidal mystery. But don't stop there. Make sure she under-stands your excessive stupidity in leaving breadcrumbs for answers instead of just leaving the fucking jewel with her. Make us all participate in a scavenger hunt. Make her *beholden to us so we have no choice but to shelter her from the violence waiting for her on the other side.*

Fucking asshole, is what Maverick is.

He's lucky he's already dead.

Pretty, innocent creatures have no business near me, yet Elara is everywhere I turn. The room is thick with dust from the old texts they've been combing through while I de-encrypt Maverick's files, creating a fog between her and me. The flickering haze doesn't do her justice, but her beauty is undeniable even in this pitiful setting.

Hazel eyes flecked with gold snag mine as soon as she senses my stare, her mouth thinning as she takes in every surly bit of me.

That tiny gesture, her small intake of breath, is enough to send my sinful thoughts spiraling. I've seen her afraid, seen her angry … and it's the fact that I'm remembering each of her expressions and cataloging them in my mind so I can return to them to think about later, that makes me look away first.

I return to the stack of books, the ancient tomes coated in a thick layer of grime that transfers to my fingertips as I flip through the pages. The musty scent of decaying paper fills my nostrils, and I'm reminded why I prefer advanced tech and computer code to fragile manuscripts.

I slam the book shut, dust billowing from its pages. "We're wasting time. Maverick's Pokemon GO game is going to get us all killed."

Elara's head snaps up. "This wouldn't be amusing to him. He was trying to protect the Heart."

"By leaving it for you to find? Brilliant plan." I mock.

"I knew him best. It would only make sense for him to give enough detail that I could find the answers without alerting his enemies, *the Court*, and that includes you."

Elara spits our title out like it's the crudest of all insults. To her, I guess it is.

"Tread lightly. Your brother chose to be part of this Court," I counter, my words lighter than the venom snaking its way through my veins.

"Chose?" She throws the word at me like a challenge. "Or was forced?"

The polluted air becomes so thick, I could slice it with the blade Elara had pressed against Wilder's throat earlier.

Her lips remain pursed, resentment burning in her eyes like an untamed fire.

I lean back in the tattered leather chair, crossing one ankle over my knee, my gaze never leaving hers. "He had a choice. We all did."

A strangled laugh escapes from her, vulnerable and acidic. "Is that what you tell yourself to justify the horrors you commit?"

"Oh, beastie."

My nickname for her lands like an untracked nuke. Even Axe stops his constant, silent brooding to start cataloging our argument.

I rise from my chair, closing the distance between us until I can see every golden fleck in her eyes.

And then I do something unexpected, something that earns me a gasp from Elara and the complete and utter stillness from my brothers. I take her hand in mine and press her palm against my chest, my sling's bandage rough against our combined hands.

I lean forward until our faces are inches apart, until I can smell the sweet scent of citrus mingled with fear wafting off her skin. "Do you feel that? It's a heartbeat. Even the most vicious have them, too."

"Not all hearts beat in the same way," she responds, pulling her hand from mine. It's a surprisingly graceful action—calm and steadfast that somehow makes it feel like she's touched me more deeply than I'd intended. "Some are ... colder."

"Is that what you think?" I ask, the nonchalance in my voice contrasting with the tension in my body. The memory of her touch still lingers on my chest, making every nerve there hyper-aware of its absence. "That I'm a coldhearted bastard?"

"Yes," Elara states.

I show my teeth. "Good."

Axe snorts from his corner. Elara shoots him a quizzical look, but he merely shrugs and returns to his task.

Elara's eyes narrow at that, preparing to rebut. But before she can utter a word, I turn on my heel and stalk off to where Wilder is enjoying a 100-year-old bottle of whiskey he found inside a broken grand piano.

As I accept the offered drink from him, my shoulder suddenly twinges with the reminder that I'm in a sling because of her—the fucking Wraithwoods.

Against my better judgment, I steal one last glance at Elara. She's hunched over Axe's phone again. The screen's light clings to her face.

Like a beacon that only draws you in to crash against the rocks.

I fight against the pull, turning away to focus on the expensive whiskey Wilder expects me to drink directly from the bottle. There's no use digging around for a glass. The burn down my throat is just harsh enough to ground me.

Wilder grins, a sardonic smirk on his face as he reaches for the whiskey.

"She's got spirit," he comments idly, tipping back the bottle and swallowing the fiery liquid.

I grunt, eyeing him in my periphery. "Is that what you call it? I call it a death wish."

Wilder shrugs, a wry glimmer in his hazel eyes as he stares at Elara across the room.

"Semantics," he says, setting the bottle down on an old, dusty tabletop with a soft thud.

Elara continues to devour whatever details Axe has typed in his notes. She could've asked me to watch the video again, but I know why she hasn't.

That would mean facing me. Asking me to give without taking.

I suppose I could also preempt and offer to replay it—but I don't.

It should come as no surprise that I'd love to see her beg.

For a moment, I allow myself the pleasure of watching her: the intelligence in her eyes; the way she bites her lip when deep in thought; how passionately she fights for what she believes in...

No, not pleasure—a quickly growing obsession. One of my favorite vices.

"Hey." Wilder interrupts my thoughts, nudging my injured side with his elbow. I cover my wince with a growl.

Wilder doesn't react. "You might want to keep those dirty thoughts off your face before she catches you."

I grind my teeth and root my gaze on the bottle beside us, containing whatever unwanted emotions are boiling beneath my skin.

"Stay out of my head," I warn under my breath.

"I don't have to be psychic to see it," he replies with a laugh, leaning back in his chair with stretched ease.

Before I can respond, Elara stands abruptly from her chair.

The sudden movement startles a murmur of surprise out of Axe, drawing all eyes in the room to her. Cav comes out from the stacks, concern etched into his sweat-dotted forehead.

I note the small droplets on his face. He's in pain.

"I found something," Elara announces.

"Don't leave us in suspense," I drawl.

Elara ignores the jibe—to the point that I'm annoyed she reduced me to it.

I fight the urge to one-up her with my progress on Maverick's files. But I bite back the impulse, knowing that any breakthrough she had will ultimately be mine as well. She may as well have her moment.

She spins Axe's screen to face us.

In half a second, Axe is by her side, swiping the phone from her and gripping the edges as he studies what she wants to show us. A flash of panic crosses his face before he quickly composes himself.

I frown, but I'm stopped from asking what has crawled up Axe's ass when Elara says, "Maverick said he made three flash drives. See?" She looks over Axe's shoulder to see the screen again. Reluctantly, Axe lowers his arm to accommodate her.

She continues. "'*There are no more USB drives. Just the three.*' Three videos. We've only found two."

Wilder's pleased expression falls at Elara's words, his bottle of whiskey pausing halfway to his lips. Cav's cool gaze sharpens in thought, his brows furrowing with an intensity overriding any lingering agony he feels.

Tickling at the edges of my mind are fingers of bruising desperation. The fear of failing our legacies, of being banished from the Court, or worse—being killed in the bloody ritual down in the catacombs by homicidal Sovereigns.

"Three videos," Wilder finally utters, setting the bottle onto the piano. His gaze moves to me expectantly. I glance over at Elara and release a slow sigh, tipping my head back and closing my eyes for a few seconds.

Fuck.

"How did we miss this?" Cav asks from across the room, voice strained.

"Distracted by lesser details," I say, raising an eyebrow at him.

I don't need to look at Elara to know I hit my mark. We're all too distracted by *her*.

"We need to find that third flash drive," Elara says, ignoring me. Again.

"But not just anywhere," Cav points out, crossing his arms over his chest, then letting out another groan as soon as he accidentally presses against his cuts. "Maverick would've hidden it somewhere significant. Somewhere meaningful."

"Cav, you should sit down," Elara says, reaching for him.

He shakes his head, his bloodless pallor not helping his argument.

Elara frowns but turns to Axe. "I've combed through your notes, but I can't find any subtext to what he's saying—if Maverick's given me a clue through his words."

I swallow a sardonic chuckle. Beastie still refuses to ask me for another look at the video.

"I found the first drive here," I say, deciding to end her suffering somewhat. "Maverick referred to this space as the Grand Library."

"And we found the second in the altar room through that bookcase there." Axe utters the sentence as if he's reminding himself of our previous footsteps.

"Where Sarah Anderton was tortured and murdered," Elara murmurs.

"By the very dark arts she was accused of practicing," Cav adds. His breathing seems to slow, his lungs now encased by those very symbols.

Axe, as well, carries scars of our Sovereigns' hobby, a practice we'd presumed started with their reign, but we're now realizing runs much deeper than our modern overlords.

"We can agree Mavvy-boy enjoys forgotten areas," Wilder says. "Places the Sovereigns haven't used or don't know about. Do you know of any more old, neglected, forsaken hiding spots, sweetwitch?"

Elara's expression goes taut.

"Could the third be around here, too?" Axe asks.

Wilder runs a hand through his unruly hair. "Am I actually going to tear this place apart in search of a mysterious third flash drive? Because the Grand Library is fucking … grand. But I'll do it."

Elara winces as she takes in the size of this underground fortress, filled with answers, yet so overbearing, it would take us years to search it.

My laptop churns where I left it on a stack of books, sorting through Maverick's files and doing everything it can to unlock them.

Maverick Wraithwood, while an asshole, was a clever one. It won't be easy getting into the files he promised would explain everything.

Of course not, I think dryly. *Why make it easy?*

"We don't have any other leads," Axe mutters, worry creasing his brow as he leans heavily against a bookshelf.

I hum my agreement. "Especially if there are other secret rooms behind bookshelves. We need to be swifter than this. It's only a matter of time before the Sovereigns call on us to either do another job for them or give them answers—"

"Oh my god." Elara hops from foot to foot, excitement curling her fingers as her eyes light up.

My brows jump at such a display of joy in this world of gray. My gaze rakes over Elara, taking in her flushed face and bright, eager eyes.

Fuck, I want to touch her. Break her. Own her, all in one breath.

"Yes, beastie?" I prompt.

"I know a spot!" she breathes out. "At my Gram's house. Behind a grandfather clock."

I suppress the urge to rub at my face but don't bother to hide an exasperated, "Somebody spare me from entering fucking Narnia next…"

"There's an office belonging to a man named William Jonquil," Elara continues. "He looks exactly like Maverick. I thought I was the first to find it, but maybe my brother did, too."

"You think your brother stashed the drive in this Jonquil's office?" Wilder asks, skepticism woven into his tone.

Elara nods with conviction. "The Grand Library was hidden behind a painting, and the altar room was hidden behind a bookshelf. This would make sense. And." Elara points at Axe's phone, where it's rested face-down since he took it back.

"Another thing Maverick said. For me to only trust family, no matter how many years separate them from me ... that's Jonquil."

Wilder snorts. "Your brother found a secret office behind a grandfather clock in your grandmother's house?" He shakes his head slowly. "That's ... bizarrely poetic."

The barest hint of a smile tugs at Cav's lips. "Guess we're off to Grandma's house, then."

You need to rest.

The statement almost escapes my mouth before I seal my lips shut. I'd never embarrass Cav like that or indicate myself in our less-than-perfect states. With my arm in a sling and his chest carved up, we both should be lying low. The impossibility of finding a bed right now and staying there is obvious—but there's also the risk that the Sovereigns can take us and use us at any time, regardless of our health.

"We'll need to tread carefully," I say instead, my mind racing, formulating plans and contingencies. "The Sovereigns have eyes everywhere. We don't want to alert them to our little field trip."

"Underestimating them is precisely why we're in this mess," Axe mutters. The same cogs turning in my head turn in his.

"Then we'll just have to be smarter," Elara says.

Her voice is a bit sharper than it usually is. Her eyes are on mine, burning with a smoky intensity.

It feels like she's challenging me, daring me to disagree. But there's something else. With her looking at me like that, the thought of destroying her seems obscene.

But I'm so good at breaking things.

Axe is silent as he pores over books we've spread out across the table. His ashen hair falls over his steel-gray eyes that have seen too much hurt in their time. It's a sight that would make any woman swoon if they didn't know the ink-black soul residing within him.

"Then we move," I say, rising to my feet in one fluid motion despite the sling hampering my left arm. "Now. Before the Sovereigns summon us for their entertainment again."

Wilder drains the last of the whiskey and slams the empty bottle onto the time-eroded piano, flashing a ferocious grin. "Do you think Granny will make us some cookies?"

I shoot him a sharp look, but he just grins, unrepentant. Typical.

Axe shoves his phone into his pocket and rises.

Cav pushes off the bookshelf, a low groan escaping through gritted teeth as his hand flies to his chest. Fresh blood seeps through the bandages swathing his torso. Elara goes to his side, concern creasing her brow.

"Cav, you're in no condition—"

"I'm fine," he snaps, shrugging off her supporting hand. He sways on his feet but stays upright through sheer force of will. "I don't need you to be my nurse."

"And I don't have the time to drag you into hiding if that intruder follows us and drops of your blood lead him directly to us," Elara retorts. "I doubt you'll be able to take him on."

I stare at her for a long moment, searching her face for any sign of doubt or fear. But there's none to be found. Only a diehard resolve that makes my heart beat faster in my chest.

My lips pull down in agreement. "She's right, Cav. Wilder, you take the bike and scout ahead—fuck."

I tear my gaze away from Elara and land on the empty whiskey bottle. "You can't drive."

"And you've got a bum arm," Wilder counters. "I'd take my tipsy ass over your left-handed punch any day."

"No," Elara says, pointing at Wilder. "No way. I know how you are on that bike sober, never mind with alcohol in your system. You're not driving anywhere."

It bothers me to no end that I can't shove them all out of the way, grab Elara, and take the lead. I've never despised an injury as much as I do at this moment.

I cross the room in three long strides and snag my laptop,

snapping it shut and tucking it under my good arm. As I turn, my gaze collides with Elara's. She radiates such fierce hatred toward me that a thrill zings into my cock.

Christ, I want to taste that fire. To possess it. To break her and remake her until she's mine, body and soul.

"That leaves Axe," I manage to say. "He'll go with you."

Axe shifts on his feet and squares his shoulders. "I can't."

"Why not?" Cav snaps.

He pulls his phone from his pocket. "The Sovereigns have asked for me."

A sharp exhale hisses between my teeth. "For what?"

Axe shakes his head with uncertainty. "More questioning. Initiate oversight. A task where I have to take an initiate with me. It could be any of those."

A resounding "*Fuck*" echoes through the four of us.

With Axe off the table for now, Cav bleeding out on us, and Wilder too much of a liability, that leaves only one other option.

"Are you volunteering, then?" Elara asks me.

A sudden nauseating wave of desire slams into me like a freight train. Lust and longing tug at my gut. Wanting Elara is a given, but needing her is new and unfamiliar territory that I refuse to navigate.

Dammit, she knows exactly how to challenge me. And I fucking love it.

CHAPTER 15
ELARA

Kaspian is a motionless, brooding gargoyle in the passenger seat as I drive us through the columns of trees leading up to Gram's house, Wraithwood Estate.

My grip on the steering wheel is the only thing keeping my composure and preventing me from being swept away by the enclosed storm that is Kaspian Valenti.

I don't bother with small talk. Something tells me he never bothers with it and considers polite conversation a waste of time.

He's focused on the rain-slicked road ahead, his expression chiseled from coarse granite. Kaspian's sharp jawline catches the dim glow of dashboard lights. Shadows from the bare branches above swipe across his face through the car's sunroof.

The manor looms into view as we round the final bend, its ancient silhouette awash in moonlight. Vines creep up the stone facade like nightmares clinging to sanity, yet Gram makes sure those vines are tended to every day by the landscapers. As hard as she tries, they remain tangled and unruly, refusing to shape to her will.

Once parked, I break our stand-off with an unintentional whimper as I lean over to unhook my seat belt. Adrenaline can only take me so far before Kaspian's carefully leashed power reminds me just how small and unprepared I truly am.

This earns me a glance from Kaspian. His eyes, previously vacant and distant, spark with an intensity so wanton, it could ignite the old manor on fire.

"Does my presence trouble you?" he queries, his voice smoother than black velvet, but laced with something murkier, like the coarse backing of a deceptively soft cloth.

"Not at all," I lie smoothly, avoiding his gaze as I push open my car door and step out into the chilly night air.

Inhaling deeply, I fill my lungs with crisp, freshly mowed grass and damp earth.

Inhale calmness, exhale fear—that's what Maverick used to tell me when I stressed out over exams, curfews, boys…

Such trivial worries now, but his advice still stands.

Suddenly, Kaspian's beside me. It takes everything in me not to jump when he murmurs into the shell of my ear, "Would you have preferred someone else to escort you?"

The menace in his voice sends a shiver down my neck, yet it's said with such tantalizing sweetness that I can't help but have the perverse desire to hear him ask it again.

"No," I blurt out, not sure if I'm answering his question or simply trying to convince myself.

There's something about Kaspian—iIn him, I see the allure of the abyss—terrifying yet irresistible, calling to a part of me I've always denied existed.

His lips curl into a triumphant smile, indicating he's 100% aware of his effect on me.

It's infuriating, knowing he takes pleasure in my discomfort.

"No one better than you to protect me, Kaspian," I retort.

I turn to face him now, chin tilted upward to keep our eyes level, then ensure I include the injury to his shoulder in my study.

His gaze shifts to a challenging sea of malachite at my insinuation.

You couldn't protect us from my own mother, I communicate when I meet his stare head-on, throwing his leashed temper back at him.

A hint of discontent passes over his lips, there and gone in an instant.

With that, he breaks away from me and strides toward the manor, leaving me in his wake and left alone with the implications of his dismissal.

I pull my coat tighter around me as I make my way up the gravel pathway. Searching in my bag for the keys to the grand oak door, I try to shake off Kaspian's overbearing silhouette.

Don't trust anyone, Maverick had said.

Among these masters of deception, trust is like than the ruby Heart—beautiful, coveted, and likely to cut.

A frigid wind blows into us before I unlock the door and step inside, making me hunch forward and stuff my hands into my coat pockets. Kaspian enters beside me, unbothered by the drop in temperature.

"Gram isn't here," I say, not that Kaspian shows any concern over our late-night mission. "She's at a charity auction in California, so we don't have to worry about making noise or being questioned."

"Good," Kaspian mutters, his curt reply swallowed by the ornate entrance hall. He glances around, taking in the high ceiling and gilded frames containing generations of Wraithwood portraits. His attention stalls on one particular portrait dead center at the double staircase's mezzanine.

My dad, Darian Wraithwood, his fiery auburn hair and hazel eyes, more gold than green, immortalized in oil and canvas.

Kaspian's bright gaze moves to me, meeting my own with a flicker of emotion—a wild desire or maybe a promise of more deceit—rapidly masked by indifference. He peels off his tailored jacket with a tiny wince and doesn't ask for my help to remove it. He tosses it over the stairs' balustrade, his white shirt sticking to his torso under his sling, revealing the ripple of defined muscles in his back.

He doesn't seem to notice—or care—about my lingering gaze on his body.

"Where's this office?"

I press my lips together, hating that his ambivalence is starting to hurt me. "End of the hallway up the stairs, at the grandfather clock."

Kaspian gives a stiff nod before heading up. I follow him closely, desperately trying to ignore the way my heart throbs erratically in my chest, like a terrified bird caged within bone and sinew.

He prowls deeper into the manor as if he owns it. Forced to keep up, I come up behind him down a narrow hallway housing dozens of portraits, both bought at prestigious auctions or custom-ordered. Gram has a thing for Renaissance-style paintings, these long-dead individuals gazing down at us from their painted prisons, their watchful eyes piercing through time and seeming to focus more on me than Kaspian.

Kaspian stops in front of the seven-foot antique clock that barely dwarfs him. He turns to me then, those intense green eyes housing more intelligence than most humans should be allowed to possess.

"Go ahead," he says in a tone that's a shade above bored.

It's then I realize my hands are still stuffed inside my coat's pockets. I pull them out, my fingers remaining icy despite the protection, and move the clock's hands to midnight. A soft click follows before the wall beside the clock opens into a stone corridor.

Kaspian shows no surprise at the revelation. Not that he would, considering the number of secrets he keeps, hidden rooms being the least awful.

Our phones' lights help us navigate the narrow passage, the ceiling nearly hitting the top of my head and forcing Kaspian to stoop forward.

We stop when we reach a worn wooden door with iron hinges.

Without a word, Kaspian extends his hand toward it. His fingers move to the rusty latch, prying it open with a grunt. The door creaks open, revealing a room the size of rich man's home office. Our lights cut through the pitch black, glinting off the large oak desk heavily ornamented with golden filigree and an eroded brass plaque engraved with the name *William Jonquil.*

Kaspian withdraws, the warmth of his body vanishing along with him as he strides in and begins exploring the room with an efficient precision that should be confidence-inducing. Instead, it sends bolts of anxiety across my shoulders.

Kaspian pauses at the desk, his eyes registering every inch of the woodwork. He doesn't touch anything just yet, scanning the room, absorbing details while his inner robot churns. His focus then shifts to a tall mahogany bookshelf stuffed with faded journals and books bound in deteriorating leather.

"This seems promising," he murmurs absently, forgetting I'm even in the room with him.

He starts pulling out books sporadically one-handed, setting them aside as they fail to meet his mysterious criteria. Kaspian's actions are swift and methodical as if he's done this a hundred times before.

To give myself something to do other than gawk at him, I get to work on the desk. It's covered in a layer of dust so thick, it mimics fur, disturbed only in the spots I explored the last time I was here. My phone's light finds an oil lamp at the desk's corner.

"Do you have a lighter?" I ask Kaspian.

Kaspian pauses in his perusal of the bookshelf. He retrieves a silver lighter from his pants pocket and tosses it to me, the small device spinning in the air before I snatch it out of midair clumsily.

"Always be prepared," he says, a hint of derision creeping into his voice before he gives me the Boy Scout salute and turns back to the shelf, resuming his hunt. "What do you suppose the Girl Guide's motto is? Cookies for world peace?"

At least I have two working hands, asshole.

I clamp down on my retort, aware it would only make this forced proximity worse for us. Flicking the lighter on, I carefully hold the flame over the wick in the lamp, waiting until it catches fire.

The room fills with an preternatural flame that turns the shadows into spider legs as they crawl up the wall.

The lamp's glow illuminates Kaspian's profile, lending him a demonic beauty. It highlights his sharp cheekbones, cut jawline, and thick lashes concealing his eyes. I feel an inexplicable urge to reach out and trace his features with my fingers. But instead, I swallow down those confusing feelings and focus on our task.

I specifically search for the diary I'd found under Jonquil's plaque, the crumbling, yellowed pages filled with Sarah Anderton's name and strange symbols reminiscent of arcane circles—a series of lines, numerals, and angular symbols that look like they were written by someone who just came off a hallucinogenic trip. Yet the repetition of certain symbols and numbers hints at a structured method to the madness.

But I go straight to the faded sepia-colored photo of William posing by his desk. Maverick's doppelgänger.

"This is what I wanted to show you," I say to Kaspian without taking my focus off the photo.

Kaspian turns and pauses, as if noticing my sudden grief before approaching me.

"What is it?" he asks, reaching over my shoulder to take the book from my hands. His fingers briefly brush against mine as he pulls away with Jonquil's logbook—and photo.

"Hey—" I grab for the photo without thinking.

Kaspian deftly moves it out of my reach, his one-handed limitation not affecting him at all. Rather, he inclines his head at the newly raised vantage point of the photo and muses, "You've been holding out on us, beastie."

I snatch the photograph back from Kaspian's by jumping for it, my fingers crumpling its fragile edges. "Yes, he's the spitting image of my brother, but that doesn't have anything to do with our current issues."

His expression shifts to one of keen interest, zeroing in on the snapshot that wavers in my unsteady hand. "Did you always know of this ancestor?"

"No," I admit, smoothing out the creases I created. "But the resemblance is uncanny, so we must be related. This manor has been in our family for centuries. I think it was built for the founding Wraithwoods, but his last name is Jonquil, not Wraithwood, and—" I shake my head. "Like I said, finding out who he is and how he relates to us isn't a priority."

Kaspian's attention drifts from the photograph to me, a trace of understanding sparking in their emerald depths. "How do you propose we discover who he is?"

I give him the once-over, certain that the sympathy I saw in those crushing eyes of his was a trick. "Nothing. Not until we solve Maverick's treasure hunt first."

At his uncomfortable silence, coupled with his piercing focus, I relent. "Fine, I'll start by asking Gram about it when I next see her."

Kaspian nods, his expression returning to his usual apathy before laying the logbook on the desk so he can sift through the pages, studying with rapid intensity.

I lean forward, my cheek nearly brushing his as I try to decipher the cramped, elegant script and linear and circular symbols. I inhale his clean, aftershave and aged whiskey scent and nearly get drunk off it.

I ask tightly, "What was he logging?"

Kaspian's finger stills on a page, his body tensing near mine. "You may want to know more about him sooner than you think. This man was practicing in the occult."

Goose bumps creep over my overheated skin under my coat. "*What?*"

"These are the same symbols the Sovereigns use in their rituals. Not the ones you saw today, but others."

My mouth goes dry. I push off the desk. Tear off my coat to help me breathe. "No. *No.*"

Kaspian sighs, his fingers tapping idly on the desk. "Nothing is impossible when it comes to the Court."

I back away until my spine meets the icy stone wall, the biting cold of it searing through my clothing. My heart pounds violently against my ribs as I grapple with Kaspian's words. My world is spinning, my breath coming in shallow gasps. "I've just been flung headfirst into a nightmare, and I don't know how to wake up, Kaspian."

My vision splits in two: the first is of Kaspian, his eyes steady on me, a rock against the tumultuous storm in my mind. He's there, an arm's length away, ready to catch me should I fall apart.

And the second is reality: Kaspian's face smoothing into his unfeeling stone and his voice following suit.

"The Cimmerian Court has existed for centuries," he explains, his voice as close to an eye roll as it can get. "No doubt your Jonquil was a part of it. Really, beastie, how are you surprised? Are you so naive that it never occurred to you Maverick's involvement is because of his heritage? Don't be so foolish."

"Stop it. You're being cruel."

"You mistake bluntness for cruelty," Kaspian counters, his voice dripping with annoyance. "You think I enjoy this? Do you think I want to be stuck in this shitty old office with you, and before that stuck in a godforsaken library with you, and before *that* shot by your fucking mom? All my problems at the moment are centered around *you.*"

"I didn't ask for any of this," I snap, my hands shaking as I dig my nails into my palms. "This type of violence has existed in your life for years. You've trained for it, and I'm positive you crave it as soon as you crack your eyes open in the morning. That's if you even sleep, you fucking demon. You basically live on scorched earth. I was thrust onto it."

"We all have our crosses to bear. Mine was being birthed into the Valenti family. Yours is being a Wraithwood."

I snarl at his relentless tone, my temper flaring hot and deadly. "It's not that simple. You act as if you're the only one who suffers in this situation."

Kaspian's lips rise into an empty smirk. He reaches into his pants pocket and pulls out an object glinting in the lamplight—a large silver locket that looks centuries old, with a broken ruby in the center.

I leap away from the wall. "The amulet—you have it?"

I make a move for it, but Kaspian is faster. He palms it before my back leaves the stone, the ruby's glimmer from the lamplight dying in his clenched hand. His eyes slide from his fist to me with a mocking slant.

"Your necklace was probably found by Maverick here, in this room," he says. "The silver has small symbols etched on its inner surface matching the ones written by Jonquil in this logbook. Your innocent Mavvy was quite the explorer."

The room tunnels into a rush of blood in my ears, his cruel bluntness wrapping around my heart and squeezing like a cold-blooded serpent.

"You had it all this time? Why did you keep this from me?"

Even as I ask it, I have the uneasy certainty that Maverick's death is far more complicated than I was led to believe.

"Because, beastie." His tone descends to a threatening purr. "You're on a need-to-know basis."

I shake my head, my pulse thrumming erratically against my throat. "That's not your decision to make. I've shared everything with you. Everything I know. Every part of—" *my body.*

An ironic smile dances upon his lips as he reads the angry flush in my cheeks. He leans back against the desk, sprawling in an audacious display of arrogance. "Yet the decision was made."

My gaze flits between the concealed amulet in his grasp and his triumphant grin. A surge of rage fills me, simmering in my veins, threatening to explode. I force my hands to relax, but my control is fading fast.

"I am not just your plaything, Kaspian. This is real to me. This *affects* me brutally."

His laughter fills the room with a sinister melody.

"Oh, beastie," he murmurs, idly threading the amulet's chain between his long fingers. "You're not my toy. You're my pet."

"And what are you to me?" I challenge him, my voice hitching. "Nothing, that's what."

He stills for a moment, his heavy-lidded stare locking onto mine with a weight that chains me to the spot. Then he straightens, towering over me like a colossal statue carved from merciless pain.

"The real question is," Kaspian says with a nasty grin, "why did Maverick keep all this from you? The dutiful sister who idolized him?"

"Don't you dare talk about my brother like you knew him," I spit out, my voice shaking with so much wrath, it's about to fracture my heart. "Unlike you, I loved him."

The green in his eyes swirls with onyx. He moves so suddenly, all shackled energy and deadly grace as he backs me up into the wall and frames one side of my face with his arm.

"And how did that work out for you?" he sneers, his breath coating my lips. His words slither out, his forked tongue coated with venom. "Did your love prevent his death? Did it bring him back? Face it, Elara, love is *nothing*."

He moves with such deftness that his hand clamps around my jaw before I can blink, his thumb and forefinger digging into my cheeks. "*You* are nothing."

Kaspian's statement clangs within my skull the same way Cav's did when he said something similar. It's like they want me to hate them. It validates what squirms within their souls, the parasite the Sovereigns implanted there, telling them they are worthless, and thus all others should be treated as such.

Especially those they start caring about.

"Let go!" I try to pull away from him, from the terrible meaning in his words, but his grasp is a bruising vise.

"I think not," he says with deep-seated scorn. "It's time you faced the truth. Maverick was part of a secret society that deals in blood rituals and murders. Your loving brother played a dangerous game and lost because he didn't have the emotionless strategy required to win. You are weak, just like he was. I will never be so fragile that I'd cry just because someone is being mean to me like you are right now. Why don't you go tattle to Mommy or Daddy? Or big brother? … Oh, wait. You can't."

His words slice through me, cauterizing my weakness for him as they cut.

"I hate you," I hiss through blurred vision, but I blink furiously, refusing to give Kaspian the satisfaction of witnessing more tears.

That awful not-smile of his returns.

"No, you don't," he says, releasing his grip on my face and pushing away from me. His cool and clipped voice is stripped of all emotion—or any semblance of humanity. "And you despise yourself for it. I'm the only one willing to give you the brutal truth, yet you *still* want me."

"Shut up!" I shout, leaping toward him with such force that his back presses against the edge of the old wooden desk with an abrupt thud.

Kaspian doesn't wince or recoil under my weight. He chuckles darkly under his breath as his free arm folds around my waist and locks me against him. "Careful now. You're making me hard, beastie."

A hint of mirth plays on his face, but something else controls it, malevolent and cruel. It sends a clear message:

The real test of my survival starts now.

CHAPTER 16

KASPIAN

THE BOGEYMAN

I'm not kind. Nor am I gentle, or empathetic, or even somewhat good.

I'm not Elara's knight in shining armor, but rather the devil clothed as one.

Not one ounce of virtue runs through my veins as I capture Elara against my front. She struggles like a mewling kitten even as I hold her with one arm. I've wisely put my legs between hers so she can't knee me in the balls like so many panicked women tend to do.

I catch her not only to restrain her, but to bottle her fury—maybe feed off it—but my body hums with a different sort of craving as soon as she's molded against me. My tongue craves the taste of her skin. My hands itch to explore under her clothes. It's such a primordial and savage need that it's rumbling from deep within, demanding a deadly price.

Elara's innocence shines through even during a temper. Like sweet nectar on my parched soul. For some damn reason, it sparks a new kind of fire inside me, possessive, protective, destructive.

"Take off my sling."

Elara halts mid-punch and whips her chin up. "What?"

"My sling." I nod to my injured shoulder. "I can't very well remove it while pinning you to my body, now can I?"

Her eyes widen, a hint of panic appearing.

"Why would I help you?"

Insubordination coats her every word.

"Because," I murmur, leaning close enough that our breaths mingle, "you wouldn't want me to use my teeth."

I can see her mind processing it, the wheels turning behind the beautiful color of her eyes.

"I'm not doing a single thing to help you until you let me go."

"Hmm," I say, dodging her forehead easily when she tries to connect it with my jaw. "That's unfortunate for you because I love it when you get angry."

When Elara's teeth go for my bottom lip, I let it happen, her sweet growl dancing along my tongue as blood bursts along hers.

Chuckling once she releases me and spits red, I lean closer to her ear, my lips brushing against her soft skin. "You know you want me to touch you, to feel you down there. You remember what it's like, don't you?"

"We're not here for that. We have to find the last flash drive."

The scent of her fear mixes with the lingering sweetness of her shampoo, making my mouth water. My lips tingle in anticipation of the mark they're about to leave.

It takes some wrangling, but I grip her hair, pushing her head toward my bloodied mouth and watching as she tries not to wince at the sight of it. She doesn't look away though, unable or unwilling.

Slowly, deliberately, I drag my tongue across the small cut on my bottom lip, then lick her mouth.

Elara trembles—a mix of revulsion and curiosity. When I pull back, my blood is smeared across her lips, marking the loss of her innocence with a crimson stain.

She tries pushing at me again, but I lean into her more, pinning her tighter until we're practically one entity.

"I'll ask you nicely one more time," I say. "Untie my sling. There won't be any hunt for a flash drive until I'm satisfied."

Her heart thumps hard against my chest, and I swear everything else goes quiet. From her throat comes a quick sound of annoyance.

I yank at the fiery mass of waves framing her face until she yields under my grip, then lower my head to taste the pulse beating wildly in her neck, all the while whispering promises of sugared torment in her ear.

There's a burst of something in her eyes then—resignation? It must be, because she starts working at the knot carefully, her small hands ripping at the linen.

"Good girl," I purr as the sling falls away from my arm and onto the floor with a soft ripple.

I flex my hand experimentally, feeling the ache resonate up to my shoulder, but it's nothing compared to the relentless throbbing in my groin at her proximity.

As soon as she's free, Elara darts away, putting distance between us. "If we're going to find that flash drive together, we need some ground rules."

The sight of a woman standing up to me feels alien, yet fascinating. I cock my head like a wolf being told about house rules.

"Rule number one," she continues, "no touching unless necessary."

A semblance of a laugh escapes past my lips. She acts as if she's got it all figured out.

"Rule number two—"

I capture her and jerk her back into my chest, a startled gasp slipping past her lips.

"Let me go, Kaspian." Elara's voice is a strained whisper, threaded with resistance.

"What if I don't want to?" I reply, cinching her tighter as I wind her arm behind her back and hold it there.

She lets out a soft whimper, free hand clenching against my

shirt, and rather close to the wound at my shoulder. "You're hurting me."

I give a slow, deep laugh at her futile attempt to dissuade me. "Oh beastie, that only tells me you're having fun."

"If you think—" Her words cut off abruptly as my fingers dig into her waist.

"Shut up and strip." My command is solid and hostile, leaving no room for negotiation.

The scent of my beastie now, sweet and tangy with her arousal, hits me like an ax head. So I bite at the hollow of her throat.

"Kaspian," she chokes out, her voice barely above a wheeze.

I lift my gaze, relishing the way the golden hue of her eyes shines with unshed tears. The very same eyes that always manage to bewitch me somehow. "Something more you need to say?"

"I ... I don't know what game you're playing." Her voice wavers.

I laugh, a deep, rolling sound that the cold brick walls can't absorb.

"I don't play games. I find them boring, because I always win," I reply, releasing her waist with one hand and tracing the contour of her jawline with my fingertips. "But I always listen to my needs, and the ache in my cock demands more pressing attention than a USB drive. Needs only you can satisfy."

"But ... we need—"

"I don't believe in asking twice," I remark casually.

"And I don't like repeating the same answer over and over again, yet here we are. *No.*"

"Shh." I cut her off with a swift, bone-crushing kiss. Tasting her for the millionth time only makes me want more, to consume every inch of her.

Elara's breath is stifled against my lips, but her hands finally come up to grip my shirt. Nails dig into the fabric, eliciting approval from the chasms within my chest.

Without breaking contact, I back her into the desk and hoist her up onto its ancient surface, my shoulder singing with the extra weight, but I ignore its screams.

Mmm, she tastes deliciously spicy tonight, all fire and brimstone. A hellcat beneath my ministrations, pliant to its master.

Elara shucks her hoodie and peels off her T-shirt, sending her auburn hair flowing across my arms. I push her pillow-soft hair to the side, revealing her lacy black bra.

I savor the sight of it, every curve and dip of her body.

My breath stalls as I trace the edge of her bra, letting my fingers graze against her skin, feeling the heat radiating off her. She quivers under my touch and gasps softly.

"Don't," she whispers. "Please remember what's important."

"Right now, you're my priority."

I pull down her bra strap from her shoulder, exposing one perfect breast. Her nipple is hard and begging for my mouth, for my teeth. I take it between my lips, eliciting a sigh as she arches into me. Her scent mingles with mine, our mutual, building arousal intertwining in a concentrated mix.

My tongue swirls around the sensitive bud, teasing it until she cries out in a throaty voice that makes me ache inside.

"More?" I ask against her skin, licking a slow path down her ribs.

Her breath hitches once more as she nods jerkily, unable to speak through the haze of lust clouding her mind. I push the strap off her other shoulder, revealing another perfect globe waiting for me. My hand slides up along her flat stomach, designing patterns that make her moan against my lips, but I pause before cupping her full breast.

"I must warn you. I am about to gladly hurt you. Make you feel agony before I allow you any pleasure, and once you scream my name at the top of your lungs, well … that will incite me to do the worst sexual things I can think up while in this forgotten study."

"Kaspian." Her pleading gaze locks with mine. "Just … don't break me again."

"Oh, but I will."

I've given her plenty of warning, yet she still sits with her legs spread for me. I don't bother with any more. I shove Elara until she's flat against the desk's surface. Papers and trinkets fly everywhere, but I push until her legs are widened to their breaking point and dangling over each edge.

With my teeth bared, I rip at her leggings until her lace underwear is exposed, wet and shining in the candlelight. Elara grits her teeth and moans loudly, her nails digging into the elegant wood paneling.

While my cock strains against my zipper, I pull off my belt and tie one of her legs to the desk's.

"Do you need me to remind you how good it feels when I touch you?" I ask her as I straighten.

I trail my fingers between her inner thighs until I dip beneath the lace of her panties, and two of my digits are met with hot, wet heat. She bucks against me when I curl them.

Elara bites her lip, trying to fight back the moan that wants to escape from deep within her chest.

An immoral grin plays across my lips, my vision hot with delight. Pulling my fingers out since I don't want her too far gone—not yet—I work swiftly, yanking her arms above her head and tying her wrists with the deceptively strong chain of her necklace bearing half the Heart.

Elara notices, tipping her head up with her mouth agape.

"Do everything I command, and you can have the ruby back," I say. "It's useless to us until it's whole, anyway. Better you have it than us for the Sovereigns to find."

"But…"

I put a finger to my lips. Her first order? *Hush.*

I use the remains of her leggings to tie her other ankle to the desk leg, leaving her split-open cunt hovering near the edge.

With the gorgeous vision at my eyeline, I unzip and release my aching cock from my pants, freeing it from its confines. It springs forward eagerly, twitching with need and hunger.

Elara is at my mercy.

I prowl around her until I'm positioned in front of her mouth, my mouth spreading wide. "Don't forget to breathe."

The head of my cock spears through her lips before she can think to clamp down, choking her until she uses every ounce of her control to suppress her gag reflex.

My hands weave through her hair and guide her back and forth at a firm pace. Elara's cheeks flush, her eyes water, and electricity lances through my groin. I grunt with satisfaction at each thrust.

And then comes the climax. I pull out just in time to spill all over her. The shock of my hot spurts hitting her face and chest startling her. My eyes remain fixed on hers, ignited with triumph as I catch my breath.

I'm not done.

Stalking around the table until I'm between her spread legs, I lift my leg until the bottom of my shoe presses against her pussy. Elara lifts her head, her mouth an angry, disgusted *O* of shock, but I'm past caring.

This girl has to get out of my head. I can't handle her dominating my thoughts or taking precedence over clearing my family's name and decimating the Sovereigns. Elara is not part of my future. I feel the need to remind her of that.

Get out of my head. Leave my fucking chest—my black heart isn't yours.

Pressing my foot down, I start rubbing her clit with the sole of my shoe in slow circles.

Elara screams out in both loathing and pleasure, her body spasming violently beneath my shoe.

Her hips buck upward, trying to meet my touch at the same time she uses her arms to pull back and recoil. I keep my pace steady, watching the way her chest heaves with each harsh pant. Her hands fumble for something, anything to hold on to, only meeting impenetrable, jagged ruby. She's tied down, a victim of my prerogatives.

I can tell Elara's close; her body is a live wire beneath me, building up more and more with every circle of my shoe. I increase the pressure, relishing the cry that rips from her throat.

"You want to come?" I ask, though it's hardly a question.

"No." Her eyes are furious and desperate. "Not like this. Not like I'm worthless to you."

She's right. Elara's anything but worthless. She's everything, far too much than I've bargained for. A hit too close to home that leaves me reeling, questioning my intentions.

She grimaces and whimpers when I rub the toe of my shoe against her clit, centering on her swollen nub.

An involuntary tremor wracks her body in response. Her outraged pleasure transforms into a stunned silence that blankets the room.

"You're not worthless," I murmur so she can't hear. "You're dangerous."

A choked moan escapes her throat, and she writhes on the desk beneath me. Heat pools between us, thick and dark as tar, every bit as deadly. She's so close to release that I can practically taste it on my tongue.

Tears slip from the corners of her eyes, running down her cheeks and into her hair. But she doesn't break eye contact. She doesn't look away from me even once.

With that, I press harder with my shoe, grinding into her with unrestrained force. Elara cries out in surprise and raw ecstasy as her orgasm crashes over her in waves of pulsating bliss.

Her body convulses and spasms against the desk, the necklace chains rattling while I watch with raptorial satisfaction. This moment belongs to me. I control it all—the whimpers falling from her lips and the quiver of each aftershock surging through her body.

Lifting my foot from her warmth, I thrust into her with my cock, riding out the crest of her orgasm inside her.

"This doesn't mean anything," I warn as I bend over her, pushing into her again.

But we both know it's a lie.

Just as our rapture peaks and we tumble into the abyss together, I can't help but whisper one final command into her ear.

"Forget me."

But even as I say the words, I know she won't. Even if she wanted to, she can't forgive this or forget me. We're bound by something darker than love, something deeper than hate. We're bound by a need that's as destructive as it is irresistible.

I watch with hooded eyes as she comes apart, my own release consuming me in a bonfire of primal sensation. Sweat trickles down my forehead as I collapse on top of her, panting and shuddering from the aftershocks that continue to rock us both.

My shoulder wound has re-opened, mixing blood and semen all over her, over us.

Once I'm sure she's spent, I push off her, leaving Elara panting and splayed, a beautifully demolished mess.

As I fasten my pants and start to collect the scattered papers, I cut a look at Elara—still tied down, still gasping for breath.

I think back to her desperate plea earlier. *Don't break me again.*

A dark grin tugs at my lips. It's what I do.

Elara tries to regain control of her shaking limbs with a weak attempt to sit up on the desk. Her lips are swollen, her eyes half-lidded from exhaustion.

Damn, she's a sight to behold.

She shoots me a glare that would have any other man ducking, but not me. That tiny ember remaining in her sends a charge through me, like some dick critical care doctor has strapped a defibrillator to my chest and said, *He doesn't get to die yet. Let him live inside his wretched mind a little longer.*

I stroll over to where the rest of our clothes lay scattered on the floor, gathering them with one arm before throwing her T-shirt back at her without any sort of warning. Her arms, lowered but still chained at the wrist, manage to catch it.

"Clean yourself up," I command, not bothering to turn around as I adjust my own attire.

"You're despicable," she hisses at my back.

I don't argue with her. I sweep my gaze over the room, taking in the debris from the desk, the open drawers, and the upturned chair. Evidence of my inability to keep myself in check when Elara is around. We need to focus on finding the other half of the ruby, not fucking my feelings out.

And that's when I see it: slightly misaligned wood grains on one section of the underside of the chair compared to the rest, and fresh scratch marks, dents, and nicks on the right corner of its underside that look newer than the overall condition of the chair.

Curiosity piqued, I move toward it and kneel, probing at the edges.

Behind me, Elara stirs. "What are you doing?"

I run my fingers along the underside of the chair until the hidden compartment slides open with a sigh, as if relieved to finally be discovered.

Inside, tucked into the corner, is a small flash drive. The third one. My attention darts to Elara involuntarily; she's still tangled amid my various bindings, watching me with a mixture of suspicion and anger. "You found it, didn't you? Maverick's final clue."

Swiftly, I pop out the flash drive and pocket it. I straighten and face her, keeping my gaze dead and emotionless. "You can have your necklace back. That was our deal."

"Deal?" Her brows pull together. "There is no *deal*. Let me see what's on there, Kaspian."

"No."

To soften the blow, I untie her legs, avoiding each foot as it kicks out to connect with my forehead.

"Not until my brothers and I look at it first."

"He is *my brother—!*"

"And *this is our freedom and reputations at stake!*" I roar back, baring my teeth. "Your brother is dead. Nothing can bring him back. But I am going to try very hard not to have my brothers die along with him."

Her expression twists with a mixture of anguish, grief, heartbreak—until I can't look at it any longer. With a flick of my fingers, I untangle the chain around her wrists, freeing her.

Elara's hair is a firestorm, her cheeks flush with humiliation and sated pleasure, her lips swollen, her body sullied.

There's an unfamiliar pang in my chest. Something akin to regret or remorse, emotions I'm not used to experiencing.

So I leave.

"You're a monster," she whispers quietly after me.

I freeze for a moment before disappearing into the dark corridor.

Perhaps she's right... as deplorable as a young Kaspian Valenti might've been, there's no denying it. I am a monstrosity.

One, who despite his dark desires and vengeful ambitions, has somehow managed to imprint himself onto a girl as radiant as the sun.

CHAPTER 17
ELARA

The cold rain bites at my skin, stinging like a thousand tiny needles, as I stumble out of Gram's house and into my car. I'm shocked Kaspian didn't take it, too.

Scanning the expansive front yard in the breaking dawn, I don't catch sight of him or any footprints telling me where he went. It's like he was never here. Just a vengeful, pissed-off aberration haunting the manor until he got what he wanted.

My body feels used and violated, the humiliation from Kaspian's cruel touch still lingering heavily on my skin. Clutching the necklace tightly in one hand, I start the car and make my way toward my mother's house.

Rain pelts my face after I park, then step out and stumble through the open gates of Farrow Manor, holding the necklace close to my heart. I don't think I've let it go since Kaspian flung his hand out in dismissal. *It's useless to us until it's whole, anyway.*

My body is a wreck, a battleground where Kaspian's crooked desires played out, and now all I crave is the safety and comfort of my childhood home.

An empty house, now that Mom isn't there.

The storm builds around my slouched form, drowning out my sobs.

"Elara!" Sasha's voice cuts through the thunder as she leaves the shelter of the porch and rushes toward me. "What happened?"

"Kaspian," I choke out.

Sasha envelops me in her arms, shielding me from the storm before she guides me up the steps and into the foyer. The door blows shut behind us, muffling the thunder to a low rumble.

I shiver, my soaked clothes clinging to my skin. Rivulets of rainwater pool on the marble floor beneath my feet. The jagged edges of the broken Heart dig into my palm.

"Tell me everything," Sasha says.

She frowns with worry as she studies my face and brushes a lock of drenched hair from my forehead.

Words clog my throat. Shame burns through me as flashes of Kaspian's heartless touch, his degrading words, play in my mind. I squeeze my eyes shut, forcing myself to breathe past the tightness in my chest.

"He used me, Sasha," I whisper. "Violated me as a punishment for—I don't even know what." A broken sob escapes my lips. "He despises me."

Sasha's eyes flash with protective fury. She pulls me into another tight hug as I weep against her shoulder, my body shaking.

"I'll kill him," she growls, squeezing me tight. "I swear to god, I will cut off his balls and shove them so far up his ass they'll come out of his eye sockets."

But the poison of Kaspian's touch lingers, a permanent brand seared into my flesh.

One that I didn't just endure--but loved experiencing. Orgasm after orgasm crashed through me while he kissed and bit and…

"Come on," she says gently, guiding me through the halls. "Let's get you cleaned up."

We navigate the house with care, avoiding the homemade traps laid out by my agoraphobic mother in her paranoid attempt to protect herself from imagined threats. Even though she's safely committed to a private institution now, her presence lingers in every corner of this house.

Sasha fills the bathtub with steaming water and pours in generous amounts of bubble bath, creating a frothy haven for me to sink into. She helps me undress, tenderly removing my shirt, before assisting me into the tub.

As I submerge myself in the comforting warmth of the water, the tension in my muscles begins to loosen. The bubbles envelop me like a protective cocoon. Sasha sits on the edge, offering me a bar of soap.

"Mom?" I ask when I accept the soap, needing to know she remains safe.

"She's fine," Sasha assures. "I've been on and off the phone with the hospital. They've made her comfortable."

"Thank god," I whisper, relief washing over me. But it's short-lived. "Thank you for being there for her and for me. I don't know what I'd do without you."

Sasha flashes me a watery smile and squeezes my damp hand. "You don't ever have to find out, El. We're in this together, remember?"

Except you have nothing to do with this. You didn't ask for this.

The guilt of dragging Sasha into this shitstorm seems to make my bath hotter. Yet she didn't balk when Kaspian pulled out a knife or when Mom shot Kaspian. She's never judged my cracked and acrid family life. And she's harbored her own secrets. Going to Thornhaven Manor at night, having anonymous sex with initiates, enjoying forbidden pleasures.

Maybe I'm not giving Sasha enough credit.

"Time is running out to find the other half of the ruby Heart." I sigh, shifting uncomfortably in the water and wincing at the tender soreness between my thighs.

"But how are we going to find it?" Sasha asks after a long pause. "Even Maverick didn't trust you enough to tell you where he hid it."

"That's not true!" I say defensively before catching myself and releasing a weary sigh. "He probably just didn't get around to it...or..."

"Or he was murdered before he could." Sasha finishes my sentence with a grimace.

"Right." I let out another sigh, but this one's heavy with dread. It tastes like iron and feels like a stone sinking into the pit of my stomach.

"We will find it," I say, more to myself than Sasha. "We have to."

I say it to assure myself that finding Maverick's killer is my top priority, but the guys' faces keep taking shape in the sifting bubbles on the water's surface. Cav, Axe, Wilder...

Kaspian.

They're bound by the same chains Maverick was. And I don't want them to die, too.

After a while, I rise from the tepid water, feeling a little more composed. Sasha hands me a fluffy towel, and I wrap myself in its comfort.

"We should start with Clover," Sasha suggests cautiously after a moment. "I looked up her name while you were gone. You know, the girl who lives with those professors and TAs."

The steam from the bath dissipates, almost like the release of a loving embrace as I take in Sasha's words.

I know exactly who she's talking about. Clover, the girl who seems to have her claws in all four Vultures, plus her brother. A part of me wants to be grossed out by it, but another part understands the need to be loved by more than one man and to love them in return. They each bring something different. Something —essential.

I bite my lip, contemplating the idea.

"Are you sure, Sash?" I ask. "It's risky, and we hardly know anything about her."

Sasha grins, her eyes sparkling with that familiar confidence

I've come to rely on. "When has that ever stopped us before? And let's be honest, we're pretty desperate."

"She could tell us more about my ancestry," I muse as we pad into my childhood bedroom, and I rifle through the drawers for pajamas. "Didn't she do that paper on the Anderton lineage last semester?"

"That's right. Professor Morgan posted it outside his class as some kind of proof that his occult studies class is awesome. Not that he has to. That class is impossible to get into," Sasha gripes.

I can't help but chuckle at her unwavering enthusiasm. Her normalcy is infectious, and maybe it's exactly what I need right now.

"Alright, we'll talk to Clover. But we need to be careful. The Vultures are just as dangerous as the Court. I don't want to get caught in their crosshairs again."

"Clearly, they already have their eyes on you, Elara," Sasha counters with a pointed look. "So we might as well use their current interest to our advantage."

I wince, knowing she's right. My encounters with the Vultures have been far from pleasant, but if Clover can give me any lead on Maverick's killer or the other half of the ruby, I'm willing to endure it.

Taking a deep breath, I lay out my plan. "Let's go to the Vultures' place tomorrow night. We need to be discreet about it."

"Why? Scared they'll peck out our eyes?" She snorts. "Sorry. Bad joke. Can I borrow some pj's?"

I roll my eyes at her quip but clench my fists tighter against the soft cotton of my pajamas. I can still feel the disturbing strokes of Kaspian's fingertips on my skin, the way I floundered underneath his touch, begging for more even as he degraded me.

What does that make me?

Sasha sobers up instantly at my sudden change in body language.

"We'll be careful," she promises.

"Grab some pj's from the drawer." I move to one side of my canopy-covered bed while slinging the ruby necklace over my head until it rests between my breasts under my shirt. "Tomorrow, we'll take more of our stuff from the dorms. This house is empty now, and it shouldn't be. Mom wouldn't want it that way."

"Wouldn't the dorms be safer than here, in the middle of the forest?"

"You think the RAs and private security guards will protect us from a violent, powerful secret society that has been operating underground for centuries?" I say after a mild snort. "This house is covered in Mom's handmade, highly illegal safety measures. Consider Farrow Estate to be like the movie *Home Alone*, except with a background in paranoia, murder, and plenty of time on her hands."

Sasha takes in my childhood room with new eyes. "Yep, okay, then. We can stay here as long as you need."

As we both settle into bed for the night, sleep comes fitfully. Each time I close my eyes, I see Axe and all the old scars on his body, layered on each other now that the Sovereigns are running out of smooth skin. And Cav, lying pale and bloodless in his bed, torn bandages around his torso staining his sheets as he roared and hallucinated. Wilder, dangling above a cliff, pretending to topple off, but a brief twist in his expression told me it wasn't entirely a joke.

Kaspian appears to me last, an inhuman slant to his lips as he pushed down on my center with the thick sole of his shoe, bringing me ecstasy under his brutal control—his irises a reflective prism of green, a kaleidoscope of emotions he couldn't keep hidden when I shattered underneath him. Regret, guilt, penitence...

The images jolt me awake every time, and it's only when Sasha's soft snores fill the room that I finally allow myself to drift into sleep, clinging onto her steady rhythm like a lifeline out of a nightmare.

A sharp gasp tears from my throat as the visions splinter into the darkness, and I'm suddenly wide awake again, heart thundering against my ribs. The room feels colder than it should, and a prickling sensation creeps up my spine. I strain my ears, trying to discern any sound over Sasha's snores, but there's nothing—just the deafening silence of an empty house.

I sit up, the necklace's constant chill an alarm to my fevered skin. The air seems to hold its breath, waiting. And then, outside the window, a faint scrape... like the whisper of leaves.

Or something worse trailing against the glass.

Holding my breath, I peel out of bed and edge toward the curtains, peering into the thick fog sifting through the yard and bathing everything in an afterstorm gray.

The silhouette is unexpected—a shape that shouldn't be there, motionless and imposing. My heart lurches as it shifts, a lurch of movement that's unmistakably deliberate. Whoever—or whatever—is out there knows I'm watching.

Fear roots me to the spot; curiosity urges me closer.

With a trembling hand, I draw back the curtain just a sliver more and come face-to-face with the reflective gaze of silver-gray eyes that seem brighter than the storm's colorless aftermath. Even more stark is the slash of red across his cheek.

"*Axe?*" I mouth in question.

I press my fingers to the cold windowpane.

The figure recedes into the mist as if he were never there at all, leaving me with a rising tide of alarm and questions.

What happened? Why is he here? Is he hurt? Is he warning me away?

Clutching at the broken Heart beneath my shirt, I know I'll never get to sleep now.

CHAPTER 18
CAV
THE PUPPETEER

I peel back the edges of the bandage, wincing as it pulls away from my skin, a sticky mix of dried blood and sweat fighting to keep it attached.

The sting is sharp, hot needles dancing across my flesh, but it doesn't compare to the burn of the symbol etched into me.

In the mirror's unforgiving light, it glares back—a jagged circular mark with multiple slashes in the center that seems to mock me.

I mutter obscenities, tracing the raised skin, each line a brutal stroke of the Sovereign's artistry. It's more than a wound. It's a brand, a sign of their ownership, binding me to their will.

The door behind me crashes open with violent force. My body snaps tight, and I wince at the angry complaint from my mutilated chest, ready for another round of torment. But it isn't necessary. Axe's form fills the doorway, and my muscles slowly unfurl.

Even so … something's wrong.

Axe's face. Fuck, his face is a map of fresh havoc.

Purple bruises bloom like sinister flowers across his skin, and a vicious cut, raw and glaringly red, splits from the center of his left eyebrow and down his cheek. His left eye is nearly swollen shut, the laceration bisecting his eyebrow and cheek still weeping blood.

In the seconds it takes me to assess him, I realize I'm gaping.

The Sovereigns have never been this ostentatious, never this bold. That scar will be a flag, a declaration for all to see.

Axe steps into the room, his movements stiff, each step an effort. He shuts the door behind him.

He eventually turns back to me, and I note the pain there, the fury.

"What happened?"

My voice, usually a weapon honed by years of scheming, now betrays a hint of something dangerously akin to concern.

Axe shakes his head. "Doesn't matter. They want the Heart. We're going too slow for them."

I nod. I'd hoped we'd have more time. Time to plan, to prepare, to find that goddamn other half. Time to find a way out of this hellscape.

I return to the mirror, my reflection a stranger's face, hard and unyielding. The brand on my chest throbs in time with my heartbeat, a constant reminder of what I am.

"They've never marked you so visibly before," I say into the mirror, watching him in its reflection.

Axe steps further into the light, and it's even worse up close. The gash is jagged, deliberate in its cruelty, a clear message from our overlords. His one gray eye is stormy, flashing with the memory of their spite. He remains silent for a beat too long, and I know this is more than punishment. It's a warning.

Axe's jaw sets, his fingers graze the angry cut as if to confirm its reality.

"They want everyone to see," he mutters, a dark edge to his voice.

I slow my breaths in an attempt to steady the rage. "Are they truly desperate enough to carve their impatience into your face?"

My hand unconsciously touches the symbol seared into my chest.

"Seems so." Axe's gaze falls away, and for a moment, he looks lost—a side of him I'm not accustomed to seeing.

An uneasiness stirs in the pit of my stomach, like a sleeping creature's waiting there and wants to crack open an eye.

"Then we need to be quicker than their desperation," I say, wrapping a fresh bandage around my torso. The Sovereigns have played with us like pieces on a chessboard for too long. But they've underestimated us. They always have.

Axe reaches out to help, but hesitates. His hand hovers in the air before falling back to his side. We've been taught to bear our wounds with stoicism because they are deserved.

Once finished, I reach for my shirt, shoving my arms through the sleeves with a grimace as the movement stretches my raw skin. Axe watches me, his expression unreadable.

Stepping away from the mirror's accusing gaze, I move toward Axe. My hand comes up to touch his scarred cheek lightly. His skin is fever-hot beneath my fingers, but he doesn't flinch.

"We're not their slaves," I say, my voice dropping even as the conviction within me roars like a beast unleashed.

Axe nods and then winces as the motion pulls at his wound. The sight reignites that flare of rage within me.

Rage at those who had hurt him; rage at myself for being powerless to prevent it; rage at our circumstances that have robbed us of any choice.

It's the curse again. It's come for Axe through the Sovereigns' wishes, and if it's anything like what befell my ancestors, my grandfather and father ... I'll lose Axe, too.

I button my shirt, each fastening a protest against my swollen skin.

"What's our next move?" Axe asks.

There's an insistent pounding at my skull—a throbbing reminder that we're not safe here anymore. None of us are until we unravel this curse clinging to our lives like a malignancy.

"We need to get out of Thornhaven," I say.

Axe breathes out a single, determined word, "Elara."

"Yes. We'll take her with us."

I haven't forgotten what Elara sacrificed to bring me back from madness, the way she sheathed my body and soul, guiding me to her light rather than raving in the dark. If we leave her anywhere other than by our side, we risk her dying next. But if I put her in our corner, fighting alongside us, the curse might find her, too…

"If we fail to bring the Sovereigns the Heart the next time we're summoned," I continue, staring hard over Axe's shoulder, at nothing, at everything, "They'll have our souls next."

Axe's forehead wrinkles, the gash on his face becoming more prominent and violent. "They can't actually take our souls."

"Yes, they can. The curse—" I pause when Axe pulls his phone from his pocket and searches for the relevant note to remind him of what I'm talking about.

I know he finds it when his forehead smooths and an emotion close to pity obscures his working gray eye.

"Don't," I snap. "I've already heard it from Kaspian and Wilder. But none of you are me. You're not in my head. You don't know what they've put there."

Rather than argue the existence of an ancient Anderton curse because I don't fucking need to, I stride to the storage trunk at the foot of my bed and throw the lid open. My fingers curl around the hilt of my favorite dagger, the engraved nightshade flower, my family's symbol, cold against my palm. I sheathe it at my hip, the movement practiced and quick.

Axe follows suit, his movements slower and more labored. He reaches for a .32 derringer and its ankle holster, then a Karambit, a curved hawk blade he can hide at the small of his back.

We continue to pocket any and all weapons that can fit to our body: push daggers for our coat sleeves, garrote wire, lock-pick set, laser breach tool.

The more I strap to my body, the further Axe's expression

settles into one of understanding. We're not coming back to Thornhaven until the matter of the broken Heart is settled. Permanently.

His lips pull into a humorless smile as he answers what doesn't need to be said. "It won't be easy."

My voice is low and fierce. "Nothing worth doing ever is."

I shoulder my pack. The brand on my chest burns, a constant reminder of my growing hatred.

Axe moves to the door, his hand on the latch.

I nod for him to open it.

Axe wrenches it open, and if it weren't for our honed reflexes, we would've slashed our weapons right into Kaspian.

He arches a brow after giving Axe the once-over. "Going somewhere?"

If he has a reaction to the state of Axe's face, Kaspian keeps it close to his chest where it will never come to light.

And as if it's not obvious, I say with a frown, "We can't live under the Sovereigns' thumb and search for the broken Heart at the same time. We've become too accessible."

"They summon us, we answer," Wilder says with a drawl as he appears beside Kaspian. "Even if it's by text."

"Then maybe we should ignore it," I challenge. "Unless you want to be under the Sovereign's surgical scalpel next."

It's subtle, but Axe shudders under all his weaponry. "If there's a good time to avoid them, it's now. It's the last semester before summer. They'll be busy culling the initiates before summer trials."

My stare cuts to Axe. I study his profile on closer inspection. Is that where he got the new scar? Helping to separate the strong from the weak in Thornhaven's basement?

It would make sense. Axe is often utilized for the culling because he's able to remain stone-faced throughout the thinning out.

"It's worse now," Axe confesses, though his face betrays no

emotion. "They've added branding this year. On the inner bicep."

"Of what?" Kaspian asks dubiously.

Axe points at my torso.

"Jesus," Wilder says.

"But a smaller version, I take it," I say with a sardonic edge.

Axe nods, a hint of grimness tugging at the corner of his mouth. "Smaller, yes. But the pain ... still excruciating."

"They're getting serious with the devil worship shit," Wilder says.

Kaspian levels his shoulders. "Where do you propose we go?"

"To Elara's," I say. "Her estate, not her dorms. With her mother gone, it could become our fortress. We'll be safe there for a time."

Confidence stains my voice, spreading its unyielding belief that Elara is the key to all this, to our rebellion against the Sovereigns, to breaking my curse, to our quest for the ruby Heart.

Kaspian isn't capable of expressing shame, remorse, or even apprehension. Yet his expression is tinged with ... chagrin?

No fucking way.

"We may have a problem with that," he says while tonguing his cheek. "I doubt she'll welcome us with open arms."

I suck in a deep inhale, hold, then let it out slowly so as not to lose my shit. "And what is that supposed to mean?"

In answer, Kaspian raises a beat-up, softbound leather book that he must've had behind his back, its delicate ties dancing in an invisible wind. "She and I found the missing flash drive as well as this logbook in the hidden office at her grandmother's mansion. It contains a lot of Anderton references."

Right.

I inwardly curse. Axe shows up in my room, his face gouged and bleeding, and I lose all remembrance that we'd sent Kaspian and Elara on a mission to find Maverick's last clue.

Wilder pushes out his lower lip in thought. "That's good news, bro. Where's the issue?"

"What's on it?" I ask at the same time. Then I clarify, "The flash drive."

"I was on my way to my room but stopped here to update you."

"You're deflecting, Kas," Axe observes under his breath, but it carries a bite. "What the fuck did you do to Elara?"

My attention whips to Kaspian.

His mouth curves into a bitter smile, devoid of humor or warmth.

"Nothing fatal," he assures us with an offhanded wave of his hand. "But she will be pissed as hell when we show up at her door."

Teeth grinding, I glower at Kaspian. "Did you harm her?"

Kaspian snorts. His smirk only adds fire to that rage swelling inside me.

"A harmless lesson, that's all," he explains with a dismissive shrug.

My mind whirls with unanswered questions and possibilities, images of Elara's terrified face flashing before my eyes. A visceral snarl bubbles up into my throat as I trespass into his comfort zone, our matching muscular frames going toe-to-toe.

Axe and Wilder make no move to intervene, their expressions intrigued as they watch the tense interaction between Kaspian and myself unfold.

"Elara is ours," I remind Kaspian with a curled upper lip. "You're supposed to protect her, not alienate her."

The Sovereigns always pitted me and Kaspian against each other to win their ear. They recognized us for what we were—feral, wild, broken leaders who could cage fight and almost kill each other, yet still recognize the other as a brother. A defender.

Kaspian usually went for deceit—underhanded maneuvers that would indicate one thing while he did another. He used false tells to convince me he favored his left side, only to unleash a blistering right spinning heel kick. I manipulated the fight choreography to lure Kaspian into over-committing, then capitalized with a savage shots.

After endless draws, I won the position of Consul by a hair, becoming the Sovereigns' second-in-command in Titan Falls.

I thrust a finger into Kaspian's chest, pressing him back against the wall. "You forget your place. She's not one of your mindless fucks."

Kaspian grins insolently but holds his tongue. He knows better than to challenge me further when I'm like this—hollow, triggered, and barely maintaining control.

His motives make sense to me in this state, and that's not a comfort.

I'm consumed by an image of Elara under me, soft whispers and pleading eyes begging for mercy I'm not sure I can grant her. Teaching her what it feels like to be at my mercy, held captive until she splinters, is a dirty, relentless fantasy of mine.

But first thing's first. We need to find out what's on that damn flash drive and make sense of this new logbook.

Dragging my gaze back to Kaspian, I growl out my final warning, "Don't ever forget who you answer to."

His grin falters, replaced by thin-lipped resentment.

"It's too risky to continue our research at Thornhaven. Gather all the weapons and equipment you can carry. Our first priority is protecting Elara until we figure out what all this black magic has to do with the Heart."

"If we're doing it your way," Kaspian emphasizes, "then we should head to Farrow Manor. Big Brother conveniently encoded this drive so it only works on his computer. Mrs. Wraithwood is institutionalized, leaving the house—and its family history—wide open. Elara will be safe at the dorms a while longer."

I stare at Kaspian sidelong in an attempt to figure out whether he thinks Farrow Manor is indeed the best course of action, or if he just wants more time before facing Elara and the consequences of whatever the hell he did to her.

Wilder comes to the same conclusion, cocking his head at Kaspian's tone, too.

Kaspian's face, so easy to read when it comes to our competitiveness, is always blank in terms of his intentions toward Elara.

"Fine," I say. "But we keep the search specific to Maverick's computer and whatever may be in his bedroom."

Before they can question my command, I turn on my heel and stalk down the hallway.

Cavernous thoughts swirl in my mind as I contemplate our next moves and leaving the Sovereigns' domain, but the largest, most commanding worry isn't fear of the consequences. It's how to plot the most effective way to protect Elara from our powerful enemies...

... and us.

CHAPTER 19
ELARA

A deafening crash jolts me awake as shattering glass and a string of curses echo through the manor. My heart tries to flee out of my mouth as I throw the covers off, legs tangled in sheets as I stumble out of bed and trip on a corner of the throw rug.

"Wh-what's happening?" I whisper through the mist of sleep.

The room spins, and I brace myself against the wall, fighting off the weight of slumber.

The floor beneath my feet feels cold and unforgiving on my bed-warmed bare feet. A sick feeling washes over me, realization dawning that something is terribly wrong.

This isn't a dream.

My breaths come in short gasps, fear scraping along my insides.

I order myself to get a grip and use every ounce of confidence and poise I usually possess when putting on a convincing facade, but it's crumbled under the weight of this sudden intrusion.

A distant sound of footsteps—heavy, deliberate—moves somewhere within the house.

Is the man in the black mask back?

I take a deep breath, steadying myself. The familiar scent of my teenage perfume invades my nostrils as I brace myself on my old vanity, bringing with it a fleeting sense of stability.

Heart pounding in my ears, I start to think logically. I need to figure out what's happening and how to handle it.

The crash, the voices … they sounded like they came from somewhere in the house. And if there are intruders, then Sasha could be in danger too.

"Dammit," I hiss under my breath.

My protective instincts kick into overdrive as I think about my best friend possibly in harm's way. Sasha has always been my rock, her warmth and laughter filling the muted corners of my life with light. I can't, *won't* let anything happen to her.

Her sleeping lump under the covers of our shared bed brings a small comfort, but not enough. *I have to protect her.*

I make my way toward the door, my hand grasping the cold metal of the doorknob. Taking a deep breath, I inch it open and slip into the dimly lit hallway. Shadows hover against the walls, cast by the faint daylight and wind sifting through tree branches filtering through the windows.

The ancient floorboards creak beneath my feet, each step making me cringe. Every sound, every wave of movement on the wall, is a potential threat.

As are the countless homemade traps scattered throughout the manor. One wrong step from my intruders could trigger an alarm or something even more deadly.

"God-fucking-dammit!" A muffled voice echoes through the halls, followed by another crash.

It's paired with a loud bark of laughter. "It's been a while since a tripwire got you, bro."

"Everyone good?" another voice chimes in from the other side of the house.

Each voice takes the form of familiar faces in my head.

"This place is like a fucking haunted mansion ride."

I sidestep a hidden pressure plate, almost invisible in the gloom. The gorgeous, dreaded enforcers of the Cimmerian Court are tangled up in my mother's knots like a bunch of schoolboys. Knowing the identities of these intruders brings me some relief, but also raises more questions.

What are Axe, Cav, Kaspian, and Wilder doing here?

"Would someone turn on the lights?" The voice sounds like Kaspian's, the voice of reason edged with indignation.

"Can't," replies Wilder abruptly. "It would trigger another trap."

I tread carefully down the hallway back to my room to wake Sasha. My mind conjures up a myriad of scenarios: Sasha and I successfully getting away from the guys, flinging ourselves into my car, and making a break for it, or one of them successfully evading a trap and grabbing me, tying me up for good this time, and teaching me what it means if I choose not to cooperate any longer.

I swallow against the adrenaline thickening my throat, every instinct screaming at me to run faster, but caution holds me back.

"Elara?" Wilder calls my name uncertainly, clearly recognizing that something in the air has changed. His voice has gotten closer. "Are you there?"

I freeze mid-step and press myself against the wall.

"Keep talking," I whisper under my breath, letting their voices guide me while avoiding my mother's traps. "It makes this so much easier to elude you assholes."

"Fuck, what *is* this sticky stuff?" Cav grumbles, clearly ensnared by one of my mother's many contraptions. "I can't move my damn arm."

"Stay still," Axe advises, his voice strained as it floats through the halls. "Kas and I have navigated this floor before. We'll figure this out."

It sounds like each one has taken a different section of the manor, spreading themselves out. I risk peeking around the corner.

"Dammit!" Wilder curses, skillfully ducking under a set of darts that whiz through the air like angry hornets before embedding in the wall behind them. Once planted, they thrum with the force of their launch. "How many of these things are there?"

I can't help the fizz of satisfaction at the look of apprehension crossing his face before he goes back to being peevish. "I'd be impressed, if I weren't the victim of the mad lady."

That does it. I step into the light.

"Do *not* call my mother insane."

The soft glow of the hazy day trickles through the shattered window on Wilder's right, casting a white sheen on the jagged glass shards that litter the floor around his boots like teeth.

Wilder turns toward the sound of my voice. His eyes widen in surprise at the sight of me, an unexpected apparition in my pink nightgown, before a crooked grin stretches across his face. "Sweetwitch. We thought you'd be in class."

I cross my arms over my chest, conscious of the thin material covering it. "What the hell are you doing here?"

The grin doesn't leave his face. "Isn't it obvious? We're here for you, Elara."

My heart gives a painful throb at his words. "You've kidnapped me once. You're not doing it again. Why do you keep doing it, anyway?"

"Because." Wilder raises an eyebrow in mock amusement. "You're special."

His tone fuels my anger. "I'd like to see you try. You haven't moved an inch since those darts went for your face."

The humor drains from his face. "I could have you by the throat in a single jump, sweetwitch. Don't tempt me. Disarm them. Now."

"Maybe," I reply tersely, the thrill of challenging him simmering just below the surface. "But first, you need to explain what you're *really* doing here."

Before he can reply, a garbled curse rings out from another room. Kaspian's steady footfalls follow before he appears at the base of the staircase, his green eyes shining with a fury that matches the fire in my own heart every time I look at him. He's meticulously extracting rusted nails from the tattered remains of his leather jacket, his expression one of aloof annoyance at having clearly wandered into some sort of improvised buckshot trap.

While unnerving to witness the violence such primitive, luck-driven defenses could inflict, there's also an odd power in watching him simply dust off the near-death experience with his typical unflappable demeanor.

I don't miss the opportunity.

"Having trouble there?" I call down to Kaspian.

Kaspian brushes off my mockery with an icy glare. "Just because you've managed to avoid your deranged mother's hodge-podge of household product traps doesn't mean you've won."

Deranged? Fuck him. He's the deranged one.

I scowl at him while he opens his mouth for another round of verbal death blows when a loud groan echoes from down the hallway. My heart skips a beat as my mind rushes to place the voice.

"Cav?" Kaspian turns and faces somewhere unseen. There's an edge of amusement to his tone that makes my skin crawl.

"I'm fucking melting," Cav snarls back.

Axe strides into the foyer from another wing, rubbing his back with a wince. "This place puts guns and knives to shame."

The sight of Axe strangles any retort on my lips. "Axe ... your face. Oh my god."

I'd thought it was a dream or a newfound hobby of sleep-walking when I saw him at my window last night, a slash spanning the entire length of his profile. I convinced myself it was because I when blinked twice, and his silhouette was gone.

But here he is, his imposing figure coming into full view. But it's the splash of red across his cheek, grim evidence of fresh violence, that weakens my knees.

That kind of gash will leave a permanent scar.

He wipes at it absentmindedly, his broad hand coming away stained with red. "It's just a scratch."

"Just a scratch?" I breathe out.

Axe shrugs. "I'll deal with it."

His nonchalance does nothing to ease my anxiety. I'm torn between leaving them here in their predicament and doing what's right.

"Elara," Wilder says, drawing my attention. "Help us out, or we will help ourselves."

His threat is calculated, designed to instill fear, but it only makes my choice easier. They break into *my* house, don't apologize when they get caught, and now rudely demand I help them?

I thought they were on my side, that we were working toward an end to the Sovereigns together. Yet here they are, implementing plans and sneaking around my house without telling me.

"Come get me, Wilder. I dare you."

His signature smirk edges back onto his face at the mention of his favorite pastime.

At that moment of distraction, Kaspian moves with catlike grace, avoiding the traps on the stairs with an uncanny presence of mind.

Instinctively, I back away but I'm not quick enough. He's on me in a blur of movement.

"Kas!" Axe warns in an attempt to stop him, but it's too late.

Kaspian grabs me, his fingers gripping my arms with biting pressure.

"Like Wilder said," he purrs into my ear, his breath hot against my skin, "it's time to disarm these traps."

The corners of Kaspian's lips twitch into a hedonistic smile at my obvious discomfort, and he yanks me forward.

I stumble against his, and this time his smile is full and

triumphant before it disappears entirely when something bashes against the back of his head.

"Stay away from my friend, you *dick*!"

Furious, Kaspian releases me and spins. I spot Sasha over his shoulder, holding the brass body of a lamp and already brandishing it for another blow.

"Fucking hell," Kaspian growls, leaping sideways as Sasha steps in front of me. Her eyes are wide, but a determined set to her jaw briefly warms my aching heart.

She stalks toward Kaspian like a protective lioness in plaid pajama shorts, her eyes slitted. Before she can land another blow, Axe materializes and catches her wrist.

Kaspian's eyes glint with annoyance at Axe's interference. He studies Sasha, looking her up and down as if trying to find a reason not to end her.

"Back off," Axe warns her. Or Kaspian. I can't be sure.

Sasha's focus moves from Axe to Kaspian, her grip on the lamp not loosening.

"Let go of me and maybe I will," she says to Axe.

He releases her wrist slowly, stepping back but keeping an eye on the advancing Kaspian. Sasha moves in sync with him, placing herself between in front of me, a fierce guardian ready to strike again.

Meanwhile, I can hear Cav's muffled curses from wherever he's stuck. Everyone stills as another loud crash reverberates through the manor.

With every second that passes, Farrow Manor feels less like a sanctuary and more like a battlefield.

Wilder seizes this moment to free himself from the trap. He sidesteps a vicious-looking dart and leaps onto a safer patch with a fluidity that hints at years of combat training.

Dusting himself off, he approaches us, his lupine gaze fixed on me.

"Elara," he begins smoothly, "you're out of your depth here—"

"Am I?" I cut him off sharply. A rush of courage floods through me. "Did you think you could just invade my home without consequences?"

Wilder says in a tone that's meant to be soothing but only irks me further, "We didn't come here to fight."

"No?" Sasha steps in before I have a chance to retort. Her voice is hard with anger. "Why are you here, then? To play catch?"

Wilder ignores Sasha entirely, focusing on me. "If you don't help us disarm your mother's traps and let us search this place undisturbed," he cautions, "we might have to find more persuasive ways to encourage your cooperation."

"There's no time for a standoff," Axe says through stiff lips.

I note with horror he can't move his mouth as he should because of the gash continuing down his cheek to his jawline.

If the Sovereigns did that to him just for failing to procure the Heart in time, what would they have done to Maverick for finding it, *breaking* it, and interfering with their sadistic plans?

Nausea hits me, fast and relentless. I refuse to blink in fear of the backs of my eyelids showing me the various ways they could've tortured my brother.

If they found out about Maverick's snooping, I have no doubt they are his killers.

"I didn't ask for your opinion," Sasha retorts to something Wilder said while I slid into an abyss of worry. Her sharp voice brings me out of it.

"Besides," she continues, "Why should we trust you? All you guys have proven is that you don't deserve nice things. *Including* my best friend's attention."

Wilder glares at Sasha and opens his mouth to reply when Kaspian beats him to it. "Because we're all trapped in this house right now, and you two aren't going anywhere until we do."

His voice swarms over me like strangling vines, stirring unwanted memories of his previous manipulations.

Kaspian's casual indifference toward our safety only proves how little regard he has for anyone.

"We are not damsels in distress," I seethe through clenched teeth.

Kaspian leers at me. "Yet here you stand," he points out, "hiding behind your friend."

I know he's trying to bait me, to make me lose my temper. If there's one thing I've learned about Kaspian during our time of forced association, it's that he gets a sick thrill out of seeing people lose control.

Either in bed, or out of it.

I won't give him the satisfaction. Instead, I square off with him. "I'm aware of every single location of my mother's creativity."

Little do they know I spent most of the last six years fighting for my life inside this home until I moved to the dorms. One wrong step and I'd literally lose an eye. "If you want to move off this mezzanine, I suggest you play nice."

The strange dance of dominance between Kaspian and me breaks when one final curse sounds out.

Cav appears at the base of the stairs, fury bunching every muscle in his exposed arms, since he seems to have lost his shirt and is in his undershirt. Light chemical burns are visible along his forearms and shoulders.

"What happened to you?" Wilder asks him at the mezzanine's balcony.

"My boot snagged on a tripwire," he bites out as he stares me down while I linger behind Wilder. "A wooden ceiling panel gave way, and a bucket of cleaning supplies, paint thinner—whatever caustic liquid Caroline got her hands on—rained down on me."

Sasha makes an impressed sound.

"The back of my jacket took the brunt of the downpour. I tossed it before it ate through the material since it was fucking *sizzling*."

"Too bad the Court doesn't allow female members," Wilder says. "Mrs. Wraithwood would fit right in."

Cav's fiery glare fades from his eyes, seeming to be a momentary lapse before the austere, calculated Cav Nightshade kicks back in, and he takes the stairs to where we all stand.

Sasha sighs next to me, eyeballing Cav's chiseled, muscular arms and the carved line between his pecs that disappears into his white undershirt.

She's clearly finding it hard we're supposed to be against these guys. I don't blame her. There's something about their survival instincts that stirs lust in anyone lucky enough to watch them work. Wrestling control from chaos seems to be their forte.

Then I remember what's hidden under the white of Cav's shirt.

Unbidden images of Maverick trapped in similar situations flood my mind. Alone, without any allies, dealing with these deadly Court members who could kill him without batting an eye. Who *did*.

Reality snaps back when Axe moves, lunging toward Sasha with unexpected speed, only to be halted by Kaspian's hand on his arm midstride.

Axe grimaces. The action looks painful with the gash across his cheek. Kaspian says something under his breath that I don't catch. His eyes soften as he talks with Axe, and then they sharpen when they land on me.

"Will you help us navigate this death trap, or should we continue to find our own way around?" He arches a brow as he asks it. "It won't be pretty and will involve a lot of destruction, starting with your precious brother's room."

"Don't you—" I'm halted by Sasha's hand on my arm.

"Don't feed the trolls," she warns. "You're giving these guys exactly what they want."

Except I have no doubt Kaspian means what he says.

It takes a second to get my emotions under control: hurt,

grief, anger, frustration … all the feelings I've refused to feel for years.

Stay positive, Elara. Your world works better when you choose pink instead of black.

"The right sequence on the wall," I begin reluctantly, pointing toward the hidden panel near the entrance, "will disarm most of the traps on this floor."

Cav steps forward, curiosity creeping into his frosty gaze as he studies me. "And how do we know you won't trick us?"

I bite back a sharp retort. "You don't. But as you've eloquently pointed out, it's in my best interest that everyone makes it out alive."

He seems to consider this for a moment before grudgingly relenting with a curt nod.

Good. If they think their safety lies in my hands, then I have some say over their actions.

Vulnerability, it seems, has become a two-way street.

CHAPTER 20

AXE

THE PHANTOM

As Elara disarms the estate's second floor, we stay close behind, wary of any missed or deliberately left behind snares, webs, or nets. Elara seems to enjoy our rare moment of weakness a little too much.

The Sovereigns would've carved into me for such a failure. Elara just smiled, her eyes glinting with refreshing, harmless amusement.

Well, harmless in the figurative sense.

Unlike Kaspian's clear distrust, Cav's suspicious prowl, and Wilder's glowering, I follow her lead with ease. Potential pitfalls barely even register to my peripheral senses, like I can sense them before Elara gets to the ones that weren't connected to the button she pressed.

"Maverick's bedroom," Kaspian barks behind me. "Take us to it."

Elara doesn't bother to turn and acknowledge him, though her back stiffens as she turns right down a hallway, Sasha throwing a glare in his direction as she walks beside Elara.

Now, surrounded by the frozen remnants of a life cut brutally short, familiar minutiae triggers visceral flashes of recollection I can't fully suppress. Maverick's overflowing bookshelf stacked with well-thumbed fantasy epics, and coding manuals; the teetering stacks of once-beloved graphic novels and gaming guides; custom-built cubbies and slots fashioned between the shelves to stash ... what, exactly?

I blink, and the room doesn't look how I just described it. It's messier, the books and manuals tossed, the stack of graphic novels tipped over, drawers left open.

How did I know what it looked like before?

I systematically take stock of the scene, my gaze roving for even the most minuscule divergence that could prove meaningf—

There. Next to the disheveled bed, nearly obscured by the room's arabesque wallpaper pattern.

To the unwitting observer, it could pass as mere idle scribbling. But the cadence of the dots and dashes subtly penned on the wallpaper rings alarmingly familiar, catalyzing a renewed sense of purpose I can't allow myself to telegraph.

My fingers twitch, begging for my phone, but I clench them until my nails dig into my palms, and they still.

I don't have to give them everything.

The cut on my face throbs, taking over where my fingers left off.

I haven't been honest with my brothers-in-arms, and that alone makes me sick. To involve Elara in the same tangled mess of lies and deceit makes my gut churn. But I have no choice.

Not if I want to keep her safe.

I stride toward the wall, ignoring Kaspian's demands to know what I'm doing. My fingers trace the pattern of dots and dashes, translating the message effortlessly in my mind. Coordinates. A meeting place. Wraithwood Estate.

Maverick knew he was in danger. He left this message for Elara to find William Jonquil's ancient office. And find it, she did.

I turn back to the others, my face a mask of calm indifference.

Elara's eyes narrow, her gaze flicking from me to the wall and back again. But she says nothing, merely nodding toward Maverick's computer.

"That's his baby, right there," she says to Kaspian. "Whoever was dressed in black and tore through this room didn't take it for some reason."

"He was looking for something else," Sasha adds. "Something specific. Is there another enemy we have to keep an eye on, or are you all popping out of the Cimmerian Court like fresh acne?"

Nobody answers. With a jerk of his chin, Cav sends Wilder to inspect Maverick's closet and me to rummage through the nightstand drawer and bookshelf, where I pull items out at random, knowing I won't find anything.

I pause, frowning. Then remember all Maverick's clues thus far have been electronic. So why *did* the intruder leave the computer for us to find?

Because he didn't want to actually take something crucial. Only for it to look that way.

Wait. How do I know that?

My head starts to ache, more related to my mental gymnastics than the cut on my face.

Kaspian draws my attention, moving directly to the fully equipped gaming chair in front of the computer.

Elara watches Kaspian warily as he activates it. His green eyes lower with an eerie calmness as he begins to type with one hand, refusing help, the sound of the keys clicking adding to the sounds of her late brother's room being pilfered.

Again.

If it breaks Elara's heart to see us put a dent in Maverick's formally preserved space, none of it shows on her face. Likely a trait she gained by spending time with us.

Any man falling for her would be saddened by that fact, but I'm glad for it.

The screen flashes alive, casting a blueish hue over Kaspian's intense expression. He leans in, reading something that prompts a low curse to slip out.

"What is it?" Wilder abandons his search and moves closer.

Kaspian doesn't answer immediately, his hand flying over the keyboard once more. Screens pop up and vanish in rapid succession before he finally leans back.

From the corner of my eye, Elara and Sasha exchange a furtive glance before they make their way toward us. Their presence is both comforting and unnerving, a potent mix of familiarity and fear that sets my senses on edge.

"Is there something we should know?" Elara finally asks, her attention fixed on the screen.

Kaspian doesn't look up from his work.

"Possibly," he replies cryptically. His face is a mask of concentration, the whites of his eyes reflecting the changing colors from the screen as he rapidly sifts through Maverick's encrypted files.

"For all we know, this could be another dead end," Cav muses from his post near the door, striking a note of skepticism among us. His hands are tucked in his pants pockets, blue eyes sharp as they move between us all.

The mild burns on his arms bloom red in the artificial light of the room, seemingly as angry as the expression he's worn since extricating himself from a caustic ambush.

Elara bristles at his words. "So far, Maverick's given us the most evidence against the Sovereigns."

"He's also the one who broke the jewel in half and played hide-and-seek with us," Wilder states.

Elara frowns at him.

"Fuck, this isn't good," Kaspian says.

I ignore the surge of adrenaline that floods my veins and instead move closer to the computer. The image there causes my heart to stutter.

It's a map—a detailed layout of Titan Falls as it is today—but it's not the geography that has my blood running cold.

There are red dots scattered all over it.

"Missing persons," Kaspian murmurs, answering our silent question. "Each dot represents a missing person case in Titan Falls."

Elara swallows audibly, her hand shooting out to clutch Sasha's. Their knuckles blanch as they grip each other, their eyes wide and fixed on the horrific constellation illuminating the screen.

"Maverick was tracking them," I surmise. "And look at the dates... this has been happening for decades."

"More than that," Cav interjects, his eyes squinting as he studies the map from over my shoulder. "Some of these cases go back to the late seventeen hundreds."

"When Sarah Anderton was alive," Elara whispers.

The sudden silence in the room is deafening, underscored by the steady hum of Maverick's computer and the fast breaths of Elara and Sasha.

"What was Maverick looking for?" Wilder asks, breaking the eerie lull. "Why all these people?"

"Not people," Sasha says, her voice strained. "Women. Look."

She points shakily to a sidebar on the screen, populated with thumbnail photos of the victims staring back at us. All young, all beautiful, all gone without a trace. With a quick glance at the information attached to each woman's photo, their ages and dates of disappearance become horrifyingly clear.

"They were all university students," Elara says, her voice flat. "All around our age when they... disappeared."

Cav turns away, cursing under his breath. There's a hardened set to his jaw as he clenches his fists, the tendons standing out starkly through his skin. Kaspian's eyes harden, his fingers pausing on the keys before he pulls his other arm out of his sling and truly flies over the keys, pulling up more information that Maverick had uncovered.

Elara's face is pale under the harsh light of the computer

screen. Questions must spin in her mind, each one bouncing off the walls of her skull but never finding their way to her lips.

I give her a nod of reassurance, hoping she knows I'm here for her. I think.

The silence breaks when Wilder throws a well-worn book—Jonquil's logbook—onto the table, a frayed ribbon marking a page in its center.

"Maverick was translating this," he announces.

The script is old English with flourishes that speak of an age when quills were common and ink was handmade. Some symbols are circled in red while others have been crossed out with black.

"See here?" Wilder adds, pointing at a list of names, faded with time but still legible. "William Jonquil was tracking missing women, too, which is probably what got Maverick started on this path."

"I've seen those symbols before," I say between a staccato of blinks. My mind is running through a microfiche of my memories, trying to find the right one.

"Where?" Cav demands.

"When…" I close my eyes, my brows tightening. "When they were deciding which ones to put on me."

Elara releases Sasha's hand, stepping toward me with a grace I don't deserve. Her gaze sweeps over me before her hands close around mine, pulling them to her chest. Delicate fingers hold my scarred ones.

Her stare doesn't waver.

"No one deserves this," she says. "Including you. Tell me you didn't have anything to do with this. That none of you are involved with these missing girls." Her throat bobs. Her eyes don't stray as they hold mine. The raw vulnerability in her gaze makes it impossible for me to look away. "Please."

My tongue swells with the need to offer her the solace she seeks. She wants my denial as much as she dreads it might be a lie.

"No," I grind out, my voice rasping against the charged air surrounding us. "I swear, Elara. None of us have anything to do with taking girls."

Kaspian nods, his fingers stilling on the keyboard. "We're monsters, but we're not those monsters."

Cav doesn't respond verbally; he only looks away, his eyes far too weary for someone who thrives in havoc.

Wilder's focus flicks between Elara and me before he adds, "We've been trying to break free from the Court for years now. But they hold our families hostage. Our heritage, reputations … curses. They threaten it all to keep us in line."

Elara's gaze softens slightly before she releases my hands and steps back. She gives a slow nod. "I believe you."

It's not relief that floods me then, but something far more profound and unsettling: *trust*.

After a beat, her forehead wrinkles and she looks to the side, deep in thought.

"Families…" she whispers, more to herself. Then her eyes widen and lock onto the back of Kaspian's head. "The Sovereigns have been doing this for centuries. Kaspian, check on these girls' last names. Are they from powerful families? Or descendants of the founders of Titan Falls?"

"Way ahead of you," Kaspian responds.

It's then I notice Jonquil's logbook to the right of the computer, where Kaspian's been cross-referencing it. "The missing women Jonquil linked together, Mary Primrose, Beloved Hawthorn, Elizabeth Thistle, Sophronia Bluebell, Mary Cowslip … they are all from the original settling families of Titan Falls."

Sasha gasps softly, her hand clutching at Elara's arm if trying to absorb some of her best friend's startling calm.

"So they knew Sarah Anderton," I surmise.

Wilder cocks a brow. "Any chance they're part of the families who hired Sarah to off someone?"

"That's not what Jonquil or Maverick were focused on,"

Kaspian murmurs, his eyes darting from page to screen and back again. "I'm forced to admit Big Brother was thorough, beastie."

"And the latest girls?" Cav asks. His attention shifts from the screen to Elara, his eyes flaring with a renewed intensity. "She's right. The victims seem convenient for the Court. It makes sense they'd target those with power or influence."

"For *what*?" Elara asks with horror.

"The fucking devil's work." Sasha whispers a soft prayer, her fingers dancing over the gold pendant hanging around her neck. Her doe eyes are stretched to their limit, but she doesn't look away from the unfolding drama.

A moment later, Kaspian pulls back from the screen and turns to face us.

"They're all connected," he confirms, his voice grim. "Every single one of them has ties to Titan Falls' founders or influential families."

Elara squares her shoulders and crosses her arms. "We need to warn the ones that are still alive."

"And what? Tell them their children could be next in a dark arts sacrifice by a secret society that doesn't exist to them?" Cav shoots back incredulously.

"We can't just do nothing!"

Cav runs a hand through his dark hair and sighs heavily. "Hundreds of people settled here 200 years ago. Since then, families have split off, names have changed, and family trees have been broken. What you're asking is impossible in the amount of time we have."

"Sacrifices," Elara whispers so quietly I almost don't hear her. She's grabbed the one word Cav used to describe why those girls were taken. "It's got to be linked to the ruby Heart somehow."

"Founding families, Sarah's legendary treasure, dark rituals." I flex my fingers to stop my hands from shaking. "Cav's and my scars … I'm just the surface of it."

If my body is any clue, the Court isn't merely a group of wealthy elites seeking power and influence; they are devotees of an ancient, occult order, willing to sacrifice innocent lives in their pursuit of dark ambitions.

"We're each a thread in whatever fuckery the Sovereigns are weaving," Kaspian adds, his voice cold and hard as he closes Jonquil's ledger with a thud.

Suddenly, Sasha whirls on Elara, her hand reaching out to grasp her friend's. "Oh my *god*, are you next? You're related to this Jonquil guy, and he—has anyone figured out what happened to *him* while he was investigating his version of these Sovereign guys?"

I grip the edge of the desk, finding it hard not to lunge for something at the thought of—"Nobody is taking Elara."

Even I'm surprised by the vehemence in my voice.

For one heart-stopping moment, everything else seems to melt away. The looming threat, the cryptic symbols, the disturbing pattern of missing women. There's only her, her natural light pulling me out of the darkness I've been drowning in.

Kaspian rises from the chair, snapping me back to the grim present. "Why not? If we could figure it out, so could they."

His attention rests on Elara for a second before he quickly looks away, as if afraid of revealing too much.

"I won't let it happen," Cav adds, echoing my sentiment.

"If they wanted to get at Elara, they shouldn't have surrounded her with us," Wilder affirms with a killer smile. Literally a *you're dead if you touch her* kind of smile.

That smile falls a second later with surprising seriousness. He's remembering what happened to the last girl he tried to protect.

Despite the situation, Elara looks at us with a soft curve to her lips. A smile that doesn't quite reach her eyes, and I understand why.

If only we'd met under different, happier circumstances.

She turns serious again. "We need to find out more about Sarah Anderton, too. There has to be a reason her name keeps coming up, and not just because she owned the Heart. I plan on finding Clover on campus tomorrow, the girl who—"

"We know exactly who the fuck she is." Kaspian cuts in, a venomous fire in his gaze.

Elara's cheek muscles twitch while she glares at him. "I'm not going to ruin your rivalry with the Vultures. I just want to talk to her and see what she knows about the Andertons. She wrote that paper about Sarah's daughter."

"Absolutely not," Cav says.

Elara opens her mouth to argue, but then Sasha rubs at her temples with a pained expression. "Guys, I need a break from this ancient, historical, serial killing spree thing. Does anyone need coffee? I can go grab some from the 24-hour place nearby. Pretty sure I'm not on this Satanic hit list, so I can drive there and come back while you continue to … uncover additional horrifying evidence."

Elara hesitates, her frustration evident in the line between her brows. She glances at Sasha, acknowledging her need for a breather, before nodding reluctantly.

"I'll take a coffee, thanks," she says.

"Great," Sasha says with obvious relief.

As she grabs the keys from Elara and heads out the door, she turns to look over her shoulder. "The rest of you take it pitch black, I assume?"

Reluctant grumbles all around.

Once Sasha is out of earshot, Elara turns to Maverick's computer now in screensaver mode, a rotating slideshow of fantasy artwork and scenery from his favorite games.

"I'd like to look at all the documents Maverick put on that flash drive." She adds pointedly while watching the screen with profound sadness, "Alone."

Kaspian's eyes shrink like he wants to deny her just for the hell of it, but I step in. "She has a right to see what her brother died for."

"Let her," Cav says. "But we'll be just outside the door."

Meaning it wouldn't do Elara any good to try anything against us. Not that I believe she would at this point. She needs us as much as we need her.

To solve the mystery behind the Heart, I repeat inside my head. *We don't need her for anything else.*

The thin fabric of her nightgown counters that thought. I cut my gaze to the side, unable to keep such sweet, seductive innocence in my line of vision.

Cav motions for us to leave, Kaspian strolling out first, then Wilder, then Cav. I linger at the doorway as Elara sits in Maverick's chair, her hands stroking the expensive leather around her thighs. From the quiet sigh that escapes her lips, I sense it's not to remember her brother but to feel the body heat Kaspian left behind.

"We forgot to think about one thing," I say.

Elara jumps, and I realize I've waited a good long while before saying anything, and she thought we'd all left.

She turns her head in my direction, clearing her throat and gathering her bearings as she does so. "What's that?"

"The recent missing girls."

Elara angles her head. "Yes?"

The fresh cuts and old scars on my skin throb with their own heartbeats. My body strains as if crying out the answer to her. "They may not be dead."

CHAPTER 21
ELARA

Reading through Maverick's notes, typed so meticulously, is like having him with me, pacing the floors behind this chair, muttering with his hands shoved in his pockets as he dictates to his computer, his eyes darting around, his voice growing more frantic while I slept in ignorant bliss down the hall…

Stop.

The vision retreats and I refocus on his words in front of me. Maverick didn't die so I could double over and wail with grief six years after his death.

God. It took me six years to uncover his final messages and who he truly was, what he was trying to do…

All because I burrowed into the darkest pocket inside myself and gave the rest of my empty space to an imposter. A happy, perfect, shiny fraud who knew so many people yet could count true friends on one finger.

And put her brother in that small, dark pocket, too.

The room is silent except for the soft humming of the computer. A chill seeps into my bones, threatening to make me turn away and pretend this isn't happening, but I keep reading until my eyes come to an abrupt halt on a scanned letter, half-burned and crinkled despite Maverick's obvious attempts to smooth it out so it could be legible when he uploaded it. The text is marred by scorched edges, as if Maverick had originally intended to burn it to ash so it could never be read, then for reasons taken with him to the grave, he decided against it and tried to save it.

Maverick's handwriting seems frantic, letters scrawled with haste. A smear of dried blood stains the corner.

I lean forward as I decipher the opening lines:

"To whomever finds this—To Elara, the only person who should be reading this, I was so young when you were born, barely out of the toddler stage myself, but the minute Dad guided me into the hospital suite, his hand firm on my shoulder, I knew I was meant to be your protector. You were so … squishy and angry-looking in your cot, your face redder than the soft pink blanket containing your tiny, wriggling form. I was terrified, but Dad just chuckled, patting my head and telling me you'd grow less red and scary as time passed.

I didn't believe him then, but he was right. You grew into a fierce and feisty little thing with a glint in your eyes that lit up the entire room. You became someone I could rely on, someone who understood me in a way no one else ever could, not even our mother.

But I have failed you, Ellie. I have failed to protect you, to keep you away from our awful inheritance.

Because if you're reading this, I'm not alive anymore.

You must know by now what our father did, what he was. He was a ruler of this sordid, elite society, a Sovereign of the Court. They cloaked his true title under layers of deceit, but it's a truth that can no longer remain hidden. And just like it was for him, the Court had its claws in me, too."

My jaw nearly hits my kneecaps.

"No Mavvy," I shakily whisper to the screen, "I did *not* fucking know Dad was a part of the Court." My heart does the entire plummet to the floor when I clarify with a thick tongue, "A *Sovereign.*"

Swallowing and blinking rapidly, I read on:

"Let me start with Dad. The kind, caring father we idolized from old photographs and Mom's stories? That was merely one face he presented to us. His true existence was spent ascending the ranks of the Cimmerian Court to become one of the Sovereigns. I didn't learn this truth until my own violent initiation at 16 years old.

They say they have no names, just the three Sovereigns, but that is a lie. They've given themselves titles: the High Sovereign, the Scourge Sovereign, and the Silent Sovereign. A trinity of the damned.

Still, I resisted believing Dad could have been party to their depravities. At least until I uncovered copies of the esoteric texts he pored over—the Court's demonic scriptures detailing their fundamental doctrine: *Truth in Shadows*. You see, they don't just crave the power, wealth and infamy the ruby Heart promises. Their obsession is rooted in an ancient occult belief that possessing the legendary jewel will finally unlock the long-sought path to the Exalted Regent.

The missing girls cases? Those go back just as far, a sickening pattern of sacrifices made in service of their cause. At first, it was just girls accused of being witches—those "lucky" few who contained the dark magic they sought. But as the centuries passed and it was no longer acceptable to burn, torture and maim village women, their desperation for the Heart's power mounted, and they grew...indiscriminate. Unbound from any code of honor.

That's why they had Dad killed when you were a baby. He finally recognized the Court's rituals for the evil they truly were, and was planning to spirit Mom and us away. I have reason to believe he was a turncoat, spying on his own Court and providing the information to an influential outside source—possibly the FBI. The other two Sovereigns viewed his defiance as a threat that needed snuffing out. But not before ensuring a bloodline replacement—my initiation—to maintain their reputational façade of being a noble legacy society.

[Illegible for one line].

Down into the hidden underground chamber where our ancestor Sarah Anderton was tortured and killed over 200 years ago.

That night, they forced me to witness a girl stripped bare and lashed to the ancient altar amid robed, chanting figures. The blade they pressed into my trembling hands, I was to use in carving their symbols into her flesh as the first sacrifice of my initiation. Her agonized screams... the blood...

When I hesitated, they turned their cruelty on me without mercy. The first lashes were bittersweet mercies compared to the burnings, the etchings, and mental tortures that followed. Rites designed not just to break my body, but to shatter any remnant of the fragile soul Dad hoped to shield. I endured until the light inside me was gone."

The screen blurs and I realize I'm crying, hot, angry tears dripping onto the keyboard. I take a deep breath, reminding myself of Maverick's strength, his resilience. He wouldn't want me to crumble under the weight of his revelations.

Wiping my tears away, I refocus on Maverick's words.

"Scholars say that knowledge is power. But right now knowledge feels like a serrated knife splitting me open from inside out. Knowledge that I'm caged by unpredictable monsters... Monsters our father allowed me to be fed to...

Because here's the really fucked part: the Court's entire goal in finding the ruby Heart is to summon some ancient, evil entity they call the "Exalted Regent." Not demon, not god ... something far worse that they've worshiped for over 300 years now. They think possessing the ruby's full power will finally rip open a permanent portal so this monstrosity can physically enter our world.

All those missing girls cases going back centuries, those were practice sacrifices leading up to their precious ritual, warm-up attempts at calling out this nightmare bastard, because they believe they can't actually summon him until they have the 2 keys, ruby the Heart of the Exalted Regent, and—[handwriting too illegible], which they believed no longer existed, but they got their facts wrong. It very much exists. To your detriment, Ellie."

A cold chill slices down my spine at his words. My focus snags on the illegible writing, too crumpled and smeared for me to read clearly.

"Dammit, Maverick, what's the second key? Why couldn't you have just *typed* this?"

But I force myself to move on.

"After the nightmare of that night, I was dead-set on taking those depraved occult fucks down from the inside. I started by obsessively decrypting all the ancient texts and codes the Court treated as gospel, looking for any clues they'd missed about the ruby Heart's whereabouts.

Turns out Dad had been secretly compiling his own research before his murder, data pointing to the ruby being stashed away centuries ago by Sarah Anderton herself. The very woman the Court persecuted as a witch was the one who'd kept their precious relic from their grasp.

It took years of following Dad's fragmented trails, but I finally traced the ruby Heart's hiding place to a forgotten subterranean vault beneath campus.

I also found Sarah's grimoire in a forgotten section of TFU's library. Anderton's writings gave clues about how she concealed the ruby. Apologies to our ever-great grandmother, but I ripped out those pages so no one, especially the Sovereigns, could ever find this vault after I did.

I couldn't risk giving those sadistic bastards that kind of power, not after witnessing firsthand the depravities they're willing to commit for their beliefs. If the Sovereigns found the Heart in its complete form, the requirements to their final ritual would be met.

And I swear, Ellie, where Dad failed, I would not. Something that monumental had to be permanently kept from their grasp. So I made the hard call to take a sledgehammer to that priceless ruby relic and shatter it into two separate pieces, putting one in Gram's old costume pieces of jewelry where a gem was missing.

The other piece, I placed back into the vault as a curse to keep the Court forever baited. Even if they somehow managed to find it, without the other, it's powerless to them. And the necklace ... Gram's been keeping it safe, unknowing of its importance. I've left enough false trails to keep the Sovereigns and even Gram off balance, but I'm worried about how long this can hold them at bay.

[illegible]

I know the risks of what I've done, and if you're reading this, then I have failed. But I couldn't let them use you as they've used me.

I love you, Ellie.

And I'm so sorry."

Maverick's final words turn my throat raw as silent sobs wrack my body. His vulnerability, his concern for me... everything was laid bare.

It's too much—it's all too much.

I wipe the tears from my face, steeling myself against the tide of bleakness threatening to drown me. Dad, a Sovereign of the Cimmerian Court. Maverick, forced to endure unspeakable horrors. And now, the burden falls to me.

I stare at the screen, at the illegible scrawl that holds the key to unlocking this nightmare. The second key.

My fingers clench into fists. I need to know what that second key is. Where this vault is.

The shard Gram was unknowingly looking after, that is the amulet. The one I have. The other half remains there.

I wrench myself from the chair and pace the room, rubbing the lump of the amulet under my nightgown. I need to do something, take action. I can't let Maverick's sacrifice, everything he went through, be for nothing.

I stride back to the computer, jaw set.

The second key the Court requires exists to my detriment... What the hell does that mean?

I enlarge the scan of the letter, focusing on that one indecipherable section. There has to be a way to recover the words. I refuse to let this vital clue slip through my fingers.

I toggle the display settings, inverting the colors and sharpening the contrast. The white text shines stark against the black background and I lean closer, eyes narrowed. Slowly, painstakingly, I make out a single word...

Then another.

My blood runs cold as the meaning registers, a scream building in my throat. I stagger back from the desk, hand clamped over my mouth in horror. Because now I know. I know what I am to the Court.

"...the Heart of the Exalted Regent and a Bloodline Vessel, which they believed no longer existed..."

A Bloodline Vessel.

The second key isn't an object. It's a person.

Me, the last female descendant of Sarah Anderton.

And the Court needs me to complete their demented ritual, and that is exactly why Maverick broke the ruby to make it worthless.

There's a sudden shift in the house.

The boys made it downstairs without further incident, their quick senses now honed to my mother's every trick. Their presence radiates throughout the old house like a tangible wave of heat. Maverick's notes blur before my eyes as I become acutely aware of them below me. Wilder, Cav, Kaspian, and Axe.

They're waiting.

A wicked gale of laughter trickles from the first floor,

sending a tremor through me. Their casual sounds weave through the quiet hallway, a tantalizing lure drawing me away from the agony cast by reading through Maverick's violent, secret life.

Taking a deep breath, I save Maverick's notes and power down the computer. My fingers lightly trace over the cold metal surface before I turn and take hesitant steps towards the door.

CHAPTER 22
ELARA

I slip from the safety of Maverick's bedroom, viewing my childhood home with fresh eyes. Each moldering, cobwebbed corner of the grand estate seems to whisper tales of deceit and power now.

As I tiptoe toward the staircase, each wooden step downward offers a cold kiss to my bare feet, a blatant reminder of the dark underworld that lies beneath my family's noble facade.

Maverick's message, his warning about the Sovereigns' grip on Titan Falls history and beyond, is as real to me as the manor's bitter draft seeping through my nightgown.

I follow the sound of low voices and laughter, unease bunching the muscles in my stomach. They're in the dining room, the crumbling Gothic architecture mourning what once was. The grand arched windows are shrouded in tattered drapes, their opulence faded and forgotten. The chandelier above casts warped prisms across the cracked plaster walls, a silent witness to the room's decay after my father's death and Mom's descent into madness.

Entering the dining hall, I find the guys clustered around the bar cart, coated with dust from disuse, but all decanters filled and untouched from more than two decades ago when Dad died.

Wilder casually shrugs off his leather jacket, draping the supple material over the head dining chair as he rolls those broad shoulders. Kaspian settles into a side chair, long legs stretched out as he loosens his tie with one finger, the subtle shift exposing the taut column of his throat. Even stoic Axe seems to relax minutely, chiseled forearms resting on the table's edge, the gash on his face clotted to the point it's almost black. Only Cav remains tense, powerful muscles visibly rippling beneath his shirt as he copes with the worst wound out of all of them. So far.

I drink in their varied states of casual undress, feeling an insistent flush creeping up my neck. Unbidden, I squeeze my thighs together as indecent thoughts cast my mind spiraling. How easily they adapt to confusion and disorder, oblivion their only coping method. Yet ... I find my own craving for escape mounting.

My eyes meet Wilder's, and I hesitate for a moment, unsure of how to broach the situation and what I've just read. Biting my lip, I steel myself and walk over to them.

Their veneer of casual diversion doesn't fully conceal the strain that runs beneath the surface, a constant undercurrent that seems to bind them together. It strikes me that they've grown so accustomed to bad news and severe punishment, they snatch any pockets of time to retain their sanity and hold on to the scraps of humanity they still possess.

"Sweetwitch," Wilder greets me, his voice smooth and at its lowest decibel.

My throat constricts, forcing me to clear it quietly. "I... I have something to share with you all."

Wilder's eyebrow arches, his curiosity piqued by my shaken state. Leaning forward, he quirks the corner of his mouth into a small, mischievous smile. "What'd you do? You can always confess your sins to me."

My gaze swings among the guys, each one a man I can't

quite decipher. Every time I think I can confide in them, they deliberately knock me off-balance.

I still don't—can't—trust them.

It's only my brother I have any remaining faith in, and he's dead.

"Something Maverick wrote." I broach the subject, treading lightly. "He mentioned our father was a Sovereign."

An ache blooms beneath my ribcage as I leave out the specifics of the location of the Heart's missing half. "He said there are three titles they hold—the High Sovereign, the Scourge Sovereign, and the Silent Sovereign. I don't know which one my dad was, but it's clear why Maverick was dragged into the Court. He's a legacy, like all of you."

I expected shock, or anger, maybe both, when I reveal that my father likely worked with theirs, what he did to initiates and Court members, before he came home to his wife and two young children and read storybooks to Maverick, embodying all the cartoon voices.

I study their expressions, desperate for a hint of their thoughts. Wilder is the first to zero in on me, his expression impassive.

Kaspian's fingers tighten almost imperceptibly on his glass. Axe's jaw clenches, the muscles working beneath his skin. Only Cav remains motionless, his eyes fixed on some distant point.

The quiet grows oppressive, pressing against my eardrums. I shift my weight, the floorboards groaning in protest as I wait for their reaction.

Wilder's the first to speak. "A Sovereign, huh? That explains a lot. And we always called the silent one … the silent one. So points to them for creativity."

The boys exchange glances, their demeanor shifting from cold apathy to various states of resignation. They're used to unwelcome surprises and have learned to ride the wave.

Kaspian murmurs, "Our fathers' sins follow us like annoying puppies, it seems."

"Does this change anything?" A rasp of irritation colors Cav's inquiry.

"I'm not sure yet," I admit, glancing at each of them. "Do you know who took my father's place? He was killed for defecting, trying to save us from—"

No. Not yet. Don't mention your crucial link to the Heart's ritual.

"—trying to escape from the Court," I finish.

"We never knew who the Sovereigns are and never will," Cav answers. "Their anonymity is closely guarded because of how powerful and influential they are outside of their leadership of the Court."

"That Maverick discovered your dad's high rank is a feat in itself," Wilder adds.

Axe's lips remain sealed, his expression a cipher while he stares out of the window into the overgrown, wilted garden.

"Most of those documents uploaded into the drive," I say, "were from my dad. Maverick found everything Dad was trying to collect as proof to use against them."

"And provide evidence to whom?" Kaspian asks, slowly raising his gaze from his glass to me. "Did your father have an outside savior offering to help him? Because no one escapes the Court. Well, they do, but … not kindly."

His eyelids lower after that statement and he glances away.

"I don't know," I answer honestly. "Maverick thought maybe there was someone in the FBI, but he had no evidence and couldn't say who."

"Show me the letter." Cav points through the wide double doors and to the staircase. "I'd like to see this for myself."

My throat constricts at the thought. I didn't tell them everything.

Their collective focus presses in on me, demanding answers I'm not ready to give. The missing half of the Heart is in Sarah Anderton's vault, and I have no idea where that is. I reason that I can delay giving that information to the guys because I want to talk to Clover first, who has basically become a historian on Anderton lore, and see what she has to say. Not that I trust her over the others, but…

Okay, I do. She was in the exact situation I'm currently in, with four intimidating, primal, trained men who always expect to get their way, yet she somehow managed to get hers to heel.

Now that's magic.

I lick my lips, my mouth suddenly dry.

"That's all he mentioned about our father," I lie, the words bitter on my tongue. "The rest was … personal. About how much he'll miss me and that he wishes he could've protected me more. I'd rather keep that part private."

That much is honest, at least.

The creases around Cav's eyes deepen, twin flames of suspicion in their depths. He opens his mouth to press, but Axe cuts him off.

"We're already wanted men," Axe points out, his steel unwavering, even with the fresh knife cut down one side of his face. "Especially now that we've decided to possess both halves of the ruby and figure out what they want with it and how to bring the Sovereigns down. Maverick was on our side. Darian Wraithwood was, too. And they're both dead. We need to stay focused on our mission before we're next."

It's the most Axe has said in weeks.

Cav purses his lips, a muscle ticking beneath the stubbled skin. For a moment, I think he'll argue, but then he nods.

I release a breath. Axe's intervention bought me a reprieve, but it won't last. I have to get my answers, and soon.

Kaspian stirs.

"And you had no idea?" he asks me, his voice bristling with an emotion I can't quite place.

I shake my head. "None. Maverick never told me, and I never suspected."

The admission tastes like betrayal, like I'm somehow at fault for not knowing, for not seeing the signs.

Kaspian rises from his chair, his movements fluid, graceful, and sling-free. I wonder how he's really doing with that shoulder wound since he refuses to treat it as anything more than a scratch.

My brief respite evaporates when Wilder speaks again, unleashing another paradigm shift.

"Better get to giving us a tour of all the traps on the first floor, sweetwitch, because we'll be staying here for a while."

I blink at him. "I'm sorry. What?"

"Yep." He grins. "We live here now."

Live here? In this crumbling mansion filled with ghosts and sadness and … me?

"You can't be serious," I choke out. "This place is falling apart. It's not safe."

Wilder's grin only widens, a flash of white against tan. "Dead serious. This place is a fortress. The Court's hunting us, and we need a base of operations."

I look at the others, searching for any sign that this is some kind of twisted joke.

"But … this is my home," I protest. "You can't just decide to move in."

Cav crosses the room, his presence dominating the space between us. "It's the safest place for us right now. Your brother's intel changes everything."

Kaspian nods, setting his glass down. "Your family's estate is secluded and defensible. It'll serve our purposes well enough."

I bite the side of my cheek. Hard. The thought of these men, these dangerous, unpredictable men, living under the same roof as me, sends tremors in places inside me that I didn't even know they could travel to.

As a last resort, I look at Axe, pleading evident in my eyes. But he gives a slight nod, confirming his brothers' words.

Worse, I can't deny the logic behind their decision.

"Fine," I concede. "But we need ground rules. This isn't going to be some kind of frat house."

Kaspian arches an eyebrow. "You think so little of us?"

I meet his stare head-on. "I don't know what to think of you. Any of you."

"Good. We've lingered long enough." Kaspian parries my verbal jab effortlessly. "You still need to show us the remainder of the manor's ... defenses, which we'll keep up since they are oddly effective against any intrusion."

My mind reluctantly catalogs everything my mother installed throughout the mansion. The tripwires. The concealed poison-coated spikes. The fake doorways leading to nowhere. The floorboards rigged to collapse beneath the weight of a man. Remnants of my mother's brilliant yet troubled mind, designed to push her imaginary intruders to their limits.

The thought of explaining these lethal surprises to four highly combustible men while wearing nothing but a sheer nightgown is overwhelming, but there's no one else left to do it.

"Alright," I say with a drawn-out sigh. "But you need to stay close and do exactly as I say."

Wilder leans against the wall and folds his arms, exposing a tantalizing glimpse of toned forearms. "Then you'd better take point, sweetwitch. Unless you require some..." His tongue darts out to graze his lower lip. "Motivation."

The blatant challenge resonates straight to my core. As I rise to meet it, the corners of his lips curl into a half smile that sends a familiar jolt down my spine. I've spent so much time dreading them, fearing the havoc they've brought into my life, but there's no denying their sex appeal.

I clear my throat of nonexistent phlegm. "Let's get to it, then. There are eight on this floor. The first one is—"

Cav moves into my comfort zone, so close I can smell his cologne mixing with the antiseptic coating his abdomen.

"Oh, we're not just going to do a walk-through," he says. His eyes blaze with a depravity that no Sovereign will ever be able to carve out of him.

His cuts to Wilder, whose grin hasn't faltered. "It's called turning lemons into lemonade, doll."

My heartbeat stutters as realization dawns. They plan to make their living here an occasion for... games.

The sort of games men like them play.

A shiver dances across my skin as I turn to the hallway. "Try to keep up, then."

"I have a feeling you're going to enjoy being in charge far too much, little witch," Wilder muses behind me.

"If you're so confident," I toss over my shoulder, trying to keep my voice steady, "why don't we make a challenge out of it? Each trap you successfully navigate earns you a reward."

Cav's falling into step beside me is casual, but the keen look in his pale eyes reveals his piqued interest. "And what might those rewards be?"

My body instinctively responds to his proximity.

Heat creeps up my neck. Inwardly cursing myself for showing how easily they can turn me on, I put space between us by striding into the lead. "Let's begin."

They follow, apex predators stalking their cute, fluffy prey.

I deliberately trigger the first tripwire, unleashing a barrage of darts that I nimbly avoided by dropping to the floor.

Of course, their reflexes are faster than mine, their lithe bodies already hunched near the ground. But Wilder and Axe share a white-hot look as my short nightgown rides up over my admittedly pert derriere.

"Eyes front, boys," I say with a half-trembling smile. "You'll need your focus for this next one."

I would've never believed it if it were not currently happening, but my mother's defenses are actually giving me confidence and a needed, pleasurable distraction from the abandoned circus my life has become.

Sashaying farther ahead, I come to an abrupt halt before a pressure plate camouflaged in the floorboards. "This one's for you, Axe."

The stoic giant steps up without hesitation, intense eyes questioning. Slowly, I circle him until I stand flush against his rigid front, my petite frame contrasting his imposing one.

"Going to need that exquisite control," I breathe against his jawline, relishing the way his pupils dilate instantly. Dragging my palms along his sculpted torso through his soft cashmere sweater, I guide Axe's stance with excruciating patience until...

"There," I finally exhale, lips brushing his nape as I withdraw. "One step at a time. Don't let me down."

A sterling hurricane whorls over his eyes as Axe advances with robotic restraint, every movement a lesson in preternatural discipline as he successfully avoids springing the plate's trap among the many tiles he was faced with. Only the faintest rasp of his harsh breathing gives away the strain.

My triumphant gaze falls on the remaining men, issuing a villainous challenge. "Who's next?"

"Kaspian," Wilder offers, still sipping his drink. "You're up."

Kaspian's assent catches me off guard, his outstretched hand a dare in itself. "And what's my obstacle, beastie?"

I point east.

My mother's twisted genius manifests itself in curious ways. Each trap is intricate and unique in design. Memorizing every trigger point has become a rite of passage.

Kaspian's moss-colored gaze flits between me and the trap ahead—a web of homemade laser triggers requiring nimble movements to bypass.

He moves closer—until the distance between us is nearly nonexistent. Raising an eyebrow at him teasingly while my heart tries to leap into his gorgeous mouth, I instruct, "You'll want to be as fluid as water for this one."

He matches my cheeky smile with his own sardonic slant, the corners of his mouth lifting ever so slightly—a beast amused by his plaything's brazenness.

He inches forward, movements as graceful as they are lethal. His tall frame ducks and lifts effortlessly between each beam—

the macabre routine enhanced by the charge of not knowing what would be triggered if he failed.

Once he's safely on the other side, I cast a raised brow Wilder's and Cav's way.

"Your turns," I quip.

My voice is teasing, but my heart is a ticking time bomb in my chest.

Cav remains motionless, his scrutiny unrelenting. His stare raises goosebumps along my arms, a silent invasion. Despite myself, I find it hard to look away from his lightning-blue eyes.

"And what," he murmurs, words dripping like warm honey, "would be the reward for successfully navigating this labyrinth you've got us in? You've yet to explain."

His voice vibrates through my body, each syllable laced with a promise of something wild and unpredictable. The tension burns in the air like an open flame. The men exchange glances.

"Continue on and find out," I answer smoothly with a shrug that lifts my nightgown a fraction higher up my thighs. My tone is light but flirty, aiming to keep them intrigued, off-balance.

With measured grace, Cav eliminates the gap separating us. I hold my breath as he leans down to whisper in my ear, "We'll be expecting something ... satisfying."

His breath tickles. A quiet moan almost escapes my throat.

I tilt my head in a needed escape. "Careful. Keep looking at me like that, and you might miss a trap."

Wilder chuckles, the sound velvet over gravel. "Our witch has a point, Cav. Best keep your eyes on the prize."

"Oh, I am," Cav murmurs.

The heat in his eyes sets me alight.

With a smirk, I saunter into the next room, the men close behind.

"Watch your step," I warn, halting before a jagged hole. Rotted planks jut like broken teeth. "Unless you fancy a tumble into the basement."

Kaspian presses close, quickening my breath. "And deprive you of our company? Never."

Pulse hammering, I navigate around the hole. The men follow, their steps precise, efficient. They're in their element.

Kaspian's fingers graze the small of my back as if he can't resist playing with the thin material of my nightie despite himself.

"Are all the traps so obvious?"

"Only to those who know where to look." I nod at an innocuous section of the wall. "Right, Axe?"

The giant freezes mid-step. He scrutinizes the wall, nostrils flaring. With a grunt, he changes trajectory, avoiding the pressure plate by a hairsbreadth.

"Well done," I praise, fighting a grin. "Seems you boys are quick studies."

"We have incentive," Wilder says, his teeth flashing again. "A witch's favor is a rare gift."

"Who says you've earned it?"

"Haven't we?" He spreads his arms, encompassing the traps they've breached. "We've danced to your tune admirably."

I pause before an innocuous door, hand on the knob. "One last challenge, then. Make it through this room unscathed, and perhaps you'll get your reward."

Kaspian leans a shoulder on the wall, arms crossed. "You enjoy playing with us."

"You make it so easy." I wink, pretending that's how it is between us, then twist the knob.

The door swings open, hinges shrieking. Darkness yawns beyond the threshold.

I gesture grandly. "After you."

Axe moves first, his tall form slipping into the black.

Kaspian follows, silent as an evil spirit. Wilder throws me a heated glance before he too is swallowed.

Cav hangs back, gaze intent upon my face. "And what of my prize, butterfly?"

"You assume you've won it."

"I'm a very determined man." He crowds me, his fever-warm presence enveloping my senses. "And I always collect on my debts."

My breath stutters. "Do you?"

"Yes." His lips hover over mine, a whisper of contact. "And you owe me."

He claims my mouth in a harsh kiss, his tongue delving deep. I moan, clutching his shoulders. He grips my hips, grinding me against the hard ridge of his arousal.

A curse shatters the air, followed by a tremendous crash.

We wrench apart. My lips tingle, bruised from his assault. Cav's eyes glitter in the dark, a panther deprived of his meal.

"Really?" Wilder barks from the other room. "A fucking bear trap?"

CHAPTER 23
AXE
THE PHANTOM

Wilder circles the deadly sharp maw of the bear trap in the center of the room and lets out a low whistle. "Sweetwitch's mama is full of surprises."

"You don't say?" Kaspian deadpans.

Elara rushes into the room with Cav on her heels.

From my stance near the door, I snake my hand out, fingers curling around her wrist. "Not so fast. You've had your fun with us. Wilder almost losing a leg should finish it."

I glance from her to the others, reading the hunger in their eyes, the wolfish intent. Anticipation fires through my veins, hot and potent.

And by the look in her eye, we're not the only ones in desperate need of a distraction.

"Then come and claim it," she breathes.

Wrenching free of my grip, she bolts for the door, nervous laughter bubbling up her throat as our footsteps pound behind her, the thrill of the hunt spurring us on.

Elara's game has reached its fevered pitch, and I'm no longer certain whether I'm the hunter or the prey. All I know is Elara craves the chase, the capture, with a deep-seated need to be pursued, cornered, and conquered, if she's baiting us like this.

I race through the halls, my shoes silent on the flagstones, my brothers' careful breaths mingling with her gasping laughter. She leads us on a winding path, darting through narrow passageways and up twisting staircases, putting all her knowledge of the manor and her mother to use.

But in the end, as I knew it would, her flight proves futile. We crowd her, caging her against the wall with our much larger bodies.

Kaspian braces a hand beside her head, lips curving. "Caught you."

Elara squirms, trapped between us, my body humming at her proximity and the arousal flushing her cheeks.

She's so fucking beautiful.

"Then do your worst," she says.

Wilder, flanking Kaspian, responds, "Oh, trust me. Our worst is better than most men's best."

"Prove it," she dares.

Cav reacts first, reaching under her nightgown and pulling at her panties. The silk fabric swishes down her elegant, toned legs and pools at her ankles before he teasingly reveals her glistening arousal. Elara steps out of them, and he tosses them to me.

I catch them with a half-cocked smile as Elara tracks the movement, her lashes lowering. She remembers my longing for the scent of her pussy, wet and inviting.

The sight of her open desire makes my pants tighten further —if that's possible.

Elara rewards Kaspian by allowing him to caress her fiery hair and cup her breast in his hand through her nightgown. His fingers gently squeeze and massage her flesh, feeling the hardness of her nipple between his thumb and forefinger, but that's all she gives him.

Elara's subtle rebuff of Kaspian becomes more obvious when she openly welcomes Wilder. She lets him take her soft breast into his mouth, his tongue flicking over the hard, sensitive nipple. His face becomes as peaceful as I've ever seen it, savoring the warm taste of her skin and the siphoning the addiction that comes with controlling her pleasure.

Fuck. Finally, it's my turn.

I place myself between Wilder and a frowning Kaspian the moment Cav peels off her nightgown. Elara is completely naked except for that cursed amulet, gleaming between her breasts like a witch's eye. I ignore it and kiss her, my tongue slipping past her lips, her teeth, to play with hers.

She cups my jaw as I tip her head back, plunging as deep as she wants, sucking up my saliva, my soul. The heat between us skyrockets. Our bodies press together. She grinds herself against me, moaning softly into my mouth.

The adrenaline from impressing her fades, replaced by a carnal lust that's as deep as it is dark.

Her scent wraps around me like a chain, driving me absolutely batshit insane. My fingers twitch with the urge to touch her and claim what's ours. I'll rip apart anyone who dares to lay his fucking eyes on her once she leaves this manor.

She's ours, she's ours, she's ours.

That's a sentiment I will remember forever.

"Can't play nice anymore," I rasp as I sever the kiss.

She looks up at me, her eyes misted over with lust. "Well, you're all so fond of playing rough."

The light in her eyes gutters after she says it before she quickly blinks it back in place.

I angle my head, reading her face. "You don't like it?"

A throat clears beside us.

"My fault," Kaspian says.

Acknowledgment from him? A rarity.

With that said, he places an arm between me and Wilder, to our disgruntlement, and scoops Elara up in his arms. Elara releases a vocal gasp of shock, her limbs flailing before he holds her hard against his chest and grumbles, "I'll make up for it."

Obviously, Wilder, Cav, and me follow as Kaspian backtracks through the manor.

Kaspian kicks open a door to a guest bedroom with more force than necessary, but right now, restraint isn't high on his list of virtues.

The bed is a four-poster draped in soft, buttery sheets. Placing Elara onto it, he peels off his shirt slowly, matching Elara's earlier tease with his own strip show. She watches with bated breath and eager, yet wary, eyes.

What did he do to her, I wonder?

With great effort, I take my attention off Elara and do a fast scroll through my phone's notes in case his fuckup was referenced earlier. It wasn't, not really.

It's hard to keep my mind on the task as I scroll through my phone, knowing that Elara is naked and waiting on the bed, that ruby glittering with no power but hers, waiting for Kaspian.

By the time I refocus on Elara, Kaspian stands between her splayed legs bare-chested, his pants hanging low on his hips and revealing a carved, V-shape arrow to his cock.

Her body arches toward him, pleading for contact, pussy gleaming.

He's potent and dominant, just like she wants it, and his body is a work of art under the soft light of the room. He towers over her, glistening with sweat from our earlier efforts.

As he lowers himself between her legs, her breath stops.

Kaspian pushes against her knees, revealing her wetness to us all. We watch as he teases her entrance with his rough fingers.

"No objects this time, beastie. Promise. Only me. Always. Me."

He pushes inside her all the way to his knuckles, grunting slightly at the tight fit, but he doesn't hesitate to push four fingers in as far as they can go.

Her moans caress the walls and fill our ears like music.

Every time he hits that sweet spot inside her, she gasps or cries out in delight mixed with pain, making our observation all the more unbearable.

If I don't get out of these pants, I'm going to bust the zipper.

Elara writhes, her hips arcing off the bed in a desperate bid for more. I spot Wilder across the room, the same famine reflected back at me.

Without further hesitation, I liberate my throbbing erection.

The sight of Elara, bare and spread beneath Kaspian elicits a rare, untamed counteraction from me.

Cav follows my lead, ripping open his own jeans with an impatient tug. His cobalt gaze settles first on the necklace, giving an annoyed eye-twitch at its presence, but for once, it's not almighty enough to keep him from choosing to focus on Elara's face instead as she cries out, her body bucking beneath Kaspian's relentless touch.

Wilder is making his own show of things; tearing off his shirt and tossing it to the side before turning his attention back to the bed. His hazel eyes are starved as he watches Kaspian's hand disappear inside her again and again. Wilder's entire demeanor is one of barely leashed restraint.

My cock bobbing high and hard against my stomach, I stride over to where Elara lies squirming, her breath coming in harsh pants. I stroke myself slowly, matching the rhythm of Kaspian's hand thrusting inside her.

As if sensing my approach, she cracks her eyes open just enough to track me before they slip shut again, lost in her ecstasy. A slow smile curves her lips as she beckons me closer.

The intoxicating concoction of their combined scent hits me, Kaspian's musky aroma of arousal mixing with Elara's sweet cunt. It's enough to drive me to my knees.

Wilder moves to her other side, his hands trailing up her thigh and toward her breasts that are bouncing with each powerful plunge Kaspian delivers, the necklace pooling at her collarbone, face down as if even it has accepted defeat when faced with us. He traces the outline of her breasts, then pinches her nipples until they stand swollen and erect.

The unspoken agreement passing between us needs no words. We'll take care of our woman.

Together. As it's meant to be.

I want her. We all want her.

Her cries grow louder and more frantic as Kaspian applies more pressure on her sweet spot. My fingers find their way to her clit, adding to the overwhelming sensations coursing through her body.

Cav gets on the bed, straddling her face.

She comes violently, a loud scream tearing from her throat as wave after wave of rapture courses through her. Cav positions the tip of his cock so it pulls down her lower lip as she shouts.

Every man in the room groans at that goddamn perfect sight.

The image of her coming undone pushes me over the edge, my own release spilling onto the floor below.

With one last shudder, her body goes slack, her heavy breaths the only sound in the room. She gazes up at Cav with awe and something deeper, brushing a stray hair from his forehead before turning her attention to the rest of us.

Elara lies in the center, a masterpiece, flushed and spent.

"Your shirts," she says breathlessly to Cav and me. "Take them off."

Cav and I tense, exchanging similar looks of resistance.

To bare our scars in such an intimate, personal setting ... well, now I have a partner in that, as terrible as it is. Cav, once as flawless as Kaspian and Wilder, and where I was once a unmarred, trained, muscular specimen like the three of them, is now asked to expose his deformity, his descent from magnificence to this gorgeous, unblemished girl.

Then again, Elara isn't like any other woman we've met. She's seen our scars. In fact, she's seen all of us—the good and the bad, the highs and lows. We've been laid bare before her.

With my lips tight, I pull my shirt over my head and toss it to the side. The air of the room hits the raw skin of my fresh scars, causing a tremor that has nothing to do with the beautiful woman in front of me. Still straddling her, Cav does the same, shedding his bandages, his characteristic poise deserting him beneath Elara's steady look once he's exposed.

There's no disgust in her eyes as she takes us in. She doesn't flinch away from our mutilated bodies. On the contrary, she reaches out to trace her fingers along the jagged lines marring our muscles. Her touch is soft as she maps out our flaws with a care that stirs an unexpected ache inside my chest.

Then she smiles that radiant smile of hers, reaching up to trace the raised outline of one of my more prominent scars with her delicate caress. The touch sends shivers down my spine and stirs something akin to possessiveness within me.

Kaspian slides off the bed to give room for me to move closer. He crosses his arms over his chest, a move that might look defensive on anyone else. But on Kaspian, it's got this raw masculine appeal that leaves no doubt he considers Elara his as well.

I reach out to cup her face, my thumb tracing her swollen lips before pulling her into a deep kiss that makes her stop breathing. The salty taste of Cav's precum on her tongue sends another jolt of arousal to my dick.

When I lean back, Cav takes advantage of her open mouth and slips his dick inside. A soft mewl escapes from her throat, and it's echoed by a deep groan from Cav.

Wilder pulls away from the bed long enough to slam the door shut. He prowls closer to kneel between her thighs and dip his head to suck on her pussy. Elara's surprise is muffled by Cav pushing himself to the hilt inside her mouth.

When Kaspian goes for her breasts, I immediately get hard again. I could watch them pleasure her all night, but then I remember that I'm part of this, too.

I can touch and taste and have my own piece of Elara.

So that's exactly what I do.

I reach for her, my fingers slipping inside her pussy while Wilder's tongue swirls, pressing against her wet folds.

She's so slick and ready that it takes a lot of control not to lose myself right then.

But instead, I take my turn, pushing into her warmth with a gratifying sigh. The men around me add their own touches, their own caresses, until Elara is a wriggling mess beneath us.

The sight of her coming apart under our hands, under our bodies, is a heady one. Her cries grow louder, more desperate as she gets closer to another climax.

Cav moves with her, his pace increasing to match the frenzy around him. Kaspian closes his lips around a taut nipple with more fervor. Wilder growls against her clit, and my fingers curl inside her, hitting the spot that makes her scream.

Eyes slammed shut, she bucks against me once, twice, then a final time, her walls clenching around my fingers as an orgasm rips through her.

It's at that moment Wilder bats my hand away, rises, and slams into her pussy with such acute force that the bed shifts sideways.

Cav groans, the muscles in his back bunching as he releases into her mouth, his hand fisting in her hair to keep her anchored. Wilder's growls deepen into long-drawn-out groans that vibrate against her skin. Kaspian's eyes flash as he watches Elara take Cav in her mouth and Wilder in her pussy, clearly unhinged by the image.

Wilder drives into her faster and harder. His hot, savage focus on Elara's satisfaction matches the bestial lust in his eyes. Wilder takes full control, using every ounce of his strength to hit that G-spot inside her again and again.

Every time Wilder thrusts into Elara, each time Cav slides deep into her mouth, Elara convulses with delight. Her hands grip at Kaspian's arm holding her leg aloft and my shoulder as she seeks stability amid a tsunami of gluttony.

Cav growls something incoherent, a slurry of curses and compliments, and pulls out from her mouth, shooting the rest of his load onto Elara's flushed face and chest. His release triggers Wilder, who buries himself deep inside Elara with a harsh shout.

Kaspian's hands are quick to smear it down her breasts, his fingers dipping into her cleavage before moving to her peaked nipples. I choke on a groan, my cock demanding its due attention.

I shift my position until my straining erection nudges Wilder's out of the way, and I can claim her wet, swollen heat.

I move slowly at first, the sensation of Elara's tight walls around me too delicious to rush. I have to savor this moment and etch it into my memories for all eternity.

Her hands, previously holding tightly onto Kaspian and me, now claw at my back as soon as Cav shifts off her face. It's a pain I welcome—a testament I'll be proud to wear.

"God, Axe," she moans as I hit a particularly sensitive spot within her.

Wilder grunts in displeasure at being forced to vacate, shifting to slide into her mouth, taking what he can while watching me claim his territory. He pulses in her mouth, his lust incurable.

Cav moves beside me, his hand snaking down Elara's body until it reaches that perfect nub of flesh Kaspian had tormented earlier.

When I straighten to gain a better thrust advantage, Kaspian takes the available space and kneels around her waist, blocking my perfect view as he slides himself between her breasts and squeezes them around his cock, using Cav's release as lubrication.

I growl low in my throat as I sink into her warmth, the friction of our bodies adding another layer to the multitude of sensations already rippling through her. My hands grip her thighs, pulling her closer until no space is left between our sexes. Elara's body welcomes me in, her soft moans spurring me on.

Cav's eyes turn a smoky blue as he focuses on me fucking her. He circles her clit amid the tangle of limbs and sweat-soaked skin. His free hand pushes against one of her thighs, keeping her open and spread, his fingers digging into her flesh, leaving marks that will remind all of us of this night long after it ends.

And he doesn't wait his turn.

Cav steadies himself by placing one hand on the bedpost before guiding his rigid cock to the place where Elara and I are connected.

He pushes inside slowly, his expression holding an intensity that borders on reverence.

The sensation of him filling Elara alongside me carbonates my veins. It's such a profound intimacy that we share with her—a perilous blend of possession and surrender that transcends anything else I've ever experienced.

Elara lifts her head and chokes on an inhale as she struggles to accommodate Cav and me simultaneously.

"Shh, we got you," I whisper, my voice hoarse with longing as Kaspian finally bottoms out.

Elara's response is broken by a cry as Kaspian lifts to his knees and shoves himself into her mouth, his ass muscles clenching. Her pussy clamps down around Cav and me, and it sparks such sharp pleasure, my vision is dotted with stars.

Kaspian's hand moves from the headboard to cradle Elara's chin as she chokes on him, his thumb swiping at the tears trailing down her cheeks, his gaze filled with uncharacteristic softness as he looks down at her.

"Come for us, Elara," Kaspian murmurs. It's a command more than a request.

And like the shattered jewel she is, she does.

She spasms around me and Cav both—a hot, tight clench that has us both grunting in satisfaction. Kaspian curses lowly as his seed shoots down her throat.

Wilder, on the other hand, was jerking off the entire time, watching intently as Elara swallows Kaspian's release, his gaze darkening to an obscure gold when, with a loud grunt, he spills his load onto her chest, too.

And then there are two.

Cav and I keep up the pace. Elara's eyes flutter open to meet us in turn.

Our breaths intermingle in the small space between us as we lose ourselves in each other's depths.

It's easy to forget that we're not alone—that Cav is still here—but it doesn't matter. I'll share.

She spasms around me and Cav both.

The moment my climax hits, it whitewashes everything else. I can't see or hear—I'm lost to her.

When we pull out, Elara is left panting and flushed on the sheets, a mess of glistening limbs and tousled hair.

For a while, nobody moves. Nobody speaks. The only sound in the room is our collective, heavy breathing and the occasional grunt or sigh as we come down from our high. The air is thick with our mingled scents—cologne, sweat, fresh blood from re-opened wounds, sex.

We all collapse onto the bed, gasping for breath and fighting off the haze that threatens to pull us under. Elara is sandwiched between Cav and me, her body limp and sated.

Kaspian is the first to move, detangling himself from the mess of arms and legs to fetch a damp washcloth from the attached bathroom. He cleans Elara with a gentleness that seems out of character after what we've just done. His touch is gallant as he wipes away traces of our time together, a trait I never thought I'd associate with him.

Wilder is silent, though his eyes speak volumes as he observes Kaspian clean up Elara. His gaze is hooded, lips pursed in a thin line. His way of regaining control after letting go so completely.

I shift slightly and pull Elara closer against my chest, relishing her soft sighs against my skin. My hand lazily strokes her auburn hair, its strands around my fingers like the shining threads of a story we're still weaving.

Elara stirs, her amber eyes blinking owlishly as she looks up at me. A soft smile curves her lips as she regards us, her gaze drowsy but content.

"Thank you," she murmurs, her voice raw from crying and screaming.

The simple sentiment resonates within the uncertain space between us. It's an acknowledgment, a gratitude not only for the pleasure we brought her but also for the trust we've placed in her…

…and she in us.

I ignore the stone in my gut, growing larger, harder, heavier. The world outside our sphere abruptly seeps back in, reminding me of its existence.

Of promises I made to the Sovereigns the last time they summoned me and the secrets I'm keeping from my brothers, Elara, because of it.

Of the looming dawn that would soon push away the cloak of darkness that had allowed me to stop pretending and just be.

I must think of Marianne.

Wilder drags himself to sit against the headboard, his kindled gaze drifting over Elara's body like a tangible caress. He looks as if he's about to say something when a knock interrupts.

Our gazes snap toward the door just as Sasha's voice filters through.

"Um … hello? I have the coffee."

CHAPTER 24
ELARA

A wave of heat rushes to my cheeks as I briskly make my way into the expansive dining room, acutely aware of the gazes that follow me. Kaspian, Axe, Wilder, and Cav all sport identical expressions of post-coital satisfaction, but it's my own mortification that has me feeling like a blushing virgin.

"Finally," Sasha says with an amused wink as she hands me a cardboard cup of coffee, "you've come up for air."

The guys let out collective, low sounds of amusement, a pride of male lions purring over their sole lioness, as they take their coffees from the to-go holder at the center of the table and recline while Sasha gives them all wry looks.

I take a deep breath to calm my nerves. It's me that's the problem, not Sasha. It's not wrong to sexually connect with more than one guy, and college is all about experimenting, right?

Kaspian lifts the lid from his coffee and inhales through his nose. If I had blinked, I wouldn't have caught the contented lowering of his eyelids, like he's happy, before he snaps his unfeeling self back into place. He glances my way, almost daring me to comment.

Wilder grabs his cup with both hands and drinks deeply—heat be damned—his Adam's apple bobbing with each gulp. His charged gaze meets mine across the rim as if making sure I'm still here and haven't escaped.

Axe casually stirs his coffee with a silver spoon, the liquid swirling in hypnotic circles without looking down—just at me, like he's dissecting my embarrassed thoughts and finds them amusing.

Cav doesn't touch his cup.

My attention darts to Sasha again, who seems utterly at ease with these men who are anything but college boys.

My heart jumps into my throat as a realization nearly makes me choke on burning-hot coffee.

Sasha's reaction to them is important to me because I am attached to these men.

What we share isn't merely physical anymore. Emotionally, too. Every smirk they share, every word, the way they drink their coffee, all of it resonates with me, strengthening my bond with them.

Fucking hell.

"You okay, El?"

Sasha's question drags me from my sex-addled thoughts—because that's what it has to be, some sort of post-coital bliss making me feel this way about them. I need to refocus and remind myself of the real reason I'm here. It's not to get tangled in the sheets with these four undomesticated men, although that's an unexpected bonus. It's to find out what happened to my brother and why he was so certain the Sovereigns want to involve me in their final ritual.

I answer, "Yep, I'm totally fine," before plopping into my seat and hiding as much of my reddened face as I can behind my cup.

"What's on the agenda today?" she asks. "Because after all this, I doubt we're studying for midterms."

I drum my fingers along the paper cup, still nursing my coffee. "I need to visit Clover Callahan."

A large, dark, masculine cloud descends upon the room.

Wilder makes himself comfortable in his chair. "You want to parlay with a Vulture?"

"Uh, last I checked, Clover was a sophomore," Sasha says.

I clench my fists in my lap under the table. "Clover is one of the few people who might have some insight into Sarah Anderton's history. My history."

A foreboding tremor quakes along Wilder's jawline. Axe just maintains his unsettling calmness, studying me with his harrowing stare. But it's Cav who speaks, his words every bit as icy as the glacier chips he's housing for eyes. "That woman is dangerous."

"I know," I say, meeting his cool survey without flinching. "But I can handle her."

Wilder scoffs loudly at that. "You can barely handle us."

Something inside me snaps at that.

Standing abruptly, I slam my palms onto the table, making Sasha jump in her seat. "What you mean is that I've dealt with far worse than Clover Callahan."

The hinges of Wilder's resolve audibly creak as he leans forward, muscles tensing under his tight black shirt. "You don't know what you're walking into. The Vultures have been bred like us, meaning they will protect their woman if you so much as exhale too close to her face."

"I'm not asking for permission." I stare him down.

A thick silence engulfs the room, so complete that you can hear the crinkling of the paper cups from their combined grips. Cav is the first to break it, the sharp angles of his face becoming razor-edged.

"You may be a Wraithwood, but that doesn't make you immune to their treachery."

Cav's voice is barely controlled, a stark contrast to his typically calm demeanor.

Probably because he's been the closest to the Vultures, worked with them even, and understands them the best.

I dive into the bottomless depths of his stare. "I never claimed to be invincible."

"You have a dangerous habit of underestimating your enemies."

"And you," I fire back, "mistake scars for invincibility."

I don't have to include his chest for him to understand what I'm referring to.

The searing brand of his scrutiny intensifies, but I endure the burn.

This is bigger than us. This is about finding out who I am and who my brother was. Nothing is more important.

Axe rests his forearms on the table, one hand clenching his phone. "Even if you find Clover, she won't be alone. She never is."

"Sounds familiar," I drawl.

Kaspian exhales a sound caught between humor and threat, lounging back in his seat. "She wants to play with the birds? Then let her."

I clamp down on my rising frustration. "You've seen more than one side of them, Kaspian."

Wilder laughs. "And what side is that, exactly? The one where they kill people?"

"No, like when Rossi and Tempest stitched up his shoulder. Not to mention, they helped me get my mother to safety instead of into jail."

Sasha shifts uncomfortably in her seat. "Maybe we should—"

"I know what Clover is," I concede, so passionate about the subject that I cut Sasha off. "But I also know that she wrote a paper about Sarah Anderton's nameless daughter—who is likely one of my ancestors, and she did a ton of research. Something is there, guys."

Kaspian's rare laugh cuts through the air, sharp as broken glass, like I'm some sort of chick following the bigger birds around, and it's the last straw.

I push back from the table. "Fine. You guys can sit around debating the risks all you want. I'm going to track down Clover and get the information I need. Feel free to join me when you're done with your little war council."

I stride for the door, but Wilder's voice stops me. "Wait."

Glancing over my shoulder, I see him push to his feet, muscles bunched tight. "I'm coming with you."

"No, you're not."

"You need backup. And out of the four of us, I'm still flawless in my execution."

He winks while the other three frown but don't argue since they sport fresh injuries. So far, Wilder's come out unscathed.

It stands out as a powerful reminder. My worry for them ratchets up to an unbearable level.

If the Sovereigns get to them before I've found the answers, if I lose these men forever and waste all of Maverick's, of my father's, efforts to bring down the Cimmerian Court … what did they die for? What am I good for?

My time is running out.

***

Wilder slings his leather jacket over his shoulder as we exit the manor and descend the stairs to the circular drive.

I glance sideways at him, my initial irritation melting away as he falls into step beside me. I'll never admit it, but his attendance is a comfort. Clover may not be a threat, but her Vulture bodyguards are. Having Wilder along could mean the difference between getting the information I need and ending up in a body bag.

We stride across the gravel drive, boots crunching, my mother's manor taking its skeletal shape behind us.

When we reach the sleek black SUV, Wilder opens the passenger door for me, a chivalrous habit even in the midst of his lawless, unpredictable mind.

Though I expect it, I still flinch when he gets into the driver's seat and guns the engine, the SUV leaping forward like a viper and me recoiling like the viper's lunch.

He tears down the long, winding road, gravel spraying from the wheels.

Farrow Manor, where I've left poor Sasha with three of the most unprincipled men I've ever come across and their assurances that they'll make sure Sasha goes to class today and finds normalcy again, recedes in the distance.

I stare straight ahead, the side of my throat hammering with my pulse. I'm acutely aware of Wilder beside me, his body a tangled spring of energy. It's hard to believe he funneled so much of his fire into me a mere hour ago.

We hit the main road, the SUV eating up the miles. Trees blur past, a green smear against the lightening sky.

As the journey stretches on, I realize that this is the first time I've been alone with Wilder since ... well, since he threatened to jump off a cliff if I dared him to. I study him out of the corner of my eye, his expression focused despite the seemingly reckless driving as he navigates the twisting roads leading out of Titan Falls.

I ask, my voice barely audible over the thrumming engine, "Why are you really coming with me?"

He doesn't respond immediately. His grip tightens on the steering wheel before his shoulders shake with subdued laughter. It sounds hollow. Haunted, almost.

"Someone has to keep an eye on you," he replies eventually, but his smirk isn't as dimpled and confident as it normally is.

I roll my eyes at his response, an action more to keep myself from analyzing the turmoil behind his features than for mocking him.

But instead of dipping into silence again, he surprises me by speaking up.

"Four years ago," he says, his voice barely floating over the sound of tires on asphalt, "I had a girlfriend. Teagan."

His revelation stiffens my shoulders in my already tense

body. "The friend you mentioned when we were at the cliffs. The one who…"

For whatever reason, I can't say the word: Died.

Or that she was his girlfriend.

He nods, understanding what I mean. "Tea was different. Bright. Alive. She had this ability to see the good in everything, even when there was none to be found. Kinda like someone sitting beside me right now."

He tries to inject humor, but sorrow bleeds into the edges of his voice.

"She's dead because of me," he murmurs, keeping his eyes on the road.

"You never explained why you believe that," I prompt quietly.

Strain ripples from his face to his hands, leaving his knuckles pale against the dark wheel. "She was innocent, unaware of the Court's existence. I was an initiate who'd just had the ceremony in front of the Sovereigns to make me a member."

He turns to me before returning to the road, and the distress in his eyes grips my heart.

"I've never been good at following orders, doing what I've been told without question. The Sovereigns knew that. They used Teagan as leverage, claimed they had her hostage and would kill her if I didn't comply." Beneath the dark scruff of his chin, a battle of restraint plays out in taut muscles. "I didn't believe them … until they sent me proof. A picture of her, bound and blindfolded with sheer fucking terror in her eyes."

"Oh my God," I whisper.

I'm fully aware of the Sovereigns' depravity at this point, yet they still manage to shock me with their callousness.

"They dared me to try to save her. Said that if I found any information about the ruby Heart, she'd be freed. They left out the part where they'd already sold her."

Wilder's voice breaks, an agonizing sound that rips through

the car's interior. I reach out, placing my hand on his arm, conscious that comfort will never be enough.

"It was easy enough to track her down. I had Kasp, Cav, and Axe on my side, using their talents to dig up where they'd put her. But when I got there..." He lets out a breath that sounds more like a sigh of defeat. "There were other girls there, too. Sold to some Mafia perv named Marco Bianchi, who was excited to spread them around to his friends. Knowing that, I lost my shit. There was no way I was going to interrogate any of those fuckers for a stupid piece of jewelry, so I grabbed Tea, who they'd stripped and drugged, and got out of there."

Raw anguish carves itself into the planes of his face, and in that unguarded moment, the facade of smirks, flirtation, and ill-timed jokes crumbles away. For the first time, I glimpse the man beneath the armor—vulnerable, scarred, and achingly human.

"How did she...? You mentioned before..." I start, but my voice trails off as I grapple with how to ask the question.

"She died in my arms," Wilder finishes for me. "I wasn't fast enough. Kaspian and Cav covered me, and Axe was in the car down the street waiting for us, but it wasn't enough. They shot her down like some kind of target practice."

His truth slams into me, an invisible force that empties my lungs and stills my heart.

"I carried her body out of there. Cradled her in my arms as her blood soaked through my clothes. And all I could think was that it was my fault. I brought her into this world because I thought she was pretty and cute, and I stupidly thought I could have her and the Court at the same time. I couldn't protect her from it." Wilder clears his throat, the sound harsh in the stillness, and I realize Wilder's eased off the gas. "I failed her. I couldn't protect her from the Sovereigns. And now, with you..." He shakes his head. "I won't make the same mistake twice."

"I'm so sorry." My voice cracks. "What happened to Teagan wasn't your fault. The Sovereigns, they're the ones who—"

"Don't." He slices through my words, that one syllable jagged with emotion. "Just ... don't."

But I understand. The helplessness, the desperation to save someone you care for from an enemy that always seems one step ahead. It's a feeling I know all too well.

"Doesn't change the fact that she's gone because of me. Because I was too much of a dumbfuck to see their game."

Wilder sniffs hard, schooling his face into practiced apathy. "After that, I promised myself I'd never let anyone else get close. Never let anyone else become a victim because of me. But then you showed up."

My hand stills on his arm, the stress under his skin bulging against my palm. His body is a paradox—present yet distant, still but far from at ease.

But I also feel strength. Resilience. A fierce, unbreakable will to protect those he holds dear.

It's then I finally figure out that Wilder isn't just coming with me as backup. He's coming with me because he cares, because he's willing to put his life on the line for mine.

The SUV lurches as Wilder takes a sharp turn, the tires screeching against the asphalt. He guns the engine, surging the vehicle forward with renewed purpose.

And I'm guessing the conversation is over.

I grip the door handle as he rounds another bend, and there, rising from the tree line, is Blackwood Manor, home to Clover and the Vultures.

Wilder cuts the engine. His hands leave the wheel reluctantly as he faces me, and his curt nod says more than words could.

Together, we exit the vehicle, striding toward the old but well-maintained structure, ready to face whatever might crawl out of its walls.

CHAPTER 25
ELARA

Blackwood Manor's weathered stones are bathed in an ethereal glow that battles with the darkness creeping along its edges. Trees cast long shadows over the expansive grounds, their gnarled branches reaching out and ready to snatch any unsuspecting soul dumb enough to venture too close.

A stain of unease spreads across the back of my neck as we approach what the guys consider to be enemy territory.

Wilder, all business now, pulls ahead with a measured cadence to his steps. He glances back at me only once, that quick study seeming to permanently etch me into his mind. A mask of grim purpose settles over his features.

I quicken my pace, falling back into step beside him. As we near the imposing front door, my unease grows. The feeling becomes stronger when I really think about Clover's men, the Vultures.

I've met two, Tempest and Rossi, but that was enough. Most around campus have heard rumors about them within Titan Falls' local gossip mill, salacious rumors and nothing more, but their reputation, even as their disguise as professors and teaching assistants, commands an intimidating respect.

As Wilder raises his hand to knock on the door, I tell myself to breathe normally. Their house might be a fortress hiding more bloodshed than anyone could imagine, but so is my heart.

The door swings open before his knuckles can make contact with the heavy wood, revealing a rather imposing man with dark brown hair and matching eyes that glint with intelligent perusal as he takes us in.

He looks vaguely familiar, but I can't quite place him. Though his carved, angular face emotes nothing as his gaze rakes over me in a way that makes me want to die a little inside.

"Elara Wraithwood and John Wilder." He moves the thin line of his mouth just enough to say our names.

His voice is rough, like the quiet thunder before a storm, and just as intermittent. And the way he forms our names is unsettling; like he's not used to communicating before strangers.

Wilder shoots his arm out, forming a barrier between me and this new player. Though it shouldn't, my stomach flutters at Wilder's overprotectiveness. I'd like to think of myself as an independent lady, but sometimes it's nice to have a man fling you behind them for safety.

It's undeniably hot.

"Who are you?" Wilder asks.

"Rio," the man answers. "And you're trespassing."

Not one to mince words, then.

I send a wary look at Wilder, unsure of how to navigate this encounter. The sound of the surrounding forest settles over us, each of us trying to decipher the motives behind the other.

Until I can't take it any longer.

"Is Rossi here?" My voice is way more high-pitched than usual.

Rio's brow twitches at the mention of Rossi, but he otherwise remains unmoved. "If it's a paper or his favor you're trying to gain, he no longer works for the university."

Wilder scoffs. "No shit. He's the new Mafia don. I wouldn't want him teaching my kid business ethics, even if my child were a rich asshole dumped in the woods as a work-around to the Ivy Leagues."

Rio cocks his head at that, appearing outright supine. "You're aware of who he is."

Wilder rolls his eyes. "Huh. And I thought you weren't one to mince words. Yet here you are, stating the obvious."

I stifle a grin at Wilder's and my parallel thoughts. But I sober and answer Rio, "He helped me and my … friend, Kaspian, out of a bad situation. And you know his name." I point at Wilder. "So you must know why we might be showing up at your doorstep."

Rio gives a single blink in answer.

"I want to talk to Clover," I clarify.

At last, a flare of emotion bursts through Rio's stone expression.

I wince.

It's the same one Wilder uses when he goes into alpha mode.

"Clover isn't accepting visitors." Rio shifts until his tall frame blocks the entrance.

"Is she sick?" I ask, infusing worry in my tone even though I'm certain he's full of shit.

Rio's eyes harden, and he takes a moment before responding. "That's none of your concern."

Wilder plants his feet beside me, too similar to a fighter shaking out his body before springing onto his opponent for my liking. "Are you going to make us force our way in?"

A hint of amusement tilts the corners of Rio's mouth. "I'd like to see you try."

Nope. Not doing this.

I cut in, positioning myself between Wilder and Rio. "We're not here to fight. I just want to talk to Clover."

Rio stares at me, his dark eyes boring into mine as if trying to peel back the bone of my skull and peer directly into my thoughts. I force myself to keep his gaze.

The seconds stretch out, the suspense tangible enough to

choke on. Wilder's body is a solid line of heat behind me, his muscles still taut with the urge to fight.

Finally, Rio's lips thin into a hard line.

"Wait here," he orders.

The door slams shut in our faces with a resounding bang.

"Well. I think he likes us," Wilder says.

I blow out a long, hard breath, staving back an anxiety attack at the thought of peeling bits of Wilder and Rio off the pretty courtyard.

"Do you think he'll actually let us see her?" I ask.

Wilder shrugs, his eyes fixed on the door. "Who knows. But we're not leaving until we get some answers."

Minutes drag by, each second stretching into an eternity. Just as my patience wears thin, the door creaks open.

Rio reappears, his expression even more foreboding than before.

"Follow me," he says, turning on his heel and striding into the mansion's depths without waiting to see if we'll comply.

Wilder circles my waist and holds me against him as we walk inside. His body language screams victory, but his tight hold on me shouts we're far from it.

But the contrast between the mansion's gritty exterior and the manor's lavish interior is staggering. I take in the high ceilings and rich woodwork of the entrance hall. My eyes catch an impressive array of framed photographs lining one wall—Clover at the center of most, which tells me all I need to know. She's the reason for the surprising warmth in this house of killers, even going so far as to lay out group photos of her arms slung around her men, or kissing the cheek of one while holding another at her side, or splayed on top of all of them on the couch, laughing freely and coaxing warm gazes from her partners, one even smiling down at her. With tattoos inked on his neck and covering the tips of his fingers, it has to be Professor Morgan.

If Sasha were here…

A smile stretches my lips wide. The elusive professor she wished more than anything would grant her sophomore wish, and I'm in his house.

Rio leads us down a long hallway to a large, open room at the back of the manor, a generous space filled with plush furniture in dark tones and pale marble floors.

On the far side near the fireplace, stands a woman. Her long black hair cascades down her back in wild waves, shining in the firelight. She's dressed in a black T-shirt and jeans but transcends the simple style with an exquisitely delicate face and liquid brown eyes that glint with copper from the flames.

And she's not alone.

Rossi stands beside her, his tall, muscled physique and stern, sinister expression hard to forget.

He wears a tailored suit, the fabric stretched over his broad frame.

Rossi watches us walk in with a guarded expression, his arm possessively wrapping around Clover's waist in a similar way to how Wilder keeps me close.

A knot forms in my throat, making each breath a conscious effort as we approach them. The sense of belonging between Clover and her men is almost palpable. It radiates, filling the room with an energy that's intimidating and fascinating to be around despite only just having met her.

I felt it when I spoke to Rossi the night he tended to Kaspian, cringed away from it when Rio directed his possessiveness over her at me, and I am now facing it head-on.

"You must be Elara," Clover greets in a light, friendly tone.

Wilder's grip on my waist tightens, his fingers digging into my skin through my coat.

"Elara. Wilder." Rossi's greeting is a low and reluctant, each syllable precise and measured. "I didn't expect to see you here."

Clover's copper-flecked eyes study me with unnerving intensity.

"We need your help," I say, my voice steadier than I feel.

Rossi's cheekbones cast knife-edge shadows over his face as he lowers his chin. "We've already involved ourselves more than we should have. Whatever trouble you've found yourself in, it's not our concern."

Wilder's fingers press into my hip, a silent warning to tread carefully and not to give too much of our situation away. But desperation propels me forward. "Please. It involves my brother's killers. And I think they're targeting women connected to the university, and Maverick got too close. Women like Clover and me."

Clover and Rossi exchange a loaded glance, an entire conversation seeming to pass between them. Rio shifts his weight behind us, his presence a hovering reminder of the precariousness of our position.

Clover faces me again, her features unreadable. "And what makes you think I can help?"

"You're practically an expert on Sarah Anderton lore. It has to do with her and what she left behind over three hundred years ago."

Rossi's stare digs into my thoughts. "We made ourselves clear the last time we met, Miss Wraithwood. You chose to deny our protection and continue your pursuit of the ruby. And now you come into my home and ask our woman to become involved in your pointless, reckless pursuit? Are you as mad as your moth—"

"Don't you dare," Wilder growls, heedless of Rossi having two decades of deadly accuracy over him. "Finish that sentence, and I don't care if I never walk out of here as long as I take you down with me."

Wilder says it with such lethal calm that I instinctively lean away, terrified that my simple request will cause these men to kill each other.

Clover swiftly intercedes.

"First of all," she says, holding up a finger, "your woman has a mind of her own. And second, Elara doesn't deserve your Mafia-level threats, Miguel."

Her voice carries a tone of command that shuts down any argument Rossi might have had ready on his lips.

"Well said," I manage.

If Clover knows anything about my reputation on campus, she's probably wondering how a girl like me, who prefers coffee dates and Meath House parties, became tangled in Sarah Anderton infamy and the legend of her blood jewel.

Clover, at least, has a whole witchy goth-girl vibe going. Me? I'm more out of place in this gory history than a lost kiwi bird.

"My brother believed in it," I say, speaking directly to Clover. "He believed Sarah possessed the ruby Heart and that it exists to this day. Maybe you think it's all folklore and fairy tales, but he didn't. He died for it."

My words hover in the air like a stalled guillotine blade.

Wilder squeezes me in warning. I'm saying too much.

"You're saying that the Heart has something to do with missing girls on campus?" Rossi asks, breaking the contemplative silence.

"Now, we said nothing about 'missing.'" Wilder tsks, and I'm reminded why he's such a valued member to the Sovereigns.

So they do know something. Rossi barely restrains a snarl at being caught out.

Clover seems to ponder my words for a moment.

"You must want answers badly to come here," she says.

"I do," I say simply. "I'll do anything to get them."

"Even risking your life?" Rio murmurs behind me.

He's standing far enough away, but it feels like his breath fans down my neck as he asks it.

"Even that."

My reply is immediate, absolute.

"This has become much too familiar." Rossi sighs and reluctantly releases Clover. "And a lot like someone I know and love."

Clover angles her head with a mischievous smile. "Sarah really vibes with the boss babes."

She happily moves out of Rossi's protective shield. Even as the pressure mounts, her elegance remains unscathed.

"It took a lot of stubbornness on my part, but my men understand that I decide what risks are worth taking," she says. Her look softens as it lands on me. "So let's leave these boys with their fangs for company and come chat with me about Sarah Anderton. Woman to woman."

She indicates for me to follow her. Wilder eyes her in half awe, half annoyance as she passes us. I have no choice but to trail in her wake, waving to Wilder and whispering, "Don't kill anybody while I'm gone," to which his annoyance is then directed at me.

When I turn back to Clover, she has her arm wound around the back of Rio's neck and his around her lower back as they kiss deeply. I correct my surprised stumble before it's noticed.

I peek at Rossi in my periphery to note his reaction, but he's busy keeping an eye on Wilder, who's inched closer to Rossi's desk. But there's no doubt he's fully aware of Rio and Clover's embrace despite not looking at them. These men don't miss much.

He simply doesn't mind that he has to share.

My attention moves to Wilder before I can stop it, and I immediately clash with his heated hazel eyes. His plans to peek at the papers on Rossi's desk have completely evaporated—his motives are solely on me. He tilts his head, including Rio and Clover in the intention swirling behind his arrogant, curious expression.

I give him a small, one-sided smile, letting him know I'm not disgusted or even confused. I understand Clover's situation. And I like it.

His stare turns ichorous in response, and I scoot out of the room as fast as I can, thankful that Clover's finished with her five-minute farewell to Rio and I can get out of there before

Wilder tears off my clothes and fucks me in front of all three of them.

Clover peers over her shoulder at me with a knowing grin as I cross the threshold, fully aware that we've left our men standing there in a state of … unease.

Wilder's gaze burns into my back as I leave.

Clover extends her hand and guides me up the staircase without waiting for me to respond, her fingers cool against my wrist. Her friendly affection fills me with anticipation, nerves, and a flicker of hope. Maybe Clover can help us in more ways than one, and I'll have time to ask her for advice on how to manage ticking time bombs for men.

As we cross into Clover's bedroom, I'm struck by the sense of intimacy that permeates the space. A grand four-poster bed takes center stage, draped in deep crimson and black silk sheets—large enough to accommodate more than just two.

In one corner stands a mahogany desk cluttered with an array of tarot cards and crystals. Against the adjacent wall, filled shelves overburdened with aging texts bear testament to Clover's fascination with the history of Titan Falls and the occult.

I study the back of her head as she moves to an ornate high-backed chair near her private fireplace.

Does she know about the Cimmerian Court leaders and their sick obsession?

Clover gestures to a matching chair across from her.

"Sit," she urges. "We can talk here without any inter-ruption."

I lower into the plush cushion of the chair. It's soft, warm, and welcoming, completely unlike the reception the guys swore I'd receive if I visited the Vultures.

And I can't shake off Wilder's parting gaze. It was too intense, smoldering with something inky and fiery. To be wanted like that … the memory of it prickles like an unattended flame, licking at my insides. I take a deep breath to calm myself down.

Clover seems to sense my discomfort. "You have to talk to them."

"What?" I blink at her.

"Your men," she clarifies, resting her elbow on the armrest, her chin on her folded fingers. "Right now, they're sharks circling your bloodied waters. You need to make them see you as their companion, not their meal." Her eyes take on a wistful glint as she adds, "Trust me, it took time for me, too."

"I don't—" I stammer, thrown off by her bluntness. But should I expect anything else from Clover Callahan?

Back when I used to hang out with a bunch of friends, the girls talked about her all the time. How Clover was more strange than popular, preferred black to school colors, and managed to score four of the hottest men on campus. And as soon as she did, two left their full-time positions so they could live with her.

"How does she cast such a spell?" I remember them wailing. "Chaos magic fueled by daddy issues? An unholy alliance with the god of morning wood?"

"They might be complicated," Clover continues, unperturbed by the thoughts that I'm positive are all over my face.

She rises to pull out a hefty bottle of whiskey from under her desk. It glints in the warm light of the room as she pours two generous measures, the scent of rich, aged liquor settling with the smell of burning wood from the fire. "But so are you."

"That's me," I say, perching on the edge of my chair as she hands me a glass. I stare into its amber depths, observing my gold-hued face mirrored back at me. "Complex and steeped in danger."

Clover laughs, easy and intimate. "You'd have to be, to grab their attention. And if you've also sold your soul to the god of morning wood, all the better."

I gape at her, now certain she can read minds. She stares back innocently.

"How did you know?" I manage to ask. This is as close as

I've gotten to openly admitting I'm falling for them. "That I'm into more than one guy?"

"As much as they refuse comparisons to their title, my guys really do chatter like birds," Clover says. "My brother, Tempest, was the first to notice since he was following you for a while."

Gripping my glass tighter, I take a deep sip, then try not to cough at the burn. "It's not easy being involved with one possessive man. Let alone four."

A wry smile plays on her lips, though there's an edge to it—a hint of battles fought and won. "You have to be sure about who you are and what you want. Establish boundaries and stick to them, even when they push. Especially when they push."

"But they must fight against those boundaries all the time?" I probe.

She nods sagely, swirling her whiskey in thought. "They do."

Clover raises her eyes to mine, their sparkling amusement giving away how much she loves it when they try.

We share a smile, and I take a moment to absorb Clover's words, the whiskey warming my throat and spreading into my bloodstream.

"I want to be with them," I confess. "But I'm afraid of losing myself in the process."

"You won't lose yourself. They'll always push, Elara. It's in their nature. But you have to know when to push back and stand your ground. They respect strength, even if they don't always like it."

I set my empty glass aside. My thoughts drift to Wilder and the sheer intensity of his presence, regardless of his mood. And Cav's chilling desire, Kaspian's deliberate crossing of moral boundaries, Axe's haunted, visceral touch.

Clover seems to read my thoughts. Again. "You have to maintain your own identity, your own desires."

I fight the urge to cough as anxiety tightens my windpipe. "And if my desires align with theirs?"

A slow smile spreads across Clover's face. "Then you embrace it. You revel in it. But you never let it define you."

She leans forward, her elbows resting on her knees. "These men, they're not just lovers. They're protectors, guardians. They'll kill for you, die for you. But they'll also try to control you, to keep you safe at all costs. You have to be willing to fight for your independence, even as you surrender to their obsession."

I let her words sink in, my heart racing at the implications. I know she's right. I've seen the way Wilder looks at me, the way his body tenses when I'm in danger. I've felt the way Cav and Kaspian watch me, like they're just as likely to kill me as they are to fuck me. And there's Axe's barely restrained triggers, unleashed when he gets near me.

"I want that," I say, my voice steady despite the nerves fluttering in my stomach. "I want to be that force."

Clover's eyes sparkle with approval. "Then let's make it happen."

She leans back in her chair. "But first, you have a mystery to solve. Tell me everything."

So I do. I explain to Clover about my brother, the circumstances of his death, and the cursed legacy Maverick dug up that he connected to the Sovereigns of the Cimmerian Court and the ruby Heart Sarah Anderton left behind in an undisclosed location before her death.

Clover listens so intently that I go into how each of the guys —Axe, Cav, Wilder, Kaspian—have a strange, horrible connection to the missing gem, and that its supposed "curse" started when Sarah Anderton was accused of being a witch and killed. I even explain my fear that if I don't find it before the Sovereigns do, Wilder and everyone else will continue to be tortured, brutalized, and sacrificed for the Sovereigns' false deity with very real consequences.

"And that's why I'm here," I finish with tremors in my voice. My throat is raw from talking, from baring my soul and the burdens I've been carrying. "I thought maybe you could shed some light on Sarah Anderton and why she'd have a ruby of that size and where she might have hidden it."

Clover's eyes are wide, her lips parted as she takes it all in.

"Damn," she says finally, her voice softer than I've ever heard it. She shakes her head slightly, as if to clear away the fog of information. "I knew you were wrapped up in some shady stuff, but this..."

Inwardly, I wince. It sounds like something out of a horror novel when said out loud. I look down at my hands clasped tightly together in my lap.

"We told Cav the Heart doesn't exist," Clover adds suddenly. "We even provided him proof last year to take back to his bosses —the Sovereigns. Of course he didn't listen." She huffs out a breath. "Now he's roped you into a mystery that is not a mystery. We solved it, Elara. I can't go into details, but Sarah ... Sarah never had a treasure. Not in jewels, anyway."

I stare at her, the words bouncing around in my head. She must be mistaken. "But Maverick—"

"Maverick was misled," Clover says gently, sympathy in her voice. "By the Sovereigns, I'd bet. You see, there is a treasure of sorts..." She trails off, her gaze conflicted.

"What is it?" I ask.

"Sarah's true treasure was knowledge," she finally says. "Her grimoire—her spells, potions, and ... remedies."

The last word is spoken with a hint of agitation like Clover isn't telling me the whole truth.

"My brother didn't die for a book," I say flatly.

"No," Clover agrees, shaking her head to sort through her thoughts. "I'm saying you're chasing the wrong thing."

She pauses, letting her words settle before continuing. "Sarah Anderton was a healer, but she was also an incredible strategist. The 'ruby Heart' might not be a real gem, but a metaphor. A symbol for something else."

"What could that possibly be?" I press.

Clover shrugs casually as though we were debating a professor's lecture rather than matters of life and death. "That's for you to discover."

Rage hits my cheeks hard. The blood under my skin grows hotter than the fire warming its surface. I liked this girl. I really thought we could form a friendship from our commonalities, our outsider-ness.

But I love the men in my life more.

In a single, sharp move, I yank the amulet from around my neck and throw it at her face.

CHAPTER 26

ELARA

Clover recoils. She throws her hands up in defense as the amulet lands in her lap.

"How do you explain this?" I ask.

Too late, I realize any squeak of distress from Clover would've brought the door down, the Vultures crashing in to defend her while they take my head as a trophy.

Then again, my Court members surround me in the same way. Wilder is nearby, lingering near the door just as Rossi and Rio likely are, but he's not the only one I can call on. Kaspian would've discovered a way to sneak in undetected by now, Cav will be circling the perimeter, and Axe will be positioned somewhere near a window to keep an eye on me, any of them able to intercept if needed.

I'm not so naive as to think they would've stayed back at the manor. Injured beasts become even more feral when they bleed.

Thankfully, none of my thoughts are put to the test. Clover's eyes flick from me to the amulet, widening as she takes in the sight of the twinkling ruby nested in the grotesque metal.

"This is half of the ruby Heart," I say, pointing at it for further effect. "Do you see the jagged edges, how they're sharp and fresh? Maverick broke it in an attempt to save me." The pain of my brother's name burns, but I swallow it down. "He said the other piece is still in Sarah's vault. He was in the midst of compiling all the documents he found to use against the Sovereigns and stop them before—before he died."

A silence stretches between us, broken only by the crackling fire in the hearth. The glow from the fire casts dancing light on Clover's face, highlighting her sharp cheekbones and furrowed brow. The ruby gleams.

Her fingers hover over the necklace, but she doesn't touch it. She whispers, "This changes things."

My heart stutters at her words. Maybe I've cracked through her skepticism.

I forge on. "My brother wanted to keep the pieces forever separate so the Sovereigns could never have it whole. Or maybe just to buy himself time to collect every piece of evidence he could before they made their ultimate move. The Sovereigns' entire plan of summoning this supposed Exalted Regent of theirs depends on the ruby being whole."

I shake my head in complete disbelief that I have to stop three grown men from initiating a murderous séance. "Setting aside the fact they think they can summon a fucking demon, I don't think Maverick had the right idea. Frankly, I don't care if the Sovereigns get the whole Heart. There's no demon to summon—they don't exist. What I do care about, what terrifies me, is the Sovereigns' utter dedication to mutilating their members and sacrificing girls in fucked-up rituals for this overlord of theirs."

And Maverick's fear that if they ever possessed the entire ruby, they would go after me.

She withdraws her hand, curling it into a fist as she looks up at me, her eyes obscured by the play of dark and light on her face.

Clover stands abruptly, the ruby tumbling from her lap onto the plush carpet. The firelight catches the jewel's facets, scattering crimson glints across the room.

Clover begins to pace. "This is bad. This is really bad. What did you say the name of this demon was? Exalted Regent?"

I stare at her sidelong and ask slowly, "Does it matter? There's no such demon."

"If what you say is true, then we need to act fast," Clover says, ignoring my pragmatism. "The dark arts should never, can never, be messed with."

Closing my eyes, I take a deep, quenching breath, recalling the tarot cards on her shelf, the crystals, and the Wiccan almanacs piled on her shelves.

She believes in this stuff.

Clover strides to her desk, throwing her hair up into a messy bun. As she does so, she reveals a small tattoo at the base of her neck—a vulture in flight. She pulls open a desk drawer and slips on white cotton gloves. I push to my feet, not bothering to hide my curiosity as I join her.

Clover carefully flips open a large ornate book, the motion carrying the most disgusting smell into my nostrils. I turn around and retch, then gulp some deep breaths before I turn back around and meet Clover's wisened, but amused smile.

"To this day, I have no idea where that smell comes from or why it's so potent after centuries," she says.

"Wait." The hand I was using to massage my throat freezes. "Is that what I think it is?"

"Sarah's grimoire," Clover supplies without looking up. "It was given to me last year. To say it changed my life is an understatement. It's written by both Sarah and Li—her nameless daughter. If you can stomach it, take a look."

Clover twists the book to face me. After a few choked breaths, I get my gag reflex under control and read the page Clover has open.

Intricate drawings, the ink faded but the designs made timeless, showcase jewelry of all shapes and sizes, recorded with such precision that I forget about the smell emanating from the page. "Are those…?"

"Jewelry Sarah was allegedly paid in? Yes. Her daughter inventoried every piece. We assumed the pieces were theoretical, or codes for the transfer of something entirely different from actual priceless gemstones." Clover slides her attention to where the amulet rests on the floor. With her features crystallizing into diamond-hard resolve, she turns back to the grimoire and flips the pages until she finds what she's looking for, her white-gloved finger landing on—

"The Heart." I gasp. "And it's in full."

Behind that page is a small gap of space before the thick, yellowed paper continues. Angling my vision, I notice pieces of pulp clinging to the glue on the spine—pages ripped from this historical book.

I reach for the grimoire with both hands before I stop myself, fingers splayed in midair.

But it's not respect for Clover's clear, gentle handling of the book that prevents me from grabbing it with my bare hands. It was purely instinctual. I don't want to touch it. It's one of the last things Maverick held when he ripped out Sarah's confession on where the Heart was locked away.

I don't want to touch this thing.

Yet my eyes eat it up. Maverick decided to preserve this drawing. The amulet is perfectly detailed, from the shading of the dark and light to the uncut angles. The full ruby.

"This is what it looked like before Maverick broke it," I breathe.

"Read what's written below," Clover says.

I do as she says, noticing the small, flourished script, written in the days when handwriting was considered elite.

"'Paid to the Anderton house,'" Clover says without bothering to read upside-down. She's memorized it. "'A ruby whose circumference is the largest we've seen. Its inner glow screams with power, a touch of the unearthly caught within its flaming heart. Beware its allure, for even in our possession, it seeks its rightful master.'"

Skeletal hands caress my shoulders. The idea that a ruby has mystical powers is laughable, but there's something in the way those words are penned that makes me jumpy.

"I never thought much of the written descriptions below the jewels after we recovered the Anderton treasure," Clover continues, almost to herself. "But you've successfully turned the Vultures' and my theory right on its head."

"Tempest mentioned finding the treasure, too," I murmur, raising my eyes from the book to Clover. "Both of you clam up as soon as you're asked to describe it, though."

"That's because, if we made what it truly is public, we'd tank Titan Falls tourism, the founding families' reputations, and ruin a lot of lives, not to mention history. People were killed to keep it a secret, and there are those that will still murder to keep it from coming out."

I point at the amulet. "Kind of like that thing?"

Clover blows out a breath. "Yes. Sarah Anderton is the gift that keeps on giving. I thought all this ended when I uncovered her daughter's name."

I gape at her. "You know that, too?"

Clover nods. "Don't ask me to tell you. I can't. It falls under the horror I just listed. Part of Titan Falls' appeal is its history, the idea that a priceless treasure is hidden away somewhere, and a woman and her daughter were persecuted for it. Finding out her name is part of that draw and part of what keeps many powerful people in the Titan Falls hierarchy. It's not worth upending. Believe me."

Her expression grows so somber, I'm led to believe Clover experienced certain atrocities herself when she became involved in the Vultures and sought to reveal the true history of the Andertons, like so many who tried and failed before her.

Yet she succeeded.

My voice drops to a whisper. "I'm related to her."

"What?"

A lightning storm of copper bursts in Clover's eyes.

I gulp. "There's a high likelihood that I'm a descendant of the Anderton line."

Clover shakes her head as if flinging away the insane thought, but she doesn't outright dismiss what I've said.

A part of me wishes she would just laugh in my face and negate my fears.

For a moment, she's so dumbfounded that she can't speak. Then, with a suspicious lightness to her tone, she asks, "How do you figure that?"

"Cavanaugh Nightshade's ancestors are the ones who accused Sarah and put her to death. She vocally cursed the Nightshades while she was tortured, and Cav believes the curse is real. His entire family line went through their lives, failing to battle this curse of theirs. But … me, Kaspian, Axe, and Wilder discovered a hidden altar room below Thornhaven, the Court members' Estate. Well, Maverick found it first, but…"

I pause, getting my breathing under control so I can stop rambling.

"Anyway, Maverick said the altar room is where Sarah died, where all these girls the former Sovereigns were taking were being sacrificed, too. I'm trying to find a link. It's why I've come to you, because Cav said the Nightshades took a baby from Sarah's arms. Her grandchild. And—sold her. That baby is where my family line comes from. I don't know if it's Wraithwood or Farrow or … I'm sorry. I'm rambling again."

Clover listens with a mixture of intrigue, pity, and concern. Every emotion flits across her cheeks, the corners of her mouth, the quirk of her brows.

Until they smooth, and she looks at me anew, as though I'm on her team, suddenly privy to a secret that sets us both apart from the rest of the world.

She reaches across the table to place a hand over my own.

"I'd like to show you something else," she says softly.

Clover lifts her gloved hand from mine, reaching into

another compartment in her desk and pulling out a cracked, leather-clad notebook.

"I found this during my search last year." Again, she finds the page she wants and spins the open book so I can read it. "Do you see the names?"

Bending closer, I read:

Lilium - Keeper of Secrets

Nightshade – The Guardian

Marigold - The Seafarer

Bluebell - The Quill

Rosemary - The Shade

Lavender - The Hearth

Sage - The Stablemaster

Jonquil - The Lexicon

Primrose - The Purse

Foxglove - The Watcher

Sweet William - The Emissary

Hawthorn - The Physic

Cowslip - The Masquerade

Snowdrop - The Frost

Daffodil - The Mason

Thistle - The Engineer

At first, I think Clover's shown me a list of herbal and floral ingredients Sarah probably used for her alchemy, which doesn't concern me. Sarah was considered the town healer before being branded a witch.

I'm glancing up to say as much when my eyes snag on a name. Jonquil.

I let out a shaky breath, pointing. "Jonquil. I know that name. I found William Jonquil's old office in my grandmother's manor. I think he's a great-grandfather of mine."

Clover hums in thought. "I was hoping you wouldn't recognize any of the names."

I look up at her then. "Why?"

"Because then your theory about being a descendant has merit, and I worry for anyone who's forced to become involved in the truth of the Andertons."

"That's nothing new," I reply tiredly. "As soon as I figured out my boyfriends fully believe in a witch's curse that includes a demon being summoned, I started worrying about my well-being."

Abruptly, I press my lips shut.

I don't know what's more galling: the fact that I so easily said boyfriends or that my life now includes curses, violence, and bloodshed.

Despite the gravity of our conversation, Clover laughs, and I share in it.

We both sober as we return to the books splayed in front of us.

"These names," Clover says, "were part of Sarah's underground network. These people helped her with her cause. That's why I'm shocked to learn the Nightshades betrayed her. I always knew Cav was a manipulative bastard, but to keep his family's betrayal a secret from us the entire time he helped to find the treasure…"

I'm unable to explain Cav's motives since I'm not quite sure of them myself.

I say, "His reasons are valid in his mind. His ancestors' destruction over the centuries and his solid belief that Sarah had something to do with it—Cav's poisoned. They've tortured him down to the marrow of his bones. I'm working like hell to rid him of it because I know who he is inside. He's not callous and evil."

I trail off, swallowing the lump that's formed in my throat, thinking about Cav. The pain he's endured, the horrors he's witnessed, are a vital part of him now. It makes him dangerous, unpredictable. But beneath that hardened exterior is a man who bears the weight of his family's sins. A man I've come to deeply care for despite what it could cost me.

Clover seems to read my thoughts, her eyes softening. "That's a heavy burden to carry for someone else, Elara."

"Isn't it what we're doing here?" I counter with a forced smile. "Carrying the burden of our ancestors' sins so we can set things right?"

She nods slowly, an appreciative smile tugging at the corners of her mouth. "You're a stronger woman than I gave you credit for."

My cheeks heat at her praise, but I quickly brush it off. The Elara I wanted to be, the one I molded myself into the minute I stepped foot on TFU campus, doesn't exist anymore, no matter how much I'd like to get that popular, social, ignorant girl back. "Turns out, I'm not just a pretty face."

"But why these men?" Clover asks abruptly. "Why Wilder, Cav, Kaspian, and Axe? Have you thought about why they were brought into the Cimmerian Court?"

"They're legacies," I supply. "Initiated because of their family lineage, dating all the way back to—"

"Oh my God." Clover gasps and turns the logbook of names clockwise. Her eyes flick up and down rapidly as she reads them over. "I'd thought the flowers were all code names Sarah used to protect her agents. Nightshade and Jonquil weren't disguised for reasons I've yet to figure out. But the others ... do you think some of these flowers could be your boyfriends' families?"

"Boyfriends," I echo, the word still sitting clumsily on my tongue. "That's a possibility..."

"These men aren't just legacies," Clover interjects, flipping through the pages with a fervor. "They could also be descendants of Sarah's allies."

The truth crashes over me, leaving me cold and shaken. If Clover's right, then that means...

"Then it isn't just me. They're all linked to Sarah, too."

A pang of fear settles in my heart as I consider what this could mean for us — for Cav, Kaspian, Wilder, and Axe. Our relationships are complex enough as it is, without the added pressure of a shared destiny.

"We need to find out for sure," Clover announces, lowering and getting comfortable on her desk chair. "Same with your lineage. Sarah's daughter was young, but not so young she couldn't have had a baby. I always had a feeling the Anderton lore went a lot deeper. There's nothing better than a good, witchy mystery…"

As Clover begins to delve into the historical records that clutter her desk, I look down, toward the broken Heart tangled in its chains. The fire gives it a sinister pulse, like it's imbued with centuries of blood.

I picture the faces of the men I've come to adore. Their peculiar smiles, their eyes in various stages of bleakness. They were taken in by the Court so young, their humanity stripped bare until glorious, honed weapons took their place.

Cav, with his eerie handsomeness and uncut sapphire eyes that see too much, yet reveal so little. Kaspian, whose beauty almost hurts to look at and whose mind is equal parts supernova and black hole. Wilder, the embodiment of raw power and bottled rage, who seems untamed, yet harbors a gentleness that touches my very soul; and Axe, his scars a timeline of his tumultuous past—cruel, blurred, and troubled.

Each name represents a life lived under the burden of past sins, profound secrets, and undeniable attraction.

Each name is now inexorably linked with mine.

CHAPTER 27
ELARA

Wilder drops me off at Farrow Manor after a solemn ride in his car.

When I left Clover's room and returned to him downstairs, he must've seen something on my face, because he didn't drag me out of the Vultures' home and insist I tell him everything. I was expecting Wilder to go so far as to lock all the doors in the SUV and refuse to let me out until I gave up every reason I wanted to meet and talk with Clover.

Wilder did none of those things.

He opened the passenger door, giving my arm a squeeze before I slid in. Then he started the car and swerved off, his face a blank canvas.

The second he pulls up to the manor, I twist toward him in my seat, unable to take it anymore. "Why haven't you asked what happened with Clover?"

Wilder doesn't face me when he answers, choosing to keep staring ahead. "Did you want me to?"

"What kind of answer is that?" I pause, using the moment to study his profile. "Did something go on between you, Rio, and Rossi to make you go quiet?"

The corner of his mouth tics as he fights off a smile. "The

only thing I did in their presence was breathe, and that's only because I have to."

His answer is curt, a typical Wilder response. But beneath it, I detect a tenderness, a refrain that's more protective than dismissive.

My gaze ricochets between his stoic profile and my family mansion, casting deep shadows over us despite the bright morning sun. I want to tell Wilder everything, as well as the others. I'd love to be with them with the sun over our heads instead of constant dark clouds.

But the truth is like acid on my tongue, the unspoken words clawing at the back of my throat.

"Danger," I confess quietly, finally breaking the silence. Wilder's focus shoots to me briefly before returning to the mansion's imposing facade. "It seems like danger is following me and always has its eyes set on the people around me."

"I know," he says simply but not unkindly. "But if you start calling it a curse, I may have to keep you and Cav separated."

It was meant as a joke, but it doesn't land. I press my lips together.

Wilder exhales heavily, turning his gaze from the manor to mine. Despite the lurking misery in his hazel eyes, there is an undeniable warmth there, too.

"I won't make the same mistake twice," he says.

I furrow my brows at him, confused.

"Teagan," he supplies.

My forehead smooths with realization.

"I ignored the signs with Tea. In the end, it cost her everything."

He swallows hard, his Adam's apple bobbing with the motion.

"You're not responsible for that," I tell him. "We're not repeating history, Wilder. You're not the same ignorant initiate you were back then."

He fixes me with a pained stare. "But I am responsible for you. We all are—in one way or another."

"I am not Teagan," I say quietly. "My innocence is gone. I'm fully aware of what the Sovereigns are."

Wilder's features lock down, disagreement clear but unvoiced. Instead, he reaches over and brushes a wisp of hair out of my face. His touch lingers on my cheek before pulling back.

"You should get inside. The guys and I will join you shortly. We have to—go."

The way he stalls on go makes me freeze with my hand halfway to the door handle. "Go where?"

Weariness drags at his eyes as his hands fuse to the steering wheel. "We still have our duties. The Sovereigns don't know where we are, but if we stop following their orders altogether, there will be trouble for our living relatives. So we play our roles from afar."

Ice, chilling and painful, fills my stomach. "What does that mean? I thought you guys were ignoring their summons altogether."

He flexes his fingers. "We need more time. Always more fucking time. Doing this for them, going after their blackmail targets, people who've crossed the Sovereigns in some way and forced to do their bidding, will buy us more. They have to be kept in line."

Before I can voice any protests, he's opening his door and stepping out.

I watch him round the car and open the passenger door.

His hand extends toward me, the movement just shy of a command. But I take it, facing him as soon as I step onto the old stone pathway, but Wilder's already moving to return to his side of the car.

"Promise me something," I state.

He stills without answering.

"Promise me you won't let them manipulate you into doing

something that will break you into pieces I won't be able to fit back together."

He levels his gaze on mine over the SUV's hood, his irises swirling with honey and earth tones and swallowing the sunlight beaming on them.

A beat passes before he speaks again.

"I can't promise that." He yanks on the driver's door. "Because I would do anything for you."

And his words—those deadly, beautiful words—are a dagger in my chest. I watch him slide back into the driver's seat and shut the door with a resounding slam before he roars off.

I let my head fall back, willing the sun to dry any tears that try to escape my closed eyes, then turn and trek inside.

The smell hits me almost immediately.

I follow the scent with a wrinkled nose, deftly avoiding all signs of my mother's evil genius, until I reach the grand, unused living room and spot the figure lounging on the Queen Victorian couch, one leg raised in the air.

"Sasha?" I creep in cautiously, stepping over the white sheets she's cast aside that were acting as dust covers for the furniture.

"Hello!" Sasha turns her head and grins at me.

"What are you doing? Is your leg okay?"

"My leg is operating as an exclamation point to my hello!"

I blink at her, trying to make sense of her words even as I take in the sight of her languishing with an open bag of gummy worms on her stomach. "You're stoned."

"Fuck yes. It's not like we're in the best situation right now. Might as well enjoy a good high."

She waves her leg in a last salute before lowering it.

I can't stop a genuine laugh from escaping at the sight of her.

"You should try it sometime," she says.

Sasha's eyes are glazed over, and she has this soft smile on her face that almost makes me want to agree with her.

Almost.

"No thanks," I murmur.

I glance around the room, and my gaze falls upon a photo frame settled on one corner of the ornately carved fireplace mantel. The sweet smiles of my innocent youth greet me from behind the glass—me hugging Mom, and Maverick on the other side, all of us smiling too brightly.

Seeing Maverick's younger self brings that familiar flutter of warmth and the ache of absence in equal measures.

My attention moves to the picture next to it: Mom and Dad's wedding day.

They looked so happy. Dad, with his wide smile and twinkling eyes, his arm wrapped around Mom's waist as if he would never let her go. And Mom, radiant in her simple white dress, her cheeks flushed with joy and awe at who she gets to marry.

The raw emotion captured in that photo slices through me like a knife, and for a moment I let myself sink back into the memory of happier times. I can almost imagine what their laughter would've been like that day, weaving through the now plagued halls of our family home.

It's odd how quick laughter can turn to tears when you realize everything's a lie.

"Hey," Sasha prods softly, jolting me out of my thoughts. Her smile fades as she sits up, replaced by a look of concern. "You okay?"

"I'm fine," I lie.

She doesn't buy it, but doesn't push either. Instead, she pats the spot next to her on the couch. "Come here."

I sit beside her, avoiding the half-eaten bag of gummies teetering precariously on her stomach. She wraps an arm around my shoulders, pulling me into a side hug.

"You don't have to be a bad bitch all the time, Elara," she says quietly. "It's okay to be scared."

A lump forms in my throat, and I blink back tears. My voice is barely a sound when I finally admit, "I'm terrified."

My family looks so happy up there on the mantel, innocent even. It feels like centuries ago, a completely different life.

"We'll figure this out, El," Sasha says, her voice solid and confident.

The strength of her words is soothing, but it only goes so far in suppressing my fears, the worrisome thoughts forever nipping at the edges of my mind.

A tear seeps from the corner of my eye, trailing down my cheek before I brush it away and slip out of her embrace.

"I need to shower and change. I'll come back down when I'm done."

She doesn't argue, simply nods and goes back to her bag of gummies with a serene expression that only pot could produce.

With one last wave, I make my way toward the grand staircase leading up but pause at the base, looking back at her.

"Hey," I say softly, "don't think about going anywhere tonight."

Sasha snorts a laugh but relents easily enough when she sees my serious expression.

"I'll load up Netflix," she declares before dangling another worm near her mouth. "Go find your comfiest loungewear."

Retreating to the comfort of my room, I find myself unable to push away the gnawing sense of dread that's been clinging to me ever since my conversation in Wilder's car. The memory of him saying those words—because I'd do anything for you—sounds too much like what I'd do for him, for all of them, and that ignites a precarious hope within my heart.

The truth is, the devastating allure of Wilder and Cav, Axe and Kaspian, their inescapable mix of aggression and desire, is a dangerous cocktail I've willingly sipped from. The heady effect it has on me is a terrifying kind of exhilaration that leaves me vulnerable, and that's exactly why I haven't told them about Maverick's last message.

That the Sovereigns want the blood of Sarah Anderton, too.

Me.

"They want to use me as a sacrifice," I say to myself,

watching the words disperse into nothingness as if they were made of smoke.

What would Wilder say? Cav? Kaspian? Axe?

Would they be shocked? Angry? Would they fight for me, or would the revelation change everything between us? They want nothing more than to be rid of the Sovereigns, but I'm not certain if their pursuit of the Heart and the downfall of the Sovereigns is truly about liberation … or just another manifestation of their hunger for power and control.

Fear, shaped like sharp thorns on vines, wraps around my heart at the thought.

Naked, under the hot spray of the shower, I yield to the memory of our stolen moments as visceral torment threats to swallow me whole.

Possessive touches, sinful whispers, strategic moves, all of them burning with a fire only for me. The heat between us is palpable, undeniable.

Yet their motivations remain shrouded in mystery as thick as the steam engulfing me.

I stay under the hot water far longer than necessary, hoping its scalding embrace might wash away my doubts and fears and cleanse me of my uncomfortable thoughts.

Finishing my shower in silence, the warmth of the water does nothing to chase away the frost coating my bones. After drying off, I pull on a pair of black leggings, an oversized shirt, and a blue hoodie, where I stash the ruby locket in its front pocket. It doesn't feel right to wear it anymore.

Downstairs, I find Sasha sprawled across the couch again, her cheek resting against one of the red velvet cushions as she snores. A bag of chips has replaced her previous snack.

I tiptoe around her sleeping figure to grab a blanket from an adjacent chair before draping it over her. She shifts but doesn't wake, a soft mumble escaping her lips. I watch her for a moment, overcome by a rush of affection for my best friend.

I can't put her at risk. Not Sasha, not the guys.

Staring down at my friend, I confront the terrifying facts.

I'm an innocent sacrifice for a power-hungry secret society. It's absurd. Grotesque, even.

Elara Wraithwood is the final descendant of a feared healer, accused witch, and suspected assassin from centuries ago.

If anyone had told me that the tales uttered in hushed tones about Sarah Anderton were true, that her blood ran in my veins, that I was destined to be a sacrifice for the Cimmerian Court's relentless pursuit to unleash a demon, I would've laughed it off as one fucked-up joke.

But reality doesn't take jokes lightly, and it certainly doesn't allow escape from its iron clutches.

Would it be selfish to shatter Sasha's peaceful reality? Could I even bear to watch the light dim from her eyes when she learns that the men she's begun to trust are entangled in a plot that could very well cost me my life?

"No," I breathe softly, feeling a boulder lodge itself in my throat. "No, she can't know."

I can't let her know.

I can't let the guys know.

Not until I have more information and understand what my brother tried to stop.

Sasha's left the TV on, and I nestle beside her curled-up legs, choosing an old rom-com to watch. Sasha had the right idea of skipping afternoon classes. Acting normal seems like a far-off goal these days.

I'm halfway to a nap when I hear a noise on the other side of the wall in the foyer.

Footsteps.

Fright doesn't hit me, not in the fortress Mom's built, but curiosity does.

I lean into Sasha's body, peering into the open archway in time to see Axe navigating the flooring in the way I taught him, a 3-2-1 step process that will bring him into this room unscathed.

"Hey," I greet.

Axe stiffens in surprise, glancing over.

I frown. Axe doesn't startle easily.

Slipping out of the blanket I decided Sasha could share, I pad closer to his still form. "Axe? You okay?"

He shoves his hands in his pockets. "Yes."

I press my lips together and give a single nod because that's the most I'll get out of him in terms of how he's feeling. "Where are the others?"

"Others?"

"Kaspian, Wilder, Cav. Wilder said you guys had a job and would be back soon." I check the grandfather clock at the top of the stairs. "That went a lot faster than I thought."

"Oh. I didn't go with them."

This time, my brows pull together and accompany my frown. "No? I thought you four did everything together. Why didn't you go?"

"Not everything."

He says it in such a low tone, such defeat, that I move closer. "Axe?"

Axe's gaze is remote, as if he's looking past me and into aspects of his fractured memories I can't begin to fathom.

"I—" he starts, then snaps his mouth shut as if biting back an unpleasant confession.

It's rare for Axe to let his guard down, and it's rarer still for him to reveal any semblance of vulnerability. I reach out, brushing my fingers against the rough skin of his hands. Axe grimaces at the contact but doesn't pull away.

A flicker of strain passes over his control as he levels a laden look at me.

"It's okay," I say, hoping to reassure him even as unease puts pressure on my heart. "You don't have to tell me if you don't want to."

Without another word, Axe covers my mouth with his,

desperate and demanding. The shock of it reverberates through me as he backs me up against the wall.

I try to protest, but the softness of his lips, the urgency of his tongue, and the sharp bite of his teeth captures all of me, and I'm lost to him.

Axe grips my hips, holding me close as he deepens our kiss, his body heat singeing through my clothes.

His taste is addictive—fresh air and sea salt. My sighs linger in the air as our lips move together, seeking an unbreakable connection.

Axe presses his groin into my stomach, hard and demanding. My fingers tangle in his hair, and I return his kiss with just as much fervor.

Sasha's still sleeping on the couch around the corner. If she woke up and decided to inspect the strange sounds, we'd be caught and I'd be embarrassed, but I can't bring myself to pull away from him. Axe's touch kindles an inferno that burns away all thoughts of caution and reason.

He trails his lips down my jawline to my neck, dragging his teeth over my skin before pressing his hot tongue against it. My pulse flutters, trapped under his teeth as he groans against it, satisfied with my response.

Axe's hands roam lower, tracing slow circles around my hips before moving to my thighs. Every brush of his hand sets off seismic shifts through my body, and I'm getting wetter by the second, soaking through my leggings.

The fleeting thought that we should go upstairs is soon swept away as Axe's hot mouth travels lower, kissing along my collarbone and down to the swell of my breasts. He pulls my hoodie and shirt over my head, discarding it carelessly on the floor. His lips trail fire across my bare skin to the lace-edged bra I'd worn, as if I'd sensed that at least one of them would strip me again today, even if my brain hadn't caught up yet.

Axe kneads my breasts through my bra, his thumbs brushing over my stiffened nipples. The sensation shoots straight through me, and I can't hold back a gasp. He looks into my eyes at the sound.

"More," he growls, sending a delicious flutter down my spine.

His voice is dark and gravelly, edged with a desperation that's like a raw, open wound. His low command paints my skin with invisible brushstrokes of liquid fire, pooling between my legs in a sweet, throbbing ache.

Axe lowers his mouth to one hardened nipple, sucking it through the mesh fabric. I moan, curving into him and digging my fingers into his shoulders. He unclasps the hook of my bra with a swift motion, letting it fall away.

"Axe," I gasp as he hooks one of my legs around his waist.

"Hate this," he mutters, tearing at the fabric of my leggings with unbelievable ease. His fingers brush against the heat of my center, and I whimper at the sudden contact. "Hate how they make you feel like you're less than them." He pulls back to look into my eyes—those piercing gray storm clouds voltaic with defiance and agonizing need.

"No..." I breathe out, shaking my head, desire churning in my throat and thickening my voice. "You're not less than anyone. You're more."

Axe studies me as I say it, something like guilt churning in the depths of his hurricane eyes. But his ruthless vulnerability, his ferocity and tenderness, all intertwine until my heart aches with the sheer beauty of him.

He slides what's left of my leggings down, bunching them along with the slick fabric of my underwear around one ankle.

I'm left bare to him. And even though I've been on this precipice with Axe and the others before, each time feels so different. So much more vital and profound.

His fingers tease along my folds, finding me drenched for him. A shudder weakens my knees at his touch. It's like he knows just what to do to unravel me completely. The pad of his thumb presses against my clit, and I whimper.

The sound seems to fuel him. Axe's fingers slip inside, curling in just the right way that makes my back arch off the wall.

A groan rumbles from his chest, resonating as though he were a seismic force and I the ground beneath him, shaking from the tremor. Then he withdraws his fingers and brings them to his lips, tasting me on them and watching for my reaction.

"Delicious," he murmurs.

I bite my lip.

His pupils dilate.

I reach out to him then, my hand sliding over the rough terrain of his scarred back through his shirt, feeling it tense under my touch.

"I want you," I whisper.

My body is burning for him, yearning for him.

Desperate.

I reach down to grip his hard length over his jeans. Axe's breath stutters and he presses into my hand, seeking friction.

He pushes two fingers inside me then, pumping slowly while his thumb continues to circle my clit with a torturous pace that has me writhing. The exquisite pressure builds, a mounting crescendo that threatens to fracture.

"Please." I almost weep, raking my nails down his back through the thin layer of his shirt.

If I cause him pain, he wants it because he tortures me further by almost bringing me to climax, then backing off.

"Say it again," Axe orders, his voice tight and strangled.

Before I can, his lips crash onto mine in a heated frenzy, swallowing my half-formed words and whispers.

Axe releases a guttural sound into my mouth, then pushes away. His fingers cease their torment, leaving me gasping.

But his focus stays on me, drinking in my disheveled state— the flushed cheeks, the heaving chest, the parted lips.

"Elara." His voice is a ragged whisper, a plea. Perhaps a prayer.

He grinds against my hand, his own coming to rest over mine as he guides it under his pants so I can stroke him bare.

The friction is maddeningly delicious, both for him and for me.

"I need you," he rasps.

The heat between us is unabated, a wildfire racing across parched land.

I pull my hand out, fingers finding purchase in his shirt's fabric, tugging it free from his body.

Axe's muscular torso is carved from pale granite. Each line and ridge of muscle is pronounced under my touch. Each brutal scar forms an obvious ridge under my hands.

I trail my fingers over him in fascinated exploration, lightly tracing over the contours of his body, losing my breath when he mirrors my actions and does the same to me.

Axe keenly observes every response I give him. Then he frees himself, unbuttoning his jeans and pushing them down in a swift move.

Axe is bared—so undeniably him—and my heart lurches.

There's nothing gentle about the way he takes me then, hoisting me up against the wall with ease as if my weight means nothing to him.

I moan against his lips, lost as he pushes me harder against the wall. The cool surface bites into my back.

With one hand, he covers my mouth, pushing my head against the wall at the same time he slips his dick deep inside me. I gasp against his palm at the intrusion, feeling myself stretch around him as he begins to move in a brutal rhythm.

It feels good—too good—and it takes everything away except pure, pleasure-pain bliss.

Axe thrusts into me harder. There's no softness left in him now, just raw force, a man drowning in torture but choosing to die in ecstasy.

I endure every punishing thrust with a smothered gasp that feels like surrender.

His relentless pace drives us both toward an edge we're teetering on. I respond in kind, my body matching his rhythm as I cling to him for support, the wainscotting halfway up the wall digging painfully into my back.

Axe's climax detonates through his body, the power of it rippling through every muscle, every vein, until all that remains is what I can cling to. He's threadbare, but his fingers claw into my hips, holding on tight as he loses the rest of himself.

He stays entwined with me, slowing his pace. Axe's lips trail soft kisses along my neck, each one a silent confession etched into my skin.

Axe slides in and out of me with excruciating gentleness, his aching need now sated, replaced with an indescribable intimacy. One that goes beyond skin and bone to touch upon something ethereal.

I'm holding back tears, but my own release finally takes hold, shattering under the weight of his touch and observant gaze.

I erupt around him, my cries muffled under his hand, my nails digging into the strong sinews of his back and creating crescent indents over his scars.

I ride out the wave of him, lapping against the shore until, finally, everything is calm.

Axe removes his hand from my mouth and lifts me off the wall, striding down the hall with my legs wrapped around his hips and avoiding my mother's disguised hazards as if he's lived here for years. The entire time, we're kissing, our tongues stroking, his dick pulsing inside me.

Reluctantly, Axe releases my lips and lays me on the bed in the guest room, then swings onto the mattress until his body is heavy on mine.

As he gathers me into his arms, he buries his face in my hair, inhaling deeply.

I gently guide him away so I can look at him. Axe's eyes are soft, gray clouds breaking apart enough to reveal rare sunlight that casts its brightness over the furious cut down his face. Its warm rays are present in the way he traces circles on my skin and how he memorizes my face.

He looks at me like I'm one of Sarah's precious, rumored jewels that he's afraid will implode under the pressure of his touch. Yet his caress is far from delicate—it's filled with a rough longing that scrapes against my flesh, carving feelings into me I've only ever dreamed about.

I want to tell him everything, the looming, god-awful truth about the Sovereign's plans for me. The dread that eats at my insides, threatening to swallow me whole. But the look in his eyes, the way he cradles me closer into his embrace, warns me not to add to whatever is currently hurting him. Silencing him.

My fingers thread through his, and then, we're sleeping. Or at least he is.

Axe's breath tickles my nose as he drifts off, his chest rising and falling rhythmically against my sensitive nipples.

His ash-blond hair is an unkempt mess on the pillow, lips slightly open in deep sleep. He looks almost peaceful, like a boyish Axe who didn't have to endure torture, fight off abuse, and face neglect.

This is the Axe who just held me, loved me … and I drift off, too, cradled by the rhythmic beats of his heart and lulled by his warm, solid presence.

***

I wake up to the dimming light of dusk filtering through the windows. My head is on the pillow, but my body feels bereft—empty—and I soon realize why. Axe's side of the bed is cold. His scent lingers on the sheets, but he's no longer there. My hand reaches out, brushing along the cool cotton where he should be.

As my heart sinks deeper into my chest with the absence of him against my skin, it's like a part of me has vanished.

Been taken.

A pang of disappointment shoots through me. Did he leave to keep me safe? Or was it all too much?

Drawn by some peculiar instinct, I turn my head toward the plush couch in the room where Cav's tall frame is sprawled, his ebony hair an unruly haystack around his pensive, slumbering face.

Kaspian rests in a chair across from him, chestnut tendrils framing his handsome features and almost making him look innocent.

I look down, and Wilder's sleeping on the floor directly beside me, his face tilted in my direction as if he had to keep me in his horizon before he was forced to surrender to sleep.

It's unlike them to have resisted crawling into bed with Axe and me, taking their rightful positions, since I've been with all of them and care for them all the same.

Perhaps they sensed in Axe the same thing I did, a vulnerability that's desperate for consolation, one they can't provide, but that I have all too much of.

It's then I realize these men can do anything, kill anyone, and I'd probably forgive them. I'm too connected to them not to.

Sitting up, I give each of them a brief survey in the growing darkness, finding none of them worse for wear. Whatever job Wilder was talking about, they all got through it unscathed.

As for Axe's absence, I'll ask Wilder when he wakes up. Maybe Axe was never meant to go with them, but I'm wondering where it was he did go that gave him a heavier dose of torment than usual. And where Axe went now.

That leaves Sasha.

Slipping out of the covers, I tiptoe around Wilder, who grunts and grabs my ankle as I try to step around him. I swallow down a yelp at the feel of his calloused palm and look down, expecting alert, glimmering eyes to be staring right at me.

But no. They're firmly shut, but he's brought my ankle to his lips and bared his teeth, nipping at it and grinning in his sleep.

I tug my limb away, though the feel of his mouth lingers on my skin.

His hand drops onto the floor, his body contorting as he lets out a low groan before resuming his restless slumber.

Heart hammering in my chest, I glance at the men one last time, confirming they're still asleep before sneaking out of the room and into the corridor, though I can feel, rather than see, Kaspian's slitted eyes following my every naked move.

Walking through one of the archways, I take in Sasha's makeshift bed on the living room sofa. It appears she's slept all afternoon and into the evening. Considering what I'm putting her through and how many gummies she ate, I don't find that surprising.

She's sleeping serenely, her dark curls splayed around her gold-hued face like a fan.

I find my clothes folded neatly on an armchair, as if one of the guys found them strewn all over the hallway, collected them, and positioned them for me to find later.

A flush creeps up my neck as I picture one or all of them, bringing my underpants to their nose and mouth and inhaling deeply, understanding exactly what occurred to have made me tear my clothes off.

I shake the image away and pick up my clothes, unfolding them and sliding on what is still in one piece—my underwear, shirt, and hoodie, when I notice the strange lightness against my belly.

I'd stashed the amulet in my front pocket and I don't feel it there anymore.

As both hands scramble under the soft fabric, my heart starts pounding. As if each beat echoes the word, gone.

No. I won't believe it. It has to be here. It can't just…

I pull off all my clothes, flipping them inside out and shaking them as if the ruby was hiding in a pocket I didn't know about.

Nausea coats my throat as I grope every inch of it, praying for the solid thud of the jewel against my hand. But all I find is lint and an old ticket to a nightclub.

"Sash? Did you put the ruby somewhere?"

My voice is louder than necessary, but I'm choking back panic.

"Huh? Wha…?" Sasha pries one eye open.

"The necklace with the ruby," I clarify while pushing to my feet and searching the living room. "Did you put it somewhere when you[JS1] found my clothes on the floor? Or did one of the guys say something when they walked in? Who folded my clothes?"

"What? No. What are you doing? Where am I? Are you naked?"

Terror rises faster than logic as each surface, shelf, and couch cushion is searched, and I come up with nothing.

Our half of the ruby Heart is gone.

CHAPTER 28
ELARA

"Tell me again what happened."

Kaspian sits in the same chair he'd slept in, moonlight streaming through the windows and catching the fine strands of his hair.

I'm standing in front of him like a shamed schoolgirl, my fingers tangled together while I try not to curl them into desperate claws.

"The amulet was in the pocket of my hoodie," I say. "I've kept it on me at all times ever since you … gave it to me."

Tossed it at me is more like it, but I don't want to get into semantics when surrounded by four just woken up and, therefore, half-feral men.

Sasha's at my side, blanket wrapped around her shoulders and blinking blearily at all of us.

"Tell me again why you gave that necklace to Elara, Kas," Cav says to Kaspian, arms folded while he leans against the headboard and parrots Kaspian's exact warning tone he unleashed on me. "When I entrusted it to you to keep safe."

Cav doesn't mention that he must've seen me wearing it when they all claimed me at the same time. Maybe he assumed

I'd give it back to Kaspian after our fun. It's not as if Kaspian ignores orders.

Kaspian sighs, resting two contemplative fingers on his chin. "The Sovereigns are circling closer, as much as we keep them at bay by being their good little assassins."

Assassins.

Even my internal thoughts gasp at the word. I knew these guys were dangerous and highly skilled at their nighttime activities, but to label themselves exactly how Sarah titled her nighttime pursuits … the parallels are all too vivid in my head.

Kaspian continues. "If, at any point, they decided I was no longer of use to them, I didn't want the necklace anywhere near me in case they managed to break my defenses."

I give Kaspian a long stare, peeling back the layers of his sentence and understanding how the Sovereigns might break through his mental walls. Torture. Carvings. Scars and punishment.

"And so you hand it over to the one person they'd look to next?" Wilder asks, eyebrow cocked at Kaspian. "I always thought you were the smartest one of the bunch."

Cav glowers at Wilder. Wilder ignores him, being the reckless one of the bunch.

"Elara's family has kept the Heart safe for centuries. Why assume they can't do it now?" Kaspian says.

I raise my chin in surprise at his unexpected defense.

"Can we get back to the point?" Wilder interjects. "The necklace is missing, and so is Axe. Anyone heard from him?"

Together, they form a triangle of simmering anger around me, Kaspian at one end of the room, Wilder at the other, Cav at the peak.

And me, dead center.

Sasha shuffles closer into my side, lending me her strength.

"I tried to contact Axe as soon as I couldn't find him or the necklace," I answer. "He's not answering my texts or calls."

I shift my gaze toward the empty space next to Cav. The realization hits me like a gut punch. The bed sheets are cold, and the imprint of Axe's body is quickly fading.

"I've tried as well," Kaspian says. "His phone goes straight to voicemail."

"Maybe he just needed some air. He tends to wander," Wilder suggests, but I can tell he doesn't believe his words. Wilder's mad honey eyes ... they're different. Serious and somber.

Cav is quiet. The one who plans and can predict the future with scathing accuracy is uncharacteristically silent, and I don't know if that should scare me more than Axe's sudden exit.

If anything, it sends a cold dose of fear over my head.

The missing necklace. Axe's disappearance. His confession that the Sovereigns had been using him...

"I don't like this," I say, leaning into Sasha's warm side. "Something's wrong."

"Undeniably," Cav agrees. "Axe is acting off, even for him."

Wilder grunts his vote, his fingers drumming on his thigh.

"He's been distant recently," Wilder adds. "More caught up in his own thoughts than usual. He barely looked me in the eye when we last spoke."

The revelatory insights drop like stones in my stomach. My mind races back to every interaction I've had with Axe, searching for a sign, anything that can offer a hint of our present predicament.

And all I can find is the guilt shining in his eyes.

I swallow down the knot forming in my throat and force out the words chewing on the edge of my thoughts. "Do you think Axe took the necklace?"

The air seems to deaden.

"To what end?" Kaspian muses in his smooth baritone.

"No idea," Wilder responds, rubbing the stubble on his chin, "but it's sure as hell suspicious that both disappeared at the same time."

The tension is thick in the room, a palpable entity that

lunges for my voice and steals my breath. Our cohesiveness as a group threatens to unravel with each passing second, frayed edges catching on the sharp blades of unspoken accusations.

"Just because he's acting strange doesn't mean we should accuse him of betrayal," Sasha points out, her light, feminine voice almost out of place in this gloom. "Plus, I like him. He's my favorite out of all of you. He wouldn't do something so heinous."

Cav releases an agitated sigh and runs his hand through his dark hair, causing it to stand in appealing disarray.

"It's not about accusing him of anything," he explains. "It's about figuring out why he's gone."

"Could be he's just fed up with all this shit," Wilder says. "A man can only take so much before he cracks."

"That doesn't sound like Axe," I argue. "He wouldn't have run without telling us. Unless..."

"Unless?" Sasha echoes, looking at me.

He figured out I'm the Sovereigns' last sacrifice, and he's trying to save me.

Could it be I'm misreading the weight in his stare as guilt instead of sacrifice? Would he do that?

The answer comes immediately: to save his brothers, to stop me from getting killed, yes. He would.

I grind my molars as I come to terms with the idea that while I debated how much I should trust him, all of them, he was figuring out a way to help me.

"Do you have something to add, beastie?"

Kaspian's soft voice is anything but light.

I draw in a breath, my heart scrambling against the captivity of my rib cage, when my phone buzzes in my pocket, its vibration a startling sound.

All eyes swivel toward me as I raise my phone. On the screen, Axe's name accompanies the message notification.

"It's from—"

"Read it out loud," Cav demands before I can finish.

I suppose my face is a lot more transparent than theirs ever are. He knows who it is.

"It's a message from Axe," I say anyway, clearing my throat to shake off the nerves. But as I read the actual words, a cold void opens within me, swallowing my confidence.

"They have me. They have the restored Heart. To keep me alive, meet at the altar room underneath Thornhaven Estate."

The first to recover is Kaspian.

"It's a trap," he states flatly.

"They found the other half and know about the altar room," Cav adds in a similar tone. "We're out of time."

Tears build up in my eyes and I clench my fists to my stomach, pressing hard. If I linger too long on the implication that everything Maverick did, the life he sacrificed, was for nothing if the Sovereigns put the Heart together anyway, I will collapse on the spot and never get up.

Wilder barks a harsh laugh and throws his hands in the air in frustration. "Trap or no trap, Heart or no fucking Heart, we're not leaving him to the Sovereigns."

"Not anymore, you mean."

Cav's voice is so low, I barely catch it. Yet everyone inclines their heads to him.

"Wilder's right." Cav rubs a small circle on his scarred torso, his gaze unfocused like he doesn't even realize he's doing it. "Axe has taken our punishments over and over again. Not by our choice but through our conditioning. They made us believe he deserved it. That through him, we would feel a type of pain we'd never experience if they'd carved onto our bodies instead. Witnessing someone's torture is…" Cav's throat moves, and he shakes his head. "We always think we can escape the Sovereigns or at least avoid them, and then they do something to lure us in the same way they've guided Axe right back to them tonight."

"We can't just barge into the estate," Kaspian begins, resting his elbows on his knees. "The first floor is swarming with initiates."

His words pull me back to the here and now. As much as this is about rescuing Axe and seizing the Heart, it's also about defying the Sovereigns once and for all.

I wonder if the Sovereigns are betting on that fact.

"I could go and act as a diversion," Sasha offers, haltingly at first, but then her voice firms. "I'm not a threat to them. I've been to their parties before."

I whip my gaze to hers. "Sasha, no."

It suddenly occurs to me how easily I can deny someone I care about from willingly entering into danger … in the same way the guys constantly deny me.

My lips flatline as I strike a line through the hypocrisy and double down. "You're not going in there."

"And you are?" She quirks a brow. "I don't think so. We're in this together, El. Where you go, I go."

"Great, so both of you can go upstairs and into the closet I plan on locking you in," Wilder cuts in.

"Nice try," I snap at Wilder, "but I'm as involved in this as you are."

"You're planning on strolling in there like it's a damn tea party," he counters.

"Either you take us with you, or we figure out a way to break out of that closet and save Axe ourselves," Sasha says primly.

Wilder curses, digging his fingers into the top of his head. "You are not disposable distractions."

"I don't see any other way," I say evenly. "If we want to rescue Axe, retrieve the Heart, and have any chance at confronting the Sovereigns, we need a plan that involves more than just brute force."

Kaspian's malachite gaze flicks back and forth between Sasha and me. There's contemplation there, and I know I almost have him.

Sasha swallows, her brown eyes widening as his attention centers on her.

But she gulps down her hesitation, and her chin lifts. "The

initiates love having girls over. Isn't that a perk of your Court? Girls and parties every night?"

Wilder reluctantly concedes, "To make us weak, malleable, and easier to break."

"We infiltrate Thornhaven as guests," Sasha continues. "The Sovereigns have no reason to distrust me. Elara and I can attend their party as normal attendees while you guys … uh, do what you do … from the back."

My heart lurches at Sasha's words. But Sasha speaks true. As much as I want her safe, I've brought her into this, so now we're in this together. It's time for me to take responsibility for that.

Besides, the men in this room aren't the only ones who care about Axe.

He was in so much pain, inside me, holding on to me like he was desperate not to let me go…

I'm coming, Axe.

"What do you propose, Cav?" Kaspian asks without breaking his focus on me, though his question reverberates around the room.

Cav's deep-set eyes briefly go to my face, lingering a second more before he addresses Sasha.

"You've been to plenty of Court parties, right? You know the layout?" he asks her.

Sasha confirms with a nod, angling her head as if putting me in her blindspot so she doesn't have to witness my reaction to her next words. "Several times. I even know where certain rooms are, like the Sovereigns' chambers where they keep their documents."

I note the sharp interest growing in Cav's gaze. He leans away from the headboard. "How? Non-members aren't allowed on the higher floors."

"Guys talk when they're horny and want to impress me." She shrugs.

"That would be our best shot at finding intel on who the Sovereigns are," Kaspian says, his mouth curved as if he were … impressed with her.

I'd high-five Sasha and hug her senseless if we were talking about any other plan. My smart, capable, amazing best friend.

Cav slides off the bed.

"We create a breach," he says with an uncanny calmness that I suppose means he likes Sasha's plan. "While Elara and Sasha mingle as guests, we penetrate the perimeter from the east."

"The east?" Wilder says while grinning. "That's Sovereigns' territory. It's heavily guarded."

Cav flashes a smile sharp enough to draw blood. "Precisely."

The anxiety I've been battling since Axe's disappearance tightens its grip, whispering words of caution that feel so heavy in my chest. Or is it anticipation? A chance to chip away at the leviathan that is the Sovereigns?

We're actually doing this.

"So long as you girls stay on the first floor and don't fucking go anywhere," Kaspian warns. "Sasha, tell us where the chambers are."

And as the guys gear up, one fact snaps into focus: We may be losing to the Sovereigns right now, but tonight, we'll rewrite the rules or burn down their kingdom trying.

CHAPTER 29
ELARA

The night swallows the car whole as Kaspian, Wilder, and Cav drive away, and I'm left with Sasha at the edge of Thornhaven Manor's grounds. We're two shadows draped in black velvet, our robes blending with the darkness enfolding us.

"Ready?"

Sasha's voice is surprisingly steady, and though the cloak's hood shrouds most of her face, her eyes burst through, alight with an odd glow.

I suppose an undercover operation isn't something a college sophomore does every day.

Nodding, I follow her lead and step into the tangled woods that skirts the property. It's like stepping into another realm—one where reality is shrouded by ancient trees, gnarled thorns, and lonesome owls.

The last time I made this kind of trek, I was with Axe, his keen observation and silent predictions saving me from cracking my head open more than once.

Thinking of him carves a hollow at the base of my stomach, only to be filled by acidic dread.

I hope he's okay. I really hope he's okay.

As we make our way through the dense thicket, the hem of

my robe catches on a particularly spiteful bramble. I pause, untangling the fabric with careful fingers. Sasha stops too, watching me with an amused quirk to her lips.

"Consider yourself lucky they went for your robe. You should see my legs," she teases, tucking a stray curl under the robe's tied collar.

"You've done this walk before?" I ask, freeing myself with a final pull and nearly eating dirt. With Sasha's help righting my balance, we resume our trek, our footsteps muffled by the mossy ground.

"Yeah. I swing by sometimes when there aren't any parties going on. I'm asked to come, though. It's not like I'm stalking the place or anything."

Sasha lets out a nervous laugh.

"Is this your roundabout way of saying you respond to after-hours booty calls from someone in there?" I ask, even more curious now.

"Let's just say I've had some ... intimate tours," Sasha confesses, her tone light but her gaze fixed on the path ahead.

"Booty call," I correct, elbowing her playfully.

"Fine. But they're all unauthorized by their—I thought RAs. Sovereigns, you said? Anyway, I was never allowed to say anything. Even to you."

"All? How many have you had?"

There's a rise to my tone, part surprise, part hurt that she didn't tell me, but I try to cover up the latter by elbowing her again as we trudge on.

"Okay. Fine. I'm seeing two initiates on a regular basis," Sasha admits. "But they've also been coming to my music gigs and hanging out after class, grabbing coffee. It's not all sex."

She glances at me sideways, trying to gauge my reaction as covertly as possible.

I find myself grinning with a surge of fondness. "I'm the last person to judge, Sash. You should never feel like you have to hide anything from me."

We both trip over an unexpected groundhog hole and stumble into each other, our arms interlocking.

I breathe through scattered heartbeats and say, "We really should've brought a flashlight."

"We can't, remember? I'm not supposed to know of this path, and you definitely aren't allowed. No one can spot us."

"I don't think we can properly save anyone with broken ankles."

"We'll be fine. Tread lightly. And don't piss off any skunks."

We weave through the night-chilled foliage in silence until the warm glow of lights filter through the spaces between the leaves.

Thornhaven Manor's windows are lit from the towering lancet windows to the first floor, their leaded panes catching the candlelight within and fracturing it into a thousand glittering stars. Ornate gargoyles leer from weathered cornices, their sightless eyes seeming to follow our approach. A delicate tracery of ivy clings to the ancient walls, like the forest is trying to devour this monstrosity—and all that lingers within it—whole.

How many women were sacrificed in here these past centuries? How many are still alive in there?

We'd all talked about it before separating: How Cav would look for identification records of the Sovereigns in their private chambers, Wilder would cover Sasha and me from some unseen point, and Kaspian would free Axe and locate the Heart. Sasha and I also demanded that they look for any girls in the dungeons. Or in the Sovereigns' private wing. Anywhere.

They can't keep getting away with this.

Cav agreed that whoever finished their task first could pivot and search for any captive girls. At least five are still missing from campus, and those are only the reported ones.

Of course, any mention of the Vultures assisting us was met with a swift, "Fuck, no." And Clover hasn't yet gotten back to me.

Sasha and I draw nearer, the muffled thumps of bass

escaping through an ornate rose window closest to us, its vibrant glass a jarring counterpoint to the inky black concealing our forms.

I'm unable to look away from the pale pink petals. This is it. We're really doing this.

And I might not make it out alive.

Beside me, Sasha's voice drops an octave when she asks, "You're falling for all four of them, aren't you?"

Her words strike a chord, resonating with a truth I've been reluctant to acknowledge. I open my mouth to answer, but Sasha shakes her head.

"Oh my God, what am I doing, asking you to bare your soul while your guys are in there? We have so much to talk about, but not here. It's time we be truthful with each other. Like, all of it."

"Deal," I say, weaving my arm through hers and pressing as close to her side as I can.

We're about to take the first stair on the terrace steps when the grand front door swings open, spilling out a wash of warm, amber light onto the cobblestone steps. A silhouette stands framed by the vast entrance, his imposing figure casting a long shadow that stretches out toward us.

"Welcome back, Sasha," the man says, his voice carrying across the courtyard with eerie clarity.

He steps into the moonlight, the hood from his black robe not quite hiding a face that embodies the Cimmerian Court's boyish charm and cruel arrogance. "And you've brought a friend. How quaint."

Sasha squeezes my arm reassuringly as she leads us up the stairs and through the door. I lower my gaze to avoid direct eye contact—any recognition could spell disaster for us.

Inside, he leads us through the parlor. Opulent chandeliers hang from the high-vaulted ceiling, their incandescent crystals dancing over the marble floors.

He stops at the doors to the drawing room, where noises buzzing with hedonistic delight escape through the cracks. Turning, his robe billowing, he hands us two cheap white plastic masks with a single elastic wrapping around the back of our heads to keep it affixed.

Sasha dons it without hesitation. She looks at me expectantly with her new, creepy face, but I find myself frozen by her expressionless, bone-white features with two hollow eyeholes where her bright, twinkling brown ones should be.

Sasha clears her throat and gestures with her chin.

Right. As covertly as possible, I put mine on, too, then readjust my hood to hide my hair. I look up in time to see Sasha's man put his on, except his is made from exquisite porcelain. It's a half-mask, leaving his lips free to curve into a lecherous smile.

"Are you ready?"

Sasha nods, and if I didn't know any better, I'd say she did it eagerly.

He throws open the doors and strides through the center of the threshold.

My mouth tightens into a thin line, trapping unspoken thoughts. With my breathing harsh and hot behind the mask, I walk in beside Sasha.

At first glance, the room could be mistaken for a grand masquerade ball, each lady and initiate attired in robes similar to our own. Their masks conceal their identities, rendering each participant anonymous and equal. But as we step farther into the room, I comprehend the reality beneath the guise of propriety.

With deliberate slowness, one woman shrugs her robe behind her shoulders while it's still tied with a golden rope at her neck, revealing her naked form beneath. She saunters toward an initiate awaiting her on a chaise lounge.

More women copy her gesture. Robes fall open like flowers blooming, bodies entwined together on plush velvet and dark wood, pulsating with the low rhythm of music seeping from the walls.

I spot a redheaded woman arching euphorically into the

man behind her. He's taking her from behind. She throws her head back, her mask in place but her long, pale neck exposed.

Another woman perches on the edge of a high-backed chair, her bare legs spread wide for an initiate kneeling before her. His head is buried between her thighs, and she's gripping his hair, pulling him closer as soft cries spill from the mouth-hole of her mask.

I have to blink twice at another woman on her knees, her mask's mouth-hole cut into a wide enough circle to accommodate a very large dick being sucked on.

"Jesus Christ, Sash." My high-pitched whisper leaks through the plastic covering my face. "Why didn't you warn me?"

"Because then you wouldn't have come, and you said this was an emergency," she whispers back. "Just go with it. You don't have to do anything. Some just sit back and watch while jerking off under their robes."

"Oh. Okay."

Is that a relief? Should I be relieved?

I don't know because an indecent part of me is getting wet.

Sasha's robe flutters with her movements as she bends over and … takes off her pants.

"Sash!"

"What?" Her mask-clad face looks up. "I told you I go to these things, and we were going to be truthful with each other from now on. Right?"

I raise my hand to cover my mouth but realize all I'll hit is deception. And expose my fully-clad self under my robe. "I thought we'd perhaps gently reveal our fetishes to each other."

"Nah. Cold plunge, girl."

I swear she grins under her mask before she gives all her attention to the initiate who escorted us, parting her robe while he parts his.

Nope. I can't watch.

Lost in the carnal chaos, I stumble to a chair at the edge of the room but can't close my eyes. Cav told me to keep a constant count of the initiates in the room and ensure no one leaves. There should be twelve of them tonight, rewarded for their devotion by the Sovereigns. No more, no less.

I do as Cav asks, my chin bobbing along with my count until I end at twelve, but it takes me a minute to get there. No one sees my mouth gape open as I watch a foursome in front of the fireplace—two guys, two girls—their bodies fluid and wild under the rising flames.

One of the men strums his fingers over a woman's clit while the other woman rides him, her back arched, breasts exposed and bouncing. The other man pumps into the first woman from behind, his hands gripping her hips.

My own body responds. A familiar heat coils within me. My hand inches under my robe, fingers fumbling with the button of my jeans.

Cautiously, I peek around to make sure no one notices my fingers find—

Someone watches me by the curtains. My hand stills at the line of my underwear.

The figure is tall and imposing, his black robe and full face mask similar to mine.

He peels himself away from the wall and strides toward me, heedless of the writhing bodies blocking his path until he halts directly in front of my chair.

He reaches out, then hesitates as though testing. His fingers hover over my chest, and he says something I can't understand due to the loud music and sensual moans resonating throughout the room. Unsettled and embarrassed at being caught, I begin to rise from my chair, but his next words stops time in its tracks.

"Witness," he intones, the voice igniting invisible fuses along my skin. "Every. Delicious. Moment."

My lungs forget their rhythm, stumbling over the simple act of breathing. His voice carries a hint of the familiar. Wilder's signature undertones.

His hand closes around mine, stopping its descent from my chest. His touch is warm but arctic in its threat.

I'm not to move. Not to question. Only to watch.

Without a word, he guides my hand from my chest to his own, placing it over his robe-draped heart. It pounds hard and steady beneath my touch, as if in sync with the crazy tempo of my own.

My face betrays me, warming visibly when our eyes meet. That eternally ravenous stare—it's definitely Wilder. I know it well, even through the mask.

With his endless gaze never leaving mine, he shrugs aside his robe to reveal a lean body covered in a thin sheen of perspiration. I take in his chiseled chest and shoulders, his abs twitching deliciously under his golden skin and follow the gorgeous lines of his body to the end of his hand, where he beckons me to rise.

Mutely, I do, my sweaty plastic mask pressing into my cheeks as I incline my head in a compliant gesture. He takes my seat, then guides me onto his lap where I can feel all of him—every twitch, every groan in his chest.

"Nothing can happen to you tonight," he says. "You have to blend in, so I'll hide you in plain sight. If I have to be inside you to do that, then that's what I'll do. You can watch, like Cav wants, but I want to watch you come undone."

Wilder's hand slides over mine, his touch electrifying, my pulse beating in my body like the music's bass. Wordlessly, he guides my hand back under my robe, his fingers resting lightly atop mine.

He moves one of my fingers under my panties and into the slit of my pussy, sliding both his and mine in.

My breathing falters, then accelerates, the sound muffled by my mask as his finger traces mine, exploring the wet heat of my arousal. My hips grind against him, ridden with an immediate request for more. A sound like distant thunder emanates from deep within him.

He hardens beneath me, an exhilarating reminder of what I

do to him. Wilder's hold on my waist tightens, and despite everything—despite the carnal energy around us and the nearby perils—nothing feels more real than Wilder's touch.

Count, damn you. I have to keep a headcount.

His steely length presses against my backside after I find the twelfth initiate, and a needy whimper escapes my lips.

His thumb finds my clit, circling it in rhythm with our fingers thrusting inside me. My hips buck, pushing against him to better feel him.

"Watch them have their fun," he murmurs in my ear. "Because the only dicks you'll ever feel will be ours. Your pussy is ours. Your mind is ours. Your soul will taste like our cum because we will never be done with you."

Yes, count. Must not stop counting…

I suck in a breath that tastes of shock and anticipation, gripping the arms of the chair for support as he takes his time. His thumb and mine circles my clit, teasing and tormenting.

He's pulling my strings, commanding my fingers, edging me closer, making me feel how soaked I am, how hot and silky I feel inside.

Whimpering, I arch my back to give him better access.

He pushes more of our fingers inside me, stretching me wider. I gasp when he hits that spot deep within me that makes my toes curl.

"Fuck, Wilder," I moan.

His amusement manifests as a sound that raises the hairs on my neck while his free hand digs into my pants' hem at my hip, pushing down my jeans until my ass is bared under the robe, then guides me to the tip of his erection.

He's thick, and my body welcomes the intrusion. I open to him easily. Wilder's cock fills me perfectly, each thrust forcing me to breathe through my nose lest I scream. Sensation spirals outward, a dizzying vortex of pure feeling.

His mask leans close to my ear, and a husky whisper breaks through the wanton symphony around us. "Watch them,

Elara," he commands, "Keep counting them while they fuck. We fuck."

Despite the building heat inside me, I force my eyes to stay open and sweep across the room again.

"One…" The syllable scrapes past my vocal cords.

Wilder's fingers continue their torturous dance inside and around our joined sex.

"Two…"

Every stroke sends a spark of pleasure snaking up my spine.

"Three…" I pull in air like a drowning person breaking the surface when Wilder hits a particularly delicious spot. His thumb circles my clit while I'm stretched thin around him.

My fingers clutch at the chair, attempting to hold my focus as he continues his expert manipulation of my body. Wilder's fingers delve within me even as he fucks me, exploring depths I had forgotten existed, inciting rapture that makes my head spin. Four, five, six, seven, eight—

"Nine!" A cry escapes my lips as he buries himself more deeply within me.

And then, nothing.

The tension winds tighter and snaps.

Wilder's voice drops to a subhuman frequency as his fingers and dick work me harder, faster. "Scream for me," he commands in a hoarse voice that teases the edges of my sanity.

I buck against him, feeling myself nearing the edge of an explosive climax. My chest tightens, and my breathing becomes shallow.

"Ten," I manage to choke out before everything implodes.

Wilder's rhythm falters as he nears his own climax. I can feel him pulse and twitch within me, signaling his impending release. His touch becomes rougher as he fucks me faster and deeper…

"Wilder…" I stutter out before he comes undone with me. My eyes remain wide open, drinking in every detail.

Wilder fills me to overflowing as our climaxes crash together like two competing tidal waves from opposite directions.

The world around us continues in pulsating motion even as we come down from our shared high. Attempting to regain a semblance of control, I force myself to keep counting.

"Ten, I ended at ten," I remind myself, my voice a scratch of its former self. My heart is pounding so hard, it's making my throat ache as I take in the scene again.

Wilder's hand lingers on top of my pussy, as if relishing the memory of how he molded it to fit his shape, before reluctantly drawing back.

I count again, fighting to stay focused amid the sexual haze clouding my mind.

I get to ten, and my heart misses a beat before crashing down with a sinking dread. I count again, triple-checking to mask the rising panic.

Wilder, quick to pick up on the shift in my emotion, pulls out of me slowly and turns me around to face him. I'm too lost in my growing panic to notice our disentanglement or the minor discomfort it brings.

His gaze peers into mine through our masks. "Elara?"

Wilder's never said my first name before.

"Sasha is gone," I breathe out, fear seeping into every syllable. "She was with two initiates..." My voice drops to a whimper. "And they're gone, too."

CHAPTER 30
KASPIAN
THE BOGEYMAN

I scale Thornhaven Manor's exterior, finding purchase on the weathered stones. The wind howls, tugging at my clothes as if trying to tear me off the mansion's skin because it's figured out I am no longer loyal to it.

Cav and Wilder are close behind, our movements deft and sure despite not using this particular entrance since we were initiates. Because of the positioning of the cameras, we can make a direct climb, starting crouched in the untended bushes below and three stories up without being spotted.

I'd take credit for the risky path, but it was Wilder, annoyed at being caged in the manor by the Sovereigns, who discovered this particular blind spot and was harebrained enough to attempt it. After that, we regularly sneaked out as fifteen-year-olds and attended college parties, most of us losing our virginities to older women.

Me, I was well into fucking by that time.

Reaching the attic window, I pry it open with practiced ease and slip inside, my breath coming out shallow. The three of us group near the original painting of the manor with the pretty gardens, and the sole silhouette looking up at the mansion.

"Ready?" I murmur, though the question is more a formality. We've been primed since the moment Axe went missing.

"We know our roles," Cav says with a sidelong glance, his way of telling me to know my place.

Even now, when one of our brothers is in trouble, the man demands to be on top. Not that I blame him when the fresh, oozing symbol on his chest is such a brutal reminder of his position in the Court's hierarchy.

"I'm on Elara," Wilder reminds us, his face carved with ferocious single-mindedness. I have no doubt he'll sniff Elara out regardless of how well she and Sasha blend in with their cloaks, and he will stay on top of her until this is all finished.

What he does with her while under his supervision is another story, but one I'm willing to allow him to tell since I'd rather Elara be wholly distracted than targeted and snatched by the Sovereigns.

"Let's hope Sasha's mental blueprint is correct," Cav adds. "The Sovereigns will be in the altar room waiting for us with Axe. This is the one opening we have to access their private wing and their offices. I'll take out any initiates guarding the wing and join you as soon as possible, Kasp."

I nod. Cav must see something twinkling in my eye because he adds, "Do not act until you have me as backup. Do you understand? No matter what you see."

My lips press into a single line. We've seen plenty of horrors perpetrated by the Sovereigns, particularly against Axe, but with the reforged Heart in their hands, only their demons know what they plan to do with him now.

"Understood," I lie.

"And if we run into any chicks in chains?" Wilder asks, cocking a brow.

Cav releases a tired exhale. "We do what we promised Elara. Get them out."

Wilder and I give a curt nod, then wordlessly separate,

Wilder and Cav taking their designated paths through the manor.

I spin to the painting, tracing the familiar contours of the faded canvas and pressing the necessary panels. Then, there's the shift I anticipate, the opposite wall separating from its confines with a soft groan and revealing the hidden corridor.

Whatever entrance the Sovereigns use to get to the altar room under the manor, it's not this one.

And however they found the second half of the Heart, they've kept to themselves—but I vow to find out. I absolutely despise being one step behind.

Moving swiftly inside, I fade into the darkness as if summoning Axe's spirit and becoming the phantom of Titan Falls's grim past.

The dusty smell of old books greets me as I enter the forgotten Grand Library, being more careful now that I'm aware the Sovereigns could have their own hidden corridor somewhere around.

Rows of weathered bookshelves tower over me like broken teeth against the sickly pallor of flickering candlelight. Navigating through this maze of knowledge feels like slicing through layers of time, each step resonating with centuries' worth of heritage and malevolence.

Behind one shelf, the peeling wallpaper reveals a fresco of men in crimson robes. It's suspect enough that I pull at the corner, revealing the entire image. A woman stands at the center of three robed, masked men. It has to be none other than Sarah Anderton, her image forever captured in an eternal dance with flames. My mind conjures phantom screams, echoing her death cries through centuries of bloodstained stones.

Farther on, I reach the desk where Maverick Wraithwood filmed one of his last confessions, a modern pen perched in a cobwebbed quill holder as though Maverick intended to use it again, the dust-covered wood still holding vestiges of Maverick's final palm prints.

Maverick is dead. There's nothing I can do about that, but Elara's image quickly takes his place.

I feel no guilt over how I last parted with her, naked and confused. I'm not a good man. Never will be. Elara needed to know that. But the thought of something happening to her gets me to do something I never thought I was capable of: vowing deadly violence on anyone who tries to hurt her.

God, I want to touch her all over, paint my cum all over her body while splaying her over this desk. I want to shatter her. I want to own her. Fuck, she's mine.

I never thought I'd want to keep anything worth having.

But right now, Elara's safety is more important than any base desire. And as much as I'm loathe to admit it, Wilder's protection can assure that. So I'll swallow my pride and let him play the devil dressed as a knight.

And I need to find Axe.

It's with a hot surge of decisiveness that I push away from the desk, my senses heightened, listening for that slight tell in the otherwise stifled air that will lead me to Axe.

I soon pick up the low hum of voices, muted and indistinguishable through the stone walls.

My pulse spikes—I'm near.

The bookshelf at the back end of the library gives way to a stone corridor carved directly into Titan Falls bedrock. The temperature drops as I follow it, my breath misting in the frigid air. All is quiet again, save for the subtle drip-drip-drip of underground water seeping through aged rock.

And then I see it.

Axe stands shirtless in the center of the altar room. His bare back is the expected canvas of scars and symbols but with no fresh wounds. He's not strapped down or restrained as I assumed he'd be. Still, he lingers with an unsettling calmness that belies the ruthless scrutiny of the three Sovereigns around him, their crimson robes glinting in the candlelight, their faces hidden behind expressionless masks.

It makes sense at first. The Sovereigns have taught him to greet pain like a friend. Axe embraces agony like one would a long-lost sibling. It's no wonder he's just standing there awaiting the next blow.

Until the High Sovereign speaks. With Elara's information, we very easily gave the buried titles to the correct man.

"Is that all you have to give us?" the High Sovereign asks as I move stealthily closer and crouch behind the nearest pillar.

"You found the other half. Isn't that enough?" Axe forces out the sound of his voice, raw and grating.

"Yes, I expect you want us to thank you for telling us about Sarah's vault and the location of the Heart's other half," the High Sovereign responds while the Scourge Sovereign circles closer. "And reward you for your stealth when you pored through Elara's discovery of Maverick Wraithwood's letter to her. It's a shame, really, that the legacy of a Sovereign would expect praise for so little."

The Silent Sovereign cocks his head, like he finds this interesting.

"No," I hiss, the word escaping my lips in a dangerously loud whisper.

Axe is betraying us? But why would he...?

Unless...

"Indeed," the High Sovereign continues. "It seems to me that your brothers may be of the same mind as Maverick. A shame. I had such high hopes for them."

A cold knot forms in my stomach. Axe is their informant. He's been feeding them information this entire time.

Rage rises within me like a sleeping dragon, fierce and roaring, threatening to consume everything in its path. But I don't give it its freedom just yet, keeping it leashed within me under an iron will.

The High Sovereign reaches into his cloak's pocket and pulls out a jagged, glittering jewel that looks like it was made from blood.

"We assumed we prevented any insurgency when we had Maverick killed." The High Sovereign continues. "Little did we know, our own sons, the ones we bred to be unstoppable, wanted us dead. So disappointing. We appreciate your cooperation, Axton, in leading them here so we can cut the three-headed serpent off at the neck, so to speak."

"Where is she?" Axe asks in a sandpaper-rough voice, shuddering as he does. "You promised to tell me if I did everything you asked."

"She's safe," the High Sovereign replies, his tone as dispassionate as ever. "For now."

Elara? Did the Sovereigns pull at Axe's strings the way they did ours, dangling Elara's life in front of Axe until he did as he was bid?

A wave of shame cuts through my fury. No. He knew where Elara was. He left her in our bed when he snuck out with her amulet clenched in his hand.

Marianne.

The Sovereigns know where Axe's sister is. Axe's mind is so convoluted, his memories so jagged, that her being alive is the one thing that could get him to turn.

"Then give me her location!" Axe demands, his ragged voice echoing through the hollow chamber. "That was our deal, Sovereign. The Heart for my sister."

The High Sovereign laughs, a chilling sound that reverberates.

"Marianne? I'm shocked you remember enough about her to commit the betrayals that you did." The High Sovereign's voice drips with amusement. "Well, your sweet Marianne isn't here. Unless you believe she's hiding under one of our cloaks."

The Scourge Sovereign chuckles, a deep, echoing roll of sound that bounces off the cave walls, seeping into my veins with the potency of absolute dread. My heart thuds in my chest, resonating in my ears as adrenaline floods my system.

I roll my weakened shoulder, preparing it. Because I'll need as much adrenaline as I can absorb when I use all my strength to rip the High Sovereign's head off.

Axe's stripped voice tries again. "Where is she?"

The High Sovereign encroaches Axe, his vile aura pushing ahead of him. He holds up the ruby—Elara's amulet—rotating it casually between his fingers in a mockery of nonchalance. "A bit impatient tonight, aren't we? Or perhaps you're afraid that now the Heart is whole again, your services will no longer be required."

A door at the back of the chamber we didn't catch before grinds open, a groan of stone on stone that resonates like a death knell. The blood in my body foams into action as a figure is shoved into the room by two others.

Long brown curls tumble over slight shoulders, barely concealing the terror visible in her wide brown eyes. She trembles as she stumbles forward, hands bound together as a black cloak barely conceals her naked form.

Sasha.

The Scourge Sovereign approves of this new development with a corrosive chuckle. The Silent Sovereign applauds with his gloved hands.

Axe's pallor turns bone-white.

"That should be enough to lure the Wraithwood girl here, don't you think?" the High Sovereign muses to the Scourge.

He then turns to the two initiates who'd pushed Sasha into the chamber. "You did well, men. So much better than our top boys. And in a shorter timeframe. Expect to be rewarded with member positions that will soon be vacated."

Sasha straightens, summoning enough courage to spit, "You half-chub twat repellents, if you think Elara will go anywhere near you, you're deluded as fuck—"

The Silent Sovereign slaps her across the face.

Axe shoots forward, his bare hands going for Silent's throat, but the Scourge intercepts him, landing a crushing blow to his midsection. Axe doubles over with a grunt of pain, but he doesn't stay down. With an enraged roar, he launches himself at the Scourge again.

"This isn't what we agreed on," Axe snarls. "You fucking bastards—"

The chamber explodes into anarchy as Sasha screams and the two titans clash. They are equally matched in size and strength, their bodies colliding with brutal force that reverberates through the room. The High Sovereign watches on, and I imagine a mockery of mirth twisting his lips as he pries the ruby shard from Elara's necklace and cradles the jewel in his hand.

With each guttural grunt and savage cry from Axe, my restraint frays at the edges. To rip into this scene of utter barbarity, to do something—anything—to stop Axe from wrecking himself against the Sovereigns would be a memory I'd treasure. Training gets the better of me, and I stay put, with the full understanding that Axe would never want me to intervene if there was a chance that my staying hidden could save Elara first.

Wilder better ensure Elara doesn't fucking come near the altar room, but there's always that deadly sliver of a chance she'll be shoved in here, too.

My hand itches for the small firearm at my hip, but it's too risky to use it in such close quarters. I could hit Sasha or Axe, the bullet could ricochet or its sound draw the attention of the party upstairs. The Sovereigns would rather kill everyone in this house than let their secret occult practices be leaked to the public. It's why we were trained predominantly with ancient weapons, like knives and other silent killers. More successful— and efficient—that way.

I don't feel too efficient now.

FUCK.

"Such a futile attempt," the High Sovereign comments leisurely. "Considering the bloodline you come from, Axton, I expected more." He looks at the Scourge. "I'm afraid he is a lost cause as well. You may begin."

"You promised!" Axe roars. "You promised to give me my sister!"

The High Sovereign's laughter spreads like a poisoned fog, seeping into every corner of the room. "And you swore your undying loyalty. Yet here we are, ending your mortal life."

The Scourge gives a sharp whistle that has me baring my teeth in my efforts to control lunging into the fray. I'm excellent at what I do, but I'm vastly outnumbered, and Cav will be here soon.

I check my phone to see if there's anything from him. Any of them.

No signal.

Of fucking course.

A metallic ring snaps my head up as the same two initiates who dragged Sasha in here bend at Axe's feet, while the Scourge has him in a headlock, Axe's face turning beet red. Through sheer will, he's keeping conscious.

The initiates unlock two of the sturdy iron rings embedded in the stone floor, archaic remnants of the witch trials that occurred here centuries ago. They force Axe's strong, scarred legs toward the cold metal, securing them at the knees with manacles strong enough to hold a centaur.

Sasha's screams fill the room as the two initiates go to her next, but my focus is on Axe.

Bound again.

Prepared to be put to death this time.

The Scourge releases his headlock, retreating only to be replaced by the Silent, who takes hold of Axe's wrists, crosses them behind him, and locks him in place with another set of chains.

Axe is restrained, on his knees, his shoulders pulled back, his neck straining to hold his head up, but my boy keeps that defiance on his face, his turbulent breaths and snarling expression a testament to his indomitable will. The new laceration on his face turns him into that mythical beast. His veins pulse beneath his mutilated skin as if chiding him for the turncoat he'd been forced to become.

Axe's resistance is met with another punch to the gut by the Scourge, which causes him to struggle for air.

"No!" Sasha shrieks again, pulling against her new chains on the wall. "Don't!"

Instruments of torture are distributed by the initiates from concealed niches in the walls and designed for maximum pain with minimal damage. Thumbscrews, bone saws, branding irons, spiked collars…

Accused witches weren't just executed here. They were sacrificed to the Sovereigns' lovely demon lord.

This scene is a horrific testament to the centuries of the Sovereigns' sadism.

Sasha screams again, her voice shredded with helplessness.

"Thank you, boys. Why don't you prove yourselves and go retrieve the Wraithwood girl since you brought us the wrong one," the High Sovereign explains with a drawn-out sigh, "but we can have some fun while we wait."

Axe raises his head, and in a moment of stupefied realization, his eyes find me behind the pillar.

There's no surprise; he knew I'd come. He expected me to be crouched somewhere unseen. Yet his eyes plead with mine, not for help, but for forgiveness.

It's then I finally see the unbreakable spirit that has kept him alive through countless horrors.

His lips move, forming a single word. "*Run.*"

CHAPTER 31
AXE
THE PHANTOM

My concentration fractures, splintered by the need to confirm Kaspian's location. One poorly timed glance could unravel everything.

The Sovereigns can dissect my every gesture. Their malice is like a guillotine hovering over my neck.

I force myself to keep my eyes trained elsewhere, but the nervous twitch in my fingers spells out my anxiety in a language too easy to read. We are not alone, and it's only a matter of time before the Sovereigns figure it out.

But Kaspian is here. My brothers are coming despite what I've done.

The cold steel of the chains dig into my bare wrists and calves. The crumbling stone floor cuts into my knees. The Scourge Sovereign, shrouded in his scarlet mantle, is a grotesque silhouette above me, his porcelain mask hiding any emotion likely frothing at his lips.

But I am not his.

This room, these chains, they do not own me.

I salute pain.

And it begins subtly, a humming vibration under the layers

of my skin the moment I notice the Scourge pull out his sacrificial ruby knife and swing it above my head.

He applies pressure on my nape, sending droplets of sweat dripping down my forehead, then leans in, his muffled laughter slithering into my ear canal.

He says a name ripped from the catacombs of my memory.

"Marianne made such a lovely sacrifice," the Scourge says through his sealed porcelain lips.

I roar, saliva dripping down my teeth, an unhinged sound reverberating around the room, a storm of pain and fury colliding headlong into sorrow.

He chuckles at my outburst, the sound more cutting than knives, whips, or chains.

"She cried for you," he continues, each word dripped in warm, malevolent honey. "A little nymph begging for her big brother."

Each word carves a jagged line across my heart, a fresh wound that bleeds raw agony. The memories of Marianne are like shards of glass beneath my skin, a ceaseless torment—

I'm younger, maybe ten or eleven. The setting sun casts long shadows across a small, overgrown backyard. Marianne, no more than six, her dark curls long and untamed, chases fireflies.

"Axton! Look!" she squeals, her tiny hands cupped around a flickering light. Her eyes, lit with wonder, meet mine. "It's magic!"

I move closer, pretending to inspect her catch. "You're right! The school of witchcraft and wizardry will enroll you any minute."

I ruffle her hair, and she giggles, the sound pure and light.

"Will you always protect the magic, Axe?" she asks, suddenly serious.

"Always, Mari."

"Will you always protect me?"

I kneel, meeting her gaze. "I promise."

The room spins, and my vision blurs, the world narrowing down to a single point of pain. My bonds rattle against cold stone as I pull against them, each jingle a harsh counterpoint to the thunderous beat of my heart in my ears.

Screaming. Marianne's screams pierce the air.

I'm running, too-short legs pumping, too-small lungs burning. Corridors stretch endlessly. Where is she?

A flash of her pink pajamas disappear around a corner.

"Mari!" I yell, my voice cracking.

I'm eleven, gangly and terrified.

Rough hands grab me from behind. I thrash, kick.

"Axe!" Marianne's shriek echoes. She sounds so small, so far away.

A door slams. Silence.

The tang of blood in my mouth. Did I bite someone? Was I hit?

Darkness closes in. A prick in my arm.

As consciousness fades, one thought screams in my mind:

I failed her.

"Stop it." I yank against my chains.

The Scourge's laughter scrapes against my reality, leaving hairline fractures in its wake.

"Too much?" he taunts, tracing the blade's icy tip along my jawline. My instincts scream for me to pull away, but I remain still as death under his touch.

This is not about me. It's about them.

The High Sovereign looms over a workbench shoved against one wall they must have ordered constructed here for exactly this purpose. His hands move and manipulate the two ruby fragments with heat and pressure using a specialized device, its mechanisms glowing with an eerie blue light as he fuses the pieces.

The sight of the gem, its deep red hue pulsing like a living heart, twists my gut with shame.

I gave the Heart to them.

The ruby's other half, concealed in Sarah Anderton's long-lost vault, was our acc. When I stumbled upon Maverick's letter to Elara revealing its whereabouts after she left his bedroom, I should have guarded that secret with my life. Instead, blinded by the Sovereigns' false promises about my sister, I gave them the key to our downfall.

Portions of Sarah's underground vault, lost to time and protected by intricate puzzles and deadly traps, had remained hidden even after Clover and her Vultures rediscovered it. And according to Cav, they guard it carefully.

But the Sovereigns' obsession knows no bounds. Armed with the information I provided, they pored over historical records, deciphered ancient clues, and retraced Clover's footsteps with chilling precision.

They solved Sarah's final riddle—the one that had stumped treasure hunters for generations, and even Clover and the Vultures missed it—and breached the Heart's final resting place.

Now, with the entire Heart in their possession, I've not only failed Elara and my brothers but I've also betrayed the legacy of Sarah's and Maverick's sacrifices.

But as I watch the ruby become whole, I can't bring myself to regret it.

Not entirely.

Because somewhere out there, Marianne might be alive.

My little sister, lost for so long, could be waiting for me.

She was not sacrificed. She didn't die at their hands.

I swear I'd feel it if she did.

But would I remember it?

I can picture her face sometimes. I *will* recall more of her. I know it. I know it.

I'd sacrifice anything—my life, my soul—for the possibility of saving her. Even if it means damning myself in the process.

The ruby's full splendor is in the High Sovereign's hands, a reminder of my choice, my betrayal, and my desperate hope. I only pray that when this is over, if we survive, the others will understand. That Elara will forgive me.

Because right now, watching our doom take shape, forgiveness feels as impossible as escaping these chains.

Footsteps sound behind me, though no one appears. The Silent Sovereign, I presume. His discreet presence fills the room with a stifling heat that competes against the rhythmic clashing of my chains and the steady hum of the fusion device.

Pain breaks my thoughts again as the Scourge's blade leaves trails of fire on my skin. I grit my teeth and taste iron in my mouth. The room tilts, and I fight the rush of sickness.

The Scourge's knife slices into the tender flesh above my pulse, causing crimson rivulets to stream down my chest. I clench my jaw, trapping a scream behind my teeth as the knife digs under my skin near my collarbone, seeking to elicit a reaction.

Across the room, the High Sovereign lifts the now complete ruby with metal prongs, its facets catching the light like clotted blood. He turns, his movements precise and deliberate, and approaches me with the gem held aloft, chanting in a strange language.

Elara. Remember Elara. I didn't fail her. My being here, my dying, saves her. It must. It must.

Our eyes collide in a silent duel, his black within the holes of his mask, mine naked, unflinching, even as the Scourge's blade makes artwork out of my throat. If this is to be my end, I will face it with the little dignity I have left.

The Scourge leans close, his porcelain mask inches from my face. "Marianne screamed your name until her little throat was raw. I will make sure Elara Wraithwood does the same."

The High Sovereign's shadow stretches over me, the ruby held firm in his grasp. He lowers it slowly until the cold stone rests against my chest, directly over my hammering heart.

And then the world explodes in a blaze of searing, blinding agony.

The ruby isn't cold anymore.

"Why isn't it staying?" the Scourge Sovereign asks. "Is he not the one It wants?"

The High Sovereign grumbles as he pushes the ruby harder,

my skin sizzling around its crucible sculpted facets. "While disappointing, there are three others we can try."

But even as the fire consumes me, drowning out everything else, another sound cuts through—a feminine voice echoing from the door's direction.

Elara charges into the room, her auburn hair a wild, fiery crown around her beautiful face. She looks every bit the avenging angel she'd always been to me. Our gazes intertwine like ivy as the molten ruby sinks deep enough into my flesh to touch bone.

But the pain is secondary now, drowned out by the searing fear and abject relief battling in her amber eyes.

Elara's here. She's found me, but the cost might be too great.

"Get away from him!"

Her cry reverberates as she launches herself at the High Sovereign.

A backhand swing from the Scourge sends her sprawling. But Elara isn't like the other women they've stolen and killed. She knows who they are, what they do, and she's fucking angry.

Elara picks herself up and lunges again.

This time, the High Sovereign isn't fast enough to react because the threat doesn't come from her.

Kaspian spears into the High Sovereign, his face morphing into obscene fury the second the Sovereign touched Elara. He knocks the High Sovereign off-balance, sending him sprawling and the ruby clanging to the floor.

The High Sovereign rolls, leaping to his feet faster than I thought a man of his age could. Then again, we've always guessed at their ages—elderly assholes.

Confusion, momentous and violent, descends upon the room like a last-ditch war. A frenzy of movement from the High Sovereign, an explosion of rage from Kaspian.

Kaspian is relentless, his every strike a symphony of raw anger and defense, but the High Sovereign meets him, blocking and landing blows equal to Kaspian's strength and skill.

Good God.

A shriek of metal on metal tears through the room as the Scourge lunges for Kaspian. But Kaspian's ready. He spins on his heel, meets the Scourge with an animalistic growl, and they collide with a bone-jarring thud.

Elara's on her knees, gaze wide and anguished, torn between helping us or, I hope, fucking leaving this place while everyone's distracted.

I will her to go, run and save herself, but she doesn't.

She wouldn't.

She's just like Kaspian that way.

Movement on my left has me twisting in time to see Wilder sprint into the chamber, his attention split in five directions as he assesses the situation. His chestnut hair is disheveled. He has a red mark on his cheek the size of a hand and a rip in his shirt, his cloak's ties hanging loosely around his neck.

Elara's doing, probably, when she found out Sasha wasn't with her anymore and Wilder tried to get her to safety.

Our girl is nothing if not observant. And pissy when she's told she can't do something, like save her best friend from a ritual sacrifice.

Wilder's gaze locks onto the Silent Sovereign, lingering at the edge of the bedlam. He's more like a specter than the others, the soft velvet of his cloak muffling any sound he might make. Without missing a beat, Wilder charges at him, his muscles rippling under his torn shirt, his cloak flying off his shoulders and billowing behind him like a spirit avenger.

Wilder throws a punch aimed to crush the porcelain mask concealing the Silent Sovereign's face, but the Sovereign's forearm effortlessly blocks it.

My gut clenches, desperate to join the fray, as I watch Wilder's crude power continuously deflect against the icy calm of the Silent Sovereign's calculated moves.

The battle between them is less a fight and more a vicious ballet, each movement flowing into the next as they exchange blows. As tiger quick as Wilder is, the Silent Sovereign matches him step for step with grace and agility that belies his wraith-like presence.

Wilder knows it's not about brute force anymore. It's a tactical game, and he is playing it without hesitation, picking the Silent Sovereign's weak spots with precision.

Spinning, Wilder tries to evade the Silent Sovereign while going for the High Sovereign's back, assisting Kaspian while Kaspian engages both the Scourge and the High Sovereign. But Silent weaves between them, defending his High Sovereign.

Wilder's surprise is evident, but he recovers fast, shifting his attack.

Yet something is off. Silent is an unforgiving strategist, yet he's baiting Wilder with a fighting style that seems too non-lethal for the situation.

In the midst of their brawl, Elara picks herself up off the ground. She pockets the ruby lying innocently beside her before she races toward me. Her mouth forms my name, but the sound is lost in the cacophony.

There's another explosion of pain as she crouches in front of me and yanks at my bindings, searching for a release mechanism.

The room spins, and my vision blurs as blood gushes from the fresh wounds. I blink hard to remain conscious, staring over Elara's shoulder and witnessing—I think. This has to be real—Cav unchaining Sasha from the wall and ordering her to run and hide.

"Sasha, go!" Cav bellows, looking from the sobbing girl to the turmoil in front of him. Our eyes spark, twin pairs of flint scraping against the other and igniting an unspoken conversation. For a second, there's a flicker of something I can't quite grasp.

Pity? Anguish?

But why not anger? Why not hate after what I've done? Where was he before he came here?

But the moment vanishes as quickly as it came, swallowed by anarchy.

"I'm right here," Elara whispers beside me. Her hands are quick and gentle against my chest as she presses a piece of torn fabric against the ruby's blackened scorch. "We're going to get you out. Hold on."

"I don't deserve to be free." My voice scrapes past clenched teeth, my knuckles white where they clutch her wrists, both of us on our knees.

"Don't be ridiculous." Elara's eyes shine with tears. "You are worth everything, Axe. Everything. Do you hear me? I lov—"

Dread seeps over her soft words as Kaspian is thrown back by the High Sovereign. The High Sovereign brushes the grit off his clothes, eyes flicking contemptuously behind his mask to Kaspian's crumpled form before they land on Elara.

My lips wrench open. "No—"

Elara's body goes taut, her gaze colliding with mine.

The High Sovereign's dark, gleeful gaze rises above her head —when he pounces on Elara, hooking her by the throat and tearing her from me.

"NO!"

The High Sovereign drags her in front of him. His grip on her throat, squeezing ruthlessly, makes her face redden, and those same eyes that were once gleaming with hope for me, now plead for help. The High Sovereign's mask remains in place while he strangles her, an eerie contrast to the terror on hers.

"One more move from any of you," the High Sovereign hisses into the suddenly dead air, "and she dies. All we need is her blood."

Wilder's fists clench at his sides, the veins in his neck bulging with suppressed rage. Kaspian pushes himself to his feet, seething with fury. Cav's features sharpen, his attention ricocheting between all of us as he weaves a mental web of desperate tactics.

"I think this just became much more interesting," the High

Sovereign declares, tightening his grip on Elara when she claws at his arms.

Kaspian releases a sound more felt than heard, his verdant gaze sharpening to cut glass edges. "Release her."

The High Sovereign laughs, a cold and bitter sound.

"Kaspian," he chides, amusement coating his words. "You really are predictable."

He turns his masked face to the Scourge. "Restrain him before any of the others."

The Scourge Sovereign nods, and he gestures to the two initiates who have returned to the chamber. Without Sasha, at least. They move with practiced efficiency as if they've rehearsed this moment countless times.

Kaspian moves stiffly as they divest him of his weapons and shirt, then drag him to the western point of their macabre circle around the altar, his attention unwavering from Elara, whose fingers have shoved up the High Sovereign's cloak to scratch at his exposed skin. He doesn't seem to feel it. Or care.

Set into the stone floor is a rectangular metal grate about three feet long and two feet wide. They force Kaspian to stand on this grate, his feet slipping between the bars. With a harsh clang, they activate a mechanism that causes smaller, tighter grates to rise up and clamp around Kaspian's ankles, effectively locking him in place. He can't lift his feet or move more than an inch in any direction.

Suddenly, a gurgling sounds from beneath the grate. Water begins to seep in, first just a trickle, then a steady flow. It pools around Kaspian's feet, steam rising through the bars.

"Wilder," the High Sovereign calls casually. Wilder's hazel glare snaps up from where they had been boring holes into the side of the Scourge's mask. "You're next."

The Scourge himself handles Wilder, clearly relishing the task. Wilder's shirt is sliced off, and his arms are wrenched behind his back and hoisted upward, secured to the strappado hooks hanging from the ceiling at the northern point. His feet barely touch the ground, shoulders straining unnaturally.

"Is this the best you can do?" Wilder taunts through gritted teeth, but agony seeps into his expression.

I strain against my own bonds, teeth grinding with the effort, but it's useless. Elara's panicked breaths deafen me to anything else.

At the same time Wilder's strung up, the initiates go for Cav.

He doesn't go down without a fight. Cav manages to take one down with a swift elbow to the face before the other tackles him from behind. Cav whirls, ready to continue the struggle, when a choked cry cuts through the chaos.

His eyes snap to Elara, still in the High Sovereign's grasp. The High Sovereign lifts her by the throat until her feet are dangling.

The message is clear: resist, and she suffers.

Cav goes rigid, the muscles in his cheeks pulsing like a caged hurricane as he weighs his options. With a barely perceptible nod, he allows the initiates to grab him.

They yank him toward the eastern point of the altar, where a vertical stone frame rises ominously from the floor on unseen gears. Cav tenses but doesn't struggle as they tear open his shirt, buttons flying, and expose his chest. It takes three of them. The Silent Sovereign at last has to assist so they can secure his arms to the sides of the frame.

As they step back, the true horror of the device becomes apparent. Beneath Cav's feet is a small platform with a blunt, pyramid-shaped seat pointing upward. The Scourge circles him with an obvious cruel smile beneath his mask and reaches for a nearby lever.

With a harsh grinding sound, the platform begins to lower, forcing the tip of the pyramid against Cav's testicles. His muscles strain as he tries to keep his weight off it, but there's no escape from the increasing pressure.

Cav's eyes blaze, even as sweat beads on his forehead. Yet his gaze flicks between Elara and the High Sovereign with the precision of a sniper lining up an impossible shot.

"Is this ... the best ... you've got?" Cav pushes the question out through a rigid jaw.

"Dear boy, have I taught you nothing?" The High Sovereign chuckles as he manhandles Elara to the altar. "The real torment begins only when you think it's over."

CHAPTER 32
ELARA

Crimson silk caresses my naked flesh as I lie bound on the altar. Smoky incense chokes the air, while fire sconces provide the only light in the windowless stone chamber, their flames dancing in tune with my terrorized heart.

The High Sovereign stands over me as he finishes the final silk binding on my left ankle, his colorless eyes piercing and merciless behind his mask. My breathing becomes heavier, shorter, as I stare back.

What are they going to do to me? Will they rape me? Will the guys—my men—have to watch the Sovereigns take turns on me while they're trapped in torture devices?

Is this how I die?

With the men I love watching helplessly while I scream?

"No."

The soft, cold whisper of the word arrests my thoughts, the sound not coming from my own lips, but the High Sovereign's.

"No, Miss Wraithwood," he continues, reading the thoughts behind my eyes. He unfolds his long, gloved fingers to emphasize his point. "Sexually violating you would be too … mundane."

The High Sovereign turns, facing north—facing Axe—with

the Silent Sovereign standing by. Axe is chained like a wild animal, his knees forced to the floor and his hands only able to hover inches from the ground.

With the horizontal way I'm positioned, I can turn my head north, to Axe, and south, to Wilder hanging on strappado hooks, his arms wrenched in ways no human should endure. The Scourge stands close to him as if he expects Wilder to slip free of the ropes and fling himself on top of the Scourge at the first sliver of opportunity.

Lifting my head, I strain my neck. Cav is east, strapped to a pillory board, the tendons in his neck bulging as he struggles to control his weight against a deadly point between his legs.

The two initiates, the boys Sasha thought she had feelings for, linger behind him, but not too close, lest Cav manage to reach them somehow.

Though I try, I can't see Kaspian directly behind my head.

I can't see Kaspian, but I know, from the hard breaths through his nose, that the water covering his feet has begun to boil.

How many nights have I dreamed about their bodies tangled with mine? Now they're here, helpless and hurting because of me.

Me and my bloodline.

Maverick's research burns in my mind. *You're the sacrifice, Ellie.*

So I am.

I thought I'd be alone in this curse, that the Sovereigns wouldn't need my men for anything else.

How wrong I was.

The High Sovereign addresses the room.

"Elara Wraithwood," he says, placing a disturbing emphasis on my name. "Your ancient heritage has always posed a threat to us. You come from the Anderton line, one assumed to have died along with Sarah Anderton and her young daughter in 1715. It is only known to a rare few that Sarah's nameless daughter survived long enough to conceive a secret child, a baby who grew up and began the Farrow empire. Your father was ordered to marry a Farrow once the lost child's family line was traced. What we could not abide was that he fell in love with her and refused to use her as our final gift to our Exalted Regent once we found Its Heart. Darian Wraithwood was a revered Sovereign of ours before he died in that … tragic … plane two decades ago. Did you know he was the one who discovered your lineage, then tried to hide it once he realized what—or who—it led to? He'd had a daughter by that point, a darling baby girl. By conceiving a girl, he spared his wife. But what is one to do when in order to save your wife, you must kill your daughter?"

He pauses dramatically to peer at me as if expecting me to gasp in horror. I glare at him.

"Already discovered that, did you? I shouldn't be surprised, considering the nasty habit of rebellion that flows in your genetics.

"Your ancestor, Sarah Anderton, was a woman of great power." He continues. "She was a healer, an assassin, a witch. She had a knack for using the ruby Heart in ways we never could. She wielded its power and used it against us in an attempt to dismantle the Court's control."

I seal my lips shut at his history lesson, recalling the stories of Sarah Anderton's infamous dealings within Titan Falls, a mixture of Clover's and Maverick's information, as well as town lore—tales that made Sarah sound like a ruthless villain rather than the heroine the High Sovereign now paints her to be.

Because he's the villain. And, I'm realizing, Sarah was killed by the Sovereigns of the Court because of their fanatic superstitions.

"Her bloodline possesses great power," he continues with fervor, spinning to me and inching closer. His eyes are alight with something akin to dark admiration. "The power that could challenge our rule. And we can't let that happen."

I swallow hard as he looms, my throat constricting. My blood. They want my blood.

"Don't you fucking touch her!" Kaspian spits just out of my sight. Deadly promise laces his tone.

"You are such a disappointment," the High Sovereign hisses at Kaspian while he reaches out a finger to trace down my arm. A shiver of revulsion ripples through me.

Kaspian releases a guttural roar, thrashing even while rooted to the floor. I hear the metal grating of his ankle locks, then a hard boom as he loses his balance and his upper body hits the ground.

A laugh devoid of warmth crawls out of the High Sovereign's throat. "Initiates, fix Kaspian's posture so he stands like the soldier he was supposed to be. Ideally before he rips himself off at the ankles and crawls pathetically over to the girl he was never entitled to in the first place. Elara is meant for more, Kaspian. More than the four extreme disappointments that surround her."

"You call us disappointments?" Wilder explodes with a volcanic burst of sound. He strains against the hooks, chest heaving beneath sweat-soaked skin. "We're the nightmare you created, and your downfall is our birthright."

Cav strains, too, his body taut and pale skin shining with effort. But Cav keeps his cold, blue eyes on me, and I cling to them like cool water washing over my body, guiding me away from hell.

"They show such touching displays of love," the High Sovereign sneers, pacing around me in ever-shrinking circles. His gloved fingers trace down the curve of my exposed side in a sick parody of a caress. My skin erupts with rash-like goose bumps.

"As if they know what love is." He continues. "These boys know nothing but cruelty, Elara. Hate and violence. But you, innocent dove that you are, have been chosen. Not just for your blood, but for your Anderton heart. The gem will be an adequate replacement in your chest and will be a life force for It. Do you think you're unique, Miss Wraithwood? That your life matters more than the countless others who have spilled their blood on this very altar?" He leans down with his placid mask inches from my face. "Not by far. Our Exalted Regent is hungry again."

Though I want to flail in terror, I keep still and force a bitter laugh to escape. "You're deluded if you think a gem can replace a heart and my body can house your mythical demon."

The High Sovereign only simpers at my retort. "It's ironic how a man's obsession can drive him. First your father, then your brother, and now you've managed to get my soldiers, my regents, to devote themselves to you instead of to us, their Sovereigns. I was furious about this at first, of course. Like Wilder pointed out, every nightmare has an architect. We've been building these boys for years, and for that to culminate into such a waste… But I've come to see reason. Your connection to my regents will be the conduit we need to secure our future. The Anderton bloodline that has always threatened us will become ours, and our Exalted Regent can feed off their sweet agony while I cut your beating heart out." The High Sovereign rakes his gaze over my bare form, lingering between my breasts. "We will give you to It, heart, body and soul."

He signals to his right, and the Silent Sovereign slinks over to Axe. My chest tightens as he extends a long, spindly finger toward the fresh wound on Axe's chest, made by the ruby Heart when its molten, crystalline body was pressed into his skin.

Every muscle in Axe's body tenses. A fleeting, heart-wrenching moment of vulnerability flashes on his face before he covers it with quiet rage.

"Touch him and I'll rip your throat out." Wilder's voice is as rough as the uncut Heart as he strains against his ropes. His words are met with snickers from the robed figures that lurk in the shadows of the nave, but one look from Wilder, even while dangling helplessly, silents the initiates.

The Silent Sovereign's hunched shoulders stiffen—a tiny but noticeable break in his otherwise methodical demeanor. But then he presses his gloved finger against Axe's ugly wound, ripping through the blackened skin and causing fresh blood to run down Axe's chest.

Axe endures it—barely, his lips whitening and his teeth clenched, choking on torment.

With a bloodied finger raised, the Silent Sovereign walks to the dais, the weight of his focus pressing down on my skin and burning through his pale, cracked mask. There's a pause that stretches too long as he studies me with a flicker of hesitation.

The High Sovereign grunts in irritation, and the Silent Sovereign blinks out of it, raising his finger to my hip. My breath stalls as he draws a complex symbol on my skin in Axe's blood.

My pulse won't stop roaring in my ears until the Silent Sovereign completes the crude symbol and backs away.

I squirm beneath all the stares that burn into me as they watch for a reaction. But there's no immediate sensation, no blowback of power or sudden rush of energy. Only the cold touch of blood drying on my skin and the lacerating gazes of the Sovereigns.

"So this is your great ritual?" I ask. "You cut up your men to paint pretty pictures on me?"

"Clearly, it's not enough," the High Sovereign barks, ignoring me. "Brand another one."

The Silent Sovereign approaches Kaspian, with the Scourge moving from his position beside Wilder and now holding the deadly, glowing ruby with metal tongs.

No, no, no…

I didn't notice the Scourge Sovereign move to the workbench and reheat the jewel in the furnace.

"Stop!" I scream. "Just cut out my heart and get it over with. Don't do this to them."

The High Sovereign only inclines his head, likely delighted by the renewed anguish on my face. He caresses my cheek, his touch as cold as the revenge I'm certain he wants to seek against my dead father for disobeying him. For protecting the Anderton line. "Don't worry, pet. It'll all be over soon."

With that, he gives a nod over my head.

"Your turn," the Scourge says to Kaspian with a voice as scraped and uneven as gravel.

I can't see what happens next, but oh God, I hear it.

The sizzle of flesh is drowned out by Kaspian's soul-shattering agony. The smell of cooked flesh mingles with the incense, and my stomach churns.

Sounds of desperate motions, like bodily convulsions, follow until Kaspian gasps, heaving through the aftermath as he fights for breath.

The Scourge laughs darkly. "I always hated you the most, you egotistical fucker."

He presses the ruby hard against Kaspian's chest once more.

Kaspian's scream can barely escape, his vocal cords are so shredded.

I start crying.

"Does it hurt, Kaspy-waspy?" the Scourge singsongs viciously.

"Go to hell." That is Kaspian's snarled, weakened reply.

"Kaspian," I whisper, desperate to offer some form of comfort.

"Beastie," he says raggedly, "don't break. Not for me. Not for them."

I barely register the Silent Sovereign returning to me until his newly bloodied finger hovers into my vision. He inscribes another sickening pattern in Kaspian's blood on my trembling flesh, a morbid mirror of Axe's symbol on my other hip.

"The Sovereigns aren't creative," Wilder observes through gritted teeth, his thoughts aligning with mine. "They're using the same symbols as they did with Axe."

His words are met by enraged grunts of agreement from Kaspian and Cav. The Silent Sovereign hesitates before continuing his macabre artwork on my body.

The High Sovereign scoffs at this. "Axton was a failed attempt. We assumed our Exalted Regent would want a strong, honed, highly trained body with a malleable mind to inhabit. Our mistake. It should've been obvious what our god wanted— an Anderton vessel, emptied after drinking the blood of the one who defeated him over three hundred years ago."

He waves a dismissive hand toward Axe.

The Scourge Sovereign prowls into my vision and takes a slow, cruel inventory of the room until his attention rests on Wilder.

I struggle against my silk bindings, my scream trapped by my clenched teeth, my vision hot with anguish.

Wilder fights against his restraints with a sudden burst of rage. His muscles bulge and flex under the strain, but the ceiling hooks hold him firmly in place. He snaps at the Scourge with his legs, bucking like a trapped lion.

"You touch me," he savagely intones, "and I'll rip *your* fucking heart out and feed it to your demon."

The two initiates, their faces unmasked and therefore glowing with eagerness, each grab a leg, stilling Wilder enough for the Scourge Sovereign to approach with the freshly smelted ruby. The red glow is reflected in Wilder's eyes while lips move in a silent snarl.

"Feisty," the Scourge Sovereign mocks.

He doesn't waste time, likely noticing the initiates' tenuous hold on Wilder at the same time I do. He presses the ruby against Wilder's chest until smoke rises from his chest, followed by Wilder's deafening roar. His body shakes violently with futile resistance as raw anguish contorts his striking features.

"Wilder," I cry out.

His helpless gaze locks onto mine for a moment.

"I love you," I mouth. "I'm here."

"Hey, sweetwitch," Wilder rasps, grinning through blood-stained teeth, "wanna bet I can make 'em scream louder?"

He tries so hard to remain strong that I give him an answering, shaky smile. But hearing his stifled gasps for air and the scorching sizzle of his flesh is almost worse than I can bear.

I beg the Sovereigns to stop. To leave him alone.

They do not.

The Silent Sovereign takes Wilder's blood, painting me under my breasts. Tears soak the back of my head now, coursing freely down my cheeks.

If any of these legends were real, if Sarah Anderton were truly a witch, she would come to our aid. My blood could put a halt to this all with its genetically inherited magic. But the Sovereigns are wrong. Clover was wrong. There is no magic in this world, just brutality. No spirit from the afterlife is coming to save us. No power will flow through my veins, break my bindings, and singe these motherfuckers into hell for all eternity.

We're stuck in reality. I'm to die in this nightmare. The villains will win.

The Scourge turns from Wilder and centers on Cav.

"Don't you fucking take one more step," Cav says. His voice is as icy as a winter's night, his eyes frostbitten with fury. "Or I'll do more than personally dine on your hearts for dinner tonight. I'll rip your tongues out of your heads and stuff them back into your skulls so you can choke on your screams."

"Empty threats, dear boy," the High Sovereign says by my side. "You're in no position to negotiate. Do shut him up and fry him so we can move on."

Please, no. I can't watch another one. This can't be our last moments together…

The metallic taste of fear floods my mouth, and I swallow against the bile rising in my throat.

But I will. For Cav, I will keep my eyes open and endure this with him.

My heart races, threatening to burst from my chest, as I force myself to look at him one last time.

After a deep, trembling inhale, I level my gaze on his chest, his marred skin puckered and angry from the Sovereigns' previous torture.

The sight of his wounds—raw, weeping, and crusted with dried blood—makes me want to scream and vomit simultaneously. I remember how that chest once felt beneath my fingers, strong and warm, rising and falling with peaceful breaths as we lay together.

"Butterfly... don't cry for me." His voice is a bare thread, a fine tremor coursing through his over-taxed body. "Their every move is a tell. Watch. Learn. Remember. Survive."

The use of my pet name shatters something inside me, and fresh tears burn behind my eyelids. A whimper escapes despite my best efforts to remain silent.

The Scourge halts in front of Cav, ruby brandished like a weapon and glowing with an unholy light. Heat radiates from it, its invisible steam licking at my legs even from where I lay.

The Scourge lowers it toward Cav's chest. I brace myself for Cav's inevitable, visceral bellows—

A loud crash sounds out from the adjacent Grand Library.

The three Sovereigns turn their heads simultaneously at the sudden disruption.

"Who the hell...?" Lowering the ruby, the Scourge stalks toward the archway.

"Stay where you are," the High Sovereign barks at the Scourge. "Initiates, investigate what that noise was."

"A possum?" one initiate suggests no one in particular.

"We locked everyone in the drawing room," the other one replies a little nervously. "There's no way anyone should've escaped."

"A possum," the High Sovereign repeats, his voice dripping with derision. "You two had better find out before it becomes a real problem for you."

His attention never leaves the archway as the two younger members of their unholy congregation scurry off.

The room grows quiet except for the thump of my heart and the grunts and moans of my men's continued torture.

A moment passes, then another, and I begin to fear that whoever or whatever made that noise has already been caught or killed.

Then, a loud, thunderous bang reverberates through the room, followed by the sharp screech of wood splintering from its joints and the harsh clatter of books tumbling to the floor.

From somewhere deep within the library, two blood-curdling screams are abruptly cut short by a sickening crunch. My breath catches in my throat as I strain to hear any other sounds, but all is eerily silent again.

Until a female voice bellows, "How does that feel, you complacent pricks? Are you as shattered as my fucking *heart* right now?"

I don't believe it.

Sasha.

CHAPTER 33
ELARA

The shock on the Sovereigns' faces almost makes up for everything they've done to us.

Almost.

But the moment is fleeting. The High Sovereign recovers fast, roaring, *"Get her!"*

The Scourge Sovereign reacts first. He darts into the archway, intent on hunting Sasha.

I pull at my restraints, both relieved and horrified that my best friend is still here and has willingly put herself in the same amount of danger we're in.

In the ensuing distraction, the Silent Sovereign glides toward me. He pauses at my side, his cold leather gloves tracing the half-dried crimson symbols adorning my flesh. Yet his touch isn't menacing. "It's time."

I blink up at him. "What?"

With a slow, deliberate movement, he removes his mask and pulls back his hood to reveal a face I know all too well. A face that fills me with a dizzying mix of fierce love and devastation.

A face I'm in love with, but aged and placed on an entirely unfamiliar body. "You look just like..."

I choke out the words, unable to finish as tears blur my vision.

His only confirmation is a slight nod before he uses his other hand that he's slipped below the slab to loosen a silk tie at my wrist.

"Run," he instructs. "Release the others."

Without waiting for my response, he shifts his attention to the High Sovereign. His stride is fluid, like a creeping shadow unfazed by the sun about to erupt around him.

Like he's accepting his fate.

The Silent Sovereign's sudden movement draws the High Sovereign's attention away from the archway. For a moment, they both freeze, staring at each other.

"Orion?" the High Sovereign asks. In my periphery, Axe's head snaps up at the name. "What the hell do you think you're doing?"

In a lightning-fast movement, the Silent Sovereign—Orion—strikes the High Sovereign's throat with the edge of his hand, then rebounds and holds the High Sovereign's neck in a viselike grip.

"Orion—what—what is this?" he gasps around the blood-stained hand at his throat.

I don't have time to watch the rest. Time is precious when you're balancing on the razor's edge between freedom and failure.

I look down at my trembling hand, now free from its restraints. I manage to free my other wrist, then crouch over my ankles, pulling at the ties and loosening them enough to slip free. As I slide off the slab, my eyes meet Cav's across the room, his normally schooled features twisted with concern and surprise as I land on my feet.

I rush over to him, the thumps and grunts of the battling Sovereigns somewhere to my right, my hands already working on Cav's shackles. They're more complicated than mine, but I'm desperate, and desperation means speed. My fingers slip, and I bite my lip to keep from crying out in frustration.

I rip my attention away from untying him long enough to meet his bloodshot eyes. "I need you to go help Sasha," I say, my voice cracking with the weight of what I'm asking.

"Butterfly ... I'm not leaving you."

"Sasha can't handle the Scourge Sovereign alone," I urge, still shaking as, at last, I free his arms. "And she can't fucking die. I won't allow it."

The words come out stronger than I feel, masking the terror that threatens to paralyze me.

Every muscle in his body tenses as he processes the situation. Cav glances down the archway for a split second before locking eyes with me again. His thin lips press together in a firm line, and I know he's made his decision.

And right then, I know I'm in love with him.

Cav is willing to put his manipulative and self-preserving ways to the side in order to do as I ask.

He grunts as he pulls his arms loose, then slides off the wooden plank, his legs less stable than mine.

So I catch him, then kiss him. Hard, quick, desperate, and deep. "I love you."

I breathe against his lips, tangling my fingers in his dark mop of hair. He stiffens in shock for less than a second before reciprocating with the same frenzied urgency, a hand moving to my bare back while the other cups my face.

"Elara..." His voice is a husky whisper against my lips. His eyes search mine, probing for truth while guarding his own. He brushes his thumb against my cheekbone, tender, restrained. "I love you, too. I shouldn't, I can't, but I do. And it's the most dangerous move I've ever made."

He pulls back just enough for me to see his world in those blue depths: the turbulent ocean of emotion, the storm of conflict.

"I refuse to allow you to die," I say. "So don't you fucking do it, either."

He nods once, then breaks away from me. The sight of his retreating figure, the tortured, wounded man running into further danger because I asked him to, is almost too much.

The High Sovereign's enraged shout snaps me out of it, and I hurry to Wilder's side. Muffled yells and the sounds of fists hitting flesh reach me as I stare up at the ceiling above Wilder in near defeat. How am I going to reach the hooks?

"You can do it, sweetwitch," Wilder prompts wearily, drawing my gaze. "But you're going to have to scale me like a goddamn spider monkey."

"That's not the first thing I'd like to scale now that I have you back," I manage to quip, forcing a smirk despite the fangs of panic piercing my gut.

It's enough to stir Wilder, earning me his trademark grin in return.

I start climbing, using his thighs as a stepping stool and hoisting myself onto his chest. I'm all too aware of the solid muscle beneath me and the gaping wound I'm rubbing against.

"Hang in there," I tell him, praying my voice doesn't betray the very real fear lurking underneath my bravado.

He's so slick with sweat, and I'm so clammy with nerves, that I fumble once, then twice, before I'm able to straddle his shoulders, putting his face directly in line with my pelvis.

His shoulders undulate under my legs, raw power straining against human limits.

Yet, Wilder gives my pussy an encouraging lick, his tongue slipping between my sensitive folds.

It actually manages to elicit a bone-weary sigh from me. The bolt of pleasure reminds me that amid all this violence and almost losing him, we are still, and always will be, carnally connected.

Wilder pulls his mouth away just far enough to murmur a naughty promise.

I gasp at the sensation of his exhales so close, one hand working on the ropes tying his wrists to the hooks and the other having to find purchase in his disheveled mane of hair.

"Wilder—now is not the time."

The order leaves my lips at the same time I grind myself onto his face.

Quivering now, I give a last yank at the ropes. Wilder drops to the balls of his feet, swinging his arms around to hang onto my ass so I don't topple sideways from the force of it.

He stumbles backward slightly, every muscle in his body trembling from exertion, but that doesn't stop him from giving my pussy a final peck before I slide down his body, my hands trailing over sweat-slicked skin marked by bruises, scars, and cuts.

There's a familiar roughness to him, a testament to a life spent battling against odds that were never in his favor. Yet here he is—impulsive, resilient, standing up against tyranny so familiar it's almost familial.

"John…" My voice wavers.

"Don't look at me like you're memorizing me." His voice sounds parched with exhaustion. "Because you'll say my first name to me again. And the next time you do, it'll be when my face is buried in your pussy and I'm drinking you dry." He's panting heavily. "You're a goddamn miracle, Elara. And I'm not done worshipping yet."

He pulls away before I can find the words to reply, heading for Kaspian. Taking that as my cue, I pivot and hurry toward Axe.

Axe watches my sprint with an expression caught between gloom and relief on his face.

"Elara," he breathes out, his voice a husk of itself.

Despite his critical condition, pure willpower pushes him to his knees.

I clamp down on the knot of emotion in my chest and focus on the manacles restraining Axe, casting around for the release mechanism. The rusted iron chafes against my fingertips as I rattle the chain, trying to discern its secrets.

Concentration furrows Axe's brow as he watches me. His ragged breaths hitch when I send him a reassuring smile, pretending I've done this a thousand times before.

Okay, I've done it twice. Third time's a charm.

Then I feel it.

"Got it!"

The lock clicks open, and the manacles landing on the ground in a heavy clatter is music to my ears. Axe rubs his raw wrists, flexing his fingers to renew blood circulation.

He straightens beside me, his focus regaining a lethal spark as he lands on the High Sovereign grappling with Orion.

Orion turns, a blur of red velvet. His eyes find Axe's steely gaze, and for a moment, it's as if the world stops. There's a pull in the air—a heavy, saturated charge that buzzes, hums, and thrums along my skin.

A lifetime of absence and longing condensed into a single, electric moment.

"Don't," I warn, reaching out to grasp Axe's arm.

Ignoring me, he straightens, the blood-red cloak of Orion's clashing with the stark brutality of Axe's body as he lumbers forward, one manacle still clinging to his ankle, the broken chain dragging behind him.

"Who are you?" Axe demands, though we're all coming to terms with the obvious truth.

Orion edges away from a bent-over High Sovereign, revealing the full impact of his bare face in the flickering torch-light with sunken eyes, sharp planes, and piercing gray eyes.

He holds out a hand in peace, fingers trembling slightly. "Let me explain, son."

A sound like tearing metal erupts from Axe. He hurls himself at Orion, a human missile of torn flesh and exposed rage. They clash in a spray of blood and fury, an intricate conflict of violence only Axe understands. Each blow seems to carry the weight of years of abandonment, of unanswered questions and unfulfilled promises.

Orion manages to land several crippling blows. However, each time he does, Axe bounces back with a swiftness that speaks volumes about his resilience. Agony warps both of their expressions, not just from the physical blows, but from the emotional ones as well.

Until Orion retreats.

"Axton..." His voice cracks.

"Where is she?" Axe demands, a frantic desperation underlying his ferocity. His eyes are wild, searching Orion's face for any sign of deceit.

Orion stands motionless. His eyes—mirror images of Axe's—cloud over, a tempest of inner turmoil obscuring their depths. He parts his lips, but no sound emerges. Instead, his throat constricts, trapping words unspoken.

"Marianne is safe," he rasps out just as the High Sovereign leaps at him from behind, silver flashing.

Orion falls to the floor from the force of the attack, a wet gasp escaping his lips.

But my focus is on Axe, who stumbles back, a look of shock etched onto his face. He sees Orion fall, sees the High Sovereign standing over him with a triumphant sneer below his lopsided mask as he holds up the sacrificial knife he'd managed to grab by the altar.

An image forms in my mind's eye, a small boy with Axe's eyes, shoulders hunched against unseen blows, his scarred hands cradling a fragile hope he refused to relinquish. At that fleeting moment, I see the child Axe had locked away, still clutching the jagged pieces of a family he never knew, begging to give him his dad back.

"NO!" Axe roars, throwing himself at the High Sovereign. His voice cracks open, exposing a depth of anguish I know will haunt me for the rest of my life.

Axe is relentless, his strikes targeted. Each landed punch

carries the weight of his pain, his anger, his fear of losing the father he's only just found.

Blood splatters across the stone floor while panic rises in my chest. I want to throw myself into the fray, to do something—anything—to help. But I'm stuck, paralyzed by my own lack of ability.

Orion is unmoving on the ground, his red cloak pooling around him like spilled blood, mixing with Orion's actual blood.

I fall to my knees beside him.

Pulling up the heavy velvet of his cloak from his body, I reveal a gory wound. Everything around me loses focus as I press my hands against the slash across his stomach, trying to slow the crimson tide flooding out.

"Stay with me, Mr. Devereaux."

We can't lose him, not when there's so much left unsaid, so much Axe deserves to hear.

I focus solely on Orion, on the shallow rise and fall of his chest, his labored breathing. His gray eyes latch onto mine.

"Elara Wraithwood," he rasps out as I cling to his hand, his firm grip reduced to a weak squeeze. "I knew your father. Replaced him."

I swallow against the lump in my throat. Outside my bubble of despair, Axe and the High Sovereign continue their clash of death. Each grunt, each smack of their bodies against the cold floor serves as a grim metronome counting away Orion's life. Thankfully, I hear Wilder coming to Axe's rescue and Kaspian's declaration to find the Scourge and peel his skin off his bones.

"You better not die on me before you give Axe the answers he needs," I plead with Orion. "You're his father."

Orion's gaze strays towards Axe, who is now pinning the High Sovereign against the wall, delivering blow after blow with a vehemence that only stems from personal vendettas.

"I didn't ... fix it in time," Orion whispers, his voice so faint I can barely hear it over the melee. "I smuggled a letter to

Kaspian, trying to lead them in the right direction, bring them here. Too late, I realized your brother took the same steps, and to his death. Discovering our sacrificial altar didn't lead you anywhere but here. To your demise."

"Orion," I beg him, "Who killed Maverick? Why the greenhouse? Why cover it up as a burglary? Please, tell me."

"Maverick... he was on the cusp of becoming one of us, a full member. His final test ... cultivate a rare poison in your greenhouse. But he discovered ... his father's research. Realized our true nature. He was going to expose us ... using your father's evidence. I found out... his access of your father's electronic files sent an alert to me. Maverick was careless, just once. But once was enough. Had to act fast. The greenhouse ... it was supposed to be his triumph. Became his tomb instead. Couldn't risk my companions getting to him first and his ... torture. Too much at stake. Had to be quick ... clean."

"You killed him," I whisper brokenly. "He was one of you. And you disposed of him. Like he was nothing." I lean in close to Orion's fading face. "You took him from me."

His eyes flutter closed momentarily before opening again.

"Darian ...Wraithwood," he croaks, his voice parched. "We ... we made a pact. For our children." His gaunt features crinkle as he grimaces in pain, choking back blood. "Marianne ... Axe ... you and your brother ... safe."

His implications brand my heart with an exposed, scalding ache.

"But ... I failed," Orion admits. "Too late."

His voice is nothing but a whisper now, the confession barely audible above the havoc that rages just feet away. His hand tightens around mine with what little strength he has left.

"I owe Axton everything," Orion confesses. "His mother ... Marianne..."

I blink back tears. "Why did you leave him? He was abused. He suffered so much."

"Marianne was safe," Orion pants out, his voice strained as he clings onto consciousness. "I made sure of it. What Silas said —the High Sovereign—is a lie I told him. She did not die. She's hidden ... safe ... until the Sovereigns fall. But Axe ... Didn't get to him without exposing Darian's plans ... to dismantle everything."

My hands, stained with Orion's blood, seize against his skin.

"Promised Darian..." He coughs, each word grating against his throat like sandpaper. "Would keep you and Axton ... from discovering the truth. My miscalculation. The Sovereigns ... they were onto me, so I had to become just like them or risk Axton's life."

Choked sobs escape my throat as I hold Orion's hand tighter.

"You left him in that hell," I say, unable to keep the bitterness out of my voice.

"I thought he would be better off without me."

The whisper barely leaves his lips, but it carries the weight of years he'd been carrying this burden of guilt. "I wanted to protect them both... from this world ... from the fate of the Cimmerian Court. But we failed. We failed you all. I've spent every moment since then trying to rectify my mistake. To help him, to guide him ... but from afar," he mumbles, each word forcing its way past his cracked lips.

How exhausted he must be.

"Can you ... Elara..." His voice falters for a moment, but he grits his teeth and pushes on. "Can you tell him? Tell Axton?"

My throat tightens. But I decide to give him a small gift before he dies. One I wish my father had received. "Axe is not a good man because of the sacrifices you made. He's scarred, mutilated inside, and hates himself. But I see him. The real him. The man who will do anything for family, who protects me with a fierce pride, who has been reforged. Axe is strong, he is loyal, and I will take up where you failed. He won't suffer any longer."

Orion's expression softens. "Thank you."

I close my mouth, wishing there was more time. Axe deserves so much more.

"I'll tell him," I manage to murmur. "If you tell me exactly where Marianne is."

His body relaxes slightly at my promise, a sigh slipping past his bloodless lips. I lower my ear to his mouth so I can hear him better as he tells me.

"I'm sorry..." he finishes, a mere whisper of sound against the cacophony of battle.

His eyes flicker toward Axe one last time before his gaze grows vacant. His limp hand falls from my grasp.

Grief for Axe threatens to swallow me whole, but I force myself to stand, Orion's final words resonating in my ears.

I have a promise to keep.

I leave Orion behind. A father who made too many mistakes and lost too much—just like my father.

Axe's ash-blond hair clings to his forehead. He's injured, wet with blood, but fights like the demon the Sovereigns were so intent on summoning.

I sprint toward the ruby Heart. It's just lying among the debris, forgotten in the turmoil.

I scoop it up, and its weight in my hand feels oddly comforting.

Axe thrashes against the High Sovereign with boundless fury. I can't hear anything as I make my way to him, clutching the ruby tight against my chest.

There's a terrifying beauty in the way Axe fights. Each movement is a sinuous dance laced with anger and grief so palpable, it's almost a visible aura. He's a masterpiece of muscle and fury, poised despite the years of cold conditioning under the Sovereigns.

"AXE!" I cry out, my voice ripping through slices of the High Sovereign's blade through the air, so close to Axe's neck.

He looks over. His attention rests on the Heart clutched in my hand and understanding dawns.

Axe maneuvers himself between me and the High Sovereign. He strikes out with a ferocity born from years of abuse. His hair whips across his face as he moves like a wraith.

I lock onto the High Sovereign's mask, and a surge of determination shoots through me—for Axe, for my dad, for my brother, for my men—

I leap, my arm shooting forward with all the strength I possess.

The High Sovereign turns just as the Heart connects, his porcelain mask cracking upon impact. The sheer force of the blow sends him sprawling backward.

Time freezes, every sound coming to a sudden halt, drowned by the sharp intake of breaths. His mask shatters, revealing his true face in all its fury and disbelief.

His eyes lock onto mine—a faded blue devoid of any humanity. I see him for who he truly is—an ogre who will stop at nothing to hoard power.

The true Exalted Regent.

His lips curl back in a subhuman snarl. "You little cunt— you can't take the Heart away from me."

"I just did," I retort.

Wilder slams a boot into the High Sovereign's chest, knocking him flat and keeping him there.

Axe comes to my side. Concern and relief fill his scarred face. Sweating and breathing heavily from the battle, he pulls me into a tight embrace.

I wrap my arms around him, clutching him.

"Elara," Axe murmurs against my hair. His hesitant voice is filled with countless emotions.

There's no victory cheer, no joyful hugs or laughter. But for once, it doesn't matter.

Out of the corner of my eye, I see something—

"Axe, duck!"

The Scourge Sovereign pounces on Axe with a vehement roar. He's caught off guard, so Axe's arms go slack around me.

But before the Scourge can land a fatal blow, I throw myself in front of Axe and slam into the Scourge with all the force I can muster.

We both crash onto the marble floor. Electric pain shoots through my body, but I grit my teeth against it and push myself up.

The Scourge Sovereign rolls until he leaps to his feet and towers over me, his hulking form blocking out the soft light of the sconces. His mask is stripped away, revealing a face that's more beast than man. He snarls, a distorted sound.

With a guttural bellow, Kaspian plows into the Scourge from the side, his body colliding with a force that'd break bones—maybe mine, maybe the Sovereign's, I don't know, because the world tilts sideways and my back slams into the cold marble floor.

Ignoring the pain radiating from my bruised body, I crawl toward the Scourge when Kaspian flings him off me, and the Scourge lands on his back several feet away.

Hatred shades the Scourge's eyes with a darkness that mirrors the monstrous deeds he's committed. It isn't victory that distorts his face but disturbance—over losing his dominance, of losing control.

My fingers curl into tight fists as I swing one leg over and sit, straddling him. Sweat drips into my vision.

I raise my arm high above me, the ruby Heart glowing with the surrounding flames, casting a crimson hue on the Scourge's despicable face.

I slam the ruby heart into his temple. Again and again, until his screams die down into whimpers.

"Elara!"

Kaspian's voice filters into my hearing, filled with a shocking amount of alarm, especially for him.

But I don't stop. Not until the Scourge Sovereign lies still beneath me, his eyes emptied.

I stand slowly, staggering a bit as waves of exhaustion wash over me. Axe rights me, pulling me into his arms just as my knees buckle.

"I've got you," he murmurs into my ear, cradling me against his chest.

His damp, blood-soaked hair frames his face beautifully. I tell him so.

A smile doesn't touch his lips, but Axe's eyes soften, and he plants a bloody kiss on my forehead.

His hold on me tightens just as the silence around us breaks. Sasha rushes over, her face a mix of horror and relief. I can feel her trembling when she wraps her arms around me, pulling me into a crushing hug.

"Holy shit, El," she murmurs against my shoulder.

"You're an idiot for staying," I whisper in return.

"You're a moron for thinking I'd ever leave you to an evil cult," she retorts.

Cav and Kaspian stride over to our little huddle, their faces unreadable as they surround us. Cav brushes my hair off my forehead, stroking with silent gratitude, while Wilder's attention stays fixed on the fallen High Sovereign.

"What should we do with this asshole?"

"Tie him to the altar in the same way he pinned my butterfly." Cav circles him, as lithe as a snow leopard stalking its prey. "I'm not done with him."

Kaspian crouches beside the Scourge Sovereign's corpse. He prods it with a single finger, lips curling. "Efficient work, beastie."

He surveys the carnage. Blood pools on the marble, seeping into hairline cracks. The tang of copper hangs heavy in the air.

I clamp my teeth together, fighting a surge of nausea. The adrenaline ebbs, exhaustion and trauma taking its place. Every breath sears my lungs, every movement ignites agony.

Kaspian's unsettling focus centers on me. Silent on his feet, he lifts me into his arms when I see it—a glint of light in the corner of my eye.

The ruby Heart.

Axe notices, reluctantly picking it up and handing it to me.

It feels oddly warm in my palm. Alive.

Perhaps it isn't cursed after all.

Maybe it's just misunderstood—like me, like Axe, like everyone in our battered group.

Axe's hand covers one of mine and gives a reassuring squeeze, his knuckles split and clotted with blood.

Wordlessly, Wilder rests his hand on one of my legs as Kaspian cradles me to his chest. Cav lands a kiss on the top of my head, stroking my long hair.

Their touches send my abused skin and my shredded soul alight. Partly from exhaustion, but mostly from that familiar spark that always ignites between us.

Sasha flanks us, her expression flitting from pride to panic as she fully comprehends what the hell we just did.

Cav's lips brush my hair as he leans in to whisper, "We broke the curse."

Kaspian pauses, his arms tightening around me. "Where to now, beastie?"

I look at each of them in turn. My warriors, my friends, my loves.

"Home," I say, my voice steady despite the adrenaline seeping out of me. "Let's go home."

Kaspian carries me, limping through the archway. Sasha assists Axe while Cav and Wilder mutter ominously about staying behind and taking care of the rest, including the High Sovereign, who is currently struggling against Wilder's bodily restraint.

It's difficult not to wonder what Cav and Wilder will do to him. Part of me wants to ask them to stop this cycle of violence, but that isn't who my men are, and I won't ask them to be anything different.

The Sovereigns took these boys when they were so young, barely teenagers, and broke them down until they were nothing but shards, with the intention of sharpening them into deadly blades. These "guardians" became fucked-up father figures to the boys, not by choice, but when their own fathers gave them over. Because of tradition and order stemming from over 300 years ago.

The consequences of this are so overwhelming, it completely overshadows the fact that I just killed a man.

The memory of the Scourge's eyes, wide with shock that an Anderton descendant was draining the life from him, and the way his face caved in, flashes through my mind.

I want to cry, to scream, to beg for forgiveness. But I also want to justify my actions, to believe that what I did was necessary.

The weight of it all presses down on me, threatening to crush what's left of my humanity. A wave of guilt, quickly followed by a sickening sense of relief and then numbness, spreads through my body like ice water.

We move out of the manor and into the dark, away from pathways and past the imposing stone buildings of Titan Falls University, their Gothic spires a monochromatic blur against the inky blackness above us.

We move as one.

I look down at the ruby heart still clutched in my hands. Light plays across the facets, refracting, fragmenting.

Sasha follows my study. "What should we do with that thing?"

"I don't know." My voice emerges hoarse, scraped raw. "Lock it away. Destroy it. Put it back where Sarah wanted it to remain forever."

My words remain in the air long after I've said them. A vow. A promise my ancestors, and then my father and brother, made to keep this ruby and its sordid history from ever getting into the wrong hands.

One I intend to keep.

The growl of the SUV cuts into my thoughts. Tires crunch on gravel.

Exhaustion drags at me, pain a dull throb. I let my eyes drift shut, surrendering to the pull of oblivion.

The last thing I feel is Kaspian's gentle release, and I dream of the solid warmth of my men surrounding me, a shield against the demons lurking in the dark.

CHAPTER 34
ELARA

I open my eyes, my body aching with every slight movement, the rest of my senses falling behind.

When I curl my fingers, the softest cotton hits my skin, coupled with my head lying on a cloud. Through slits of vision, I realize I'm in a bed with a red velvet canopy above me and gold tassels swinging gently from the open, half-round windows on either side.

Golden rays stream through the grime of the window's panels, showcasing a figure in a sofa chair by the bed, head dipped low and thick, black hair curtaining her face.

The sound of pages turning comes next, a type of noise that calms my breathing and prevents the instant panic at the thought of someone in the room with me—I killed a man—while my memories resurface.

I must make a rustling sound because the face becomes clear through her cascading ebony waves, and Clover smiles. "You're awake. How are you feeling?"

I swallow, my throat dry. "Like death warmed over." Each of my men, branded with a skin-melting ruby. "The guys. Sasha. Where are they?"

"Alive. Rossi's tending to them downstairs. They're ... resistant to treatment."

A ghost of a smile touches my lips at the thought of my men submitting to Rossi's surgical instruments. "Sounds about right. They need Rossi's help, though. If I have to go down there and make them—"

—sounds of them screaming while the ruby was torched into their skin—

Clover rests her hand on mine, giving it a reassuring squeeze. "It's all right. You don't have to go anywhere. They'll be okay."

Too exhausted to fight, I lean back against the stacked pillows. "Who called you to come help us?"

She gives a wry half smile. "Kaspian. He refused to leave your side when he brought you into this room. Even cleaned you up himself. But I think it was when his blood started dripping on you during your sponge bath that he thought to call in reinforcements."

Despite everything, I feel a flicker of warmth at the thought of him doing all that. Stubborn idiot.

"He must've been desperate to call the Vultures," I say more to myself.

"You've all been through a lot, and we've experienced something similar. I'm glad that man saw sense because I'm convinced Kaspian prefers to live on scorched earth."

I respond with a quiet laugh. Now that I know my men are safely tended to and I've figured out where I am—Mom's bedroom—my attention drifts to the old, leather tome on Clover's lap filled with cracked, yellowed pages. "What are you reading?"

"This was in the library down the hall. It confirms what I've discovered about your ties to the Anderton line."

Clover closes the book and shows me the cover.

Though she found it in Farrow Manor, I've never seen it before.

She explains, "It's a ledger from the 1700s, kept by a

midwife named Agnes Briar. She recorded every birth she attended, including some... unofficial ones."

My interest piques despite my utter depletion of adrenaline. "Unofficial?"

"Births that wealthy families wanted kept quiet. And an entry here is particularly interesting." Clover lays the book on the space beside me and points. "A baby girl, born to a 'Miss L' in 1715. The same year Sarah Anderton was tortured and executed."

I push myself up, ignoring the protest from my battered body. "And you think that's related to the lost Anderton baby?"

Clover nods, her eyes shining. "I wanted to wait until you felt better to give you all the information, but if it were me lying in bed talking to someone with all the answers at her fingertips, I'd want to know."

I nod eagerly. "Yes. Yes, tell me. Please."

"Your father must have seen this book. It's part of how he pieced together your ancestry."

At my how did you know about my father? look, she explains, "Kaspian's a chatty Cathy when he experiences blood loss. But really, he just confirmed what I was already piecing together. But there's more. The midwife wrote something else— something that explains why the Cimmerian Court has been obsessed with your bloodline for centuries." Clover's finger traces the faded ink. "The midwife's notes mention something extraordinary about the baby. She wrote that the child was born with eyes that seemed to shift color, 'like the facets of a fine gem.' At first, Agnes thought it was a trick of the light, but as the days passed, she became convinced it was real."

I frown, trying to process this. "But how is that possible?"

Clover leans in. "Your father connected this to something called tetrachromacy—a rare genetic condition that's predomi- nantly in women and allows people to see a vastly broader spec- trum of colors than normal. He found medical records in your family line showing a higher incidence of this trait, starting from that time. Including you."

"So we can ... see more colors?" I ask, still not understanding the significance.

Never in my life did it occur to me to ask others how many colors they see versus what I can. And my mother certainly hasn't told me anything about it, nor has Gram.

"It's more than that. This heightened perception seems to manifest in other ways, too. Enhanced intuition, an uncanny ability to read people and situations. Sarah Anderton's renowned insight, her skill at seeing through deception—I call it witch-craft. But to pragmatists, it's this genetic quirk, passed down through generations."

The implications start to dawn on me. "And the Cimmerian Court..."

Clover nods grimly. "They've been searching for this trait, believing it to be the key to ultimate power and control. Imagine having someone who could unfailingly detect lies, who could see hidden patterns others miss, creating the ultimate vessel for their demonic patron."

I struggle to sit up straighter. "So that's why they wanted me. Why they've been hunting my bloodline for centuries."

My entire life, my very existence, has been shaped by this centuries-old obsession. The Cimmerian Court's relentless pursuit, my father's desperate efforts to protect me, the losses I've endured ... it all traces back to this genetic quirk, this supposed 'gift' that feels more like a curse.

Clover, so immersed in her discovery, doesn't notice my crestfallen expression.

"Your father was a genius. He traced the link through your maternal side, the Farrow line, but in the 18th century, there was a second link."

I clench my fists, ignoring the throb of pain from my knuckles.

"William Jonquil, also one of your ancestors. He was the key. He's the baby's father."

"The secret demonologist with a hidden office in my house? That Jonquil?"

"The very one. His occult practices weren't bad, per se. He was trying to sever himself from his servitude to the Exalted Regent. He wanted more than anything to whisk the love of his life away and start a family with her. But he was caught and, uh, quartered for his crime against the Sovereigns."

I stare at her.

For the first, and only, time, I understand why Orion had my brother swiftly assassinated versus the alternative.

I'm able to recover enough to ask, "Did Sarah's daughter have to witness that?"

I couldn't imagine watching Maverick torn apart, limb by limb while he screamed.

"I don't think so. Sarah didn't approve of the older man's relationship with her daughter. She did everything she could to keep them separate, including involving her daughter in her underground activities and tried to smuggle her granddaughter out of Titan Falls. It backfired. There was a turncoat in her ranks—Jackson Nightshade. Sarah realized that too late, but she perceived the threat against her and her daughter before Mr. Jonquil did, and hid her daughter before Sarah was arrested and dragged away from their house."

"The baby. Do we know what happened to her?"

Clover's expression softens. "Her name was Evangeline. Jackson Nightshade sold her to a wealthy family in France."

"Yes, I remember. Cav's ancestor was one of the founders of the Court and helped murder Sarah and her daughter. But why? Why would he do such a thing?"

"From what I gather, he was the first Nightshade to acquire an interest in demonology and an obsession with greed, power, and control. I believe he sold the baby because of Sarah's last words while she was dying—she cursed Jackson Nightshade and all his descendants. He believed in that kind of thing and must've been paranoid, so he sent the child as far away as he could while still making money off her. Of course, that was before his obsession grew and he realized he needed Anderton blood to destroy Sarah's curse and summon his demon overlord."

"I'm surprised he didn't kill the baby," I mutter, feeling sick all over again.

"I think Sarah's curse really got to him. Doing anything to Evangeline would've made it more devastating in his mind. But here's where it gets interesting. Someone in the Court destroyed the records of the sale. Jackson was never able to find her once he sold her."

I furrow my brow. "Why would they do that?"

"Guilt, maybe. Or they saw the madness in Nightshade's plan and wanted to protect the child. Either way, it worked. Evangeline disappeared from history. The family changed their name and moved around. They protected her, knowingly or not."

"So how did my father figure it out?"

"That's where it gets fascinating." Clover continues. "He cross-referenced this information with old Court documents he'd 'acquired' through less-than-legal means. He discovered that Evangeline's protector was none other than Hope Blackwood, Jackson Nightshade's wife."

My breath catches. "Nightshade's own wife betrayed him?"

Clover nods. "Hope orchestrated Evangeline's sale to a trusted friend in France, then systematically destroyed all records of the transaction. She even planted false leads to throw off anyone who might come looking."

"But why would my father risk everything to uncover this?"

"Because of you, Elara," Clover says softly. "When he found out the Anderton line was in his own blood, the blood of his wife and children, he wanted to protect you by understanding the full scope of your heritage and the danger it posed."

"Oh, Dad." I close my eyes, tears breaking through. "And now?"

Clover gently closes the book, lays my hand over it, then squeezes mine with her own. At the same time, she lowers and picks something off the floor.

A glittery, blood-red ruby.

She lays the Heart on the book and beside our joined hands.

"Now, you have the power to reshape the Court's future. Your father's work, Maverick's death, Hope's sacrifice—it all led to this moment. The question is, what will you do with it?"

I gaze at the terrible jewel.

The gem's rough, uncut surface forms an irregular, heart-like shape, its edges jagged and uneven. Deep crimson dominates, but streaks of darker red run through it like veins. Where the two halves were rejoined, a thin line is visible, like a freshly healed wound.

I can't bring myself to touch it.

As I turn my head away from it, light catches on countless tiny imperfections, each one a little firefly witness to the blood spilled in its name.

Fear and disgust clench around my neck like a noose. I have the desperate need to hurl it across the room, to smash it until nothing remains but dust. Yet I can't let it go, can't stop staring at the legacy of pain and greed I've literally held in my hands.

Clover watches the horror play across my face.

"I ... I don't know what to do with it," I stammer, looking up at Clover with a wretched gaze.

"There's no right answer," she says kindly. "But I suggest you consider what your father and brother would have wanted. They protected this heritage for you."

"And Sarah?" I ask, my voice barely above a whisper.

"Sarah wanted her Heart to be used for good. I can promise you that." Clover breathes out slowly, her stare unwavering on mine. "She wanted it to protect her family. And from what I've come to understand of you, Elara Wraithwood ... you are the embodiment of that wish."

"I want it locked away," I declare, my voice choked with emotion. "Forever."

Maverick found Sarah's vault and kept a piece of the ruby there, hidden deep within Titan Falls University's catacombs, where the Heart was safely locked away for centuries. No one should wield such obsessive power.

"Back to the buried vault it came from," I add.

Clover raises one nearly perfect eyebrow at me but doesn't object. She studies me for a moment before nodding once, as if affirming a question within herself. "I might know of a better place to hide it."

I incline my head quizzically, which she responds to with an enigmatic smile.

"Sarah's daughter. I found her," Clover says. "And I know where her body rests."

My chin dips. My eyes widen. "That's a very important piece of information you left out of your thesis paper."

"I don't plan on ever revealing it," she explains. "Whether you believe in dark magic or not, so much bloodshed, violence, and terrible downfalls have come from the Anderton deaths and their hidden jewels. Sarah wanted her secrets buried with her. I stand by her wish."

I nod. "Me, too."

Clover gives me an understanding smile.

My thoughts whirl and stumble over each other as I process this information. "So you want to bury it with her?"

"Yes. The Heart should rest beside the first innocent life lost."

Clover's solution hits me like a blow to the chest. It's beautiful, hauntingly so—just like the tragic tale surrounding it.

"The ruby will go to Sarah's nameless daughter," I say, tasting the syllables on my tongue.

The decision feels right. It feels just. The Heart has brought nothing but pain and sorrow to my family line, spiraling down through the centuries from Sarah to me. Now, it will bring closure—a silent end as it's buried deep within the earth alongside Sarah's daughter.

"Nameless to many, but not by all," Clover says. "Only the Vultures and I know who she is, and it will die with us."

"Will you bring it there? To her?" I ask Clover.

Her approval is immediate and without hesitation. "Of course. We could put it there tonight."

"Do it."

I put as much steel into my tone as I can muster.

When I voice the decision, I feel closer to my brother than I have since his murder. It's as if he's standing beside me, whispering in my ear.

You've done well, Ellie.

CHAPTER 35

AXE

THE PHANTOM

The stinging sensation over my heart draws me back to reality, and I glance down at the blood seeping through the bandages Rossi wrapped around my chest. It's the only thing I wear other than white boxer briefs. Any other piece of fabric touching my skin is too much stimuli.

It's all too fucking much.

I was the most docile of the four of us, so I was treated by Rossi first, then ushered into a guest room by Tempest before the real fun began with the rest of my brothers. No one has shared with the Vultures all of the homemade traps Caroline laid, so every now and then, I hear a genuinely deplorable curse before whatever dared threaten them is broken in two.

In the quiet of one of the forgotten, upper-level bedrooms, the fresh, ugly burn pulsates in time with my heartbeat, a constant reminder of the ordeal I put us all through.

And even though I sit on the edge of the bed, safe and cleaned up, this peace does little to comfort me.

My eyes scan the room, taking in the moth-eaten curtains and once ornate wallpaper of roses and gold crests. The dark opulence is undeserved. I should be rotting in the ground along with my father.

Then the door opens, and Elara walks in.

She crosses the room gracefully, dressed in cotton shorts and a white tank, her fiery auburn hair dancing around her shoulders like a living flame.

I can't bring myself to look at her face and see what's reflected there. The pain, the heartbreak, or even worse, the hatred.

So I keep my gaze locked on my hands, resting on my thighs.

There's a moment of silence when Elara doesn't speak, and neither do I.

The rustle of her clothes precedes the slight weight on the bed beside me.

She's chosen to sit next to me—that has to mean something, right?

But what does it mean if she can't look at me either?

"Are you alright?" Elara's words are soft, almost drowned out by the muffled threats downstairs.

Her face is still turned away from me. All I see is the soft silhouette of her profile caught in the dim light filtering through the threadbare curtains.

"What's one more scar?" I say with a jaded curve at the corner of my mouth.

The attempt at humor falls flat, and I am ashamed for it. Closing my eyes, I recall the block of text I forced myself to memorize before seeing Elara again.

"Elara ... I was the one who broke into Maverick's room that night. The Sovereigns, they'd just told me of my sister, that she was alive, and I remembered enough to know it was true. I had to discover what Maverick was hoarding, give them evidence so they wouldn't track Mari down and kill her—"

"You did what you had to."

Elara lifts her hand, gently tracing the edges of my new bandages.

"It doesn't justify it," I reply, still unable to meet her eyes. "I messed up his things. I sullied his memory. I broke your heart."

"Did you have a choice?"

"Always."

I say it with such vehemence, I almost believe it.

"It's not about forgiveness, Axe."

Elara's fingers entwine with mine, and every dark impulse within me quiets underneath her touch.

"It's about understanding that we were all forced into corners. And when pushed into a corner, we do what we need to survive."

I feel her gaze on me now, ever watchful, ever caring, and for once in my life, I hope she sees the truth. Not the hardened, unfeeling brute I've been led to believe I am, but the man underneath who, despite his hardened exterior, cares deeply for the people he's wronged.

My silence stretches on, but Elara's patience is unending, her understanding infinite.

A woman, a miracle, I do not deserve.

"You're not a monster, Axe," she whispers, squeezing my hand gently.

A keening sound catches in my throat, and I blink rapidly against a foreign sting in my eyes.

Elara's words bring no relief. Rather, they carve deeper into my soul as a hopeless truth that's hard to swallow—but I want to believe her.

A hesitant nod is all I have to offer as a reply.

"I know what you're thinking," Elara murmurs. Her thumb rubs comforting circles onto the back of my hand. "I've seen it in your eyes every time you look at me, at your brothers... You're asking yourself if there's still redemption for a man like you."

"Yes," I whisper roughly.

It's an admission that costs everything.

Elara pulls me closer until her head rests on my shoulder. "And the answer is yes."

Her response is firm yet gentle, confident yet empathetic. It's as assertive as she's always been, unwavering in her belief that there's goodness in everyone.

"Killing ... it stains your soul," I tell her.

"And you think that stain is permanent," she counters.

She releases my hand to cup my face, turning it toward her, forcing me to look. "If that's true, Axe, then I have blood on my hands, too, so deeply ingrained that no amount of scrubbing will ever clean them. I killed the Scourge. Violently. Viciously." Her eyes sheen over with tears as she voices her brutal actions. "Do you think I'm undeserving of forgiveness?"

"Never."

The strained word is strangled, tormented.

"Then why," she breathes, her voice steady even as tears drip from her amber eyes, "why can't you accept that you deserve forgiveness too?"

"I..." I falter. All I can do is stare at her in disbelief.

I work my jaw, trying to voice the fears and doubts that have caged me for years. "I've done so much..."

"So have they," she interjects fiercely. She pulls away slightly, holding my gaze with the force of her conviction. "The Court— the Sovereigns. The same way they forced their ideas onto Wilder, Cav, and Kaspian. They've hurt us enough. It's time we stop hurting ourselves."

I look at Elara, really look at her. She is a bittersweet symphony of regret, hope, bravery, and punishment. She is pure, even when covered in gore. She shines brightly amid shadows. She is good and kind and compassionate, even when forced into violent actions. And me?

I don't deserve her, yes, but I have her.

Elara's gaze holds mine captive, refusing to let go even as I try to break away. Her fingers trace the outline of my face, pausing at the slash down my cheek, brushing my lips, before running through my unkempt hair, grounding me in this moment with her before she closes the gap and touches her mouth to mine.

"I want to believe you," I confess as almost a silent plea against her lips.

The kiss is not one of possession, not this time. It communicates in ways my words can't, my lips moving with something akin to dark and sweet desperation.

When we break apart for air, she rests her forehead against mine.

"I know you do." She breathes out the words so softly that they almost get lost in our stillness. Her hands, warm and steady, continue to cradle my face.

Time stops as I allow myself to drown in her warmth, in her faith in me ... in us.

And then she drops another bombshell.

"Axe, I need to tell you something," she says. "Before he died, Orion told me where your sister is. She's alive."

I hold my breath as uninvited images assault my mind—of family dinners we never had, of school races I was never a part of, of laughter that never echoed in our home because we were separated, bartered with, sold.

But Elara continues like a gentle salve soothing my open wound. "She's safe. Living in Montana. She got into college there on a scholarship for dressage."

"She ... rides horses?"

"Always has," Elara replies, her voice tender. "I asked Clover to look into it earlier. Your sister's even won a few competitions. She goes by Melody Parsons now."

I sit there, stunned into silence. An equestrian. It seems so gentle, so delicate. But then again, it's fitting.

My hand instinctively reaches for the wound on my chest—a reminder of my past mistakes, the price paid for my imagined redemption.

"She knows she has a brother somewhere, Axe," Elara

murmurs, stroking the stubble on my jaw. "Orion made sure of it."

Her words punch through me like a bullet, leaving me momentarily breathless. My little sister ... alive ... and she knows about me.

"Write to her," she whispers, bringing a hand up to push back loose strands of hair from my forehead. Her touch is heaven. "Let her know that you're alive, too."

I hesitate, studying Elara for a long moment before I finally nod. Elara's face softens a small but genuine smile as she fetches paper and a pen from a nearby drawer.

The blank page stares back at me as I place the pen onto it. It feels foreign and unreal. The whole concept is dated, one born from a time when people trusted their hearts to mere parchment and ink.

Elara's arms encircle me from behind, her chin resting on my shoulder. Her body molds against mine like it's made to fit. Soft where I'm hard, curved where I'm sharpened.

Because of her, I begin to write.

Dear Melody,

Fuck, it feels strange to write her name down, to acknowledge that this person exists, that she is a part of me.

I've wasted so many years believing we were alone in this world…

The words flow from my mind, through my hand, and onto the paper. It's a confessional. It's healing. It's terrifying. But every word is worth it.

After finishing the final sentence and signing my name, I carefully fold the paper and turn to Elara.

"Thank you," I say. "For everything. For being here, for not giving up on me."

Setting the letter aside, I pull Elara onto my lap, careful of my injuries. The pain is there, but it's dulled by Elara's warmth. My hands find her waist, steadying her.

Her lips meet mine, soft at first, then with increasing passion.

"I'm broken, Elara," I confess while losing myself in her taste, her scent, the feel of her.

"We're all a little broken," Elara responds, punctuating the end of our conversation by sliding her tongue in my mouth.

Her body is the best kind of fire, a blackening I'll gladly allow to seep through my bandages and into my skin.

Elara's hands are tangled in my hair, pulling me closer, deeper. She straddles me with absolute certainty, her thighs on either side of my hips. My hands slide up from her waist to the small of her back, pulling her flush against me.

My hands find the hem of her tank top, and I pull it off in one swift motion, her softness contrasting with my calloused, scarred exterior. Her attention flicks downward briefly before she goes back to my face while reaching into my boxers and palming my dick.

I groan at the intimacy, but there's nothing quick or fast-paced about her shifting her shorts and underwear to one side and exposing her pussy while she guides me into her in a single, fluid motion.

I hold her tight as we move together, the sensation of being inside her shattering every wall I've built around myself over years of loneliness and despair. I bury my face in the crook of her neck and release a guttural groan.

This is Elara, the woman who has captured my dark heart and refuses to let it go.

My fingers dig into her waist as the pressure builds up inside me—that sweet agony just before release.

And I give her a scar while I come, biting just above her heart and proving to her, to myself, that I'll never let her go, either.

CHAPTER 36

KASPIAN

The soft hum of computer towers fills the sitting room section of Farrow Manor's library as I stand at the center, surrounded by multiple screens displaying the digital lives of each Sovereign.

Silas Morcant, the High Sovereign. His digital life is as austere as the man himself. Bank accounts brimming with ill-gotten gains, a calendar meticulously filled with coded Cimmerian Court meetings, and a cold correspondence style.

The Silent Sovereign, Orion Devereaux and Axe's deadbeat dad. His online presence is even more elusive, which isn't shocking, considering how he ghosted his children. His transactions are conducted through intermediaries, proxies, and throwaway accounts, leaving me to sift through layers of encrypted messages and transactions that leave only the slightest digital trace.

And then there's the Scourge Sovereign, Evander Verlane, whose e-life blatantly reflects his sadistic nature. Graphic photographic exchanges and financial transactions linked to underground fight clubs and black-market arms deals are only some of what I sift through.

My fingers dance on the keyboard, hacking into their accounts, draining their coffers, shrouding my and my brothers' bloody deeds in a veil of cyber deceit—changing camera footage, manipulating data files, planting false electronic trails. It's a kind of ASMR that somewhat satisfies my thirst for revenge.

"Rossi would not approve."

Elara's voice drifts from the doorway, soft yet laced with concern.

I swivel in my chair to face her, covering my wince of pain just in time. Fucking bandages. I'm certain Rossi and Tempest used too many strips and mummified me on purpose.

But thoughts of those featherless birds go out the window when I fully take in who's standing in front of me.

Elara's dressed in a tight white tank and tighter blue shorts. Her thick hair is finger-tousled in all the right ways, falling around her shoulders in tangled waves. But beneath all that sex appeal is something else—worry.

Ah fuck, it better not be for me.

"Are you going to tattle to Daddy?" I ask, drawing out the question.

"No," she says, stepping into the room. "I've come to understand why you're not resting."

Her bewitching eyes hold mine.

My chest constricts in a way unrelated to the horrendous burn under all the gauze. It's the sight of her trying to piece together the enigma that is Kaspian Valenti that does it. Such a futile effort. Even I can't unravel myself fully.

Elara's asking me, without uttering the words, to let my guard down and let her in. But dammit, vulnerability isn't a language I'm well versed in.

So instead, I scoff, rubbing my temples as the headache that's been steadily building since our final encounter with the Sovereigns throbs behind my eyes. "And what's your theory, Dr. Wraithwood?"

Elara crosses her arms, narrowing her eyes. "The only person who could make the death of three leaders somehow worse is you. You're nursing a brainchild of mischief over there."

My mouth tugs up into a half smile. "Always so quick to assume the worst of me."

She moves closer, the faint scent of her spicy perfume teasing my senses. I try to focus on the screens around me, but it's damn near impossible when Elara's standing within snatching distance.

"I'm not assuming," she counters. "I know you."

The silence that follows her statement stretches on for an agonizing moment. She knows me. The thought should be terrifying.

What's more frightening is that it's … not.

"Then you should know," I say finally, forcing myself to break eye contact. "Rest is a luxury we can't afford right now. I have deaths to cover up and a Court to fix."

Elara sighs softly, stepping closer until she's leaning against the back of my chair. Her fingers brush against my bare shoulders, and despite myself, I stiffen at her touch.

"Your body needs rest to heal."

"And your point is?"

Elara's quiet for a long minute, her fingers trailing lines of heat on my skin.

"My point, Valenti," she finally says, "is that you're not invincible. You couldn't even put on a shirt, could you? All you could manage was sweatpants because your body's been through too much. And God forbid you ask for help the way you help others. Like me."

I chuckle coldly. The sound slithers over the surrounding bookshelves before dying out.

"I'm still invincible where it counts," I retort, leaning into her touch and rubbing my palm over my growing erection through those sweatpants.

Her hands freeze on my shoulders.

"Kaspian…" she warns.

Fuck. The sound of my name on her lips does things to me that no assortment of bandages or painkillers can alleviate.

I shrug out of her hold and utter the biggest lie of them all. "I'm fine, beastie."

"Stop being so goddamn stubborn and let me help you."

Her words tap against the walls surrounding my heart with more force than a battering ram. I can't deny the sincerity burning in her eyes or its effect on me.

"Help?" I ask, looking over my shoulder and forcing a smirk that doesn't reach my eyes. "I didn't realize being shot at and branded made me eligible for a spot in your charity case lineup. You've got your hands full with Axe, anyway."

Her face smooths, then turns cold and bloodless. If I weren't coldblooded myself, I'd be genuinely concerned over what I just unleashed.

Until she buries her fingers in my hair and yanks my head back until I bang against the chair, leaving our faces inches apart.

"I dare you to put him before yourself again, Kaspian," she hisses through gritted teeth. "You're as important to me as he is."

I laugh at that. A low, harsh sound.

"You amuse me, Wraithwood," I say, muscling past the knot in my chest. "Your misplaced sense of duty is certainly entertaining."

"Is that what you think?" Her voice is softer now, the rage in her eyes slowly replaced by something akin to hurt, but she doesn't let go of me. "That I consider you a duty?"

"I'm a liability, Elara."

I regret my words as soon as they slip from my lips. It's unlike me to let anyone in like this.

But with Elara ... everything's different.

Her fingers soften their grip on my hair, and she uses her other hand to trace a soothing path down to the side of my jaw that almost makes me purr.

"I don't deserve your faith," I say grimly, even as I close my eyes to her touch, trying hard to ignore the fluttering feeling in the yawning pit of my stomach.

"But you have it."

Regrettably, her hand leaves my face to rest on my shoulder. The pressure is gentle but firm.

A silent promise of staying right here.

"Why are you so hell-bent on saving me?" I snap, ignoring how my voice weakens on the last two words.

It's pathetic how desperately I want her answer to be different from the one that's trumpeting in my head.

Elara scans my entire face, from my crown, to my eyes, to my mouth.

"Because," she murmurs. "You're worth saving."

"Elara." It's my turn to warn her.

She places her hand gently over the layers of bandages protecting my heart—that traitorous organ the ruby should've melted along with my skin.

Elara stares down at where we're connected, noting the pounding underneath her hand. "There's your answer."

Her eyes rise to mine with such conviction, it steals my breath.

I can't push her away. Not now. Maybe not ever. Instead, I grab her wrist, intending on pulling her off my chest and slipping out of her shockingly strong grip on my scalp, but I pause.

"Your definition of worth is skewed," I mutter, my gaze fixed on my hand wrapped around her small wrist. I notice the difference of her delicate fingers against my battle-worn skin, the purity of her touch against the grit of my life.

Sensing the slack, Elara moves her hand lower, tracing along the edge of my sweatpants. "Is this what you want, Kaspian?"

The little beastie is testing me, pushing boundaries.

"I'm not afraid of you," she says, circling to my front, still keeping me in her hold. "And you shouldn't be afraid of yourself."

Anger flares.

I abruptly rise, sending her staggering back, then yank her

against me with all the strength of a wounded, cornered animal until we're toe-to-toe.

Elara pulls her head back to glare at me while I dig my fingers into her hips, locking her into place. Her cheeks are flushed with a color that rivals her hair, her eyes bright with—good—hatred.

But she meets my gaze head-on, and that's when it happens.

A moment. Just a second when my facade cracks enough to reveal a sliver of the uncertainty brewing inside me. My fate, our future, everything hanging in an unsteady balance.

There's a hushed silence as Elara takes in the change in my demeanor, that fleeting vulnerability that makes rare appearances even when no one's looking.

But she's looking now.

"And if I prove you have every reason to fear me?" I challenge darkly, every muscle in my body turning into thin, taut sinew ready to snap.

"Do your worst," she dares with a defiant chin tilt, although her voice wavers just slightly.

I immerse myself in the intoxicating scent of her, spice and honey, the scent that's been driving me to insanity since the day she first walked into my life.

I close my eyes, pressing my forehead against hers in a rare moment of surrender. Her pulse quickens under my hands, warm and alive.

Then, in one single arc, I spin her around and pin her against the desk, a monitor crashing against the floor and cracking the screen, its picture turning into flashing, pixelated colors.

Elara doesn't struggle or try to break free. Her hands snake up the clasp around my neck, pulling me closer. My teeth snag her lower lip until my taste buds burst with her blood.

"Still unafraid?" I question, running my tongue along my teeth.

After a second of silence, she says, "Always."

I descend onto her lips with all the brutality that has gnawed at my soul. Elara returns my fervor with surprising strength. Our bodies collide, fight, struggle, and eventually find a rhythm only star-crossed lovers understand.

Elara's moans fuel the poison burning inside me. I grip her hair, pulling her head back so she can watch me grind against her. Elara bites down on her lower lip, leaving a bruise over my bite mark, and I nearly come on the spot.

I slide a hand up her thigh, teasing her clit through the thin fabric of her shorts and eliciting a sharp gasp from deep within her throat. Her inner walls clench around my fingers once I edge around her clothes and stroke her closer toward orgasm—but I can't give in yet.

With one last forceful push into her wet heat, I pull out abruptly, leaving both of us panting heavily. Elara's eyes burn with unshed tears but also desire, pleading for more punishment —for release from this tormented lust that consumes us both.

"Please," she says between ragged breaths. "I beg you … fuck me harder."

Without warning, I lift her and slam her onto the desk— keyboards, towers, and monitors crash to the ground as I pin her down with a firm hand on her neck, the other ripping away her shorts and undergarments.

Her legs spread instinctively, and I position myself over her trembling body. She arches into me. Her fingers claw at my back in a desperate attempt for contact, loosening my bandages until the blood-soaked gauze covers her chest instead of mine, exposing me at my most raw, ugliest self.

I thrust in all the way to my hilt.

Her welcoming heat envelops me, robbing me of any lingering sanity I may have clung to.

Elara's screams reverberate—a blend of shock at how fast I've stretched her and her unadulterated pleasure.

I can't help but match her cries with my own throaty grunts as I drive into her with unrestrained force. She grips the edge of the desk as if she's clinging onto her very existence. Each time I thrust, she pushes back.

"Kaspian..." she breathes out, her voice coming out in shuddering gasps as she wraps her legs around my waist.

My calloused hands grasp her hips tightly as I pull out and slam back into her, each thrust harder than the last.

Elara whimpers slightly, but it's not out of pain. No, it's pleasure that has her tossing her head back and gripping my shoulders with white knuckles.

I kiss her wildly, sucking on her bruised, cut, swollen lips. I pull away so my tongue can lick along the column of her neck, tasting the salty beads of sweat dotting her skin. She squirms beneath me, panting, writhing, and it only drives me deeper inside.

"Say you want more," I demand between grunts.

"Yes," she sobs.

There is a sick satisfaction in knowing that she wants more of my carnal hunger. A vindication that I have succeeded in marking her as mine. I withdraw and surge deep within her, rewarded by her cries, her whimpers, and the way her eyes roll back in pure electric pleasure.

I press my forehead against hers as I continue to find home inside her. Elara's nails rake against my back, drawing blood that trickles down my spine. She watches every expression cross my face; each wince, each clench of jaw that marks moments where control slips from me, and each hiss through my teeth when I plunge deeper into her.

Her hand wraps around my hilt and moves rhythmically along with our bodies' forceful collision. Her thumb brushes over my tip just as I pull out and crash into her, making both of us groan aloud.

My teeth find her bare shoulder where I bite down hard enough to make her shout, but the taste of her skin drives my primal need.

Relentless, I drive into her harder and faster with each

passing second. Her legs tighten around me as her moans turn into high-pitched screams. Elara's walls clamp down on me, sending sparks along my spine and pushing me closer to the edge.

With one final thrust, we fall together.

Entangled, our bodies heave and shudder. My fingers press into the flesh of her waist, anchoring myself as I try to find my bearings in this fugue only Elara can escort me through.

While I'm working on being able to see again, Elara lightly probes around the flayed, charred skin on my chest.

I watch her exploration for a while before snatching her wandering hand.

"I didn't think it was possible," she whispers, her voice haggard.

"What's that?" I ask, feigning indifference yet unable to break away from the intensity of her study.

"For you ... for you to let me touch the worst parts of you," Elara murmurs.

She leans forward to capture my lips with hers in a surprisingly gentle kiss.

My heart stammers at her words, at the accusation and finality they carry. But instead of retreating behind my usual barriers, I find myself admitting, "I can't help it around you."

Her eyes widen slightly at my confession, but instead of retreating or pushing me away as others might have done before her, she smiles and traces my lower lip with her thumb.

"You don't have to wear the mask with me," she says softly. "Not anymore."

Elara's words are my antivenom, seeping into the most eroded sections of my soul, where no one dares to tread, lest they never come out again.

A breath shudders out of me at her acceptance—Elara's downright stubborn insistence—to see me as I am.

And love me.

CHAPTER 37
CAV
THE PUPPETEER

The decadent, cobwebbed study inside Elara's family manor should have felt like a respite after our night's barbarisms, but the plush Persian rug does little to absorb the stench of blood and offal still clinging to Wilder and me like a second skin.

We'd strolled in when Rossi was finishing up re-stitching Kaspian's bullet wound in his shoulder. As soon as Kaspian shoved him off and stormed out of the room, Rossi took one look at Wilder's gore-streaked face, matted hair, and the jagged edges of scorched flesh peeking through the multiple tears in his shirt, and pointed at the scarlet fainting couch while I reclined in an armchair near the hearth, sipping on bourbon and thinking about what we'd done.

"You know, Cav," Wilder rasps once Rossi finishes up, "when you described peeling away the High Sovereign's eyelids, I didn't quite appreciate the artistry until I experienced it myself." An ugly, satisfied grunt punctuates his words despite the obvious strain. "The way the screams evolved ... absolutely exquisite."

I shrug, rolling my shoulders to loosen the knots of tension. Even now, with the High Sovereign's life having fled his mutilated husk, I can still perfectly recall the crescendo of his death agonies.

Rossi rises, Tempest pushing off from the wall and muttering, "Thank fuck we're done," before shoving his half-full bottle of whiskey at Wilder and striding for the doors.

I'd express my appreciation for their assistance but know it's wasted. The Vultures trade in favors, much like the Court does, and Rossi will call in our debt soon, I'm sure.

Rossi dips his chin in farewell, his impassive expression hiding any exhaustion he must feel after dealing with three extremely rabid animals. His focus switches from surgeon to Mafia don as he searches for his woman in an instant, the doors clicking shut behind them.

Bottle in hand, Wilder rises to a sit and kicks aside a viscera-stained fragment of the expensive rug. "Did you have to leave quite so much of the High Sovereign on the study's imported silk Aubusson?"

"What, and rob you of the chance to lick it up later?" I shoot back.

The room falls silent but for the crackle of flames in the hearth. It's a quiet moment between us, fractured warriors each nursing our demons.

"Do you have any regrets?" Wilder breaks into my thoughts, nursing the bottle of whiskey.

"None."

Wilder runs his free hand over his stubble-covered jawline. "This is what I was born to do. It's what you were born to do."

A smirk tugs at my lips, the taste of the High Sovereign's defeat still fresh.

"Fulfilling our bloody destinies?" I muse.

"But what now?" Wilder becomes engrossed in cleaning the blood caked under his nails. "With the Sovereigns gone and us holding the reins…"

I consider this while swirling the amber liquid in my glass. We'd spent so much of our lives, sacrificed so much, only to unseat monsters just to become them ourselves. The irony isn't lost on me but neither is the opportunity.

"No more Sovereigns," I declare.

"Won't that be a bit like letting a dog off its leash?" Wilder's brows come together in contemplation. He carefully rests his back against the couch, grunting through stiffness and the residual ache of Rossi's stinging disinfecting techniques.

"Not if we change its nature." I propose, staring into the dancing flames inside the fireplace.

"And how do you suggest we do that?"

"We remake it." I sense Wilder's gaze on me, but keep my own locked onto the mesmerizing swirls of orange and blue. "Reforge it into something harder, leaner than those depraved Sovereigns could have ever conceived."

"You sound awfully sure that turning boys into swords will end any differently this time."

I tilt my head in minute acknowledgment.

"I'm counting on it not ending the same. That's the whole point."

Wilder barks a harsh laugh. "Isn't it, though? Years of the Sovereigns breaking us down, remaking us in their grotesque image ... and for what? So we could put our own fresh brand on the stock?"

"Have you already forgotten the first obligation we owe?" My voice is pitched low, gravitational. "We control the herd, not slaughter it remorselessly."

That seems to give Wilder pause.

"You expect we can just ... temper ourselves?" Wilder scoffs. "After all the depravities the Sovereigns slashed into our bodies?"

I lean back in my seat. "We have Elara now."

Wilder stiffens, eyes narrowing. "Elara is not a tool to repurpose our darkness, Cav."

"No," I agree, shifting my gaze from the fire to him. "But she reminds us of what we are underneath all these layers of blood and grime. Men with hearts that still beat for something other than violence."

She is the end of my curse.

Wilder takes a long drink, eyes never leaving mine. "She's our saving grace, then?"

"She's our hope," I correct him quietly.

Wilder's gaze turns distant then. An emotion flickers in his eyes before disappearing as swiftly as it came—regret maybe? Guilt? Remorse? No doubt thinking about Teagan, his lost love who fell prey to this savage competition we're all caught up in.

"Do you think…" Wilder trails off.

"We'll make it right," I assure him before finishing my drink in one swift gulp. "Part of that means swearing our devotion to her, vowing our protection. Nothing will happen to her with the four of us surrounding her, Wild."

His rugged features soften, easing the tension along his jaw slightly.

"Thank you, Cav," he grinds out, his voice low and gruff. "I'll hold you to it."

Before I can lighten the moment, the door swings open and Elara walks in, the soft glow of the fire casting a warm shimmer across her face. Her approach brings a halt to our argument, capturing our undivided attention as we both straighten up, instinctively trying to diminish the effects of our recent injuries.

"What are you two arguing about now?" she asks playfully, taking a seat beside Wilder.

I give her my best smirk while Wilder counters with an easy grin. We know this dance all too well; the subtle battle for her approval, a silent contest of flirtations when Elara always emerges as the victor.

Elara raises a brow at us before her attention drops to the bandages covering Wilder, then my dirtied, bloodied clothes I'd refused to remove so Rossi could take a look at me.

"You two should be resting."

She says it as if she's requested it multiple times before.

I suppose she has. She would've passed both Axe and Kaspian on the way downstairs to us.

I laugh humorlessly. "Resting? Wounds are a part of the life that we live, butterfly. We'll be all right."

Wilder joins in with a wry chuckle, the corners of his mouth twitching upward in a semblance of a smile. "Yeah, we're as tough as they come."

An odd quiet descends. Wilder's mock laughter fades away as quickly as it started.

Elara seems to sense the shift in mood and reaches out tentatively to touch Wilder's bandaged arm.

"John," she murmurs, her voice barely audible over the crackling fire.

His hazel eyes snap to hers, and for a moment, all I see is a man laid bare. Not the wild child of Titan Falls, not the rakish enforcer of the Cimmerian Court, but John Wilder, the boy who lost his first love too soon.

"Sweetwitch."

His tone matches hers.

I mean to say something casual, maybe downplay the heavy moment with another witticism. But Elara's stern glare in my direction stops me.

She can see through our deflections, our worn defenses crumbling under her scrutiny like brittle autumn leaves.

"Cav," she says.

Elara's eyes are golden pools of worry and challenge, an unspoken demand for sincerity that somehow tugs at the hardened armor around my heart.

"God help any man who tries to hurt you," I say. The sentence comes out in a quiet exhale, our gazes unbroken.

She looks startled, taken aback by the unfiltered confession in my voice. No deflective jest or charm-laden pretense. All minefields cleared and walls crumbled. A man ready to die for her.

"I don't want you to be okay because you're tough." Elara's

focus drifts to Wilder, then back to me. "I want you to be okay because you're loved."

Her words hit me square in the chest, a punch worth more than any physical blow.

I blink at her. It's all I can do.

Wilder stares at Elara with the same expression, his hand buried in his hair, looking younger than I've seen him in years.

He reaches for her hand resting between them and lifts it to his lips. Wilder's kiss upon her knuckles is tender, achingly intimate. It's a side of Wilder few truly get to see.

I stand, then extend a hand out to her. She eyes me, her gaze alternating between Wilder and me before slowly reaching out and slipping her other hand into mine. The softness of her fingers sparks a surge of emotion in my chest.

I pull her up and toward me, our bodies flush. Wilder rises as well, wrapping an arm around Elara's waist and pulling her back against him while I hold her from the front.

"Both of you," she breathes out, looking at each of us in turn, her voice shaking with emotion. "I want you both."

Her declaration is bold as the bloodstained altar room Wilder and I strolled out of, but tender as a kiss.

We're filthy, but Elara makes us clean.

Wilder brushes his lips against her neck. I lean down to capture her lips with mine. She tangles her fingers into my hair, pulling at the strands as Wilder nuzzles into the crook of her neck.

Her taste is sweet, tangy, and mixes with the blood on my face and our bodies. Wilder's hand trails down her front, tracing a path over her top, then her shorts. She visibly shudders, as both Wilder and I find that tender spot beneath each of her earlobes while our hands continue to explore.

I tighten my grip on Elara's waist, pulling her closer until there's no more room between us—until she's consumed by us.

Wilder hooks the hem of her shirt and pulls it over her head, revealing my butterfly finally out of her cocoon. It's then I notice the bite marks, one on her chest, and one on her shoulder, and I recognize the patterns immediately.

Axe. Kaspian.

We all are laying claim to her.

Wilder cups both her bare breasts, drawing circles around her nipples before capturing and pinching them. Elara moans, arching her back while her nails dig into my shoulders.

My name is a tattered gasp against her lips. I release her mouth, and Wilder takes over, his tongue sweeping in as he teases her breasts.

The thought of Wilder tasting me on her lips makes my erection form a heartbeat. I trail my fingers down her stomach, dipping under the waistband of her shorts.

Elara squirms as my digits discover just how ready she is for us.

"Cav," she moans, turning away from Wilder's kiss only to have him latch onto her pulse point with a low growl. The sight of his teeth grazing against her skin ignites an insatiable hunger, spurring me on.

My thumb strokes over her swollen nub, drawing a strangled cry from her as I push down her shorts. Elara's bare underneath and so damn wet, it makes my head spin.

Wilder lifts Elara onto the coffee table, scattering whatever drinks, bottles, and first aid items lay there. He parts her thighs wide, settling between them. His eyes find mine over her writhing form and an unspoken understanding passes between us as we take in the sight of Elara—our woman—spread for us.

Wilder dips his head to kiss down her stomach, and Elara arches upward with a low cry. Her fingers tangle in his hair while I lean forward and maintain my rhythm on our butterfly's most sensitive spot. His tongue circles around my ministrations, swirling through her folds, drinking all of her.

My cock throbs, begging for a turn with this beautiful creature. As if reading my mind, Wilder looks up over her pussy and smirks before standing and guiding Elara to her feet.

I take the lead, returning to the armchair and pulling out my cock while Wilder helps Elara position herself to straddle my lap. She gasps when she feels my hard length pressing against her wet entrance, and without any hesitation, I give in to my greed.

Elara cries out when I bury myself inside her but moves in sync with me, just as ravenous, her tits bouncing.

And then there's the sight of Wilder behind her, his hand on himself, watching us ferociously.

"I want in," Wilder grinds out, his meaning sending a shudder through Elara's body that I feel deep within her.

He drops his pants and steps forward, positioning himself at her back entrance.

Elara sucks in a breath as I pause. She feels Wilder pressing against her but doesn't protest, instead spreading her legs farther apart for him.

I get to witness Elara's eyes widen when Wilder breaks through, stretching her in ways she's never felt before. But she takes him all, moaning in pleasure while wincing with the sharp, sudden pain.

Every nerve is alight within me because I feel him coming close to me inside her, and I have a front-row seat on what we're doing to her.

Slowly, Wilder's buried as deep as I am. He sets a torturous pace, slowly pulling out and pushing in while I thrust up with increasing urgency.

Wilder's strong hands grip her hips, guiding her movements, matching mine. His head falls back, his eyes closed tight as he mutters something unintelligible under his breath. I wrap my hands around Elara's waist, holding her tightly as I increase the pace. Each thrust gets harder, deeper.

Elara tenses, her breath catching. She's close.

Wilder and I share a knowing glance: we won't last much longer either—how can we when the woman between us drives us to insanity? Her eyes flutter shut, and she bites down on her lower lip to keep from crying out. But there's no way in hell I'm letting her silence herself.

"Let go, butterfly," I tell her. "We want to hear you."

Wilder rumbles his agreement from behind, lowering to swoop her hair to one side and place a kiss on the back of her neck.

The tenderness in the act makes me realize how much things have changed between us—how we care for her like she does for us.

And only her.

I'll carve into my future with ruthless precision, but at her altar, I'll always kneel in devotion.

"I'm ... I'm..." she gasps out a warning before going over the edge.

Her release triggers ours, and we are lost, my cock emptying into her in powerful spurts. Wilder's groan tears from his throat as he buries himself fully, his own climax pulsing through her.

When our breathing slows and our heart rates return to normal, Wilder pulls out, leaving Elara to collapse against me. My butterfly is exhausted, but she's wearing such a sated expression that I can't help but smile, brushing a strand of hair off her sweaty forehead. When I also pull out slowly, she winces a little at the sudden emptiness but doesn't complain.

Elara sighs deeply, sinking into my chest while she reaches for Wilder. He moves closer and wraps an arm around her shoulder, pulling her into a tight hug from behind.

We sit there in silence for a while, lost in each other's company. Bound together in a way we never thought possible, while the darkness outside fades into first light.

CHAPTER 38

ELARA

THE JEWEL

The aftershocks of pleasure still ripple through me as I sink into Cav's warm, lacerated chest. My body bears the imprint of Wilder, Cav, Axe, and Kaspian's touch, a map of sensations I'm still learning to navigate. Even as I catch my breath, it feels like a dream—a dark, twisted fantasy that I never knew I wanted until it happened.

"Quite a sight to behold," Kaspian drawls, his voice dripping with sarcasm as he saunters into the room. His gaze flicks over the three of us, a wicked grin on his lips. "I must say, I'm almost disappointed we missed the main event."

Axe follows close behind, rolling his shoulders as he walks. The atmosphere in the room shifts with the arrival of Kaspian's silky menace and Axe's lethal quiet, but not in the way many would think.

They complete my home.

Cav shifts underneath me, propping up on one elbow to regard Kaspian coolly. "It's not our fault you were late."

I move to cover myself, a sudden surge of self-consciousness washing over me even as I ache from letting these guys do what-ever they wanted while I got off each time. But Cav's arm tightens around me, reminding me that I'm all of theirs, now, and have been for a while.

Only Wilder remains still, his eyes closed and unfazed by their entrance while he reclines on the fainting couch.

Axe moves deeper into the room, bypassing Cav and me to settle down next to Wilder. His bulky height dwarfs the other man's lean shape, but their connection is undeniable, a bond formed from years of brotherhood.

"Do you need them to draw you a picture?" Axe's baritone rumbles the question to Kaspian, but his steel-gray eyes don't waver from mine, forcing my heart into a wild gallop.

Kaspian eyes me sidelong with a suspicious quirk at the corner of his mouth. "The show may be over, but encores are never off the table."

A blush burns my cheeks, but I don't shrink back from his statement. I am no innocent dove to be coddled and protected —not anymore—and these four men have made sure of that.

As different as they are, each man resonates with a purpose, an unspoken oath to protect me and what we share.

It feels like I've become their hallowed ground, and they're the devils I let dance on it.

And then, just when I sense their collective need to pounce on me again, the sound of bare feet padding on the floors heralds Sasha's arrival.

She appears in the doorway, a tub of ice cream clutched in her hands and her soft curls all frizzed out like she'd stuck her finger in a socket.

"Oh, my sweet baby Jesus," she says, the whites of her eyes obvious as she takes in the sight before her. "I go away for a few hours to drown my sorrows in mint chocolate chip, and I return to find..." She pauses, her gaze sweeping over the room. "Well, it looks like some sort of sinful Renaissance painting."

Her faux-scandalized tone has Cav breaking into laughter, his chest shaking beneath me. Wilder cracks an eye open to regard our intruder with lazy amusement before closing it again.

Sasha sidles closer, arranging herself onto one of the plush armchairs as if she's settling in for a movie.

"I think I'm going to need more ice cream," she mutters, staring hard at what's left of her pint.

Kaspian counters with a sly grin. "Ice cream won't be enough to erase this image from your mind."

"Yet," she shoots back, "it's a scene that keeps entering my reality."

She takes another dramatic scoop of ice cream.

Axe pulls off his shirt and hands it to me. I accept it gratefully, enjoying all too much the warmth of his body heat and the smell of him lingering in the dark green fabric, its oversized length swallowing my thighs.

Sasha's jaw drops at the sight of Axe's mutilated chest, obvious even through the multiple strips of gauze. "Okay, I definitely need more ice cream and maybe a few shots of vodka."

Wilder snorts at that, not bothering to open his eyes. "Innocent is the last thing you are, Sterling. You helped save us by putting your two boyfriends in a coma."

Sasha points her spoon at Wilder. "Don't make me come over there and do the same to you, pretty boy."

Cav loops his arms around me as I resettle on his lap, his body a shielding presence against my back. "Seriously, Sasha. Are you okay after … everything?"

Sasha looks up. She stares at me, her usual spark of mischief dimmed by the weight of recent events. I can tell she's considering her response carefully, weighing the gravity of what's happened against the instinctive pull to lighten the mood.

A soft sigh escapes her lips. "It's not exactly what I had in mind for a Saturday evening. I mean, I was hoping for maybe a movie night and some popcorn… Casual human sacrifice wasn't really on my agenda."

A tidal pressure enters the room at her words. Wilder's eyes open, Kaspian's snide expression falls a fraction, and even Cav's grip on me tightens while Axe's mouth thins to an even grimmer level.

Sasha simply meets their gazes head-on.

"But hey," she continues, managing a shrug as if we hadn't just spent the night fighting a murderous cult, as if she hadn't just been chained and forced to watch me almost die. "Upside is, I got a pretty good workout, and I'm pretty sure I lost like five pounds from the stress alone."

The tension eases slightly at that. Axe huffs out an amused breath.

"We owe you, Sasha," he murmurs.

"Are you okay, El?" she says next.

Sasha's simple question stirs the four men, like they've been reminded that I am, indeed, not just theirs but also a woman who has faced terrors previously foreign to her.

"I'm more than alright," I reply, reassuring her and myself.

Sasha's gracious nod confirms she understands the pretext under my answer—that this entanglement with these men is my choice.

I linger on each man in turn, drinking in the sight of them.

Alive, safe.

And perhaps this is what it takes to create something real, something that matters.

As if reading my thoughts, Kaspian says, "We've got a lot of work ahead of us. The Court won't fix itself."

Wilder grunts his agreement from his sprawl on the couch.

Axe, watching the exchange with a thoughtful expression, adds his input. "We need to ensure that what happened tonight never happens again."

Cav says, "We stand against an entity that has wielded power in Titan Falls for centuries. Victory won't come easy."

Everyone nods.

Kaspian continues. "We can all agree that the title of Sovereign died with them. If we're to take over, we need a name.

Something befitting of what we've done and what we'll continue to do."

Wilder chuckles, nudging Axe with his foot. "I didn't realize we were starting a band."

Sasha laughs, a delightful sound that bounces off the walls and softens any of our flashbacks. "Oh my God! Yes! I vote for Sinister Skulls."

"Pass," Cav says almost immediately. Sasha throws him a mock glare.

"Barbarians, then?" she suggests next, which earns an amused snort from Axe.

I'm quiet for a moment, idly circling my thumb on the chair's velvet arm.

"The Regents."

Wilder sits up at my voice. "The Regents?" he repeats.

"Yes," I say with more confidence as the name takes hold. "As in governance without a monarch." I glance at each stunning, devious face in turn. "Isn't that essentially what you are? Leaders without sovereignty?"

Kaspian gifts me with a rare smile. "It has a certain ring to it."

Cav nods, a deadly glint in his eye. "The Regents. Simple. Powerful."

"Unforgettable," Axe adds, his smile sharp enough to cut.

The name settles over us like a mantle. These men are no longer nameless survivors or rebels. They aren't just 'the guys' to me anymore, or even the Untouchable Four that my sweet, ignorant past self dubbed them.

They're the nightmare other monsters fear.

I study each of them—Cav, Kaspian, Axe, and Wilder. My Regents. My monsters. My lovers. My family. They sense my stare, and I see everything they've been through in their multicolored eyes, everything they're capable of.

I've walked through hell with these men. Now, I'm ready to rule it.

The Regents aren't the heroes of this story.
But they're mine, and I finally feel whole.

EPILOGUE
THE REGENTS

Thornhaven Manor breathes differently now, its grandeur no longer cursed by the Sovereigns' death grip. The mansion, a decrepit source of power and menace in the heart of Titan Falls and the initiates within it, now live under the firm grip of the Regents.

Cav stands by the expansive window in the former High Sovereign's bedroom, his eyes reflecting the untended landscape bathed in moonlight. The moon, as in love with him as I am, caresses his aristocratic features, but his intentions are as sharp as his cheekbones.

He's traded his role of Consul, second-in-command for that of de-facto leader. But none of the four are subordinates to each other. They're each a force that protects their shared vision.

Weeks after disposing of the Sovereigns, Kaspian took the Scourge's quarters, and as soon as Axe entered his father's, he didn't emerge for days. I moved back in with my mother for a week after she was released and put on proper medication and counseling, unlike the private doctor she used before. He ended up being on the Sovereigns' payroll after Kaspian went through their records that Cav managed to uncover before joining us and finishing off the Sovereigns. At the time, Cav also discovered the

Silent Sovereign's identity after rummaging around the private wing, but was saved from having to personally deliver that brutal blow to Axe when Orion admitted it himself.

Today, I've moved in with my men.

Kaspian reclines in a chair—more like a throne—behind a carved wooden desk, typing on his laptop with an air of casual irreverence, those spectral green eyes of his now free of the casual boredom they held under the reign of the Sovereigns, gleam with a corrosive delight that mirrors his newfound position of power as he writes up a new Code for the Cimmerian Court to follow. His hair, groomed back from his face but not quite enough to tame one thick strand from falling onto his forehead, makes him appear deceptively approachable.

Wilder paces the room, a wolflike grace to his movements. Teagan's loss crafted him into an impulsive creature of vengeance and ambition, but with his brothers and me by his side, he's only impatient now because he wants to meet with the initiates waiting downstairs and get the new Order started.

Meanwhile, Axe stands apart—away from us—but his nearby presence sweeps toward me like a thundercloud directing its lightning shot. His complexion matches the marble busts lining one wall, my previous words of forgiveness as effective as whispering to a statue. He needs his brothers to voice their mercy, too.

My heels click against the wooden floorboards when I enter. Each man stills, their movements compressing into a small universe that includes only us. Kaspian's fingers halt on his keyboard, the silence in his corner oddly deafening. He leans back with practiced nonchalance to watch me over the screen. Wilder freezes mid-stride, an incorrigible smirk tugging at his lips as he leans against the front of Kaspian's desk, crossing his arms over his chest and eyes dancing as they rake over me, showing no remorse for the explicit appraisal.

Even after their proof of utter devotion, I still turn red under their scrutiny.

They like my new outfit.

Donned in a flowing white cloak with a gradual ombre effect fading into the Regents' chosen color, midnight blue, I come into the room. I have to fully turn my head left and right to see all of them due to the custom mask I'm wearing that obstructs my peripheral vision, but its beauty is worth the partial blindness. Cav crosses the room to get to me and Axe's towering figure stays put in the far corner, eyes fixed on me. Axe chose the rose gold finish of my mask while Cav, Kaspian, and Wilder argued over how best to reflect me in its design. They decided the mask's shape would resemble an uncut gem, with subtle, asymmetrical facets. These facets wouldn't be sharp or defined, instead choosing gentle slopes and planes that catch the light.

With my hood up, I look like I've stepped out of a fabled labyrinth. I would know, because I couldn't stop staring at myself in the mirror for over an hour.

And … I may be wearing nothing but white lace lingerie underneath.

Cav reaches me first, his hand coming to rest on the small of my back. A whirlwind of emotions radiates off his potent form. Pride, possessiveness, a hint of wonder. His touch grazes against the silk of my cloak, sending pleasurable zings up my spine.

"Butterfly," he murmurs. "You look stunning."

Kaspian abandons his laptop and strides over to us. He uses a finger to lift my chin, just enough to peer beneath the mask and catch the yearning in my stare. His own is a fractal of its usual acidic burn.

"You make power look irresistible," he says, his smile hinting at the wickedness that slithers under his skin.

Wilder joins us, a spark in his step as he circles us and pays particular attention to my backside before stopping in front of me. He takes my hand and raises it to his lips, planting a soft kiss against my knuckles.

"You were always a queen," he says. "Now you have an army."

Axe remains where he is, his voice absent from the conversation. I break free from the circle, the three men surrounding me understanding my need to confront their renegade brother. They felt the same sting of betrayal I did when he gave up our secrets to the Sovereigns, but they also share the same depth of forgiveness in their hearts. They just may not recognize it as forgiveness yet.

If I have to smack them on the heads to initiate a heartfelt conversation between the four of them, then I will.

Axe follows my every move until I'm standing before him. I lay a hand on his chest, feeling the steady thump of his heart beneath the layers of fabric and muscle. His hands remain at his sides.

"Your brothers know what you did, the information you gave up to save your sister," I say, keeping my voice level despite the racing heart against my palm. "They may have hated you for it, but they love you in spite of it. Mostly, I've missed you because of it. Come back to us, Axe."

His eyes darken, hardened marble melting into a churning sea. Axe's expression wavers, torn open by my words.

"There's no shame in asking for forgiveness," I gently insist, "and even less in accepting it."

Axe swallows, his Adam's apple bobbing with the effort. He lifts his hand, fingers brushing against my own where they rest on his chest. His touch is tentative.

From behind us, Cav speaks. "Axe, we've already forgiven you."

Cav's voice holds an edge, but his words are softer than I've ever heard.

Cav moves beside me, his hand coming down to rest atop mine and Axe's. Wilder and Kaspian wordlessly come up behind us, adding their hands to the pile.

The five of us combined as one unit.

There's no rule book for this strange, beautiful connection

we share, only the knowledge that we are stronger together than apart.

"We're family," Wilder says to Axe, reading my thoughts. "For better or for worse."

Axe tenses under our interwoven hands. His stoic expression breaks, exposing a vulnerability I've only caught fleeting glimpses of before.

"I'm sorry," he says, his open gaze holding mine captive. "Elara, I'm so damn sorry."

He lets out a breath, his chest concaving, the feel of it twisting something in my chest. But Axe finally moves, his hands settling around my waist under my cloak, almost as if he's anchoring himself.

"Join us as a Regent," Wilder says, his tone vibrant despite the seriousness of the moment. "You weren't meant to stand alone, bro, no matter what you think."

"Let us help you carry the weight," Kaspian encourages, his sharp barbs conspicuously absent.

Axe's gaze cuts to Kaspian then back to me. His heart-rate slows.

"Thank you," he says on a whisper of breath.

The cool moonlight may bathe our forms, but the warmth coming from within us grows stronger. We move, as if the pull is magnetic, toward the gigantic, canopied bed.

Wilder is the first to pull at the ribbon tying the cloak at my neck. Kaspian grazes the unfeeling metal of my mask—

"Wait," Cav says. "Leave the mask on."

Cav retreats into his expansive closet for a few seconds, his erection leading the way, before emerging with a large black case. Laying it on the desk, he pops it open to reveal four unique gunmetal masks.

"I was going to reveal these during our ceremony downstairs, but now is the better time," he says, turning to us with a delicious grin.

"Cav…" I breath out in awe as he presents each man with their Regent mask.

They're not mere disguises. They're symbols, tangible representations of the identities they've carved for themselves within our group. Cav's is thin and sleek, with faint lines etched into the mask resembling strings and converging at the eye. Wilder's has subtle, canine-like contours around the cheekbone and jaw, with a pointed edge near the nose. Kaspian's has angular lines etched into the surface, creating a fragmented appearance that's hardest to read and slightly unsettling. Axe's has almost imperceptible depth changes across its smooth, pristine surface, creating the illusion of a smiling face fading in and out of view.

All four slip their masks on, their identities merging with the designs crafted by Cav. They are the Puppeteer, the Hellhound, the Bogeyman, and the Phantom.

They are mine.

And within seconds, they're wearing nothing but their masks.

Axe comes behind me while I kneel in the middle of the bed, sliding the cloak off my shoulders and tossing it aside. He reaches out and brushes my hip, his thumb running along the edge of my lace underwear. His touch is softer now, no longer hesitant but still cautious, as if worried I may vanish like smoke under his fingers.

That's why I take his wrist, guide his hand beneath the front of my underwear, and make his fingers wet between my folds.

With a groan, he slips a finger all the way in to the knuckle and drags it out. His other hand cups my breast, pinching and rolling my nipple through the lace as I let out a soft moan and clench around his fingers.

Wilder kneels before me, taking my other breast as Kaspian spreads my legs wider. Cav prowls onto the bed to join, replacing Axe's hand between my thighs with his own and slipping inside effortlessly because of Axe's careful preparation.

Cav watches me through the darkness of his mask. My face

is hot under mine, but I don't dare take it off. If I'm finding it so damn sexy to see them in theirs, they think the same of me.

Axe, no longer restricted, spans his hands over my waist and trails them higher until they caress the swells of my breasts just left bare by Wilder. Wilder's chosen to move lower, tracing the ladder of my ribs before settling between my thighs and joining Cav, making me squirm in anticipation.

Cav's fingers move in slow, deliberate circles around my swollen bud, enhancing Wilder's teasing fingers underneath. A sigh escapes my lips, rewarding their efforts.

From behind me, Axe's hands venture lower, tracing the delicate lace of my lingerie until they find the strap's edge. With a quick snap, he removes the barrier.

I'm fully exposed now, to him, to all of them. But I've been like that for a while.

Kaspian has been watching with an unsettling intensity that sends a current close to an orgasm through my center, just by his blackened stare alone. He leans in now, joining Wilder and Cav by sliding two fingers inside me, matching Cav and Wilder's rhythm.

I don't just gasp. I almost pass out from the crippling, unbelievable sensation of being finger-banged by three masked men.

Not to be outdone, Axe prods at my backside, inserting his thumb.

It's undeniable—they have me encased and surrounded. I'm theirs, claimed in a way that transcends the typical bounds of intimacy.

My head falls back on Axe's shoulder as their pace quickens, fingers plunging deeper, movements growing more frantic as they respond to my gasps and trembles.

Sensing my impending climax, Cav picks up speed, swirling in tighter circles. I'm spiraling toward the edge, my release building and ready to crash down on all of us. Wilder changes his rhythm, plunging higher inside me. Kaspian pulls out and presses the edge of his palm on my mound, using a grinding pressure that joins Cav's and has me panting his name. Axe's thumb pushes deeper into my ass and I think I've gone blind.

The world fades away, leaving only the biting feel of the mask, the tempo of their movements, the heady scent of male musk, and the spices of sex. But I keep my eyes open, watching them through the slits in my vision as their metallic faces look back at me.

The knot in my belly tightens.

They press in until they become a wall of heat-soaked skin and domination. My faded world unbearably sharpens when I reach my peak.

My toes curl and my hands clench into fists. Kaspian notices first, and with a loud, carnal growl, he strong-arms Cav and Wilder away and spears into me with his dick just as my orgasm crashes over me and my scream takes over the room.

Kaspian filling me through the wave of my climax is special, fucking addictive. He's relentless, thrusting in a rhythm that matches my own quivering spasms, drawing out my pleasure until I'm whimpering his name over and over.

Not to be left out, Axe plunges into me from behind, sliding into the wetness he created with his spit. His entrance is so deliciously unexpected that it reignites the fire burning low in my belly. He moves in a rhythm different from Kaspian's—a slow slide—each thrust shifting Kaspian inside me.

There is a unique intimacy in this act, heightened by the way Axe's breath catches in his throat and he buries his masked face into my hair. I'm filled and emptied simultaneously, Kaspian and Axe's dual invasion driving me to another peak far too soon.

Cav shifts, moving around Wilder and stands on the bed until he can position his cock at the mouth of my mask. He flicks my mask off with an impatient, tight grunt, revealing my sweaty, overtaxed face and lax jaw, because I'm a boneless puddle.

Of course he takes advantage.

His arousal slips into my mouth. Cav's groan vibrates

through my body. He tastes salty, delicious. I circle my tongue around his length as he sets an unforgiving pace until each thrust hits the back of my throat.

By now, my body has tuned into their movements. I suck Cav in time with the pace Axe and Kaspian set, spit flying. The taste of Cav makes me want to conquer him in a way he's never been before.

Wilder gives a warning at my side and takes hold of my free hand, bringing it to his erection. I wrap around him, matching my harsh strokes to the pace the others have created.

Their control wanes as their greed takes precedence. Kaspian's thrusts become more erratic, and the noises from Axe come closer to rabid snarls than human utterances. Cav's cock twitches in my mouth and Wilder's hand locks around mine, increasing and shortening my strokes.

I'm helpless, surrendering to the climax about to shatter me. It's an overwhelming wave that has me arching my back, spasming around Kaspian and Axe. I scream around Cav's length and he chokes out a muffled curse, his own release coating my tongue.

Axe follows suit, his frantic drive slowing down as he fills me from behind. And Kaspian…

My name is a resounding oath from him, one that causes a tremor coursing through me. His climax is an intense burn that has him gasping, the power behind his thrusts never wavering. Wilder is the last to surrender, his grip on me rigid and painful until he's swearing under his breath and pouring himself into my closed hand.

But even as their climaxes taper off, they refuse to leave me.

Cav slips out of my mouth with a satisfied sigh while Axe guides me to lie down while he and Kaspian shift lazily inside me, making their own Elara sandwich.

Our bodies are slick with sweat, the room thick with the scent of sex. We're all panting, but it's surprisingly peaceful to hear as Cav, then Wilder, climb into bed on either side.

"Fuck, sweetwitch."

Wilder's voice is hoarse from exertion and deep with contentment as he rolls onto his side and discards the mask. He reaches over Kaspian to cup my face and force me to look at him.

"You good?" he asks. There's a tenderness in his voice that contradicts his gruff exterior.

I manage a nod and moan, "More."

Wilder smirks as if he knew the answer before he asked the question. He leans down to kiss me, ignoring audible displeasure at Wilder's looming over him, his lips rough on mine.

Cav stretches out on his back, watching us with hooded eyes. "We have a meeting to get to, but hell, you are the blessing that removed the Nightshade curse and returned my heart. You can have whatever the fuck you want, whenever you want, butterfly."

Kaspian, mask gone as if it were never there in the first place, pushes Wilder back so he can lick my neck. "We'll never be done with you."

And I wouldn't have it any other way.

Maybe it isn't normal to get off on this—being used by four men. But then again, what the hell is normal? Normal is for people who haven't seen the things I've seen or done the things I've done.

Axe grips my hips and flips me onto my belly. His hands are strong and unyielding on my flesh as he raises my ass into the air. He parts my thighs, his fingers skimming against my sensitive, swollen pussy.

"Axe...," I breathe out, clutching the sheets beneath me.

Cav pushes himself up, stroking his impressive length. Wilder kneels on my other side, his eyes slitted as he calculates where to go next. Kaspian bides his time, watching, commanding.

And I oblige them all.

These men, they're awful—murderers in cloaks and masks

who are determined to keep ruling their underworld—yet behind the scenes, I have them wrapped around my finger.

Because I, Elara Wraithwood, am not the popular girl on campus, the tragic victim who lost her father and brother, the Anderton witch descendent, or the demonic sacrifice. Not anymore.

I am their coveted jewel.

ALSO BY KETLEY ALLISON

all in kindle unlimited

If you want more secret societies, read:

Rival

Virtue

Fiend

Reign

The Thorne of Winthorpe:

Thorne

Crush

Liar

If you want mafia with your dark, why choose romance:

Cruel Promise (M/F)

Broken Beauty (Why Choose)

Loyal Vows (Why Choose)

also writing as S.K. Allison,

contemporary romance:

If you like your bad boys and bullies as standalones (no series, one book, a happy ending), read:

Rebel

Crave

If you like a grump turned into a protector for his woman, read:

Rock

Lover

If you like your playboys with tormented hearts and scars, read:

Trust

Dare

Play

If you like small-town, angsty vibes:

You Will Want Me